Books by B. V. Larson.

STAR FORCE SERIES
Swarm
Extinction
Rebellion
Conquest
Battle Station
Empire
Annihilation
Storm Assault
The Dead Sun
Outcast
Exile
Gauntlet
Demon Star

REBEL FLEET SERIES
Rebel Fleet
Orion Fleet
Alpha Fleet
Earth Fleet

Visit BVLarson.com for more information.

Crystal World

(Undying Mercenaries Series #20)
by
B. V. Larson

Undying Mercenaries Series:
Steel World
Dust World
Tech World
Machine World
Death World
Home World
Rogue World
Blood World
Dark World
Storm World
Armor World
Clone World
Glass World
Edge World
Green World
Ice World
City World
Sky World
Jungle World
Crystal World

Copyright © 2023 by Iron Tower Press.

This book is a work of fiction. Names, characters, places and incidents are either products of the author's imagination or used fictitiously. Any resemblance to actual events, locales or persons, living or dead, is entirely coincidental. All rights reserved. No part of this publication can be reproduced or transmitted in any form or by any means, without permission in writing from the author.

ISBN-13: 979-8864401118
BISAC: Fiction / Science Fiction / Military

In memory of Manuel Fonseca, 2023.

"Count no man happy until he is dead."
– Heraclitus, 501 BC

-1-

On a fine autumn morning, my tapper started buzzing around 7 a.m. This was unusual, as I'd set it to ignore all communication except from my closest contacts, friends—and of course, official business from Central. That was only because I couldn't turn that off, no matter how much I wanted to.

Therefore, receiving an early morning call was weird. Especially at this hour. My friends knew better than to disturb me in the mornings.

My eyes snapped open as I grunted and heaved, and Tessie rolled off me onto her side of the bed. Lately, she'd gotten into the habit of sleeping at my place on my fold-out couch bed. She didn't like the bed much, despite the fact I kept telling her it was a big upgrade. I'd improved my living quarters, moving up from a single crusty couch to the fold-out a few years back.

Unlike old-fashioned fold-outs, it wasn't a torture rack. This modern contrivance was relatively comfy—but there's just no pleasing some people.

Tessie's continued presence was the second big surprise of the morning. It dawned on me as I yawned and scratched and contemplated answering my tapper, that she'd been around for weeks now. While such a long-term romance wasn't entirely unknown in my life, it certainly wasn't the norm. It was always a pleasant surprise when a woman didn't get sick of me after a dozen or so nights of passion.

Tessie, while not exactly clingy, was definitely committed to sharing some good times with old McGill. Apparently, our shared near-death—and actual death—experiences had imprinted on her during the Jungle World campaign. A switch had been flipped in her brainstem someplace, and she really liked me.

I'd been enjoying the experience myself, so I hadn't kicked her out. I'd even done my damnedest to hide all signs of my restless spirit.

Shrugging and getting up, I pulled on some clothes. The smart straps wrapped around my body as my tapper continued to ring.

"Damnation…" I muttered.

The fuzziness of sleep was fading. I wondered who this could be and whether I should answer. Knowing in my heart I shouldn't do it, I looked at the name on my inner forearm.

"Imperator Galina Turov…" it read.

I sighed, but then a moment later frowned.

The situation was somewhat mysterious. If this had been an official call—a call initiated in the name of duty—Galina would have forced it through.

Why hadn't she done so? Anything governmental in nature, whether reactivating my contract or requiring me to report to Central, wouldn't have involved this arm-twisting nonsense. She would have just forced the call through.

But she hadn't.

"There's a new mystery for you…" I said to myself as I scratched my head.

By this time, of course, the call had rung through, stopped buzzing, and then begun again twice over. That meant we were on… what? At least the third call she'd made in a row? Was she chain-calling me? Really?

Finally, heaving a sigh, I raised one oversized finger and hovered it over the screen. I was finally ready to swipe and answer.

"If you answer that call," I heard a small female voice behind me. "I'm going to kill you in the exercise room during our next campaign."

Tessie wasn't sleeping anymore. Probably all my buzzing, thinking and scratching had woken her up.

"Uh..." I said. My finger still hovered hesitantly over the screen.

"That's Turov," she said, "this can't be an official call. She would have just buzzed through and forced it to answer."

"Well..." I said. "Yeah, probably."

"There's no probably about it, James," she said, her small fists were planted on her small hips. It was a nasty look, a look I'd seen on so many women.

I had to turn away, despite the fact she was buck-naked and looking pretty good. Tessie was a small-breasted woman, but what she had was perfectly proportioned. Normally, I'd be admiring that view, but right now, I was too befuddled by all the circumstances crashing in on me all at once.

"Hey," I said to her as the phone call from Galina stopped its third round of buzzing and began the fourth. "I've got to go outside for just a minute, see. I need to take a piss."

Tessie glared at me, her fists were planted on her hips, and her eyes were narrower than ever.

"James," she said, "this has got to be a booty call. I don't want you taking off on me to chase some old flame of yours."

There was possessiveness in her tone. Why did this kind of moment always come along after spending a couple of nice weeks with a girl? Was it preordained that the outright evils of jealousy had to rear up and spoil all the fun?

It seemed to me, after damned-near a century of life, that it was unavoidable.

I slashed my finger across my forearm decisively. I'd declined the call. "See? She's gone."

Tessie examined this suspiciously, but then she relaxed a little.

"Now," I said, "I really do have to go out and pee."

I felt a set of small eyes boring into my back as I walked out the door, letting the big screen door slam and rattle behind me. I went out to the yard and, sure enough, started to take a long and convincing piss.

Now, unbeknownst to Tessie, I had taken the precaution of hitting the mute button on my tapper while I'd made this grand display of hanging up on Galina. Having known Galina for many years, I got the feeling that she wasn't through yet—she was a persistent woman. No one knew that better than me. Sure enough, that sixth call came in before I could even shake it to hang up.

Looking as innocent as a trout in a cold mountain stream, I surreptitiously opened up the phone call and half-mumbled, "What the hell is it?"

There was a squawking sound from my forearm. As a necessary part of the subterfuge, I reached down to grab myself. I had to continue the illusion of taking a super long piss out in the yard.

"What's this?" Galina squawked, looking through the camera at something that she knew rather well, but which she had no desire to witness at this moment. "You ignore me for half an hour and then you start off with a dick-pic?"

"Whoa," I said, lifting up my forearm, so that I could pretend to scratch the back of my head and rub up my neck while I spoke into the microphone.

My back was still turned toward my shack, where I felt Tessie might just be looking out the window or the screen door to watch me.

"What the hell do you want so bad, Galina?" I asked.

"I need help," she said, "and not the kind you just displayed to me."

Right then, I felt a mite disappointed. Apparently, this wasn't a booty-call after all. I mean, sure, I had Tessie—but Galina and I—we went way back. We hadn't been together for months and—

"Well?" she demanded suddenly. "Are you going to help me or not?"

I was a bit taken aback. "Listen, it's the first thing in the morning. I'm not on duty. I'm on vacation, and you haven't even told me what the hell you want me to do yet."

"Oh…" she said, "so that's how it is. You're whispering and showing me your neck. There must be someone else there. You're a goat of a man, McGill."

"That may well be," I said. "But still, if you want me not to hang up this call, you'd better tell me what this is all about."

"I don't have to," she said. "I'm calling in my favor."

"You're what?"

"Do you remember, James, at the end of the Sky World campaign?"

"Uh…" I thought, vaguely remembering having experienced something called the Sky World campaign. "You mean out there in the frontier province, fighting with Rigel and all that?"

"That's right, James," she said. "Do you remember what you told me?"

I thought of a bunch of things. None of them were all that pleasant. She'd gotten me killed multiple times during those days. She'd always had a bad temper, even for a highly-ranked female officer in Earth's military service, and even for a woman who'd had to deal with the likes of me for so many long years.

"I remember you getting mad at me and killing me over and over again and all that," I said.

"Yes…" she said, "that's right. And do you remember why I did all that?"

"Oh," I said, thinking about it. "You had some crazy suspicions about me and revolutionaries and all that nonsense."

"Not just that, James."

"Uh," I said, remembering what she must be talking about.

Her sister Sophia and I had had a fling back then. I know that sounds bad, but it was very brief. No more than a few hand-holdings, pecks on the cheek—and one glorious night. I'd confessed all this to Galina, and then she'd said something about how I owed her one. Something like that.

"But wait a minute," I said. "I know what you're talking about. You and I came to a nice conclusion over all that. You forgave me for Sophia, and I forgave you for murdering me over and over again. Do you remember having me strapped to a wall and whipped to death? Repeatedly?"

"Vaguely..." she admitted.

"Well, then... we're even-steven."

She growled. I got the feeling that she'd hoped maybe I'd forgotten the details of that day. At least enough so she could bamboozle me into yet another favor based on my indiscretions with her sister.

Nope, that wasn't going to work.

Right about then, I heard a soft voice calling from the screen door of my shack, some thirty or forty feet behind me.

"James?" Tessie called. "Are you done pissing yet? I need to get some breakfast."

I grimaced. Tessie was watching. I had to be careful with this fakery.

"Oh yeah, sure," I shouted over my shoulder. "I'll be there in just a second. I need to check on something out at the shed."

I began ambling away toward the toolshed, which stood at the edge of our property before the swamp proper began.

Most of this so-called farm my family possessed was unfarmable. It consisted of bogland, trees, thick brush, and very wet ground. There were ponds and a couple of creeks scattered over the acreage as well.

There were a few fields that were level and plantable out closer to the road, of course. We also possessed a huddle of animals and fruit trees, a big vegetable garden—that kind of thing. But most of our land was a dark, primordial swamp.

"So," I said to Galina again when we were safely out of earshot of Tessie, "what is it you want me to do for you so badly on a Wednesday morning?"

"First of all, it's Thursday, James. Second, I want you to find out what happened to Drusus. Last, I want you to... I want you to kill me."

That stopped me. My jaw dropped low, and I gaped. I lifted up my tapper and looked her square in the face. I could tell at a glance she was serious—and she wasn't all that happy about it. Galina wasn't a girl who enjoyed dying. She took such events seriously.

"What in the hell?" I said. "You don't look that long in the tooth, girl."

Immediately, my mind jumped to the conclusion that she wanted a beauty treatment, essentially using death and a revival machine to regenerate herself back to the prime age of nineteen again.

That sort of extreme measure seemed premature to me. She was actually looking pretty good. Casting back in my memory, I recalled that she'd died recently. The last time had to have been when *Dominus* had blown up, destroyed by Hegemony because it was being chased by an angry Skay at the end of the Sky World campaign. The same Skay had gotten itself blown up over Jungle World just last year.

I smiled at the memories. Unlike that behemoth of an AI being, we humans had been revived. There was no revival machine in the known universe that could revive a Skay. As far as I knew, they didn't back up their minds, either. If you died when you were a planet-sized evil alien monstrosity, well, I guess the rest of them figured you were a bad piece of software to begin with. They rerolled with a fresh install and probably some variations in the software, in an attempt to perfect their own weird species.

"I'm not looking for a facelift, James," Galina said, snapping out the words. "I need to disappear for a while. I need to go somewhere where no one can find me. And I want you to help me get there."

I blinked at my tapper, as befuddled as I could be.

Right about then, I heard a rustling behind me. I turned slowly, using one finger to quickly mute my tapper. I faced Tessie and gave her a big, fake grin.

She gave me a glare in return. She lifted up an arm, holding her upraised hand high. That hand ended with a single, ugly finger.

"I'm out of here," she said. "You've been looking at every girl that goes by at the market and that crappy poolhall you keep dragging me to every time we go to town. And now, here you are having a whispered conversation with one of your exes? If I can't hold your attention for two weeks, you're just as bad as every girl in the legion says you are!"

"Oh, now hold on, Tessie," I said, but that was it.

She turned around and stomped off, marching through the tall grass. I watched her small, angry butt as she left me, and I heaved a sigh. She climbed into a tram she had parked out on the roadway and drove off.

I lifted my arm again to frown at Galina. I unmuted her, even though I was regretful to do so. She'd been carrying on for quite a while, apparently delivering an angry tirade of her own.

"Well?" she demanded. "Are you going to help me or not?"

"You just chased off a good thing for me."

She grumbled and rolled her eyes. "Yes... Yes. I heard all that. I apologize for interfering in your personal life yet again. But James, you know she wasn't woman enough for you. She was just a bit of fluff that you were entertaining yourself with."

"You don't know that," I said, even though we both knew she was right.

It partly had to do with the realities of aging in the twenty-third century. Physically, Galina and I looked like we were in our twenties, but in reality, we were quite a bit older. A big stack of decades older.

As a person aged and gained experience, even if you looked young on the outside—you really weren't. Even if your body was still physically capable and full of the vigor of youth, I'd found I couldn't seriously connect with someone so much younger and inexperienced.

"All right," I grumped to Galina at last, "what do you want me to do?"

-2-

My morning started off on the wrong foot. After Galina gave me her laundry list of tasks, we disconnected, and I went in to take a shower. Tessie had cleared out by this time. She'd taken her minimal belongings with her, including a small bag of clothes and a large bag of makeup.

While I was in my bathroom, I noticed a considerable number of various and sundry items she'd left behind. Many of these I was unable to identify, but all were definitely feminine in nature.

Using my long arms and a trash can, I scooped them all into the bin and stashed it under the sink.

Why, you might ask, would I undermine a rekindling with Tessie later on? Because I understood ladies rather well, that's why.

If Tessie returned before anyone else showed up to replace her, I could always say that I'd experienced an imaginary fit of rage and grief over her departure. That I'd thrown away her stuff in this addled state of mind. Then, she could have the fun of buying new stuff to replace it, all the while thinking about my emotional state and how much her absence had affected me.

If, on the other hand, a new girl showed up—Galina or someone else—well sir, that girl would never want to see some other chick's stuff in my bathroom.

Therefore, I scooped it all into the can. There, it would hide until trash day, and that was that.

After I took my shower and cleaned up, I said goodbye to my folks. They were looking a little down in the mouth and long in the tooth, but I knew they'd get over it. My mom made an appeal, urging me to make sure Etta came home from Dust World for the holidays. The girl hadn't been home for more than a year now, and this was really beginning to upset the old lady. I filed that away for future reference. Maybe it would happen, maybe it wouldn't. Etta was definitely her own woman now. She was in her thirties—older than me physically—and easily as stubborn as any McGill that had ever lived.

I took the family tram to the airport and gave the old rust-bucket a kick in the butt to send it rattling back to the farm on autopilot. I bought a cheap ticket heading north, climbed onto a bench seat next to a fat, snoring dude, and settled in for a long sky train ride.

Mentally, I pushed aside all this baggage about Tessie, and my mom, and Etta. I turned my thoughts instead to focus on what Galina had suggested.

She wanted me to find Drusus, first. Now, one would think that heading up to Central and locating the whereabouts of an extremely famous and important personage, one who had recently been the consul of all Earth—essentially a dictator in the flesh—would be easy-peasy. But old Drusus had fallen from grace. The moment he'd abdicated his position in front of the Ruling Council of Public Servants, his accomplishments had transformed into a steaming pile of crap, as far as Earth Gov was concerned.

Apparently, according to Galina, his tapper wasn't even in the registry any longer. In my modern world, anyone could do a search on anyone, using nothing more than the computer implanted in your forearm. Most people, depending on their privacy settings, could be located physically on the globe in an instant.

Drusus was no longer locatable. I tried it myself while riding in the sky train, just to make sure. No dice.

He'd been disappeared—or he was hiding. Either way, it gave me a qualm.

This realization sparked a secondary thought, which caromed around in my mind. I had to wonder why the heck

Galina wanted me to find Drusus for her? If her real mission was to have me kill her for various inexplicable reasons, why did it matter if I located Drusus first?

Frowning about that on the long flight up to Central City, I took the time to tap out a message to her asking this precise question.

No answer came back.

Frowning again, I did another check. Where was Galina herself? It's one thing to find Drusus, but what about this woman I was supposedly doing a favor for? Where the heck was she?

Moldova—that was the answer. She was in her hometown, in the old Western Russia Sector.

Huh... that was kind of weird. She was at her dad's place, or somewhere near it. She came from deep eastern Europe, a dark patch on maps in any age.

I thought about calling her directly, but then I decided not to. After all, it was the middle of the night on her side of the globe. She was probably asleep. She'd called me quite late in her time zone, in fact.

Shrugging my shoulders, I decided I'd ask her about all these mysteries later on—maybe before I drowned her, or whatever fate she had in mind for herself this time around.

The sky train landed at the spaceport and transformed into a ground train. Most people got off, but not me. The fat snoring guy woke up and left, and I was happy to see him move on. The train began to rumble and roll, then it quickly transformed again into an underground train as I rode my way to Central. There was a station underneath the earth, several floors down, where regular folk could disembark. I went through security with a dismal pack of yawning low-level officers and non-coms, and gained access to the building. The hogs guarding the gate frowned at my identity when it was flashed up on their screens, but they shrugged and let me through. Something in the datacore AI knew I was often allowed into Earth's military headquarters for murky reasons.

For once, none of the hogs arrested me and escorted me through the big, squatty building. This time, my mission was entirely my own.

Thinking back, I could hardly count the number of times I'd come here without being coerced to do so. It was an odd feeling, kind of like going to work on the weekend, or shopping at the feed store on Christmas Day. Such an act was both boring and unnecessarily self-abusive—but I soldiered on for Galina's sake.

When I got to the elevator lobby, there was another checkpoint. I was given a few strange looks as I was technically off-duty and off-contract. One particularly bony hog even took a moment to ask me about it. "Centurion McGill, huh?"

"That's right, hog," I said with a smile. "I'm from Legion Varus."

He looked up at me, a bit startled. My legion didn't have the best reputation. In fact, it definitely had the worst.

He narrowed his eyes at me and squinted. He seemed not to even have registered the fact I'd called him a hog to his face. "There's no funny business going on in the building, is there, Centurion?"

"Nothing you'd like to know about," I told him.

He nodded his head as if he understood some hidden meaning I'd planted inside that cryptic statement. Of course, I knew he didn't understand it, as I had no intended meaning. I just wanted him to stamp "approved" on my forehead and let me through the damned gates.

"We don't usually see your kind around here," he said with a hint of suspicion, "especially not on the weekend—and when your contract is deactivated."

"Is that right?" I asked. I lifted my tapper and made a show of swiping through some very heavy-duty names. "So, would you like to be talking to my tribune? His name is Leonard Winslade. Or perhaps the ex-consul is more to your liking? He's a praetor now. His name is Drusus, in case you've forgotten."

The hog in question was busy draining all the blood out of his face as I kept on talking. His smile, his curiosity, and those furrowed-up eyebrows faded all away and smoothed out real nicely.

"Or maybe the new consul," I continued, "the up-and-coming Galina Turov. She might be more your style. She's easy on the eyes, too. There's even a few Public Servants here in my favorites directory."

The hog almost shit himself right there. "Never mind, Centurion, never mind," he said quickly. He tapped his long fingers on everything in a flurry. He never met my eyes again, but he approved my tapper to open every door he could.

Smiling and nodding, I touched my cap as I walked on through. Of course, I'd taken the time to put on my uniform in the shitty sky train bathroom. You didn't want to walk around in your civvies in Old Central. Every third hog would stop you, and the rest of them would at least frown.

Marching as if I knew where I was going, even though I didn't, I took a few seconds to think about where my search might begin. Now, a normal person would probably start off by consulting various records and official listings of individuals. An even more discerning individual would probably start by phoning up their friends and asking them for advice and tips.

I did none of these things. That's because I was an experienced and seriously paranoid individual. When dealing with mysterious disappearances at Central, a man had to proceed with caution. Anyone who thought it was a good idea to go around telling people what your business was when you were looking for someone who had quite possibly been disappeared due to political machinations was an outright fool. So, I had to investigate without *seeming* to investigate.

Thinking it over, I began to appreciate the sheer genius of Galina's approach to this entire affair. What had she done? She'd enlisted the aid of one fearless and rather ignorant ape—I'm speaking of myself here—to do her dirty work for her. That way, she could have complete and total deniability should the operation go to shit. She could claim she didn't know why I was interested in Drusus's whereabouts. As far as she was concerned, I was plumb crazy.

As I didn't have my own handy sidekick with any kind of pull or punch left in this building, I couldn't follow her example. The important people I'd known at Central were all gone now. Drusus had been the most important of them.

Second had to be Floramel, who was now living on Dust World with the Investigator doing God-knew-what. The last would have been Etta, who now worked with Floramel.

None of those three were in this building anymore. I was on my own. Hmm…

I squinted at the crowds and the hallways for a good five seconds, hoping my mind would conjure up a plan.

Fortunately, this time it did. When it comes to things like subterfuge, deception, and even downright skullduggery, my mind was fertile ground indeed.

Turning on my heel, I marched straight for the elevators. The fairly high-level approval the bony hog had given me down at the train station allowed me to access a wide range of floors. All the public areas, all the legion base levels and even some of the upper echelon zone in the three hundreds were in reach. Those were usually reserved for primus or tribune-level officers.

But, most importantly of all, the first one hundred levels *below* Central were within my reach. That was a real break. Those were the prison levels all the way down to the Situation Room. That's where, when Earth was threatened from space, critical decisions were made for her defense.

One might think I would head for the brig first. After all, it stood to reason that any disappeared person would have spent some time there. That's where they had the torture chambers, the auto-judges—all that sort of thing.

But I skipped the security and detention zone entirely. Instead, I headed down past them, all the way to the Situation Room. Why? Because, with Drusus gone, I wanted to know who had replaced him—even though I already suspected who it was.

After a considerable ride down into the depths of the Earth, the elevator dinged at last. The doors opened, and I stepped confidently forward.

Two guards met me at the lobby exit. They seemed to be in an unfriendly mood. Their rifles were unslung and aimed in my direction.

I walked up to them as if they'd waved, smiled, and offered me a beer.

"Hey boys," I said. "I'm looking for Praetor Wurtenberger. Is he down here?"

The two hogs exchanged glances. "If you have orders to be down here at the Situation Room, Centurion, you'd better show them to me right now," said the hog on the left.

Obligingly, I lifted my tapper, paged through some high-level red contact names, and stabbed at the one that said Wurtenberger. Naturally, this did not ring through straight to the old man himself, but rather to his office, which was located far above us, probably near the peak at the five hundred level. That's where Drusus had once held court.

I talked to a couple of secretaries, identified myself, and then proceeded to bore and annoy the two hogs. They watched me with growing impatience as I sweet-talked my way through a few sneering sidekicks of primus rank.

Finally, I dropped the bombshell that I'd been shaping up inside my devious mind. I had a trick that I knew might get me through all of this nonsense.

"I'm supposed to be meeting Praetor Drusus down here," I told Wurtenberger's chief sidekick lady. "In fact, I'm standing right here at the door of the Situation Room right now."

"That isn't possible, Centurion—"

"But—here's the weird part—I'm not getting a signal on my tapper saying that he's here, and I'm just trying to find out what's happened. Has my appointment been changed?"

These statements were finally breaking through to the hogs upstairs. "You have an appointment with... um... the previous commander?"

"That's right, sir. Do we have a bad connection or something? I guess maybe I should inquire elsewhere. I'll use your name when I ask around."

That statement was somewhat electric. Wurtenberger's crony glanced around as if she'd been caught with her hands in the cookie jar.

"Um, well, Centurion, I'm not sure that's going to be possible right now."

"Right, right," I said, "but isn't Drusus in charge of planetary defense?"

17

"Um... that was his charge last time I checked," the secretarial primus said diplomatically. She was walking on eggshells because we were talking about a nonperson. There was all kinds of AI listening in these days to every type of communication imaginable. Anyone mentioning something—or someone—who was unmentionable, could become the subject of an investigation.

"Okay then," I boomed at her, pretending not to understand her state of mind at all. "If Drusus isn't around, well then, the second-in-command will have to serve. As I understand it, that would be Wurtenberger himself. That's why I'm calling your office. My appointment is with whatever official is serving as the chief-of-defense."

The primus formed up a tiny rosebud—or as I like to put it, butthole-type mouth. A pink bud that was very tight indeed.

She looked at me for a moment as if thinking things over. Finally, she released a wheeze of air. "All right. I'm ringing you through. Hold on."

I held. Some soft music played.

The two hogs looked on. They seemed mildly intrigued, but also annoyed. I could tell they really wanted to arrest me, and I could hardly blame them. Their job was to stand around down here all day like robots, a hundred levels below the world of light and air. They were like two dogs, wondering if they were going to get to go out for a walk today.

"You know what?" I told the hog on the left, the one who'd dared to speak to me in the first place. "You should think about joining the legions, boy. This is so dull down here. Aren't you sick of it? Wouldn't you rather earn an honest paycheck out among the stars?"

"No," he said flatly. "I was in the legions once. I was in Solstice. I didn't like it."

"Ah, too bad... The legion life's not for everyone. Not all of us can be a starman."

He eyed me sourly after that, and I knew I was going to get no help from him, but I didn't care. I hadn't really expected much. There was no way he was going to let me pass him unless he was ordered to, in any case.

Finally, Wurtenberger himself came on the line. It'd been quite a wait, but I was a patient man when circumstances demanded it.

"McGill?" he said in his thick euro accent. "Centurion McGill? What are you doing here at Central? Your contract isn't even activated. I checked."

"That's right, sir," I said. "I had a private meeting scheduled with Drusus, but I can't find him."

He glared at me for a while, not saying a word. Finally, just like his secretary had before him, he released a little gust of air. This gust, however, was quite a bit more generous and voluminous, as he was an obese man.

Only about a year or so ago, he'd been thin and trim. Ever since his last death, he seemed to be dead-set on putting back on every pound he'd lost. It required all of my tact and goodwill to not mention this fact.

Instead of an insult, I was thinking of calling in a debt if I had to. I'd gotten him out of purgatory the last time we'd met, so by my way of thinking, he owed me one.

This, of course, was largely why I'd bothered to go this route. I'd wanted to find Drusus. That was my goal. Who would be more likely to know where Drusus was but the guy—the man who'd assumed the top defense post in his absence?

Of course, it wouldn't have worked to simply walk up to Wurtenberger's office, tap on his door, and ask to be seen. No, no, no. High-level officers were extremely adept at avoiding contact with their various sycophants, bootlickers, and simps. You had to give them a damned good reason to *want* to see you. There had to be something in it for them.

In this case, I'd given him one: curiosity. He had to be wanting to know why I was here to talk to Drusus. That would give me a chance to find out from him what had happened to the man in the first place.

Smiling, I waited until he finally made his inevitable decision.

"He's not in the Situation Room, fool," Wurtenberger said. "Even you should know that by now."

I shook my head, and my jaw dropped low. "I don't know anything, sir. Like you said, I've been off duty. I'm just here reporting for—"

"Yes, yes, yes, shut up about that. Do not mention that name again."

"You mean Dru—?"

"Silence, idiot! Come up to my office. Don't stop anywhere and don't pester anyone else on the way."

"Yes, sir!" I said. I gave a little salute, but he was already gone.

Tipping my hat to the two head-shaking hogs, I turned around and marched back to the elevators from whence I'd come.

-3-

The ride up from one hundred floors below ground to four hundred fifty above was quite a long one. I entertained myself by playing with my tapper and sending messages to various members of Drusus' dissolved staff.

That had been the one place I'd considered starting, actually. Primus Bob, for example. He might have been forthcoming with information.

To my mild surprise, however, the names of his staffers were all listed as unreachable. In fact, as I sent off one text after another to every one of those people that I could remember the existence of, I found all of them bounced back with things like, "message sink full," "unknown address," and my favorite, "mailbox not found."

This made me pause. Just for a moment. Whatever had happened to Drusus had apparently happened to everyone else he had been personally associated with.

Huh… This could not bode well…

Ding! The elevator stopped. I stepped off and marched down the corridor as if I belonged up here in the stratosphere of offices. We were one notch below heaven, and my ears were popping with the air-pressure change.

A pair of hogs challenged me immediately. I showed them the message which I'd transformed into wallpaper on my tapper. It was from Wurtenberger, ordering me to pester him in his office.

The hogs melted away reluctantly, and I kept walking.

The female primus who I had talked to, the one with the butthole mouth, was front-and-center the second I opened the doors. Her hands were both up, fingers splayed in the classic stop-gesture.

As she checked my ID, her lips tightened up another notch. They were bloodless and barely pink by this point.

"Right this way, Centurion McGill," she said.

There was resentfulness in her voice, and maybe just a touch of fear—but whatever. I didn't care. I'd made my way into her praetor's office, and that had been my plan. It was my life experience that you rarely achieved anything you weren't supposed to unless you were bold and annoying.

At the door of the inner sanctum, the primus lifted up a delicate-fingered hand. She rapped on the door.

I sped up the whole process by reaching down and popping the handle open. The doors swung wide automatically.

The primus secretary stepped off to my left side, her eyes flashing at me angrily. "Your appointment has arrived, Praetor Wurtenberger," she said formally.

"Ah, yes," Wurtenberger said. "Centurion James McGill... Yes, yes. Step this way."

I walked into the place and had a look around. I had to admit his office wasn't half-bad. Not as big as Praetor Drusus' or Consul Drusus' had been, mind you—but pretty damned nice. These four-stars did well for themselves.

The office didn't take up an entire floor of Central, but I would say it had to be at least a quarter of whatever floor we were on. Yessir, old Wurtenberger was doing all right.

"Hello, Praetor," I said. "Very kind of you to see me, sir—and to help me out."

"Don't say that, McGill," he hissed.

"Why not, sir? No one else in this building would give me the time of day."

He glared underneath beetling brows. "There are good reasons for that, as you should know by now. Only an imbecile could be so undiscerning."

I endeavored to look as clueless as possible. This was rather easily achieved, both because I *was* clueless, and because my face naturally looked that way.

He waved irritably for me to sit across from his massive and overly ornate desk. Looking around, I thought to myself that Praetor Wurtenberger had taste that was somewhere between Drusus at his most fanciful—and Galina Turov herself. There were even a few of those red velvet curtains with gold ropes hanging in the corners.

The more I looked, the more I gawked. The room was like something you'd see on the grid selling you on a trip to Old Europe. It fairly reeked of opulence. The double doors were *real* wood. On both sides of the doors were all kinds of honest-to-God printed books on bookshelves of polished mahogany. I wondered if Wurtenberger had ever cracked one of the books for reals, or if they were just for show.

That's when I caught sight of the biggest shocker in the room. There was an actual, no-shit fireplace with a grand marble mantle in one corner. A large mirror with a gilded frame hung nearby. In front of the fireplace were two high-back chairs upholstered in the same red velvet as the curtains. I could only imagine Wurtenberger ate his snacks right there when he wasn't lording it over a pack of his underlings.

While I was rotating my head around like an owl and leering at things, Wurtenberger dove right into the matter.

"McGill," he said, "let me come directly to the point. I feel a certain debt exists between us. That's the only reason I'm seeing you here today."

I rotated my head back toward him, and I stared. "How's that, Praetor, sir?"

"You were instrumental in getting me out of purgatory some months ago."

"Oh, yeah… that… You would have done the same for me, I'm sure of it."

Wurtenberger looked furtive for a moment, then he changed the subject. "Listen, just as I was in purgatory then, Drusus is in purgatory now. You should have been able to figure that out on your own and avoided coming here. Anyone with half a brain could have made this small leap of logic."

I pointed a big finger at him, and I waggled it. "I think you hit the problem on the head right there, sir," I told him. "I have somewhat less than half a brain. In fact, my grandma—"

"Shut up, Centurion," Wurtenberger said, rudely interrupting my homey prattle. "What you need to do now is go back to wherever you came from. Hide there and hope that no one comes looking for you."

I shook my head slowly. "I don't know about that, sir. I'm not really good at pissing my pants and shivering in a hole. You should have probably figured that out by now. I tend to stick out like a sore thumb."

Wurtenberger sighed. "All right, why are you here? And what did Drusus want to meet with you about?"

I shrugged and spread my hands. "About Earth security, of course."

This perked Wurtenberger up. He was, after all, not just a fancy interior decorator. He was in charge of Earth's defenses. If a man such as myself knew about a threat against our world, he wanted to hear about it.

"All right," he said, "I'll bite. What is your mission? Why did you come here to pester Drusus?"

"Well, sir, I've been operating as a visual aid."

"A what?"

"An individual who's able to give… ah… firsthand accounts concerning threats from abroad."

He blinked at me. "You're a spy, then? Is that what you're telling me?"

"A rude word, Praetor. Rude."

"All right. Where have you been spying, and what have you seen?"

I hunkered forward and lowered my voice in the manner of a man imparting great secrets. Wurtenberger didn't fall for it and lean in to meet me, but I kept going anyway. "Did you know there are rebellious feelings, sir? Not just toward the Empire itself, but out amongst the possessions of good old Mother Earth?"

Wurtenberger looked at me sourly. His fat lips pursed up grotesquely. "Of course. There are always sour feelings, rebellious mutterings. That is the nature of man and alien alike."

"Right you are," I said. "Where do you think these, ah, *mutterings* are the worst right now?"

He shrugged. He clearly wasn't all that interested. "Well, out in Southeast Asia, there have been rumors. The same for the tip of South America. Then there's—"

"No, no, no, sir," I said. "Not here on Earth. I'm talking about people who can actually do something about it, people who are on other worlds."

He frowned at me. "What do you know of the other worlds?"

I laughed. "I tend to get around. I travel a bit. I have both a wandering eye and a wandering foot."

"Yes, yes," he said, disgusted. "Whatever. Give me specifics or get out."

I spread my hands and shrugged. "I've actually been charged to do this service for Praetor Drusus, sir. So, if you could produce him, or tell me where—"

"I told you, you idiot! He's in purgatory. He has been incarcerated indefinitely."

"Are you saying that he was executed? That's he's being held on ice?"

"Of course, that's what it means. According to my records, that fate befell you before the Sky World campaign. Don't you recall?"

Wurtenberger paged away at his tapper for a moment, throwing a slew of files out onto the desk. There were unflattering images of me dying on the dirty puff-crete floor of a cell, being given the last rites by a circle of laughing hogs.

"I would think," he said, "you know the process rather well."

"Oh, yeah… When's the trial date?" I asked.

"For Drusus? His trial date has been suspended."

I stared at Wurtenberger, and he stared back at me. "Suspended until when?"

"It's suspended… indefinitely."

I began to frown. I was smelling a gigantic rat, here. And that rat's name was Public Servant Turov. I'd been there when he'd ordered Drusus arrested and thrown out of his own office.

"Uh, sir?" I said, "this doesn't smell quite right to me. Mind you, I'm a country boy, so I'm quite familiar with things that don't smell right."

"Listen, McGill," he told me. "Drusus and all of his staff have been placed under arrest, executed, and been put on hold until their trials. Those trials will never come. Never."

"That's not justice, sir."

Wurtenberger shrugged. "If you want to join Drusus out of loyalty, I suppose that can easily be arranged—"

"Uh... no thank you," I told him. "I'm not interested in that."

"Right. I didn't think you were. Now, if all of your absurd questions have been answered in a satisfactory manner, I suggest you exit my office and do not return. If you persist in this matter, I will not intervene on your behalf again."

I shook my head ruefully. "I can see now why they picked you for this post, sir."

Wurtenberger bristled. "What do you mean by that?"

"You're a compliant man. The kind who does what he's told without question. Drusus wasn't like that. He just couldn't leave well enough alone. He liked to poke under rocks and overturn them. That gained him the rank of consul, but it also, in the end, was his downfall."

Wurtenberger looked troubled.

I stood up slowly, saluted, and began to walk away.

"Wait," Wurtenberger said. "Come back here, McGill."

I did so, and I stood before his desk quietly. I knew he had a big decision to make.

"I want you to report to me as you would have reported to Drusus," he said at last. "I have his job now, his role. As of today, you are my spy. Give me what you know."

And so, I told him what I'd seen. I told him about the rebellion that was simmering out at Dust World and about another rebellion, which I suspected was bubbling out at Death World. Elsa, Kattra, and all the Edge-Worlders from their tribe—they weren't happy stuck on that planet, and the colonists who lived in the hellish heat of Dust World, they weren't all that happy either—and they had a new leader who might be leading them to new dangers.

Of course, I made no mention of the bunker that had been found on my property. Nor did I bring up the fact that Boudica had been interred in that bunker. I didn't even talk about her having been a brain in a tank, or what her real name was—which I didn't know, anyway. But I did talk about the unhappy feelings percolating on those two worlds.

Now, this might seem like a treacherous act—and perhaps to some degree it was—but no one in Wurtenberger's shoes could have avoided hearing of these trouble spots before. They had to be blinking red lights on anyone's map. Plus, I had the added credibility that I'd been to both these planets recently.

Finally, when I finished speaking, Wurtenberger thumped a fat fist on his desk.

"It isn't right," he said. "Drusus was a good man. In fact, as you suggested, he probably deserved the role of consul more than I did. Here I am, cowering in fear. Here I am, sitting behind my desk, facing another man with more bravery in his soul than I've ever had in my long career."

This was quite an admission for Wurtenberger. These facts were, of course, obviously and blatantly true—but the amazing part was that he could admit such a thing. My estimation of his character rose up two notches higher—perhaps even three.

"Listen, McGill," he said, "I want to know a little bit more about what happened to Drusus, just as you do. I want you to work for me now, as I am holding his office in his stead."

"Uh... okay. What exactly do you want me to do, sir?"

"I want you to go down into the Vault of the Forgotten, and I want you to find him. I want you to talk to him."

I blinked a whole bunch of times as these words sunk in. "Down *there*, sir? You mean...? Aw, jeez... Did they really put him with the floating brains?"

Wurtenberger stared at his thick carpet. He nodded slowly. "I told you, the incarceration was permanent."

Right then, I got it. I got it all. This was why Wurtenberger was being such a chicken-shit. What they'd done to Drusus... oh, it was so much worse than just murdering him and leaving him dead for a few years. Much, much worse.

They'd taken him down to where they took their worst offenders, the people they wanted forgotten forever. He was one of those people whose mind they wanted to study, whose intelligence and knowledge they wanted to keep.

They had stored him like canned peaches on a shelf in the Vault of the Forgotten.

-4-

Wurtenberger kicked me out of his office with a mandate and a lot of permissions. Unlike this morning, when I'd been bullshitting my way around Central based on old credentials and fudgery, I was now legit. Too legit, you might even say.

I was a bit concerned about my new, highly visible status. Getting people to notice and respect you wasn't always a good thing around Central. I had no desire to join Drusus and find myself floating in some fish tank at his side.

My first step was to dutifully head for the lobby and the elevators. What followed was a long, long ride down to Central's main floor, which looked like Grand Central Station. There had to be about a thousand people milling around every which way. Most of them were in uniforms—but not all. The place was confusing, energetic, and very loud.

Naturally, my next obvious step was to cross the main floor, go through another round of security, and then take the other elevator system—the one that plunged downward. Some said that the secondary elevator system went down another five hundred floors or more. Others said it went all the way down—to the very gates of Hell.

The first hundred levels below were essentially for storage, prison, and other nefarious, unknown purposes. At around minus one hundred fifty, the labs began. That's where all the secret stuff Central came up with was invented.

In between the prisons and the labs—that's where the intel boys squatted in their dark lairs. From one hundred on, there was nothing but spooks and geeks down there.

But things got really weird down around level minus five hundred. That was supposedly the limit, the furthest depths which they had ever dug—but I knew better. There were more things down there, in the dark, and some of them didn't bear thinking about. That's where Wurtenberger had told me to go.

I'd been down there before, and I didn't want to go back. Most people who'd lived and worked in this building for decades had no idea about the strange goings-on deep in the belly of the Earth under our feet.

Down somewhere around level five hundred twenty-five— negative five hundred twenty-five, mind you—things got warmer, and stranger. Far beneath the Earth's surface, there was something known as the Vault of the Forgotten.

I'd been down there a couple of times, and I'd talked with some of the strange, ghostly beings who inhabited that aquarium of forgotten people. They squatted in their jars with bubbling fluids flowing past them, existing without a clear purpose. Those jars fed them somehow, providing nutrients, oxygen, filtration—everything a soul needed except a body.

These human jellyfish were in a state of mind similar to that of a dreaming person. It was a cruel, weird place. An abomination, really. I'd hardly ever seen any aliens do anything so bizarre to an enemy, much less their own kind. But here we humans were, keeping people in a suspended state for a century or more.

The idea that Drusus had ended up down there in a place like that… It was so unfair, it was sickening. I didn't want to contemplate it.

Stepping off the elevator at the lobby, I glanced toward the place that Wurtenberger had ordered me to go—toward the next, darker set of gates.

Then my fool head turned the other way. Something better had caught my attention. The great glass entryway that led out to the open streets of Central City. It was glorious out there. All sunshine, blue skies, buildings, streets, moving vehicles, gliding aircars—everything was visible through the front entrance.

Central City had been rebuilt. She was rich—fat with money. Most of that wealth was probably stolen from some colony or another. She was a capital city like no other.

So, I had two options, two stark contrasts—and I decided to take neither.

Instead, I stepped toward the public bathrooms. I pushed open the doors marked with a marching man.

Inside, I relieved myself with noise and gusto. During this process, I took several surreptitious glances to my left and right.

I lingered, and a dozen patrons came and went. But there was one guy—a tall, lanky fellow with a thin mustache.

Had he followed me into the restroom? I thought he had. But he was still here, holding his cock and staring down at it like he was expecting fireworks or something.

I decided to wait him out. I stood there long after I'd finished hosing down the urinal, clutching my own dick like it was a crucifix in a cathedral.

At last, a minute or two later, the other fellow shook off. He took his time at the sinks, but finally left.

Satisfied, I sauntered out myself a minute or so later. I glanced around without seeming to—and there he was.

That skinny, wispy mustache gave him away. It was distinctive.

There were always a lot of wimps and weasels hanging around inside Central. They were hogs, mostly, along with a few legionary wannabes. There were also loads of support personnel who were just government contractors, not really military at all.

But this fellow was wearing a uniform—an unusual one. I looked him over carefully. Sure, he had the blue patch of Hegemony on his shoulders. The blue globe of our Mother Earth. There wasn't anything odd about that.

But the uniform itself... What was with those black slacks? Those tight cuffs?

Then I had it. He was Intel. He was a spook. I was instantly on guard.

The lanky man was lingering at a vending machine that stood outside the restrooms, and he appeared to be arguing with it. He insisted on telling the machine he'd given it money. The machine argued back with typical robotic self-certainty. "No, sir. No vending has been initiated. Sale canceled."

"Look, machine," the skinny spook said, "I've given you money and you're going to give me my cigarettes."

"Sir, I do not vend that item."

I had a certain level of sympathy. That was a vending machine for you these days. They might forget what was happening in the middle of a transaction. Sometimes they lied about things, too. Sometimes, they just flat-out stole your money. I didn't trust any of them.

I walked up to the fellow and struck up a conversation. "Hey," I said.

He glanced at me, startled. "What do you want?" he asked. His voice was a bit like a jockey's and distinctly unpleasant.

"Is this machine giving you trouble?"

"No, it's nothing. It's fine," he said, turning away.

"Wait a minute," I said, grabbing him by one skinny arm. "Don't I know you from someplace?"

"Certainly not, Centurion. Unhand me."

He wasn't scared, and that was a bit bewildering. The reality was I was at least twice his size and wearing a Legion Varus uniform.

Sure, Intel men held their own mystique. They *were* spooks. They knew lots of secrets. But Varus guys like me? We were just plain killers.

Still, this guy wasn't afraid, so I let go of him, somewhat impressed. I squinted at him.

"Do you know a man named Dickson?" I asked.

His eyes widened a fraction. Those two narrow slits opened, but then they sealed back up again. He returned to his poker face.

"Never heard of him," he lied. "I must be going."

"No problem," I said to his back. "The next time I talk to Dickson, I'll give him your regards."

The man stopped and turned around, cocking his head quizzically at me. He took a few steps back toward me. "Are you looking for trouble, Centurion? Because if so, I believe you've found it."

"Oh," I laughed. "Now I *know* you're a spook, just like Dickson. All you Intel boys have the same M.O.: big swaggering attitudes. You're all like small-town cops with your first hard-on."

As I spoke, the man's slitty eyes widened to an improbable size. In fact, they almost bulged. I don't think he was accustomed to being accosted and talked to in my unique fashion.

"As long as we're name-dropping, McGill," he said, finally admitting that he knew who I was. "Oh yes, of course. I know your name—and I know that you know I know your name."

"Huh…?" I said, a bit confused by this exchange.

He sighed. "Ah, yes. That was in your file as well. 'Likes to play the part of an imbecile but is sharper than he seems.'"

He read this bit off his tapper and looked up at me, cocking his head again. "I dare say that must be true. No one could have reached the rank of centurion or spotted an Intel man tailing him unless he had at least two brain cells to rub together inside his oversized skull. Therefore, you must be faking idiocy."

"That's right," I told him. "I'm a genius with bells on."

He nodded. "Anyway, now that we understand our roles, I'm here to escort you down deeper into Central. I've been charged with making sure you arrive at your destination in a timely manner."

"Oh yeah? To what floor?"

He shrugged. "Minus one hundred and six."

It was my turn for my eyes to squint. That wasn't right. I was supposed to go all the way down to five hundred and something.

One hundred six below? That deep in the Intel zone. That's where spooks like this dude ruled. Heading down there could be unsafe for a man like me. It wasn't just your run-of-the-mill torture center with detention cells. Down there—that's where people who knew things were questioned.

"What do you want with me down there?" I asked.

"Nothing," he said. "Wurtenberger's office simply informed me they were sending a man down into the region of my personal office. That's on the one hundred sixth. There's an approval process to be done before you go any… farther."

"Ah," I said, as if catching on at last. "Okay," I said, extending my hand to shake. "Since you know who I am, tell me your name."

"Brinkley," he replied. "Agent Brinkley."

We shook hands, then we marched off toward the dark tunnels that led to the second elevator lobby—the one that led downward.

On the way through more security, I kept the air full of harmless banter. Brinkley seemed bored, but at least he wasn't alarmed.

He should have been. If he'd known me better, he might have realized I was having some very dark thoughts.

I didn't like how things were going. I'm an independent man, and when I embark on an independent mission, I like to *remain* independent. In fact, few men like Brinkley had survived attempts to follow me pretty much anywhere. One of them was Bevan, a guy I knew and liked—someone I'd met on the Moon years ago. He was such a harmless and clueless hog that I'd let him keep breathing.

But Brinkley? I wasn't so sure about him.

We breezed through the checkpoint, as both of us had perfect credentials. In no time, we boarded an elevator alone and rode down into the abyss.

"What do you know about Dickson?" Brinkley asked.

I shrugged. "He joined my legion for a while. You know, I think he drifts through a lot of them. Didn't he serve for a time in Victrix?"

"That information isn't widespread."

"I get it. I get it."

Around the fiftieth floor below the surface, I decided it was time to make my move. I held out my hand to Brinkley, as if wanting another shake. He took it slowly, looking kind of bewildered.

"What's this?" he asked.

"Just a farewell and a hearty well-met. Give my regards to Dickson next time you see him, okay?"

"Farewell? I don't think so," the smaller man said. He frowned at me with fresh irritation. He lifted his tapper again and read from my file.

"Boobish, rude, and prone to ham-handed trickery," he said aloud. "I'm certainly beginning to understand this report. You, sir, are going down with me to floor minus one hundred and six, where—"

I hit the emergency stop before he could finish his sentence.

It was the end of the line for Brinkley. I murdered him quickly and efficiently, crashing one fist into his skull and the other at the base of his neck at the same moment. I snapped a number of his vertebrae like crackling twigs.

This kind of kill wasn't always as clean as it sounded, of course. It's a matter of severing the brain from the spinal cord, disconnecting the nervous system itself. You didn't die from the broken bones themselves, but rather from not being able to draw breath or pump your own heart.

It's not the quickest death, but it's definitely a humane one. I suspect people were relatively numb while they were lying there, suffocating and going through cardiac arrest on the floor.

With a couple of sweeping motions of my size-thirteen boots, I kicked his body into a corner.

There were cameras on us. Naturally, I knew that. I was now on a timer to get out of Central before I was caught.

I'd stopped the elevator at floor minus fifty, which I happened to know was a quiet maintenance level. I'd been down in this region many times due to insubordination and countless punishments, both fair and unfair, so I had the layout of the place in mind.

I stepped off the elevator, spotting only a single, distant figure. He was wielding a robotic cleaning machine of some kind.

"Hey," the janitor shouted at me, "you can't be down here. This is a maintenance level. Who are you, anyway?"

I waved to him as if he were an old friend. Tapping the buttons and hopping clear of the elevator car, I sent Brinkley's corpse all the way down to the very bottom levels that my newfound security clearance could reach. That was somewhere around minus five hundred—which, believe you me, was going to take a long time to reach.

"Sorry!" I shouted to the janitor, who was now heading my way, wagging a finger and lifting his tapper to make a report. "Sorry! I just got off on the wrong floor."

Fortunately, another elevator—there were four of them—stopped soon thereafter. I was allowed to step aboard.

The janitor was glaring at me and prattling about clearances.

"Don't worry," I said, "I've got the run of the place."

Then the doors closed, and the elevator whisked me away. This time, however, it was going upward rather than downward—back up to the main floor.

Let me tell you, I was a bit nervous during this long ride. After all, I'd just committed my first murder in months, and the victim had been a stranger from Intel, no less. Would I make it out of the building? Only dumb luck or a nod from the heavens could help me now.

Why had I struck Brinkley down? You see, the simple fact was I didn't trust the Intel community. Brinkley had suggested he was there to escort me on Wurtenberger's behalf, but Wurtenberger had mentioned nothing of the sort. He hadn't said anything about putting a man on my tail to ensure I'd go anywhere.

In fact, that wasn't Wurtenberger's style. He was a very direct man who thought in straight lines. If he'd wanted to assign me an escort, he'd have probably sent that little butthole-mouthed primus down with me—and in that case, we'd have gone all the way to the bottom.

I was mistrustful. I didn't believe anything Brinkley had told me, except possibly that he actually knew Dickson.

At the main floor, I stepped off the elevator and walked quickly, marching directly toward the exits. I wanted to get out of Central right the hell now.

As I walked, I stripped off my beret and, with one hand, reached up and ripped the identity patches off my shoulders. This is easily done. In my time, insignia like this were designed to be removable. After all, we died frequently, and when we returned to duty, they issued us fresh uniforms and fresh badges. The uniforms and the insignia had to be interchangeable.

The nanofiber material had a very firm grip on your shoulder when applied—but it could be removed with a firm hand and a harsh tug. I left on the centurion patch, of course.

I also pulled on Brinkley's cap, which I'd stolen. It was an Intel cap.

Although it wasn't large enough for my head, I squeezed it onto my skull, anyway. These days, most clothes were smart clothes. They really were one-size-fits-all, as they could alter themselves physically. A given piece of clothing could fit most men of varying dimensions. This was fortunate indeed for me.

In the lobby area, there was a security alert going. It was silent, but you could tell. A group of four armed men had formed up, and they were looking sternly at everyone flowing in and out of the lobby gates.

I marched purposefully toward the gathered squad of hogs.

"Who are you?" The lead hog said, challenging my approach. "Move along."

I looked at them, as Brinkley might have—as if they were idiots. "I'm Intel," I told him, as if this explained everything.

The head hog frowned at me. He glanced at my lack of patches, noting my rank of centurion and the Intel cap.

"That's not—" he complained.

"Listen, Vet," I said, "who called you?"

"Intel…"

I smiled, and I tapped at my cap, which was so tight it was hurting my skull right now. "That's right. I'm here to support you. I'm here to identify the culprit and bring him back downstairs."

The men frowned at one another. I was lucky, because none of them seemed to have gotten my picture on their tappers—not yet. Intel didn't like sharing anything about anything if they didn't have to. Of course, it was only a matter of time before they got desperate.

"I won't be any trouble," I said. "I'll stay right here." I moved to the left, standing at the flank of the leftmost man in the line. "I'll let you know when we see him."

They looked at me somewhat grumpily.

"Eyes front!" I boomed. "He might be here. He might be walking right by. He's a master of disguise."

Confused, they gripped their weapons, staring in every direction.

Before making my next move, I waited until a particularly attractive young recruit wandered by. She looked as clueless and sweet as Tessie had on her first day, when she'd been tricked into joining Legion Varus.

Under normal circumstances, my eyes would have been glued to her butt, just like all four of the hogs I was standing alongside. But today was a different day.

Instead of gawking, I put a big hand on the leftmost hog's shoulder and reached down with my other hand, popping the pin out of his plasma grenade. He only had one, but I was surprised they'd allowed him to have any explosives at all.

Unfortunately, I had to give it a hard tug. He was a veteran. He knew what he was doing, and he'd bent the pin so it wouldn't slip out too easily.

"What the hell?" he said.

"Look! There he is!" I said, pointing at a random guy with big teeth and curls. My chosen victim was tall at least, and I guess in another universe, someone could have been convinced he was a McGill.

The hogs were fooled. They rushed forward as a group to arrest the hapless guy, who was backing up, lifting his hands and facing a circle of carbine muzzles.

"Whoa, whoa," he was saying. "Hey, dude, wait!" he said, pointing at the man on the left.

The hogs ignored him. One of them reached out, grabbed his wrist, and clamped a gravity cuff on it.

But then, all of them noticed what the teeth-and-curls victim I'd fingered was blabbing about. He was pointing to the glowing, radiating, blue-flashing light of the plasma grenade on the hog veteran's belt. It must have been set for the default: a long fuse with a slow burn.

Desperate, they began to scatter. They tried to back away, to run. The guy with the grenade on his belt fought to get it off, but there really wasn't time.

A moment later, all of them went up in a blue glare, along with a few startled passersby.

I began shouting random things about aliens and terrorists. In the confusion, I fled the building with a hundred others. We headed for the emergency exits in a panic.

I was really screaming. My mouth was wide open, my lips blubbery. Spittle flew as if I was truly terrified.

The crowd hit the panic-bars, and a moment later sunshine hit my face.

Soon after, most of the others stopped, as the disturbance seemed to have dissipated. Most turned back, bewildered. But I kept right on running.

Unlike them, I never bothered to turn. I never bothered to pause. I simply raced off into the city and disappeared.

-5-

Marching down the streets of Central City, I snatched a coat off a drunk and stuffed some credits into his hands when he woke up and started complaining. It wasn't much of a disguise, and it was flat-out filthy, but it would have to do.

I don't mind telling you I was seriously worried about my new status as a fugitive. Of course, I'd been a fugitive many times before, but the circumstances were different this time. Instead of doing something stupid on my own, for my own goofy purposes, I'd been tricked somehow into doing someone else's dirty work.

And for what? The potential future benefit of intimacy with Galina? Well… that wasn't all of it. I'd agreed to help her because she was an old friend.

Still, on the face of it, I'd been shit-off crazy to get involved at all. Sure, she'd asked me nicely. But she'd also managed to run-off Tessie just by calling. Now, here I was on the edge of being disappeared—just like Drusus.

Overall, I wasn't totally sure how I'd gotten into this sad predicament. I had to chalk it up to persistent ignorance and my pridefully stubborn nature.

Trying to think clearly, I paused in an alleyway and took stock of things. No one seemed to be following me—not even a drone. That was something, at least. But it was only a matter of time.

I decided it was time to contact Galina. I tapped away at my tapper fruitlessly. She wasn't accepting calls. In fact, there was no way to locate her.

"Girl..." I muttered, "goddamn it..."

It was as if she didn't exist, as if she wasn't even on Earth—but I knew that was nonsense. She'd called me just this morning. I thought about it and soon came up with a way to flush her out into the open.

I sent a three-word message to her inbox instead of using the instant-messaging service. I knew my note would linger until she read it—and I knew she eventually would.

Galina was the kind of woman who got curious about things, and couldn't leave them be—not even when it was best to do so.

After that, I searched for a dive bar. That took me several long blocks of walking, as the area around Central was all pretty upscale these days.

I found what I was looking for in the old alien sector—the Gray Sector, we used to call it, although that was considered a slur these days.

Some humans lived here now, not just Cephalopods, Blood-Worlders, Saurians, and the like. So, it wasn't all that odd when I stepped into the dingy bar, ordered my first drink of the day, and a big plate of cheese fries to go with it.

I munched on the fries, drank my beer, and pondered how likely it was that I'd make it out of this city without being arrested. I'd killed a slew of people, which tended to piss off law enforcement anywhere you went.

Now, sure, I was out of Central itself, but I was still in the most photographed, surveilled, and AI-swept city on the planet. No city on Earth was less secure for a man like me. Naturally, I'd ditched the stolen cap from Brinkley, torn off my insignia again, and swapped my uniform for a bum's raincoat. The coat was unseasonable, but I didn't care. It allowed me to hide everything except my sheer size as I huddled in the bar, hoping for the best.

About half my plate of fries and my third beer were gone when my tapper buzzed. I glanced at it. The message read: "This had better be for real, McGill."

That made me smile. My ploy had worked.

The three words I'd sent to Galina had been: "I found him."

That's all I'd sent. Nothing else.

One of the keys to communicating with people who are not in a communicative mood was to give them something they wanted—but not all of it.

Sure enough, her curiosity had gotten the better of her in about ten minutes. She'd emerged from hiding and sent me a message in return. She'd probably done so using a myriad of protective security measures—private network settings, with proxy bots set up all over the place. Maybe she'd even taken *extreme* measures, like deep-linking a message to another planet and then bouncing it back to Earth. Such messages were untraceable in terms of their point of origin.

But whatever she'd done, she *had* responded.

Now, a less discerning man—or a more desperate man—might have tapped out an instant demand for help. I didn't do that.

Instead, I ate some more of my cheese-fries. I finished off the plate and ordered a fourth beer. Several minutes later, as if it was a nonchalant afterthought, I sent another text to her.

"It's legit. I found him."

Then I waited. Sure enough, my tapper buzzed. She was calling me direct. I lifted my arm, so I could surreptitiously look down without making it too obvious.

The screen didn't brighten with her pretty face this time. Instead, it stayed black.

"James?" she said, "tell me what you learned."

"Nope. Not until you get me out of this city."

"What do you mean? Just take a flight—to anywhere."

I shook my head and sipped my beer. "That's going to be a problem," I told her. "Things didn't go perfectly."

She hissed and fussed for a bit, then she sighed. "All right. I can see by the grid reports—did you have to kill people? That was you in the lobby—right?"

I shrugged noncommittally. "I can neither confirm nor deny."

Galina sighed, realizing with utter certainty that I'd caused the devastation at Central. Normally, I would have denied everything vehemently, even when I was obviously guilty—but there wasn't any point to that today.

"Okay," she said, "I'll extract you. Stay right where you are."

That alarmed me. Did she know where I was? If she'd figured it out, then surely the spooks back in Central would have done so by now.

My tapper went blank again. She'd disconnected, and I was left with little choice other than to order a triple-meat hamburger and my fifth beer. Before these delicious items could arrive, there was a disturbance at the entrance.

No fewer than four hogs walked in. They were all human, and they all looked ornery.

The bar's bouncer, a Blood-Worlder ex-heavy trooper by the look of him, stood eight feet plus tall. He probably weighed as much as all four of the hogs combined. He tried to block their way, throwing out his arms just as he'd been taught to do.

The hogs, unfortunately, were in no mood for it. They drew out shock-rods and began stinging him with them.

This was probably not the best plan. Blood-Worlders didn't feel much in the way of pain, but you can anger them with it if you push hard enough.

I didn't feel an ounce of regret when he dashed one hog to the deck, backhanded another right out of the door of the bar, and then cocked his fist to nail a third. The massive guy was just trying to do his job.

But that's when a single shot rang out. The squad leader had put a round right between his eyes—a bolt big enough to take down a Blood-Worlder in one shot.

The bouncer flopped back, stone dead.

"Shit," I whispered to myself.

That seemed plain unfair to me. After all, he wasn't going to get a revive anywhere, and he'd just been doing his job. But that's how hogs acted in Gray Sector—like bullies, as if they had the right to stomp on anybody's territory and do whatever they wanted.

The whole bar was emptying out by this point. Aliens were fleeing, clambering over the tables and chairs, knocking them over in their urgency to escape the premises. Most of them went out the back, since the front door was choked with hogs and one giant carcass.

For my own part, I didn't bother to get up. I didn't bother to flee. What was the point? If they had a squad at the front door, they probably had another squad at the back.

Instead, I chugged my fifth beer and let myself be arrested. I didn't make it super easy for them, however. I seemed docile at first, then I put a man down on the deck.

"Sorry about that," I said. "Things like this just happen when a man has big shoes."

Another guy stabbed me with a shock-rod. He seemed to be in a bad mood due to the dislocated jaw that the Blood-Worlder had given him earlier.

"Hey, hey, settle down with that thing," I said. "He tripped. I swear, he tripped!"

The guy on the floor climbed back to his feet with a growl. He happened to be the leader of the group, and his mood was almost as ugly as his face.

"McGill," he said, "our orders are to bring you in alive. But just like you, I've been known to bend my orders into something I like better."

I smiled at him, daring him to do it. He flashed a gun under my nose, and we eyed each other. He considered blasting me, even though we both knew full well I didn't care if I died right now.

The delay I'd managed to cause by messing with the hogs actually turned out to be beneficial. Right about then, some of the aliens began to drift back into the bar. They came in from the rear entrance, from behind the bar, from the bathrooms, and two more even walked in through the front door, hopping right over the swollen, massive corpse of the bouncer.

I couldn't help but notice one thing about them: they were all Saurians. Now, lizard-folk weren't entirely unknown in the city, especially in Gray Sector. There were a fair number living in town—probably numbering in the low thousands. But to see three, four, five—no, make that six—of them all in one place, at one time, all walking together? That was outright strange.

The hog police around me noticed this, too. One turned and pointed a thick finger.

He managed to distract the squad leader, who still had a big pistol in my face, long enough for him to look around irritably. "What the hell's wrong with you, Jacobs? What do all these cold-blooders want?"

The business end of his weapon shifted away an inch or two. I was glad for that because a single bolt from that high-caliber weapon had put the Blood-Worlder back on his rear in less than a second.

This seemed to me as good a time as any to get back into the game. I grabbed the leader's wrist, twisted, and yanked him off his feet.

Utter mayhem commenced after that. Six oversized lizards charged at us from all directions all at once.

Startled, the human guards dropped their shock-rods, pulled out their pistols, and began to fire. The Saurians had no guns. Maybe that was because aliens weren't allowed to own weapons—but then again, it was also illegal to attack the police in the pursuance of their duty.

Two of the Saurians were flattened by big, booming pistols before they reached us. Then they were in close, and things turned nasty.

The conclusion was foregone, because three normal men couldn't stop a pack of Saurians in close combat. I'd already taken care of the fourth man, having yanked his big pistol out of his hands, placed it to his skull, and fired it. His brains now decorated the tile, much like the Blood-Worlder's had done not five minutes ago.

Once all the humans were dead and gone, I looked around at my new circle of even uglier friends.

Had I traded four hogs for four Saurians? Was that a good deal? I wasn't sure yet.

They were all looking at me with hostility, perhaps equal to or beyond the level of rage that had been exhibited by the hogs themselves.

"Hey, boys," I said, "good timing. Thanks a bunch. I'll be heading on out now."

The pistol was plucked from my hand. I'm a strong man, but when faced by Saurians who were easily equal to me in strength and general physicality, there was no stopping their powerful claws short of killing them. And I didn't want to do that. After all, I didn't know yet if these guys were friend or foe.

Finally, a seventh Saurian entered the bar. He came in from the back, near the restrooms. He walked in, exhibiting an unhurried nature.

This alien was wearing a hood, unlike the others. But when he came close, he threw back that cowl, and I was surprised.

He had blue scales, and I recognized him in an instant.

His name was Raash.

-6-

Raash was an old friend of mine. Well, perhaps the word "friend" isn't exactly right. We'd killed each other as many times as we'd shaken hands—or tails, or whatever the hell you do to make a Saurian feel like he's your buddy. But in any case, we were well known to one another.

"It is McGill," Raash said to me. "Blood follows you, human. It follows you the way shit follows one of Earth's tasty rodents."

It was a weird statement, but not out of character for Raash. His mind, like the mind of all Saurians, was different from that of a human. In fact, Raash's mind was even *more* different than that.

Some years back, Raash had gone through a very difficult revival process—one in which I was directly involved. This had given him a look and an outlook that was unlike anyone else in his species.

He'd never been a particularly friendly fellow, mind you, but now he was outright hard to tolerate. He was a creature of the kind I understood best: a driven being, a creature of elemental habits, appetites and attitudes.

Both Raash and I were impulsive, violent, and we tended to rub people the wrong way. We both had trouble telling the truth most of the time as well. One significant difference between the two of us was that Raash was a terrible liar, while I considered myself something of a master of the art.

"Hey, Raash, old buddy," I said, ignoring the bloody lines that four sets of claws were driving into my forearms. His Saurian sidekicks were hauling on my arms, which were outstretched on either side of me. "It's really good to see you. Is all this your idea? You're my extraction team, aren't you? You're my knight in shining—"

"Shut up, human," Raash said. "You screech and chatter as would a mindless ape in the trees. This is your nature, but it is not ours."

I sensed, in that moment, that Raash really wanted me to shut up. Maybe he didn't want the others in this group to consider me and him as friends. So, I kept quiet.

"Okay, Raash," I finally said, "this is your show. What happens next?"

He stared at me with hostility for a moment. "I should," he began, "by all rights, gut you to pay a tiny portion of the debt we all owe our two comrades."

Raash gestured toward the dead Saurians sprawled on the barroom floor.

"Here they lay supine, their tails forever motionless. It is an abomination that this ape-descendant still draws breath while they do not."

The other lizards shuffled a bit, and I got the feeling they agreed with his sentiments.

"That's not my fault, Raash," I said. "I didn't command anyone to come into this bar and tear up these hogs."

"That's not true," Raash countered. "In a way, you did exactly that. But for now, this debt must go unpaid. We must leave here before more of these pesky humans come and seek unfair vengeance upon my people."

We went out the back then, and all of us stuffed ourselves into a single aircar.

Now, perhaps you've never been in an aircar with three Saurians in the front, two in the back, and you wedged into the "chick spot" in the center of the backseat. If you haven't, you can count yourself lucky.

One universal physical attribute shared by every Saurian from Steel World that I'd ever met was an overwhelming stench. I don't think they've ever even pondered the concept of taking a bath, brushing their teeth, or even wiping after they dropped a deuce. No, none of these things were in the playbook for Saurians.

On top of that, they're quite sharp-elbowed—literally. They're covered in raspy scales and have broad shoulders, hips, thighs—broad everything. So, to sit with them shoulder-to-shoulder, with my soft, normal human skin rubbing up against the rough, horny surfaces of two reptiles—it was no picnic.

I suffered in silence in the back. I'm not an ungrateful man. After all, these stinky nightmares had come and rescued me.

We flew out of the city in a highly illegal fashion. The normal traffic rules on Earth were simple: aircars were for the air, ground cars were for the ground. This seems like a simple enough concept, even if you were born with cold blood and a slow brain. But these Saurians seemed not to get it.

They flew right down on the deck, inches from the surface of the road. This allowed the aircar, of course, to move much faster than any ground vehicle possibly could. Every now and then, the pilot, who did seem to be an expert at his craft, hopped over ground traffic that got in his way. Then he went straight down to the deck again and sped along at high speeds.

Red lights were for suckers, as far as this group was concerned. Robocops with whirling lights and squealing wheels? Utterly ignored.

Surprisingly, the air traffic control system didn't seem to come after us. Apparently, it wasn't engaged, as we weren't being chased from above.

I realized this was a brilliant way to get out of town fast—if you didn't mind losing your license afterwards. I mean, we were doing something like two hundred kilometers an hour most of the time, if you didn't account for sudden screeching slowdowns and wild bounding jumps over garbage trucks, taxis, and the like.

As soon as these momentary slowdowns passed, the pilot immediately sped up again. Within a few minutes, we were out of town. To my surprise, we weren't racing over the main highways or into the skies.

No, sir. Instead, we were down at the docks.

We whizzed by the giant ships—the super-massives—where I'd once worked as an cargo inspector.

"Look at that," I said, whistling. "There's at least three fat ladies in the harbor from Europe Sector. That's unusual, you know."

"Shut up, human," one of the Saurians said.

It was the one to my right. Damn, this guy's breath did stink the worst of all—probably because of sheer proximity.

If you can imagine rotten sardines mixed with a hot, skunky undertone to flavor it up. That was the nature of the humid, fog-like cloud of stench that rolled over my face when he spoke.

Just to discourage him from continuing to gas me, I went ahead and shut up.

At the end of the pier, after sending a few fishermen diving over the side into the waters of the Atlantic, we drove right off the end of the pier and into the water itself.

Not *into* the water, not exactly. We skimmed over the waves, perhaps two meters above.

Soon, we reached new high speeds. We were doing about three hundred now. That's what the speedometer seemed to indicate as I craned my neck and peered toward the front.

"Uh…" I said, "you guys wouldn't mind telling me where we're going, would you?"

"There is a floating contrivance ahead," Raash said.

A floating contrivance?

I thought that over to myself, peering through the windshield, which was splattered with salty sea spray.

Then, I thought I saw it. There was a yacht out there. A large yacht, dead ahead. Could that be our destination? I believed it was.

Something like seven minutes later, I stood on the deck of the yacht. I marveled a bit because it was actually pretty cold out here in the open ocean. The sea always seemed to do that, reducing the temperature of the land or raising it by several degrees once you crossed that border we call the shore. No matter where you were on Earth, the oceans stabilized the temperature.

The aircar rested on the deck behind me, its engine ticking as it cooled. There was a light rain and a growing wind. I ignored the storm because none of the Saurians seemed interested in it, and it wouldn't do to appear weak.

Raash went below, leaving me with two Saurians, who were both still painfully clinging to my bloody arms. When a big swell came up and lifted the deck under our feet, I thought about flipping one of them into the sea. I genuinely did. I figured I could probably pull that off with a sudden, unexpected move.

But then the other guy would be on me, and it was going to be a tough fight. Sure, I might win—or I might get my throat torn out. This was probably the only opportunity I was going to get to escape these lizards, and I seriously considered taking it—until a small figure appeared.

She was directly in front of me, coming up from below decks. Behind her, Raash lingered—or rather, malingered.

"Galina?" I said, shocked to my core. I'd kind of expected to see more lizards, or possibly some other alien lifeform, but no. Galina was here, on this ship. It made a bit of sense, as her father was incredibly rich, and the family doubtlessly owned a half-dozen yachts as nice as this one.

"Hello, McGill," Galina said. "This is not how I expected to meet you. We must get you below before you're traced." She turned to Raash, and her tone became commanding. "Raash, get this aircar off my deck, and don't allow it to be traced back to me."

"Yes, mistress," Raash replied.

That startled me and even raised my eyebrows a bit. Was Raash working for Galina now? What a pair!

Raash directed one of his lizards—I think it was the one who'd been expertly piloting through town before, although they all looked like gators to me. He told him to climb back into the aircar and fly off in a random direction.

This was immediately done, and we headed below decks.

Like steps on most ships, these were rather narrow and made of metal. At no point did the two Saurians, who still had firm grips on my arms, allow me any semblance of freedom.

My mind wandered anyway, and I considered once again performing a move of sorts. Stairways could be dangerous places—just ask anyone. That went double for narrow, steep, ladder-like steps that were wet with seawater.

A lizard fellow who slipped and fell here... well, he might just dash his brains out on the way down...

But again, I passed over this opportunity, as I had with the other such fleeting moments. I reminded myself sternly that these reptiles might smell bad, but they seemed to be rescuing me.

The fact there was blood running down both of my forearms wasn't really their fault. They were likely just following orders—Galina's orders.

So, I let them drag me down into the interior of the yacht, which was quite sumptuous inside. The main lounge had floating sofas and chairs with smart-padding.

"Oooh, those look comfy!" I exclaimed.

Galina glanced back, slightly pleased. "They are. They even have embedded AI systems within them that can offer massages or temperature adjustments as desired."

"Just what a tired man needs!"

She hesitated, then shook her head. "Not yet. Let's talk first—down below."

We went down another level. This was even more inviting. The deck itself was a translucent material that could turn opaque or transparent, giving guests a startling view of marine life swimming right underneath.

The walls of the yacht were odd as well. They were adaptive partitions that could turn opaque or transparent depending on the need. I vaguely hoped the bedroom walls were solid, at least...

We passed the dining area, and I felt a hunger pang. I pointed and grunted at the fine foods, but Galina was unrelenting.

There were a few human crewmen in sight here and there, but they avoided eye contact with either me or the lizards.

They seemed quite terrified of the aliens. Creatures like Raash didn't think like humans, not even like rabid wolves. They thought in an alien manner. Anything might set them off.

Anything might be considered an insult or a grave personal injury.

I, on the other hand, had no such reservations. I asked the chef what was for dinner, flirted with the wait staff, and generally annoyed people until we were led down three decks to what must be Galina's personal stateroom. There, the Saurians finally released my arms and pushed me inside.

Galina ran her hand over a translucent wall. "These surfaces are constructed of smart adaptive glass," she said. "I can alter the opacity at my whim."

"Can you play a ballgame?"

Her nose wrinkled. "I probably could, but I never tried."

I ran my hands over a wall. It was firm, and it felt as smooth as glass—warm glass. "Wall, show me the bathroom."

An arrow appeared, glowing and green. It pointed me to a doorway that hadn't been there a moment earlier.

Galina watched as I ambled in there and applied some towels to my bloody arms. When I started to take a leak, however, she squawked and urged the walls to transform into a solid again.

The door to the stateroom shunted open violently.

"What's this?" Galina demanded.

"I heard you cry out in anguish," said a familiar raspy voice. The hulking individual who stood in the doorway was Raash himself. He was breathing heavily and staring at me as I came out of the bathroom. I waved and smiled at him.

"That will be all, Raash," Galina said. "Thanks for your concern."

I touched my middle finger to my forehead in a salute, but he didn't seem to get the hint. Instead, he stared past me toward Galina.

"Mistress," he said, "I know this one. He's an ape of unrelenting negativity. He might abuse you, or worse yet, trick you into allowing yourself to be abused. I cannot recommend that you socialize with this rogue for any length of time. It's a grave mistake on your part to do so."

"Yes, yes, Raash," Galina said. "I know McGill very well. I've known him longer than you have. Close the door and get out. You're getting my carpet wet and stinking up my stateroom."

Rasch slammed the door and stomped away with poor grace.

"Galina?" I said, spreading my dripping arms wide and stepping toward her as if we were about to embrace.

"Your arms are torn up," she said in disgust.

"Just one more small sacrifice I've made for you tonight, my Lady Fair," I said.

"Shut up, McGill. This is business."

As I could tell I wasn't going to get any sugar from her, I went looking for something to eat.

"So," I said conversationally, "when did you take up with Raash? You and him aren't doing the nasty, are you?"

"How disgusting," she said, giving a little shudder. "Don't even suggest such a thing."

"Okay, okay," I said. "Then how is it that you and him… uh… hooked-up, so to speak?"

Galina glared at me. "That's a poor choice of words, McGill. We haven't 'hooked-up', as you put it. I'm not like that freak Floramel you used to chase after."

She was, of course, speaking of Raash's one and only human girlfriend. Floramel had, strangely enough, become the wife of the Investigator out at Dust World. That made her my relative, more or less.

That was the kind of thing that living for a century could do to a man. Relationships, personal histories—they tend to get all mixed up and entwined over time. It was like marrying a girl, divorcing her, and then twenty, thirty, or fifty years later, meeting her all over again and remarrying. That's what happened in my world.

I finally found her snack drawer and began chewing on nuts. I poured myself a stiff drink. Galina watched me with crossed arms, her fine butt propped up against a dresser.

"You haven't changed."

"Nope."

"Are you going to talk to me now? I've rescued you."

It was a reasonable request, so I complied. I told her pretty much everything, all about Wurtenberger, the spook named

Brinkley—the works. When I got to the details about Drusus floating in a tank down somewhere under Central, she gasped.

"That's horrible. I hate that place."

"It's worse than horrible!" I complained. "It's unforgivable. We have to get him out."

She looked thoughtful and worried. "It might not be so easy..."

"Not if you take the job of consul. The way your daddy wants you to... then you could do it with one signature."

"I can't do that, James. Don't you see that? If I do that, I'll only be a puppet. My life won't be my own."

"A puppet with teeth. Drusus got away with a lot."

She chewed on her pretty lower lip. "Don't think that the Ruling Council won't deal with me just as harshly as they did Drusus in the end. One of them is my father... but that won't save me if I'm too much trouble."

I nodded. I couldn't disagree.

"Well then, where does that leave us? What do you want me to do next?"

She hesitated, then finally spoke in a quiet voice. "I want you to kill me. In public."

-7-

"What?" I demanded. "You want me to kill you—*in public*? That's crazy, girl!"

"Yes, in public, James. What would be the point of having you kill me right here in this room? I could do that myself. I could drown myself in the toilet or tie a chain around my neck and throw myself overboard, sending myself to the bottom of the ocean. Utterly pointless."

"Well… but what's the point of making it public, then?" I demanded.

"Try to think, James. My death must be witnessed by a wide group of people. A crowd has to see with their own eyes that I'm no longer alive."

"Okay, okay," I said, "I get that… but so what? Why do it at all?"

"That's how I'm getting out of becoming Earth's next consul. I will disappear and be revived somewhere else, the way Claver always does it."

"Claver?" I asked, as if I didn't know what she was talking about. But naturally, I did.

The Clavers were a crazy branch of humanity who liked to clone each other and make lots of trade deals. In any case, their classic method of moving about the universe wasn't to fly somewhere in a ship, but rather to be killed in one place and then revived in another. Within twenty or thirty minutes, they could be across the entire galaxy that way.

"Uh… where are you going to go?" I asked. "I mean, if you did die and disappear, what's the plan after that?"

Galina rolled her eyes at me. "I'm not going to tell you…" she said. "That way, even if you're caught and tormented, you won't be able to tell them anything."

I stared at her, slack-jawed. This woman was the queen of the big ask. First, she'd had me expose myself to all kinds of abuse at Central, and now here she was asking for more. I hadn't even gotten a proper kiss out of her yet, just some peanuts and a drink.

"No," I said firmly, "I'm not doing it. There's nothing in this for me. I'm already wanted by the police. I'm in all kinds of trouble at Central, too. What's more, I don't even feel like killing you today."

"Are you sure?" she asked. "What if I became unpleasant?"

"Well…" I admitted, "yeah… there certainly have been a few times… but nope. I'm not gonna do it, anyway."

She pouted for a moment, then she slyly slid across the room, coming closer to me. "I can see you're going to make this difficult." She reached out a hand and ran it up and down my biceps. "I really should tend to these wounds of yours."

"They're just scratches."

"Yes, yes, but with these aliens, you don't know what kind of pathogens they might be carrying. They could give you some weird infection."

I let her get out a first-aid kit and go to work on my arms. She really was good at that sort of thing. Everybody who served in the legions for decades eventually became a medic. We'd been injured so many times we'd all learned to do field dressings. We could even stitch up our own skins if we needed to.

Things didn't go that far in this case. She applied antiseptic, wrapped up my arms in a few bandages, and that was that.

But during this process, she got very close to me—disturbingly close. Pretty soon, I was smelling her hair without even trying to.

She smelled good, so much better than those stinking lizards from the aircar.

"If you want to die so badly, why not get Raash to do it?" I asked her as she lingered and put her rump down on my lap.

She shook her head slowly. "No... Raash is incompetent. I can't trust him. He did an okay job extracting you from Central City, but you know as well as I do that he's not really 'all there' in the head."

I knew exactly what she meant. The crazy lizard was unpredictable and moody. He might change the script in a dramatic way that didn't work out at all. Besides, he wasn't known for his kindness or his clean kills. He'd once murdered Natasha in the streets of Central City, and the whole affair had gone quite badly for her. She had been somewhat traumatized by the experience and still couldn't meet his snake-like eyes when they were in the same room.

Girls were like that sometimes. They just couldn't get over being killed as easily as the guys did. They took it personally.

"Huh..." I said, thinking things over. My thumb was on her thigh now, gently touching her. "I've got an idea. How about we stage an accident instead of an assassination?"

"I thought of that," she said, "but it won't work."

"Why not?"

"Because I need a reason to disappear, to hide from the public at large. I want to go somewhere no one can find me. If I get drunk and fly my aircar into a mountain or die in a lifter crash—something like that—people will see no reason for me to disappear. They'll simply revive me and send me back to my job the next day. No, I need a reason to be running scared."

I nodded. I kind of got that, as crazy as it was. Then, I got another idea and I frowned, squinching up my eyes tightly. I examined Galina. I noticed she still had zero gray hairs, but there was a line or two on her cheek.

"How long has it been since you died?" I asked her.

She shrugged noncommittally. "I don't know... Four or five years, I guess. Maybe longer."

"Huh," I said, thinking back. I knew that Galina really didn't like getting to be older than twenty-five—physically, I mean. Her skin was pale, her hair was light, and her kind tended to age fast and badly.

"You aren't just doing all this to get yourself a revive, are you?" I asked. "It could be so much easier."

"No, James," she said, "that's not it at all. Not this time."

"Okay, okay," I said, deciding to believe her.

Now, if she'd been showing a straight-out lock or two of gray hair, then no. I wouldn't have bought it. Not for a second. But that wasn't it, not this time. She seemed to be earnest. She wanted to get away from the public. She wanted to get away, probably from her father and from this job he had hung over her. She didn't want to be consul of all Earth—certainly not as her father's puppet.

I knew it was the fate of Drusus that I'd relayed to her that had really freaked her out. She didn't want to become like him. No one thought a brain squatting in a tank was pretty.

"Hmm," I said, "exactly what good is it going to do you to hide? And how long are you planning on hiding?"

She shrugged. "I don't know. Six months... a year?"

"How's that going to work for you?"

She smiled. "I know my father. I know the Ruling Council. They absolutely *must* have a puppet on the throne. They must have an executive, who of course, they control. They won't allow the throne to sit vacant for long."

"The throne?" I said, laughing. "It's not a throne, you know."

"Are you so sure?"

I shrugged, not liking the thought of it. Technically, Hegemony was a republic, not some kind of monarchy. Sure, we'd just announced the temporary need of a consul, a singular ruler—but that was just temporary, wasn't it? Until the crisis was over?

The situation reminded me of the Galactics. They had endless civil wars because they didn't have anyone on their throne. They'd been unable to agree on who to put into the role of emperor. Because of that, they were disorganized and decaying.

Maybe that's what the Public Servants of Earth really feared. They wanted that single, strong figurehead leader. They had selected Galina for the role and were pushing her toward it, but she was resisting, seeing it as a dead end.

At some point, Galina and I started kissing a bit. I was still thinking, though, which was unusual for me. Most of the time, when I had a pretty girl in my lap, my mind stopped functioning entirely.

I thought I finally understood her plan. She wasn't disappearing forever, just for long enough. She was betting the powerful on Earth would lose patience. They'd turn toward someone else. The spotlight would fade away from her and fall upon another.

Since there had to be someone in charge, they would choose another victim and install their puppet.

An assassination… An actual, legitimate, assassination… that would give her an excuse to run, to hide, to avoid the public eye. It was a bizarre plan, but I could understand it.

I finally nodded my head. "You know, I think I might be able to come up with a plan for you."

Galina stopped kissing my sweaty neck, and she smiled. "I knew you could."

She got up, and I was reluctant to feel her warm touch leaving my legs. She went to the cabinet and poured two strong drinks. Then she came over and offered me one. Her hand reached out to its fullest extension with the glass in it.

I took the glass, but I snagged onto her wrist, too. I didn't let go of her hand. I drew her down into my lap again. She squeaked lightly, but then sat across my knees and allowed me to put my hands on her.

We sipped our drinks, and soon we went back to kissing, and I began sliding my big hands into her clothes.

"Wait," she said, putting her small hand on top of mine. I stopped moving, reluctantly.

"What is it?"

"Tell me your plan. Tell me what you're going to do."

I shook my head. "You asked me to do this because you trust me," I said.

"Yes," she admitted.

"So… trust me."

She sat there in my lap, stiffening up for a moment. Then, finally, she relaxed.

It was, after all, an undeniable truth. If you couldn't trust the person whom you had tasked with the sacred mission of assassinating you in public, who could you trust?

-8-

We enjoyed a few nights of passion on the voyage across the Atlantic. Her yacht actually transported us faster than I had hoped, moving along at a pace of something like fifty knots. With a rate of travel like that, crossing the entire ocean only took a few days. The voyage was disappointingly short and come to a close all too soon.

A few days later, we reached the shores of Europe. We sailed into the harbor of Lisbon, then took a sky train ride to Geneva.

Now, this was a flat-out, ballsy move, and I knew it. Central City was the main hub of military power on Earth, but Geneva was the city that the civilian government called their home. This is where the Servants met and decided the fates of billions of citizens.

The town was full of huge, gorgeous buildings, meeting halls, and cathedral-like structures. The largest of these wasn't a pyramid, but rather a sphere, and that's where we were headed. The outside of it was a high-resolution screen that usually displayed an image of Earth's globe. The entirety of the building wasn't quite as tall as Central was, but it was nearly as big in overall bulk.

I suspected that underneath the Great Globe of Geneva, there were dungeons full of howling prisoners, just as there were beneath the roots of Central.

"You're a madman for bringing me here, McGill," Galina hissed at me.

"No one's going to recognize us," I told her. "That's what the illusion boxes are for."

Galina had always been one who liked to collect special alien artifacts, especially ones that were illegal for humans to have in the first place—items that could be used to enhance her personal power. One of these was the Galactic Key. That device was probably the most infamous thing she'd ever possessed.

Another, which she'd lost some years ago, was a battle suit. A dragon, as it was known. She liked to keep that hidden aboard her various ships, just in case things ever went south and became violent.

As far as I knew, she was fresh out of dragons, and she only had one Galactic Key. But another artifact that she'd occasionally found useful was the illusion box.

Normally, these were produced by the people of Tau Ceti, otherwise known as the Tau. The Tau used them instead of clothing. The various colors and shimmering illusions that wrapped around the individual Tau citizen affected those around them and showed their own personal moods.

We humans had devised more nefarious purposes for this technology. We'd used the boxes to impersonate one another, upon occasion. Of course, the image projected was an imperfect illusion, only able to fool the eyes, not all the senses. But it was good enough for walking through towns, riding sky trains—that kind of thing.

"Why did you have to make us so ugly?" Galina complained.

It was true. We were both middle-aged: me, a large, somewhat fat, farmer-looking fellow, and she, a frumpy wife. Neither of us appeared to be in top condition.

"You could have at least made me cute."

"Nope," I said firmly, "we don't want to attract anyone's eye. That's the whole damned point."

She grumbled, but acquiesced to my point, and we made our way ever closer to the Great Globe of Geneva.

Now, why, you might well ask, were we headed there of all the places on this vast Earth? Why not somewhere remote?

Why not fly to Stonehenge, or Easter Island? Anywhere but the center of culture, government and technological devices?

Well, there was one clear reason, and that was transportation off-planet. There were gateway posts in the Geneva Globe, just as there were inside Central. These posts cheaply connected Earth to other remote locations. All of our colonies and outpost worlds were reachable from here.

Gateway posts weren't cheap, mind you, far from it. They didn't have a set in every county seat all across every sector in Europe, North America and the Asian continent. No, they were in rare places, and they were always under guard.

Fortunately, the individuals who regularly marched through them weren't under such intense scrutiny. As long as you were leaving Earth, not arriving, the officials didn't give much of a damn why you were emigrating away from the homeworld. It was my private contention that, even if you were some kind of criminal, they figured they'd rather have you off-planet than here, causing trouble.

It was getting close to dusk as we approached the massive globe, but that didn't matter. The gateway posts operated night and day. In fact, it had become so common for people to transport themselves from one planet to the next, some folks used them to make their daily commute.

I marveled at the idea that people would get up in the morning, transmit themselves to another planet, and then transport themselves back again at 5 p.m. when their shift was done on some distant world.

So, the lines were long, but the process itself was relatively quick. It was also painless and inexpensive. For a few thousand credits, you could teleport yourself just about anywhere in Earth's growing region of influence.

For all the expense of developing and deploying gateway posts, they were far cheaper than starships. Therefore, the regular populace used this method of transport far more often. Starships were now reserved entirely for the military and for large freight deliveries, that sort of thing.

We still needed starships, of course, for commerce to distant worlds and other provinces in the Empire. We also still needed to defend our skies against invaders. But as far as just moving a person from one planet to the next—there was no technology better than the gateway posts.

"I don't like this, James," Galina complained. "Why do we have to leave Earth at all? Just kill me right here, right in front of the Geneva Globe."

We now stood at the base of the sphere. It was a glorious thing to behold. I'd never been here before, not in all my long years, and it was jaw-dropping to describe. Galina, on the other hand, didn't even glance up at it.

The sphere, with all its glorious colors and flashing lights didn't interest her in the least. She was like a kid who'd grown up right next door to a theme park—jaded and unimpressed.

To get her into the building, it took some coaxing, cajoling, and even a few threats of abandonment. At last, she followed me inside, grumbling all the while.

Fortunately, the security checkpoints weren't as thorough as those at Central. We were able to fool them with a combination of illusion boxes, some biometric hacking, and two of those burner-tappers criminals sometimes wore. You could slide these polymer sleeves over your skin, and that way your fake tapper would report a different identity.

The bored guards waved us through, assuming we were yet another set of tourists wandering around the great sphere on a day when the government was closed and no officials were present. They made sure we had no explosives, and no questionable backgrounds—which our fake tappers confirmed. Then we were ushered on with a wave and a curled upper lip toward the exhibits inside.

I took Galina by the hand. Although she tried to work her grip out of mine, she, of course, couldn't. I didn't *drag* her along—nothing like that. I slowly walked at a sedate pace while she cursed and mumbled beside me. Every time she caught sight of a mirror or any other reflective surface, she exclaimed about how ugly she was. Nothing else seemed to occupy her mind more than that.

At last, we reached the central plaza inside the globe, and she looked at me in concern.

"Where are we going?" she asked.

"It's better that you don't know."

"This is absolutely crazy."

"Come on," I said, urging her along.

At a grungy booth decorated with dancing holograms depicting exotic locations tourists could go to, I bought our tickets. Galina was fussing about something or other, but I wasn't listening. The robot in the booth, despite being AI and not an actual person, seemed startled, even bewildered, by my choice of destinations.

"Are you certain, sir?" it asked.

"Yep, that's right. We've had relatives go out there. They say it's the best honeymoon hideaway in the known galaxy."

"I can almost assure you, sir, this is not true," the AI objected. But I kept on pressing, even as the machine brought up objections against the trip.

"This is a very inexpensive destination," it argued, "but I can assure you there's very little of cultural or natural significance to observe there. Tourists are not recommended."

"Come on, machine," I demanded, pounding a thick fist on the countertop. "Are you gonna take my credits or not? Two tickets to Dust World, pronto!"

The machine finally acquiesced and fired out the tickets, which came in the form of transmissions to be caught by our tappers.

"Dust World?" Galina said as we walked away from the booth. "Are you kidding me? You're taking me to frigging *Dust World?* No wonder you didn't tell me where we were going. That planet sucks, James."

"I think it's perfect," I said. "Think about it. Where else could I more easily escape after performing a public assassination?"

"Well, yes… it's probably good for that," she admitted. "But you're just thinking about yourself. You know people there—you like it there. It's a disgusting place. I was hoping to vacation a bit, you know… have a little fun."

"Come on, do you want me to kill you or not?" I demanded.

Here we were, bickering like an old couple about who was going to kill whom, and how it was going to happen. Why did little social trips like this with Galina always end in argument and rancor?

Finally, she allowed herself to be coaxed to the non-existent queue that stood before the Dust World gateway posts. They had a yellowy glow about them. It wasn't a golden color, mind you, but more of a dirty, slimy yellow. It was the kind of color you might see forming a ring in a urinal.

A bored attendant tried to wave us away. He was watching a ballgame on his tapper and didn't want to be bothered by lost tourists asking questions.

"Sorry, folks," he said. "The information booth is that way."

"We don't want information," I told him sternly. "We want to be transmitted to Dust World. See? We already bought our tickets—they're right here."

He frowned, stared, checked, and then double-checked. Finally, he shook his head in defeat. "Okay, it's your funeral. They aren't the friendliest bunch out there. Whatever you do, don't make fun of them. The locals will shiv you as fast as look at you."

"It sounds charming," Galina said.

The attendant looked at her. "She's with you, huh?"

"She says the darndest things," I commented.

"You've got yourself a cheapskate, lady."

I glared at the attendant and tugged at Galina's hand.

"I'm well aware," Galina said.

We stepped through the gateway posts. There was a bug-zapper noise and a strange tingle. Then, what seemed like a moment later, we stood in a very different place.

It was night on Dust World, but sure enough, there was dust falling on us, anyway. That was the first thing we noticed, a drifting cloud of dust. It was drifting down from far above where bright smudges represented stars.

The surface of Dust World was a cauldron of sand and sandstone, with little else of note. There were two suns in the star system, but neither one was up right now.

We were in one of the sheltered spots down deep, in what amounted to the crater of a great volcanic lake. The lake was surrounded in a circle by scrubby, rubbery plants and hot, humid air. Around that was a kilometer-high cliff that encircled the green valley.

On Dust World, this spot was a veritable Garden of Eden. There were only eleven such green holes punched into the surface that could support life as we knew it.

Galina made spitting noises. She squinted and complained bitterly. Her hands flapped before her face. "What is that stuff falling on me? I'm breathing and eating it!"

"That's dust," I said, as if surprised she didn't expect this extra treat. "We don't always have a sandstorm going on Dust World up above the rim—but it's not an uncommon thing. I think that's how this place got its name."

"Hello folks," said a hog guard. We noticed him for the first time. He was a tall fellow, standing tiredly at his post near the gateway. "I've just got to check your IDs—it's a formality, really."

We waved our fake tappers to him. He identified us with a bored expression and was surprised to see we'd never been to this planet before.

"Tourists, huh?" he said. "Actual, honest-to-God tourists? We usually get a few traders, maybe some relatives who want to try to convince a fugitive to come back to Earth and turn himself in."

He laughed at this, as if he'd laid a howler of a joke. Galina and I squinted at him sullenly. Neither one of us was in the mood, besides which, his joke was hitting too close to home. Dust World was the kind of place only a fugitive would seek out purposefully.

The hog cleared his throat. "Um… sorry, we don't get too many regular folks here."

"Can you direct me to a good restaurant and the best hotel in town?" Galina asked.

The guard laughed again. He straight out laughed at her. "This is Dust World, lady. We don't have hotels. Restaurants, maybe… sort of. You can probably find a bar that will serve you a sandwich. A fungus-slab sandwich, that is. And don't ask where the meat inside came from, either. Not if you want to finish it. Anyways, it's down the hill that way."

He pointed off into the darkness, where we saw a glimmering row of faint lights.

I led Galina away before she could cause more trouble. We soon set ourselves up with hats and goggles—necessities on Dust World, which I'd taken the opportunity to buy back in Geneva before we left.

"This is disgusting, McGill. Absolutely disgusting. I don't know how you can come out here. I think your daughter and the rest of your family—they're all crazy to be here at all. Even the heat is of the unpleasant variety. I'd thought it would be a dry, oven-like sensation. But it's kind of muggy. I hate it."

"Yeah, well, that's 'cause it's nighttime. In the daylight, it's downright broiling. It feels like walking inside a sauna set on high."

"Wonderful."

We headed down toward the town, such as it was, but we never made it there. After a few hundred steps, when I judged that we were beyond the interest and scrutiny of the guard at the gateway posts, I made a sharp right-angle turn. I led a stumbling Galina off the road toward the tall, dark cliffs that surrounded the valley and the central lake itself.

"Where are you taking me now? I want to get something to eat," Galina complained.

"We'd probably just get robbed down there in town—and possibly poisoned by their food."

"Where are we going?"

"I know some folks up this way."

"Oh no… you're not talking about that horrible Investigator-person, are you? That walking corpse of a man?"

"Settle down now, Galina. Those people are my relatives."

She allowed me to lead her off into the dark, and eventually, I spotted a pair of lanterns surrounding a dim-lit opening in the cliffs. We passed between these fixtures and wandered into a vast maze of echoing caverns.

We used our own tappers as a light source to guide ourselves deeper into this labyrinth. Less than a thousand steps inside, we were suddenly surrounded by strange men with knives.

Galina gave a single, loud squawk of alarm.

None of the men spoke. They were bare-footed and bare-chested. They wore nothing but what looked like long leather pants, and they carried nothing in their hands but knives.

"Hey boys," I said, "remember me?" I flicked off my illusion box.

They took a step back in alarm, their eyes widening. A few of them peered, some nodded and pointed.

"McGill," someone said.

Another echoed, "The McGill!"

Apparently, it was their only word of English. That made me feel a touch of pride.

They gestured, and we followed. We didn't have much choice, being surrounded by better than a dozen of them now.

Galina fiddled with her illusion box, but I put my hand over hers.

"No," I said, "not yet. Keep the look you have for now."

She stared and nodded. She was finally afraid, finally worried for her own skin, no longer simply complaining about anything and everything that happened.

Eventually, the strange, tribal men led us to one of the large central chambers. There, we met others who didn't look like they belonged to this illicit pack of half-naked clones. They were the Investigator, Floramel and Etta.

"We were told you had come," the Investigator said, "but I didn't believe it."

"Why not?" I said. "It's been months. I like to visit my relatives."

"James, this is not a safe place or a safe time for your special brand of nonsense," Floramel said, taking two steps closer toward us. "It really is a dangerous time."

"Dangerous? How? There's nobody here but these clowns with their pig-stickers." As I said this, I reached out and snatched away one of the knives from a man who had been distracted. He'd been looking at the other normal humans, not me.

"You see this?" I said, flipping the blade around and brandishing it with a laugh.

This man looked ashamed and backed away. If I didn't know better, I would've thought he was going to cry or something. The others showed me their teeth in snarls.

"You see?" the Investigator said to Floramel. "That's exactly the sort of thing I was talking about." His bony knuckles were on his hips, and all his skin seemed stretched tight.

Was he getting old again—so soon? Man, it had only been... What? Twenty years since I'd last seen him die?

"Daddy?" Etta said, walking closer. She was making her own appeal to my almost nonexistent sense of reason. "Why did you bring this woman here? This is crazy. These people don't like outsiders."

"Then they'll be more than concerned about her," I said, pointing at Galina. "She's worse than an outsider."

Finally, for the first time, everyone's eyes moved to Galina. She'd had the smarts to stand there and be quiet this whole time. With the illusion box on, she was unknown to everyone present.

I couldn't blame her for that. After all, she was surrounded by unknown, crazy-looking savages with knives, and a pack of McGill relatives. No one in their right minds would have felt comfortable with this bunch. To demonstrate her feelings, her nails were digging into my palms—but I pretended not to notice.

"Perhaps we've made a mistake, James," Galina said, shifting her voice slightly. "Maybe we should be going back to town now. Maybe you shouldn't have brought me out here with these nice people performing their quaint little ceremonies in the dark—or whatever is going on out here."

"Yes," the Investigator said. "You should leave—now."

"Daddy..." Etta said, "why did you bring her here?"

"Yes," Floramel said, "I too, am astounded. She's not a physically attractive specimen."

Galina bristled, despite the fact she was wearing essentially an ugly suit. "I wouldn't talk, you tall, skinny—"

I reached out a big hand and put it in front of Galina's equally big mouth. She shied away angrily—but she did quiet down.

It was too little, too late. Floramel was frowning at her now, and so was Etta. Could there be a hint of recognition? These women have both met Galina—many times. An illusion box can only hide so much—it certainly couldn't clothe an entire personality.

"Hey ladies," I said, "settle down! Why is it always the women who get excited in these situations? I just came out here to show her around. There is one more person, though, who I've promised to introduce her to."

Everyone froze, except for Galina. The others must have all realized who I had to be talking about.

Then, I fatefully spoke a name: "Boudica."

Everyone froze, except for the nearly mute guys in the leather pants. They opened their mouths to snarl. They seemed to think it was some kind of mortal sin to utter the name of their queen out loud.

Behind that crowd, however, a new voice rose high. They all turned to crane their necks.

We looked at a dark opening. There stood Boudica, bare-chested, redheaded. Her hair seemed even longer than before, reaching past the middle of her back. She wore only leather pants, just like the men who worshipped her. She was barefoot, with skin as white as milk. Tall, imposing and attractive, she had eyes that seemed both intelligent—and slightly insane.

"James… McGill…" she said, gliding forward with slow, steady steps. "So, you have returned, and oddly enough, with a… friend? Many are the stories of your idiocy, your whimsy, your schemes, and your tricks. But how can you explain the rationale behind this visit? Especially the foolishness of bringing a stranger into our midst?"

I smiled and made a grand gesture. "Boudica," I began, "I have come, and I bring you a fine gift."

Her eyes widened slightly. I could tell she, like just about all women ever born in the history of humanity, liked presents.

"A gift? And what is this gift?"

I reached towards Galina, but she protested, "James, don't!"

Ignoring her complaints, I flicked off her illusion box.

"Behold," I announced, "this is Galina Turov. I just knew all of you would want to meet her in person."

That was it. That was the only thing I had to say, the only action I had to take.

Boudica's eyes blazed with intensity. Then she revealed a sort of grin, but it resembled a death's head grin—the kind you see when lips pull unnaturally away from teeth. She bared those pearly-whites like a predator ready to strike.

"Seize her!" Boudica ordered.

A dozen hands reached out and grabbed Galina, who squawked in terror. Knives hovered menacingly close to her, their points aiming at her throat from a dozen different angles.

"Oh no!" I shouted. "Look out, she's got a blade! She's here to kill Boudica!"

Sure enough, there was a knife in Galina's hand. She looked as stunned to see it as the rest of the crowd.

Then those strange savages—those dim-witted, leather-pants wearing maniacs that Boudica kept close—responded as dogs might when their master makes a sudden move. They sensed the heightened tension and animosity from their mistress as she stalked close to Galina. The sudden appearance of a weapon was too much for them.

They all plunged their knives into Galina, from a dozen directions at once. She was stabbed in the neck, the eye, the throat, the guts, and the heart. She gargled and died within moments.

Boudica kept stepping forward. She was blinking, confused. She looked at the knife, and then she looked at me.

"What happened to the knife that you had in your hand just a moment ago?" she asked.

"Uh, that's quite a mystery…" I said. "It must have jumped right out of my hand."

Boudica nodded slowly. I think she understood, even if no one else in that strange, dark, smoky chamber did.

-9-

After Galina's brutal murder, I made a big show of being all broken-up about it. Naturally, that was all nonsense. I'd just managed to get these people to do my dirty work for me.

To my mind, I'd fulfilled all my promises to Galina and then some. On top of that, I'd solved certain conundrums of my own.

She'd been assassinated, just like she'd wanted so badly. That was checkmark number one.

The deed had even been accomplished in public, too. In front of a staring crowd, no less. I'd call that checkmark number two—and that was the big one. It had been, if you asked me, the hardest part on her wish-list to pull off. Killing people was easy—any Joe could do that. But doing it in public and getting away with it? That's where things got tricky.

Naturally, I could see where she might complain about some of the details... For example, I hadn't performed this miracle personally. Sure, I'd instigated it, but I hadn't actually done the knifework myself. That would have been checkmark number three, I guess...

So, no... things hadn't gone *exactly* the way she'd imagined.

But that was because, in my expert opinion, her ideas were dumb. I'd been forced to make important deviations to her original concept.

There was one more trouble spot—and I will freely admit this is where I missed checkmark number four by a mile—she wasn't going to be revived wherever she'd planned to be.

You see, Dust World was kind of in the boonies. This was no sprawling urban landscape. That meant devices recording people's minds and bodies carefully for later revival were few and far between.

It was even more isolated here than a place like the back-forty at the McGill compound. Sure, we had a big swamp full of gators, with lots of spots that were off-grid or with poor reception—you were lucky to get one bar even inside my parent's house.

But out here... on Dust World... there were zero bars in most places. Right now, to make it all worse, we were deep in the warrens. It was a region largely unexplored beyond the underground living spaces for Dust-Worlder locals.

The people here took the business of hiding seriously. Back in the old days, before we'd liberated them, big Cephalopod ships had come every year to collect human specimens. The colonists would hide underground and only come out to fight a guerrilla battle whenever they had to.

These caverns and galleries of crumbling apartments deep underground weren't just uninhabited, they were completely cut off from the rest of the universe. No signals escaped, because the builders hadn't wanted them to. If the alien raiders had detected anything like that, they'd have sent in slavers to drag away colonists to use off-world as breeding stock for their various abominations.

Those days were long gone, of course, but the warrens and deep bunkers remained. That's why the Investigator, Etta's strange grandpa, had decided to set up shop in these tunnels.

So, although some of us might've recorded the details of Galina's demise with our tappers, the broader world would remain oblivious to what had befallen her. It didn't matter anymore where she had planned to be revived, because those people would have no way of knowing where she'd gone to.

I cast aside these complaints as soon as I thought of them. She was solidly dead, and people had witnessed it. She'd damn-well better be happy with that.

Taking a moment to touch my tapper to her wrist, I pretended to comfort myself and grieve over her fallen form. In reality, I was storing her data—just in case. I had to work fast before all life could exit her body, and the organic computer in her forearm shut down completely.

When this performance was finished, I turned to note the growling circle of Boudica's simps. I waved them back as a man might do with a circle of hound-dogs.

Beyond this group were the smarter folks, who numbered exactly four: the Investigator, Floramel his wife, Etta my daughter—and of course, Boudica. They were all giving me looks that ranged from bafflement to suspicion.

"James," the Investigator said, approaching me first, "I'm sorry for this misunderstanding. I don't know why they were so deadset on slaying Galina."

"Because," Etta said, coming forward, "he announced she had a weapon. Didn't you, Dad?"

"I simply didn't want her to hurt herself or others," I explained.

Etta showed me a set of twisted lips and a look that clearly indicated she didn't believe my words for a minute—but she didn't immediately contradict me.

"I can't believe what a mess you've made in my laboratory," Floramel said in an accusatory fashion. "You've only been here five minutes,"

Of the four, Boudica was giving me the strangest looks. She was the only one not saying anything.

Finally, she stepped forward and eyed the corpse, even toeing it with one sandal.

"Is this truly Galina Turov?" she asked.

"Yes, that's her," Floramel said. "I can identify her in case you're feeling distrustful toward McGill."

Boudica gave her a glance and nodded. I knew right then and there that Boudica had already figured out that Floramel virtually always told the truth. She was truthful to a fault, whereas I did not quite hold the same reputation.

"Of course, it's Galina," I said, trying to muster up a few tears. It didn't really work. "We were on vacation, see. I just thought I'd bring her out here to show her the family digs…"

"Well, James," the Investigator said, "in that case, you've failed miserably."

"You certainly have, Father," Etta agreed. "What are you going to do now? Go home with her information on your tapper and get her revived?"

"Well…" I said, "that is one possibility… but I actually had something else in mind."

All four of them looked at me. No one said anything for a long moment. Then Boudica began to smile. "You want us to revive her, don't you?" she asked.

"Wow! What an offer!" I said brightly.

"An off-grid revival? Do you trust the Investigator's arts so greatly?"

"I surely do," I lied. Then I sighed and shook my head. "I don't think we have much choice. She was going to be declared the consul of all Earth, you know."

This startled all four of them. Boudica, in particular, cocked her head at me. "I see now why you brought her here and caused her death. You wanted to stop this ascension to the throne because you saw it as wrongful, as evil."

"I did it to protect Galina," I said, as if confessing to a great crime. "She would have taken the job, see, and then maybe she would end up like Drusus, the last guy to hold that title. I couldn't risk that."

"So, you brought her here and engineered her death?" the Investigator asked incredulously.

"Yeah, well, no one's going to put a crown on top of a dead body, are they?" I said.

Boudica nodded. She waved for her knife-wielding maniacs to back away from me. They did as she commanded, shuffling and snarling. A few of them emitted low growls from deep inside their throats, but none attacked me.

She then began to circle me, giving me occasional touches on my dirty uniform.

"You intrigue me," she said. "Let's exit this place and discuss matters."

"Uh… Okay."

Etta and Floramel frowned while the Investigator fussed over the corpse on the floor. Boudica led me out of the place and down a lonely passageway.

I glanced over my shoulder and saw, sure enough, a few of the simps with knives were peeping around corners. They hadn't completely left me alone with their mistress. I thought about bragging to them they were too far away, that I could kill their queen right here and now if I wanted to—but I didn't see how teasing them would give me any advantage. So, I managed to quell the urge.

"James McGill," Boudica said, "you are a strange one. Do you remember when we first met in the bunker on the back of your property?"

"I surely do, ma'am."

"Do you know that I thought you were an imbecile at that time?"

"Expectedly so, ma'am. I commonly produce that reaction in people."

She nodded thoughtfully. "I no longer hold that opinion of you. There have been too many strange mistakes that have fallen your way. Events have gone in your favor in a most surprising and alarming fashion too many times. That doesn't happen entirely by accident—at least not repeatedly."

I stopped walking. She faced me, and I raised one hand high, palm out, and put the other on my chest, across my heart.

"Hold on there, miss," I said. "Don't let my exterior fool you. I'm a card-carrying moron, just like everyone says I am."

"I wonder…" Boudica said, "did Galina suspect this would be her fate when you brought her out here?"

"Uh, no… probably not."

Boudica inclined her head. "I like this gift you've brought me—an evil woman from the most evil of families. You've dragged her here and slaughtered her on my carpet, the way a cat might show off a captive blue jay. I think you have deeper aspirations. I think you want to earn favor with me."

I blinked a couple of times before nodding. When a person—especially an attractive woman—got a completely wrong idea about me, well, sir, my instinct was to go with it and to go hard.

"I do try to impress pretty ladies whenever I can," I confessed. "It's a matter of basic policy with me."

"You have succeeded in this rare instance. I would never have had the guts to send an assassin to kill this vile woman, but here you've laid her at my feet. You've given me a great prize. After we revive her, we'll imprison her. We'll keep her here in secret, where no one would think to find her. Then, we'll confront the elder Turov with this fait accompli. He'll have no choice but to give up on his daughter and her consulship—or suffer the permanent loss of her."

"Uh…" I interrupted, "wait a minute. Did you say something about 'permanent?'"

"What of it?" she said, turning sharply.

"Well, um, I didn't necessarily intend the whole imprisonment part. I just figured we could keep her dead for a while… You know, on ice, so to speak."

"For how long?"

I felt a little itchy, but I chalked that up to the dust and the nanites in the region. One finger scratched at the base of my skull. "At least until the government moves on and stops focusing on her."

Boudica pondered this. "Let's put that matter aside for now. She's no longer your problem. I'll let the Investigator work on the revival process. In the meantime, I want you to take me somewhere—but not in order to suffer the fate you gave your previous consort."

"Take you somewhere?" I asked. "Like where?"

She smiled wickedly. It was an unsettling expression. I'd known a lot of evil women in my lifetime, but this girl might just take the cake.

"I want you to take me to Death World, James McGill."

I was almost as befuddled by Boudica's request to take her to Death World as I was by her half-naked body, which she'd been parading in front of my eyeballs continuously. I hadn't spent much quality time with ginger girls in my long and storied life, but I was beginning to see the possible advantages after spending so much time in her personal proximity.

"Will you do it?" she asked me as I stared at her bare breasts.

"Do what, now?" I asked.

She looked a bit exasperated. "Be my consort. Be my bodyguard. Help me reach Death World."

"Um, why would you want to go out there, ma'am, if you don't mind my asking?"

"There are others there, like-minded leaders, who I'd like to entreat with."

"Oh…" I said, and I got it.

She had to be talking about Helsa and Kattra, two other female leaders of a lost people. They led a million or so people known as the Edge-Worlders—although they should probably change their name to Death-Worlders these days.

They were ex-nomads from the edge of the province, and they were unhappy campers. Now, I'd hazard a guess that women like Helsa and Kattra weren't normally happy, even on their best days. But after Earth Gov had arranged to dump them out on L-374—a world that lacked practically all fauna and instead had only ornery megaflora to contend with—they'd become jaded. Worse still, they were forced to trade their revival machines to Earth on the cheap in order to purchase essential goods to survive on their adopted shit-hole planet.

I nodded my head. "Seeking out the disaffected, huh?" I asked.

"Is that an idiom among your people, James?" Boudica asked me.

"No, ma'am," I said with a hint of pride, "I just made that up on the spot."

"Well spoken, in any case. I'm not sure what your goals were in bringing me this prize," she said—speaking, I knew, of Galina's dead body, which was cooling on dusty stones a few hundred meters behind us. "But you've gained my trust to some extent with this single action. One problem with my retreat to Dust World was that I've been essentially trapped here. I've built a small personal army—but as you've just proven, they aren't terribly effective. They're not well-trained. They're not well-armed. I'm sure Legion Varus would find them no trouble to defeat at all."

I nodded, because I knew what she said was true. Legion Varus—or, in fact, just my own unit—could probably kill all of these jokers in a few minutes. Knives and bare feet were simply no match for hardened legionnaires.

"I've been unable to leave here. The only connection points are directly to Earth, and I have no provable citizenship."

"That's right," I said, "there's almost no way off this rock—and I think that's by design."

She nodded. "I didn't realize when I first came here what a dead-end Dust World truly is. But now, despite the fact that I've gained a considerable level of power here on this planet, I find myself frustrated trying to leave it, to move on, to meet with other similarly rebellious colony worlds."

"Well... Death World would certainly qualify as one of those."

"Exactly. Can you take me to that planet?"

I thought about it, and I squinched my eyes shut tight for a moment. Then, after a dramatic period of fake thinking-time, I nodded. "You know, with great difficulty and a lot of personal risk to myself, I think I could pull it off. For a few favors, of course."

Boudica raised her eyebrows. "Favors? What's the nature of these favors?"

"Well, first off, I'd like to get my daughter off this planet as well."

"Your daughter, Etta? Isn't she an important assistant for Floramel and the Investigator?"

"Yeah, sure," I shrugged. "But she needs to go home and visit my folks."

"Hmm... That's your condition? It seems almost absurd, but of course, I will grant it. What else?"

I smiled, because for me, that was the most important thing: to get my daughter out of Boudica's clutches. Even if Etta wanted to stay on Dust World, I no longer thought it was a safe place for her to be.

"What else...?" I thought to myself. "What else...? Oh, yeah. Of course."

I stepped closer to Boudica, and she recoiled, backing away a half-step. Then I encircled her slowly with my long, ape-like arms. Gently, I began to kiss on her.

She was as stiff as a board at first. I figured I'd genuinely surprised her—but then she relaxed and went with it.

We came up for air nearly a minute later.

"Is this truly your second condition?" she asked. Her eyes were wide and wondering.

"That's right," I said. "I'm a simple man with simple tastes."

"You may find me a more complex taste than you imagine," she warned.

We continued to make out in that dark, dingy cave. Distantly behind us, I heard the discontented shuffling of calloused feet.

I figured I was probably breaking some hearts back there—but I didn't care one whit about her simps. They'd never had a shot at her, no matter what their fantasies had been.

In the end, we found a quiet spot off in one of the side passages in an ancient, crumbling apartment. The place was empty. There weren't even any bones on the stone floor.

We made love there. It was dusty, dirty, and glorious.

I got the feeling that Boudica had a lot of pent-up sexual energy. With a million simps and tough Dust-Worlder locals around, why couldn't she have found a partner? She'd been out here for years, now…

Maybe none of them had appealed. It was a strange thought.

As I explored her, and we shared intense moments, the simps even dared to scratch around the doorway. They peeped, they growled, and they shuffled.

Boudica threw a handful of dirt at them, and they raced away. I could only imagine how badly I was disappointing them, and it made me laugh.

-10-

As a pro tip to all the men out there in the universe seeking a unique experience, you might want to try this: leave a tough-minded lady floating in a brain-tank for a century or so. Then, give her a shapely new body and follow-up by *still* allowing her no release for a couple years longer.

Boys, let me tell you, you'll be in for a unique experience when you finally light that bottle-rocket.

After a long, glorious night—which, I have to say, was a pretty rewarding experience for old McGill—dawn finally came. In the morning light, I went looking for Etta. I found her near the big, circular lake.

As I approached, I started off smiling… but that faded away quickly.

I began to frown because it seemed like she wasn't alone. It took me a minute to reach her on the shoreline, pushing through the last mess of rustling reeds.

She stood there, ankle-deep in the waters of the great lake, staring off into the rushes in the direction of town.

"Etta?" I said. "Who's out here with you?"

"No one," she replied immediately.

She'd spoken too fast, I thought. I knew she was lying. Fathers almost always notice when their kids lie. It's one of our powers.

But I took all that in stride. Etta could have her secrets, just as I had always had mine.

"Well then, come on back to the cave. It's breakfast time."

With some reluctance, she followed me back to the warrens.

"Hey, girl," I told her, "I've got some news for you."

"What's that, Daddy?"

"You're heading back to Earth—with me."

She looked at me, startled. "What if I don't want to go?"

I shook my head. "Well… that's the other thing…"

She stopped walking and glared up at me. "What did you do?"

"I did absolutely nothing, girl. Boudica just up and decided we need to go back to Earth… and she wants to come along, too."

"What are you talking about?"

I explained to her about traveling back to Earth with Boudica in tow.

"How are we going to manage that? She has no identity on Earth. She'll be labeled an alien, essentially."

"Don't I know it," I replied. "Fortunately, I can cover for her."

"How?"

I showed her the fake tapper that Galina and I had used to escape Earth. She was impressed by the technology.

"You've got two of these?"

"I do. One is on Galina's body right now. The Investigator has probably found it by this time, but I'm pretty sure, with Boudica's help, we can get it back."

"Well…" she said, "Okay, I see how that could work for Boudica."

"There's just one more thing—one more special reason why I need you on this trip."

She squinted at me. I could tell she was concerned. "What's that, Dad?"

"You're pretty good with gateway posts, aren't you?" I said.

"What's that supposed to mean?"

"Some of those times I used the casting couch, when I was transported down into the depths of the Moon, you were the one crunching all the numbers? Right?"

"Yeah, yeah. Get to the point. I'm not liking this."

"Well... what if you and I were able to change the programming of a gateway post?"

"What are you talking about?"

"Galina had one more device on her, one more trick up her sleeve. But she's dead now. So all those tricks technically belong to us, don't they?"

She shook her head in bafflement.

"I'm talking about the Galactic Key," I said, lowering my voice as if I was talking about a crime—which I was.

She frowned. "But that works mostly on Imperial technology."

I agreed. "It'll work to hack the gateway posts. I've tried it before."

"That's just insane! Where do you want the posts to go, anyway?"

"Well... I don't want to change the destination. What I want to do is change the tapper information they record."

Etta blinked at me and frowned. "You want to change... oh. So, you don't want the gateway to report that you've returned to Earth. Is that it?"

"That's it."

She thought that over. "That's still illegal hacking."

"So is my returning to Earth. You see... there were a few unfortunate events that preceded my trip out here. There might be... um... some alarms tripped when I go back."

She nodded, and she sighed. She was used to this kind of trouble following her dad around. "I'll see what I can do, I guess."

My next visit was with the Investigator himself. He did, in fact, have possession of Galina's various artifacts. Floramel was toying with them, identifying them. The only thing she didn't understand was the Galactic Key itself. I'd never revealed it to her, and neither had Galina.

"Mr. Investigator, sir?" I said.

"Not now, James. I have no time for nonsense. I'm setting up one of my baths for your fine friend."

I looked around and noticed that Boudica was nowhere to be seen. Perhaps the poor lady had been tuckered out by the night before.

"I need to take Galina's belongings with me," I told him.

He turned slowly, eyeing me and cocking his head. "And where are you going, James?"

"Not just me… it's time for Boudica and I to leave Dust World."

His eyes immediately flicked toward the various knife-wielding, maniacal simps that prowled the passages. "It's best not to talk about such things, James. Do not attempt to kidnap her. Do not attempt—"

"No, no," I said. "You misunderstand. This is Boudica's idea."

"It is? I'll believe that when I hear it from her lips."

"You will," I said. "You will."

"Very well," the Investigator said. "As to your first request, yes, you can have her belongings. I have no need of them. In fact, they represent a danger that she'll be recognized or traced in some way."

"We'll be taking all of it with us."

He laughed. "You're very ambitious. So, you bring us Galina Turov, leave her with us to revive, and then take Boudica and our best gear. Is that it? Is that the nature of your plan?"

"No," I said, "my plans are even deeper than that. I'm taking Etta with me as well."

The Investigator turned to Etta as if seeing her for the first time. "Indeed, you do have high ambitions. My granddaughter is one of my greatest helpers. What about Derek, Etta? How does he feel about this?"

"Derek?" I asked, turning to look at Etta. She was sheepishly staring at the ground.

"Has she not told you?" the Investigator asked. "Etta here plans to be married—very soon, I should think."

My jaw sagged low and stayed there.

"James?" Floramel said, coming close and putting up a hand near my face. She didn't quite touch me.

Touching, according to her kind, indicated a desire for sexual contact. I was pretty sure she had no such desire, especially as she was already married to the Investigator who was standing right there.

"James?" she whispered again. "I don't want you to have any temper tantrums. Etta is my granddaughter now, remember?"

"Yeah, yeah, I remember. Who's this Derek guy?" I demanded. "Was he the one down at the swamp, running off into the reeds like a plucked chicken?"

"Daddy, I knew you'd react like this. I knew you would be jealous and upset about my boyfriend."

"No, no, no," I said, "I'm not feeling that way."

But suddenly, inside my own head, I was putting things together. Etta had stayed out here on Dust World for a long time. She'd never done that before. She'd missed Thanksgiving and Christmas with my folks for years. What with Boudica, the Investigator, and Floramel for company, plus all these weirdos with knives, I would've thought she'd have gotten tired of it and come back home once in a while. But she hadn't.

"You must be pretty serious with this guy," I said. "Right?"

She nodded.

"Are you worried I'm not going to approve of him? What's wrong with this guy—has he got just one eye, or no balls under his kilt, or what?"

"He's a fine young man, Daddy," she said.

"All right, all right. You've certainly endured enough ornery women coming in and out of my life. If you've found someone you really like... well... I can't complain, especially at your age."

Etta seemed to sigh in relief. She'd apparently not expected the best reaction from me. Of course, I hadn't met the boy yet, so I was, more or less, withholding judgment. For the moment, I would pretend he was going to be her knight in shining armor.

But I was worried. I had a deep-down, gnawing worry that he wouldn't be what I hoped for in a future son-in-law.

"Is he, uh..." I asked, "a Dust-Worlder?"

She shook her head, staring at the stone floor again.

"Okay..." I continued, "he's not a Dust-Worlder, but... Oh, hold on. Don't tell me he's one of these lunatics with a knife, running around here in leather pants?"

"No, Daddy, he's not one of those. I'm not marrying a clone."

"So, you really want to marry this guy, huh?" I asked.

"Yes, I do. If you must know, he's from Earth, Dad."

I blinked and looked dumb. "Well, what's wrong with him, then?"

She avoided my gaze again.

Floramel lingered behind me. "Be kind, James," she whispered, "be kind."

"There's something wrong with him," I said, suddenly certain. "I can tell. There's no way you'd all be acting this strange if he was a normal, two-eyed, one-dicked, straight-walking dude. So why doesn't someone fess up and tell me what the trouble is? I'm getting annoyed."

Etta continued to study the floor, but she finally heaved a sigh. "I guess you're going to find out eventually, Dad. His name is Derek... and he's from Hegemony."

You could have heard a pin drop after that revelation.

"What?" I demanded. "Are you saying he's a frigging *hog?*"

"Dad, you can't just use that word around him, not around Derek. It's just not fair. He joined the service, just like you did years back. Eventually, they posted him out here on Dust World. Over time, I've had a few conversations with him and... you know..."

"Yeah," I said. "I know. We're talking about one of those sunburnt, bored, half-witted dorks who stand around all day next to the gateway posts, right?"

She fidgeted. "That's one of his duties... sometimes. But he's more important than that, Daddy. He's kind of like a sheriff here on Dust World."

I was in shock. She was talking-up a hog—trying to sell him to me. My own daughter had reached low, choosing someone who was worse than any Dust-Worlder alive.

I could have respected one of the local colonists. These folk were sneaky, mean, smart, and resourceful. You wouldn't typically want to bring one home to dinner, mind you, but you had to respect them.

If she'd told me she was seeing one of the clones, the weirdos with the knives, I would have been upset. But even those guys were respectable in my eyes. They were dedicated, and you just knew upon meeting any of them they'd fight to the death for whatever it was they believed in. You had to respect that.

But nooo, she hadn't even chosen a civilian, or another scientist nerd-boy. Nothing logical and dull like that. Instead, she'd picked the one type of person among all humans that I reviled the most: a fricking hog.

The very idea of me having a Hegemony man for a son-in-law… it made me want to puke.

I managed to hold back some my initial reaction, but I knew she saw the look on my face, and I knew it hurt her. So, I forced a smile—one of my finest fake smiles.

The corners of my mouth were hard to lift. It was like I was lifting weights with my cheek muscles, but I managed it.

"All right, honey," I said, "let's go meet this Derek fellow."

"Really?" she asked. "You want to meet him?"

"I absolutely do."

"Not to kill him, right, James?" Floramel inquired, still standing beside me and half-whispering.

"Of course not," I scoffed.

However, in the back of my mind, I still held onto the possibility of murder for this hog. In fact, I was already devising various heinous, underhanded ways I could do it.

-11-

Etta took me to meet Derek in person that same day. To my chagrin, she informed me he wasn't even a veteran, much less a man of means, like an officer. No, he was just a lowly specialist.

Now, among the hog ranks, specialists were similar to those among the regular legions, but there were a few types missing and a few other types added.

They had tech-specialists. I'd met quite a few of them, in fact. These are the kind of hogs that fluffed up your casting couch before they mailed you off into oblivion, or who made sure the charge in your teleport harness was in the green.

Another common type of hog was the bio—the medical people. I usually hated them, and they usually hated me, especially when I bent their fussy rules.

A couple of types that were missing were weaponeers and ghosts. They normally did not issue specialized heavy alien weaponry to Hegemony troops, and as far as I knew, there was no reason for any hog ghosts. The very idea made a man want to shudder.

However, there were some other types: Intel boys, like that guy Brinkley, whom I'd slaughtered back at Central just the week before. There were also security hogs. These were possibly the most common type. They functioned as guardsmen, sometimes working in the various prisons. The most sadistic of them liked to work with shock-rods down deep in the torture centers underneath Central.

Derek, as far as I could tell, was a standard-issue security hog. One of the guys that stood around in corridors and looked bored all day, asking to see people's IDs as they went by.

"Now," I said, marching along the path back toward the local Dust-Worlder village, "how exactly did this Derek-guy get assigned to Dust World?"

Etta was walking with me, and no one else. She seemed a bit squeamish, as if she wished she could skitter away and hide someplace.

I knew why. She knew I didn't like hogs, and she knew I was putting up a good front. I could tell she was really hoping that I was going to behave myself. I was hoping that too, but I wasn't ready yet to make any promises in that direction.

"What do you mean, Dad?" she asked. "It's just a job, like any other. An assignment. Legionnaires don't always choose where they get assigned, do they?"

"Of course not," I said. "But there are good assignments in security, and there are bad assignments. One might call some of them 'cushy' and others 'shit-work'. That's the technical term."

Etta winced. She knew exactly what I meant. Dust World was no garden spot. In order to be assigned to a guard post out here, you pretty much had to have whizzed on every shoe you could find back home.

"So, I'm asking again," I said, "and I'm asking real nicely: What did this Derek fella do to get his ass shipped all the way out here to Dust World and assigned to this post? No one wants to guard a gateway no one cares about all damn day long."

She shrugged. "Well, I don't know... he used to work at Central."

"Is that right?"

"Yes."

"So... did you originally meet him back there?"

She glanced over at me, then turned back to examine the dirt road in front of us. At first, it sort of appeared as just a rocky trail, barely discernible as it left the front caverns from the catacombs where the Investigator held court.

Like a creek turning into a stream, the path we were on grew from an almost negligible series of rounded rocks and gravel into a broadening dirt track. After a kilometer or two, it transformed into something you might consider a country road. There were even vehicle tracks on it here, where various farmers had traveled upon it, no doubt checking on their alien fields.

Most farmers here grew fungi—or animals that ate fungi. If you didn't like mushrooms out here, well, you were fresh out of luck because that was about all there was to eat. Except for the few animals that also lived on fungi.

"Yes," she said at last. "I originally met him on Earth."

"Okay then," I said. "I'm piecing this story together. The boy used to work at Central. Apparently, he pissed on his supervisor's shoes so badly that he got himself posted out here."

"He didn't get reassigned for bad behavior."

"Aha," I said. "So, you've been dating this boy for years?"

"No, not really. We went on a few outings—"

"But nothing!" I laughed. "Girl, remember who you're talking to."

She frowned and looked down at her shoes. We trudged along for a while. Etta had never been as good at lying as I was. She certainly wasn't good enough to fool an old master like myself, and she knew it.

"Okay," she said. "We met at Central, we had a few dates, and then when I came out here, we got separated. And that was that, or at least I thought it was."

"Oh," I thought, sensing something new here. "Wait a minute, are you telling me he followed you out here?"

"I wouldn't say that, not exactly."

"Wait a minute now. Let's get this straight. Did he request a transfer to Dust World?"

"He might have…"

I laughed. "There's only one reason a boy would request a transfer from a place like Central to this shithole."

She threw me a glare at the term shithole, but she didn't argue with it. No one really could.

"That's because," I went on, "he was hot to check up on his little Etta."

She sighed. "You make it sound so tawdry."

"No, actually, it makes me like the boy a bit. He seems to know what he wants, and he's willing to sacrifice for it. That's never a bad thing in a father's eyes."

"But belonging to Hegemony is..."

"Yeah, well, that is a problem," I admitted.

"You can't kill him, Dad," she told me again. "If you do, I'm not going to speak to you for years."

"Years, huh...?" I said, and I rubbed at my chin for a bit.

She looked alarmed all over again. "And if you perm him, that's it for us. I'll have no father from that day onward!"

"Oh..." I said, and I began considering another plan.

I'd been thinking that it might be worth it if the price to pay was a few years of shunning. Sometimes, I didn't see her for years as it was. There was no point in just killing him without finishing the job, so now that Etta had made it clear that wasn't an option she would accept, I dropped the idea... for now.

"Okay, okay," I said. "So, we've got a starstruck security hog who used to check you into the lower depths underneath Central. He probably watched you walking by to the labs every day. You two flirted a bit and then eventually fell in love."

Etta seemed embarrassed. "Daddy..."

"I'm just piecing it all together. One day, you changed into a new body and disappeared. What's a boy to do? Maybe he tried to find you. Maybe he got access to some security files, huh? He found out somehow that you were out here at Dust World, that you had relatives out this way..."

"Dad," she said, "hold on. Let me have my say."

"I'm just hypothesizing, here. Then he decided to get himself transferred out to Dust World. Now, that's got to be the easiest thing to do for any hog. Everybody who works out here puts in a transfer request instantly, just waiting for the next fool and/or victim to get sent to this dismal butthole of the universe. So, pretty quick-like, Derek got his wish and came out here. What was his reaction when he saw you and noticed how different you look?"

"He was shocked," she admitted, "but kind of in a good way. I think he kind of liked the changes. Before, I was as tall as he was, but now he's taller."

I smiled. It was true. Etta's original form was rather impressive. Amazon-like. She'd been a brute of a girl, taller than ninety percent of Earth's women at least. She'd never been skinny either. She'd been rather stocky in her build—still pretty, mind you, but definitely bigger than average.

All that was my fault, of course. With a two-meter tall dad, she'd followed my genetics in that regard. But girls rarely wanted to be big. They usually wanted to be small and cute—that sort of thing.

Well, her new regrown form was exactly that—a bit smaller and a bit cuter than the old one. She seemed to have a good handle on living in this new body of hers, which admittedly looked like the old one, but which wasn't quite the same. I was glad she'd come to like herself again.

This hog-boy Derek must have been all grins and giggles. He'd come out here looking for his smarty-pants Amazon girl—but found something better.

"I have to admit," I said, "I'm slightly impressed."

"How's that?"

"Well, if this guy Derek worked so hard to find you and has been willing to put up with living in the desert to be near you… that definitely puts some points on the board in my book."

"You haven't met him yet."

"I know, I know. I'm reserving final judgment, but I like a boy who shows dedication and a willingness to roll with the punches. That's a very good thing for anyone who's involved with our family."

Etta couldn't help but agree.

Right about then, we came into view of the gateway posts. Sure enough, there was a lone hog standing there, looking bored and hot. He stood under the shade of one of those big, waxy, orchid-looking trees that were the size of saplings. The big blossom, which was bigger than a man's head with flesh-like petals spread wide, loomed above him. The plant provided just enough shade to block out the rays of the local suns.

"Hey, Derek!" Etta yelled.

He left his post and waved to her. They approached one another. Then Derek caught sight of me, and he frowned a bit.

"Etta?" he said. "Don't tell me this is—?"

"Yes," she said, "it's my father."

It took me a moment to realize that Derek, in his mind, had never met me before. Sure, he'd checked Galina's tapper and mine as we stepped through the post late one night, but we'd been wearing illusion boxes then. I'd looked like some tall, lumpy farmer, dragging my frumpy wife along. I hadn't looked like James McGill at all.

Today, I wasn't bothering with any such disguises. The only fakery about me was the big Georgia grin I'd pasted on my face as I met the hog who'd recently deflowered my daughter.

"That's right, Specialist... uh..." I said, realizing I didn't know the hog's last name.

"It's Jensen, sir. Derek Jensen. I've heard a lot about you."

The hog stuck out his hand. With only a moment's hesitation, I grabbed it and pumped it.

The two of us smiled at each other, and Derek had no idea I was fantasizing about murder.

But I think Etta did. She was watching the two of us, her eyes darting back and forth quickly, wondering if anything unpleasant was about to happen.

But I kept talking nicely with Derek, and he did the same with me. He made sure to be respectful and complimentary. He went on about how I'd raised the finest daughter he'd ever seen.

Slowly, Etta began to relax. She was starting to hope that there would be no violence—at least not today.

-12-

Less than a week later, the four of us set out to return to Earth. We did it in two staggered ways. This required quite a bit of careful maneuvering on my part.

First off, I explained to Etta that Boudica had never been to Earth before, and she wanted to do a little sightseeing. Therefore, we weren't going to go straight through Central, but rather through the Great Globe of Geneva. This kind of baffled Etta, but then, thinking it over, she realized that I was trying to romance Boudica. After an eye roll, she accepted my motivations.

We were all supposed to meet up a few weeks later at our family farm. Derek managed to wangle a furlough, so they went off to Earth first. Etta took Derek home to meet her grandparents, with my remote blessings to the relationship.

Now, if the truth were to be told, I was still feeling a bit resentful about this security hog dating my daughter—but a father's got to be realistic. Etta was thirty-something years old—pushing forty in chronological years.

She didn't look that old... so I pressed a bit. She admitted that she'd gotten herself killed one more time just to back herself up to mid-twenties. All that, just so she could date Derek.

Talk about dedication. Both these young kids had actually demonstrated quite a bit of sincere interest in one another. Derek had given up a cushy post at Central, and Etta had given up a death. As my mama always used to say, "Don't listen to what people say, watch what they do."

Both of these kids had to be serious about each another. As a consequence, I couldn't find it in my heart to commit murder to separate them. In the darkest corners of my mind such ideas still lingered, mind you, but I avoided that easy solution.

I figured that at the very least, these two kids visiting Georgia Sector would do my parents some good. They'd been kind of lonely over the last dozen years.

Me and Boudica were a different matter entirely. Boudica wanted me to take her to Death World, and I'd agreed to do so. I'd calculated privately that if anyone was a match in sheer bitchery for Boudica, it had to be Helsa and Kattra, the queen and princess of the Death-Worlders, as people were starting to call them these days.

So, after Etta and Derek had taken their leave, I introduced Boudica to the fake tappers and the illusion boxes. We donned both, simulating the same frumpy pair who'd arrived here nearly a week earlier.

Then we said our goodbyes to the Investigator and Floramel. They were busy stirring up a fresh new batch of what looked like bubbling turds in a big ceramic tank.

"Is that Galina?" I asked, wrinkling my nose.

"It will be. It will be," Floramel said. "Just give it some time."

"That's right, McGill," the Investigator said. "At least six weeks, possibly eight. If you're back by then, we should have Imperator Turov as our guest."

"Plenty of time," I said. Then I left with Boudica.

Boudica was unaccustomed to wearing something on her tapper arm, and she constantly fidgeted with the rubber sheath that covered her real tapper with a fake one. She seemed to be having even more trouble with the shirt I'd gotten her to wear. It wasn't illusionary, as I didn't want any chance of a failure and a big surprise at the Geneva Globe.

"Why do I have to wear these tight, scratchy, irritating garments?" she asked.

"Look," I told her, "there are about a billion cameras in Geneva City these days, and I do mean a billion. Every citizen has one. Every street corner has one. Every door has one."

"Yes, yes, yes," she said. "What's your point?"

"So, you're going to be filmed, categorized, AI-scanned, and identified probably a hundred times between the Geneva Globe and the sky train port. We have to fake out every one of those computers, every one of those electric eyes. We can't leave anything to chance."

"All right," she sighed. "This better work. But I don't want to go to the sky train port. I want to go to Death World."

"Just straight out?" I said. "Just like that? You don't want to come back to the Georgia Sector?"

"Hell no," she said. "I spent nearly a century in a tank on that property. I never want to see your stinking slice of swamp again, McGill."

"All right, all right. Suit yourself. We'll buy you a ticket, switch directions, and put you on a one-way flight to the second most reviled spot in the human zone of influence."

She eyed me strangely. "Why do they call it Death World, after all?" she asked. "It's not a very enticing name if they want to bring colonists there."

"No, I guess it isn't. The name just stuck. It was originally L-374," I said. "Kind of a nondescript world. It was taken over by the Wur."

"The what?"

"The Wur are these weird, plant-like aliens. They spring up now and then like a weed in the driveway. We killed their brain-plants that control the rest, but they still have giant growths there. Anyone who lives on that planet has to deal with immense flora, some of which still roam about."

"Oh…" she said, "and they kill humans frequently?"

"Yes…"

"Not a very pleasant set of living conditions…"

"That's right. Lots of death. Lots and lots of death. I'm not sure I ever died more times in one short stay on a planet than I did on that one. Every soldier I've spoken to agrees with me, the place sucks. In fact, when we invaded the planet the first time, we were reduced to a single lifter and about five hundred men. We managed to revive the rest back, but it was a near wipe for the legion."

"Plants...?" she said wonderingly. "Plants managed to do all that?"

"Yes, ma'am, they sure did. You'll see. I'm certain the current inhabitants will be willing to tell you all about it."

As I spoke, she suddenly stopped walking and clamped a hand onto my wrist. Now, even though she had a stately stature, she certainly wasn't a strong brute of a girl in the arms.

I felt a pinch and looked at her quizzically. "What?"

"You're talking as if you're not coming with me."

"Whoa, whoa, whoa," I said, "No, no, I'll escort you there. Just like I promised."

The truth was, I'd almost blown it. She searched my eyes, her own darting side-to-side, squinting just a bit.

I'd been scrutinized by countless women in this fashion. She was searching my face for a lie. As any man knows—especially a philandering scoundrel like myself—a suspicious woman has a lie detector built right into her head that's superior to anything the AI boys have yet concocted.

At last, she seemed satisfied. "All right," she said, "I'll chalk it up to your general idiocy. Let's continue."

We went through the gateway posts and arrived moments later. The bustling halls of the Geneva Globe struck Boudica hard. She halted, gaped, and swiveled her head around like an owl for about a minute. She was in sheer disbelief.

"This is an amazing structure," she said.

"Yep. Over the last century or so, things have moved along a bit on old Earth."

"It's beautiful," she admitted, "but it's also an ostentatious display of stolen wealth."

That was Boudica for you. If you showed this girl a golden fork, she'd mourn the mountain from which the gold had been stolen, or maybe the unfortunate soul she imagined had been forced to mine and craft it. There wasn't a construction, man-made or divine, within which she couldn't find some injustice to lament.

After a few moments of gawking, I coaxed her into moving again. We left the Dust World posts, passing the lone attendant who was shaking his head and giving us odd looks. He scanned our tappers, realized we were the couple who had left about a week ago, and waved us through. He cracked a few jokes about the "worst honeymoon in the history of humanity," but neither Boudica nor I paid him any mind.

I led Boudica toward the central booth to buy tickets to another infamous world. But before we got there, a shout broke out. It was a shout of recognition, of alert, of alarm.

Turning, I saw an approaching group. To my surprise, it wasn't just a pair of hogs. It was a big team, and leading them was a Saurian.

This particular Saurian was all too familiar. It was Raash.

Trailing him were no less than six armed men. With a pointed claw, matched by his upright tail, he directed the hogs to spread out and move cautiously.

"That's the one," Raash rasped, his voice dripping with the glee of a predator closing in on its prey. "Don't be fooled. He's not fat. He's not slow. It's an illusion. He is: *the McGill*."

Boudica stood tall beside me. "Kill them, McGill," she said. "Kill them all. I order it. I *command* it!"

"Uh…" I said, "That's kind of a tall order, ma'am. I count seven of them, and they're armed. We aren't. Maybe we should try talking first, huh?"

"Talking? This isn't the time for talk. It's the time for action. I won't be captured to have my brain ripped out again. I won't!"

"Okay, but right now, you need to shut up," I told her. She threw me a glance full of instant hate. I lowered my voice. "If you want to get out of here, I need you to do one thing."

"What?" she snapped.

"Take off your top."

-13-

Boudica hesitated for only a moment before she whipped off her shirt, a garment she'd hated all along anyway. While she was doing this, I reached across to her bare midriff and flipped off her illusion box.

This display caused the hogs, who were now converging on us from several directions, to misstep. Some of them even staggered.

Somehow, I'd changed a dumpy middle-aged woman into a topless stunner, and that transformation had stopped them in their tracks.

"That doesn't look like Galina Turov, sir," one said to Agent Raash.

Raash halted as well, glaring at me. "What have you done, you chattering apes? Are you both falsities?"

"Uh… what?" I asked.

"Have you been duped into misrepresenting yourselves?" he demanded. "For the benefit of a tall ape that befouls every tree he squats in?"

I'd finally managed to gather from Raash's odd statements that he was wondering whether I was really James McGill or not.

I threw my hands high and haphazardly, shaking my head. "I'm nobody, sirs," I said. "Just a farmer from Wisconsin who—"

"Silence," Raash interjected. "I know of your device."

He stepped forward, reaching out. Had it not been for the half dozen guns aimed at my face, I might have made a move. As it stood, I was tempted to face-plant Raash just for fun—but I thought the better of it. It wouldn't have been fair to leave Boudica on her own, while I died in a hail of power bolts.

So, I let him switch off my box. There I stood, James McGill in the flesh.

Raash smiled, revealing more teeth than seemed natural. "So," he began, his foul breath washing over me, "I have captured you. What is this female? Another trick?"

He reached for Boudica's waist, fumbling with the box, which was already off. She tried to fend him off but to little effect.

Joining in with Raash's horny claws, the group of hogs examined her quite closely—too closely to my mind, given her state of undress.

Unembarrassed and seemingly unaware, she made no effort to let the red locks of her hair shield her chest. Compared to when I first met her, Boudica now sported a slight tan, which honestly looked even better on her bare skin.

"She's clean," the hogs finally declared. "She's no one—probably a Dust-Worlder illegal. But she's not Turov. There's no way."

The hogs continued to take liberties, feeling it necessary to touch her bare skin, ensuring it was indeed real and not another illusion. They were perhaps too enthusiastic about this, but I held my tongue. Boudica, for her part, shot them glares and hisses through clenched teeth.

"We've got no arrest record for her," one hog said to Raash.

"I don't care about his mating toy," Raash said, turning back to me. "She's not the one I seek. McGill, where is Galina Turov?"

"I don't know," I said.

Raash snarled. "She was my charge. You stole her from me. You've been gone a week, and I've been punished for my gullibility. I will not let this happen again, McGill."

"Punished?" I asked. "By who? I thought Galina was your boss-lady."

"I'll ask the questions," Raash interrupted. "You'll speak only when commanded to do so."

"What do we do with the girl?" the hogs asked Raash.

"I don't care," he responded. "If she's committed a crime, then do your duty."

The hogs contemplated that. "Well... she could technically be called an illegal alien. She must be a Dust-Worlder, but she doesn't look like one. Probably just an illegal sneaking in through the gates."

"No," Boudica interjected, "I am not. I am an Edge-Worlder, and I want to return to my new home on Death World."

"L-374?" The hogs seemed amazed.

"That's correct, fools."

The group huddled for a moment. When they returned, they were shrugging and nodding. "According to our regulations, anyone wanting to trade one shithole colony for another can do so. They just can't stay here on Earth. This waystation is technically a legal public space for even a non-registered citizen to pass through, so... as long as you're transitioning from one colony to the next, we can't hold you. Just don't try to leave this building, ma'am. That would be a crime."

"Whatever," Raash hissed. "Complete your perfunctory procedures and leave McGill to me."

Boudica, satisfied with this outcome, caressed my cheek briefly.

"Don't try to pass information or weapons to him," Raash warned her sternly.

She ignored the fuming lizard. "You've served me well, McGill. I won't forget this," Boudica declared, then turned towards the ticket booth. I supposed I'd helped her to reach Death World after all, even if it was indirectly.

I shrugged and faced Raash. "Hey, old buddy," I began, trying to reset the nature of our relationship. "Now that everything's settled, how about you and me go grab a beer?"

"Again with your ape noises," Raash chided. "You won't confuse or charm me. And you certainly won't mate with me, as you probably did with that stray female." He pointed after Boudica, noting her exposed back.

"Don't worry," I chuckled. "I have no intention of doing any of that. What brings you out this way?"

"I'm here to locate my lost charge, Galina Turov," he declared. "I have to find her and return her to Central. I shouldn't have trusted you with her well-being."

"Now, hold on," I interjected. "I was under the impression you worked for Galina."

"That's correct. However, my salary comes from someone of higher rank."

I stopped, pondering his words, before a realization dawned on me. "Servant Turov...? Alexander Turov? You really work for him, right?"

"Yes," he confirmed. "Who did you think paid for the yacht, for my services, for everything she possesses? Did you honestly believe a mid-ranking military officer could afford an ocean-going vessel the size of a Wur megagrowth? If you thought that was possible, it's clear proof of your lack of intellect."

His words settled in, and of course, they made sense.

I continued talking to Raash as we left the Geneva Globe together and boarded a sky train headed for Central City.

It had to be true, what he'd said. All the wealth in the Turov family was firmly under the control of Alexander Turov, Galina's father. He'd probably allowed her to use some of it, but ultimately, he held the purse strings.

So, when Galina had disappeared and Raash inevitably informed her daddy of this event, he must have begun to suspect that she was trying to flee from him. She'd rejected the promotion to consul, dodging the destiny he'd meticulously planned for her.

Old Alexander wasn't a man who was accustomed to being thwarted. Thus, he'd ordered Raash, the last agent to have had personal contact with both of us, to act.

I had to hand it to Raash on this point: he'd figured out where we'd gone and staked out our last known whereabouts. The moment I'd returned to Earth, Raash had been waiting to nail me.

I shrugged off these reflections, as they weren't pressing at the moment. I'd managed to hide Galina in the safest place I could think of. In her current state, she was dead and practically "permed" out on Dust World. That was about as safe as safe could be.

Raash was welcome to take a team of hogs out there and search that valley all he wanted. He wouldn't find a thing.

"Okay, Raash," I declared, "we'll head back to Central. I have a report to file with Wurtenberger, anyway."

"A report? What are you up to, human?"

We had reached the sky train, paid our fares, and boarded. Raash eyed me warily as I operated my tapper—my genuine tapper. I'd removed the false sheath, exposing the sweaty skin underneath. My original tapper was somewhat damp, and it burned a bit where numerous hairs had been yanked out. But that was a minor inconvenience.

I contacted Wurtenberger's office and, after being redirected for a good ten minutes, finally persuaded the prim secretary, the one with the butthole expression, to connect me to Wurtenberger himself.

"McGill?" he said. "I question your wisdom in contacting me this way."

"Uh…" I responded, "what manner is that, sir?"

"By calling me directly."

"Well, sir, I am in your employ, remember?" I reminded him of the charge he'd given me: to investigate various rebel sentiments on different worlds. "And in fact, sir," I added, turning my tapper to show Raash's face, "this gentleman right here has been a hindrance."

Raash hissed and wriggled. But due to the closeness of our seats, he couldn't escape the camera's view.

"You see this peculiar lizard? The one with the sky-blue scales?"

Raash hissed louder at the mention of his unique hue. He'd always been sensitive about it.

"Well, sir," I continued, "he's been obstructing my work. I'd just left Dust World after completing my sweep and preparing my report. I was on my way to another destination when this joker tried to have me arrested."

"On what charge?" Wurtenberger inquired.

"You might recall some… uh… misunderstandings back at Central."

"Ah, of course," Wurtenberger acknowledged. "Misdemeanor deaths, destruction of property…"

"Just part of doing business," I said.

Wurtenberger looked sour. "So, you claim to have finished the first part of your report? You've visited Dust World?"

"Yes, sir."

"Any interesting findings?"

"Yes."

"Make your report, then."

I shook my head. "Can't do that—not with this lizard beside me. He's a known agent for Steel World, you know."

Raash hissed so fiercely now that he sounded like a forgotten kettle on a red-hot stove.

"Stop talking, human," he threatened, "or I'll rip off your arm and destroy that device you're using to defame me."

Wurtenberger squinted at us. "You're saying he's a spy?"

"Absolutely. He's been deliberately hampering my attempts to execute your orders."

Wurtenberger examined both of us, his gaze flitting between our faces. "I'm unsure who to trust between you two. Here's my directive: as the commander of Earth's Defense, with the consul's office vacant at Central, I order both of you to report to my office immediately upon arrival in Central City. Submit yourselves for arrest and questioning. Wurtenberger out."

The call ended, and I turned to Raash with a smirk. "So," I teased, "looks like we're both arresting each other now, huh?"

Raash glared, his face contorted with rage. "You've maligned me and misled Earth's naive officers. This will slow me down, but my mission remains unchanged. I work for Alexander Turov," he declared. "No human is mightier than him."

"I thought you were with the Steel World princes," I commented.

"I was, but they discarded me. Now, I'm what you'd term a 'free agent.' I serve the highest bidder in the cosmos."

Chuckling, I pointed at him. "You're a mercenary, a freelancer."

"That's precisely what I said. You're not only repetitive but also dim-witted."

That was classic Raash. The ornery lizard was always full of piss and vinegar.

I leaned back in my sky train seat, eventually managing to ignore his putrid odor and drifted off. After all, it was going to be a long ride back to Central.

-14-

It was the following morning when we arrived at Central City. I was a tiny bit concerned about the reception I was going to get when we landed in the spaceport. After all, there had been some serious misunderstandings and a number of unfortunate deaths since the last time I'd been here. Some folks, especially those of a Hegemony persuasion, might have wrongly attributed these accidents and unlucky coincidences to James McGill.

Naturally, during the last hour of my flight, I'd attempted repeatedly to contact Praetor Wurtenberger's office to make sure things were still all-clear—but I didn't have much success. Perhaps it was predictable then that, when we landed at the spaceport and I followed Raash toward a small shuttle train that would take us all the way into Central, we were greeted by a rather large team of hogs. In fact, it looked to me like a full-blown squad.

"Look at that, Raash," I said, feeling my chest swell with pride. "By my count, there're fifteen hogs coming!" To my knowledge, I'd never been arrested by such a large group of angry Hegemony men before.

"Hey boys," I said as they crowded around, "don't be in a rush. There's enough of me to go around for all of you."

Gravity cuffs clicked on both my ankles and my wrists. They even put some kind of weird dog collar on me with a puff-crete chain leash, just in case I tried anything in the way of escaping them.

I didn't make a move, as it only would have brought them joy to beat me down. Any such effort was doomed to failure anyway against so many.

Just to irritate, I kept up a steady banter. I talked about the funny looks on the faces of the men I'd blown up with a plasma grenade in the lobby, for instance. Some of the hogs drew shock-rods after a while, which crackled in their hands. The pain-delivering devices matched their snarls of rage.

"Halt," Raash said, serving as my protector on this strange day. "Do not damage the McGill. He is my property."

"Who the hell are you, alien?" the adjunct hog who was leading the arresting party demanded.

"I am Raash, the minion of Alexander Turov. Check with his office."

They did, and his credentials were cleared. Grumbling, the hogs listened to him, although you could tell it wasn't making them any happier. I guffawed at them and made jokes about how they were all kissing up to a lizard.

Eventually, they got me onto a train. Oddly enough, the train had been cleared of all other passengers. I was the only one aboard—besides the hogs and Raash himself.

"Why do you always make things so difficult?" Raash complained. "Just keeping you alive is proving to be a challenge. I should let them slay you just so I can watch and be entertained."

"Now, now, Raash," I admonished him. "None of that talk. Your boss, Turov, doesn't want me escaping that way."

"Escape? Impossible."

But still, Raash seemed concerned at the idea that I could escape him via death. Such things had been known to work before for the Clavers. Raash seemed to put me in that kind of category of extreme trickiness.

None of them trusted me half as far as they could throw me—which wasn't far at all.

They took me to Central, and I was frog-marched down to the detention zone. There, for the first time, I was met with a truly unpleasant sight.

It was the twisted-up face of a gentleman known to me as Agent Brinkley. He had such a vicious snarl on his mug that it gave me a moment of concern.

"Hey…" I said. "I know you, don't I? Did you get a chance to talk to Agent Dickson for me? Huh?"

"As a matter of fact, he did," another voice said, having walked in and joined us.

By this time, the hogs had all disappeared. Now only Raash, Agent Brinkley, and this third man remained.

The last guy was also known to me. It was Agent Dickson himself.

"Holy crap!" I exclaimed. "I haven't seen you for years, man! Have you been hiding down here in the guts of Central all this time?"

"Indeed…" Dickson said in a silky, sinister voice.

I took no note of this and continued on like we were besties.

"Hey! Hey, seriously Dickson," I said. "I want to apologize up front for making you wet your pants so bad out there at Sky World and all those other places. You really didn't deserve that level of embarrassment."

Agent Dickson nodded slowly. "You get an 'E' for effort, McGill," he said. He turned toward Agent Brinkley, who had blood in his eye. "You see this performance? He never disappoints. Not with one word, not one utterance, not one syllable."

"Huh?" I said. "How's that again?"

"I predicted it, didn't I, Brinkley?" Dickson said.

"That you did, sir. That you did."

Agent Dickson was walking around me in circles now. They'd chained me with gravity cuffs to a chair made of stiff metal. I wasn't going anywhere.

"Will you abuse him now?" Raash asked. "I wish to observe."

"You may do so," Dickson replied, "but make no videos or other recordings."

"I will not," Raash confirmed. He stood quietly in a corner, a string of saliva dribbling from his nasty, snaggletooth-filled mouth. I figured he was probably getting excited over there, hoping these two agents would torture me or something.

"McGill is acting just the way you said he would," Brinkley told Dickson.

"Yes," Dickson said, "it's my belief he's already working on us, trying to make us lose our tempers and kill him. See the genius in that? He doesn't banter, deny, simper or beg. No fearful wetting of the pants, and no angry threats or brave statements about the future—none of that utter nonsense. Instead, he chooses to enrage us right from the outset by demonstrating a supreme confidence bordering on near-lunacy."

"It's like we could write a whole new textbook on him, sir," Agent Brinkley added.

Agent Dickson nodded and walked around me a few more times. His behavior reminded me faintly of Boudica's weird snake-charming tricks.

I had to wonder, could she have been part of this government at some point? Maybe she was a spy in a past life? It was an intriguing thought, but I had no answers. Nor did I want to give these two clowns any hint of her existence. So, I just grinned and craned my neck like an idiot while he circled me.

Finally, Dickson made his move. He leaned in and pricked me with something tiny. I grunted. It wasn't much, so I didn't react strongly. But then the real pain began.

"Whoa," I exclaimed, "I recognize that! It's one of those little wasp stings you used on your troops? Right? Back when we thought you were just some kind of sadistic lunatic playing the part of my adjunct."

"I'm pleased that you remember my techniques," Agent Dickson replied, "you'll soon become intimately familiar with them."

Oddly enough, that statement of his did kickstart a greasy sweat under my armpits. The pain wasn't intolerable. It was like getting stung by a wasp—it was burning and hurting, not from any physical damage, but from the tiny toxin he'd injected into the back of my right scapula.

As anyone who's been stung by a wasp knows, a person isn't too excited about waiting for the next jab. I recalled the single campaign Dickson had shared with Legion Varus. He'd frequently used this technique on the light troopers, earning him a high-level of discipline. Everyone in his platoon listened to his orders and acted on them immediately.

However, they also did everything they could to screw him over and bring him down. They hated him. I was beginning to understand why.

"Alrighty then," Dickson said, "there's really no need for unpleasantness, McGill. With a single, paragraph-long statement, you can end this process before it even begins."

"That would be highly disappointing," Raash boomed from his corner. He still stood there, salivating and enjoying the spectacle to the fullest.

Dickson glanced at him. He gave the lizard a disapproving pouty lip, but then he turned his attention back to me and smiled.

"What do you say, McGill, my old centurion? Let's set all this aside. No woman is worth so much fuss to a man like you. After all, we aren't going to execute her. We simply want to know where she is. Her father only wants to know of her whereabouts. He has that right, both legally and morally. Don't stand in the way. Tell us what you did with the girl."

"Uh…" I said, "which girl are we talking about, again?"

Another sting landed. This time it poked the opposite side of me, on my cheek. I felt like it would leave a red spot and a welt. I winced and scrunched up my face. I tried to act like it didn't bother me—but it did.

"Oh no!" Dickson said, "I'm so sorry! I believe I've spoiled your favorite expression. That big, shit-eating grin of yours just vanished like magic!"

He was right. It was awfully hard to grin when doing so made the pain worse.

"So that's the goal, here?" I said. "This is all to find Turov's daughter? There's no point to that. She's unfindable. I don't even know where she is. Honestly, I don't think she exists at all right now."

Agent Dickson frowned at me. He turned toward Agent Brinkley, who was fiddling with some settings on his tapper. I'd assumed the guy was watching a ball game or a porno-feely, but it turned out not to be so.

"Brinkley, what are the numbers on that statement?"

"Five-by-five, sir. The machine says he's telling the truth."

Agent Dickson flashed some big white teeth in frustration. Then, he turned back to me, frowning even more deeply.

"What did you *do*?" he demanded.

"He is a fiend!" Raash burst out unhelpfully. "It's best that you torment him to death for the good of humanity and Saurians alike. Once he's dead, leave him that way. That's my best advice."

"Raash, old buddy," I retorted, "settle down over there. Don't forget, I brought you back to life with great effort."

"Yes," he shot back, "but you cursed me with these blue scales."

"Oh, the blue scale thing again?" I sighed.

"Shut up! Both of you!" Dickson exclaimed, growing tired of the bickering. "Raash, according to my orders from the Public Servant, you're allowed to attend this interrogation if you're useful. So far, you haven't been useful at all. Since you're here at my discretion, I'm about to kick you out if you don't stop interrupting with useless suggestions and comments."

"I refuse to leave," Raash countered. "My master has given me orders as well. I am to observe this operation and report directly to him."

This statement seemed to give both agents pause.

I laughed, even though it hurt my cheek where he'd stung me. "Two scaredy cats with your tails tied together, huh?" I told the agents. "I just knew all you guys were pussies underneath. Hey, Brinkley, I never had a chance to tell you how Dickson performed when he was working for me as my adjunct in Legion Varus. It was pretty pathetic. One time—"

That's as far as I got before I was stung again, three times, fast. *Jab, jab, jab*, all across the back of my neck. I had to admit that stopped my tongue, and I started hissing like a snake.

"I'm allergic to bee stings," I lied. "Did I ever tell you boys that?"

"Don't worry, McGill," Dickson said. "I actually take the time to mix a mild antihistamine in with the toxin. That way, you get the pain, but very little of the later swelling and illness that would normally come from this kind of venom."

"Venom, huh?" I said, not liking the sound of that. What the hell was he sticking me with? Rattlesnake bites or what?

I never did get to find out because, at that moment, Dickson's tapper began to buzz. He glanced down at it, and his eyes widened. Red text was flashing. A moment later, the same thing happened to Agent Brinkley's tapper.

"He's coming," Brinkley said.

"Shit," Dickson said. "We were supposed to have the full hour. We've only just started the process."

"Can we speed it up?" Brinkley asked.

"No, not on this subject. It would never work."

I laughed and looked at Raash. He'd been working on his tapper quite a bit lately.

"It was you, wasn't it?" I asked.

"Nonsense," Raash said. "I have done nothing that I was not ordered to do, and you could never prove otherwise, gullible humans."

That's when I knew for sure, because Raash always lied in a completely wrong fashion. His lies were always complicated, brazen, and overstated, giving off a dozen red flags. I hooted with laughter.

The two agents both stared at me, then at him. Their narrowing their eyes told me they'd figured out what had happened.

Raash had tattled on the agents to Alexander, possibly telling him they were blowing the interrogation.

Now, the old bastard was on his way down here.

-15-

A few minutes later, an old man walked into the chamber with us. It was none other than Galina's father, Alexander Turov. Now, you might think that after dating his daughter for decades, having saved her life more times than anyone else alive today—probably even more times than I'd accidentally or intentionally killed her—this old coot would like me by now. But you'd be wrong.

"James McGill..." Old Alexander said. The words always sounded like a curse coming from his mouth.

I moved as if to stand and salute. Of course, the chains holding me down prevented it, but I grunted and attempted to take action, anyway.

"Sorry, sir," I said. "I can't properly greet you. I'm playing a little game here with these two hogs, and I'm ashamed to say you've found me indisposed."

Alexander nodded. "Agents," he said, "get out."

They didn't utter a word. They simply tucked their tails over their buttholes and slid away like shadows in the night.

Turov's eyes moved to Raash in the corner next.

"You too, Saurian," he said.

"Have a care with this one, Servant of Earth," Raash said. "He is far more deceitful and devious than can be easily imagined."

"I'm well aware. Get out."

Raash left, although he did so with poor grace. His scaly tail scraped loudly across the floor. I could tell he was disappointed that he hadn't gotten to watch me writhing in agony.

I had to wonder about old Raash's motivations as he left. Had he called in Old Alexander to benefit me in some way? I doubted it. Raash pretty much lived to serve himself and Steel World. But every now and then, when our purposes aligned, he could be a good ally. He had, after all, helped extract me from Central City while working for Galina. And just now, he'd alerted Alexander when the agents from Central were getting a little frisky. I shook my head, unable to figure that lizard out.

"You're puzzling over our alien friend, is that it?" Alexander asked.

"Yeah," I said. "One might think that you or I were a big mystery, but that lizard, he's more complicated than either one of us."

"A nonsensical utterance," he said. "And yet, I sense that you believe it's true. Interesting. Do you know why I'm here?"

"I surely do, sir. Somebody must have told you that it's my birthday in two weeks' time. Nothing could be more welcome to this loyal centurion of Earth than a visit from a high-ranking official of Earth Gov."

Turov nodded slowly, as if he'd expected some such line of bullshit from me. "You were there in the room when Drusus resigned his post as consul."

"I was, sir."

"You didn't like the manner in which he was... removed from office."

"I can't say it was Earth's finest moment."

"Is that why you've chosen a path of treason today?" he asked.

I gaped and blinked. "I've done no such thing, Servant!"

"You have thwarted my will," he said. "Galina is to be our next consul. You have opposed this at every step. Have you been acting out of loyalty to Drusus?"

I thought that over. The truth was, I was mostly trying to protect Galina from her own mean-ass daddy. I shrugged. "Not really. Galina doesn't want to be Earth's consul. She asked for my help, so I helped her."

Alexander muttered curses and paced around the room a bit. "Galina has never told me this. But she has obviously gone to great lengths to avoid her new role. It's highly upsetting." He snapped his eyes back to me once again. "Do you know why she is running from this responsibility? Do you know why she has defied me in this strange and unexpected manner?"

I frowned, thinking that one over. "I think she's scared, sir."

"Scared?"

"Yes. She's not the bravest soul in the world. I think she saw what happened to Drusus, and she didn't like it."

He laughed. "You expect me to believe that she thinks I would do the same thing to my own daughter?"

I shrugged and shook my head. "It's a sad state of affairs when a father and daughter have such a powerful misunderstanding."

Alexander seemed somewhat troubled by this, and he kept looking at his arm. I'm sure his tapper and mine were in cahoots, flat out telling him I was being honest.

Finally, he grunted, and looked away from his tapper and toward the bare walls of the interrogation room. "What am I to do with you, then? The man who has so clearly defied me?"

"Defied you, sir?" I said, feigning surprise. "I don't recall receiving any commands about your daughter, one way or another, that I was in any position to act upon."

Alexander considered that. He nodded. "I see your point. She is an imperator of Earth's military forces, and although you two have an inappropriate relationship, she can still order you around."

"That's right, sir," I said. "And you gave me nothing else to go on."

He nodded again. "All right, I'll accept this from you. But if I do give you an order—and I'm about to give you one now—you must follow it. Otherwise, McGill, you'll be in a dire state."

When he said that, I immediately thought of the Vault of the Forgotten. I remembered Drusus was down there floating in a brain-tank, just as Boudica had once been. It was a fate I wouldn't wish on anyone.

Boudica seemed forever changed by the experience. In fact, she still seemed somewhat insane. I could understand going mad after spending a long time in that sort of purgatory.

I felt a few trickles of sweat right then, and I won't deny that this was worse than the five burning sting spots that Dickson had applied to my skin not fifteen minutes earlier.

"What are your orders then, sir?" I asked.

"Legion Varus is going on deployment. In fact, *Scorpio* has already shipped out."

"What?" I exclaimed, my eyes widening in shock for the first time.

He nodded slowly. "That's right. You've been hiding from your tapper for days now. You've been off-world without permission, and with your location services turned off. As a result, you missed the mustering call."

"What's the emergency, Servant sir, if you don't mind telling me?"

"The effort we're undertaking is a secret one, but it's a joint military strike against the Crystals."

"Oh," I said, perking up a bit. "We've finally found their home world then, have we?"

He shook his head. "No, I don't think so. We've found a planet which is indisputably a forward base, from which they've launched numerous attacks against our worlds. It is a hundred lightyears or so beyond Rigel, out towards the edge of the galaxy. We've discovered a planet there that I believe is hospitable only to their kind, not to ours. An unpleasant place, it is unsurprisingly carpeted with geological anomalies."

"Uh…" I said, trying to think of an intelligent question to ask, but I drew a blank.

Old Alexander didn't seem to mind. He simply continued talking. "Legion Varus has long been a spearhead, an expendable sharp point to stab at any new enemy. Your outfit is serving in that role even now."

"You mentioned other participants, sir? That this was a joint military effort?"

"That's right," he said. "Rigel is sending a small fleet with transports of her own. This includes primarily Armel and his Saurian legion, along with a contingent of actual bear troops."

"Oh…"

"That's not all. The Clavers, in order to demonstrate they are part of this joint task force, have mounted another ship full of various hairy abominations they've grown in tanks, apparently." He shook his head and even gave a little shudder. "I believe you call them 'dogmen' and 'ape-aliens'."

"Oh yeah…" I said, "I know those boys. They're a bit dumb—and way too likely to sniff a man's butt—but they're tough fighters in a pinch."

Alexander nodded. "In any case, this fleet will rendezvous and strike at the Crystals, who have dared to attack us many times."

"Huh…"

"You have a question? I can see it in your eyes. Speak to me."

I thought about denying that, but he was checking his tapper again. Lying wasn't going to do me much good when the other guy absolutely *knew* I was lying. Damn these intel spooks and their tricky devices. "Well, sir, I was just wondering about this change of heart of yours."

"Change of heart? I never have a change of heart."

"I didn't mean it as an insult, sir," I said. "But you've been dead-set on crushing Rigel out like a cigarette that's burned down all the way to the butt."

"Yes," he said, "I do see Rigel as an implacable foe which must eventually be utterly defeated."

I nodded. "And for my part, I want you to know that Squantus has said the same thing to me. He views Earth as no less of a mortal enemy."

Old Alexander made a dismissive gesture. "Go on. Go on. So what?"

"Given all this bad blood, I'm just wondering why we're now taking a joint military effort with the Rigellians?"

"Because," he said between gritted teeth, "many have appealed to me to do so. I have a strong grasp on this planet's government, but it isn't complete. I have those in power whom I must please, just as all leaders do."

I nodded, understanding what he was saying and even believing it. "So, you've decided to shift gears to destroy the Crystals before you destroy Rigel?"

"I've just said as much, McGill. I also said that it wasn't actually my decision—but I've made peace with it. Now, here's what I want you to do."

I perked up. Finally, we were getting to the part that mattered.

"The moment you finish destroying the Crystals," he said, "you must cause a disturbance."

"Uh... exactly what do you mean, sir?"

He shrugged. "Some kind of unfortunate accident. You're a master of such things, aren't you?"

"I like to think so."

"Good enough, then. Sabotage, perhaps. Blow up Legion Varus's ship. Whatever."

"What?" I squawked.

"Or, if you don't want to do that, perhaps destroy another ship. The vessel transporting the Clavers, maybe. That could work. *Something* must be destroyed, and it must trace back to the Rigellians. It must be their fault."

"Why in the nine hells would we do that, sir?" I demanded.

"Can you be so simple? It's tiring to explain basic geopolitical realities to you all the time."

"I apologize for my idiocy, Mr. Servant, sir. But could you indulge me just this one more time?"

He grunted. "I obviously want to guide everyone away from fighting the Crystals. We must get back to our real enemy, the Rigellians. To accomplish this change of direction, we must break this alliance. There must be distrust and discord among the members."

"Oh..." I said, not liking his ideas too much.

"In return, McGill," he said, "I will forgive you for having thwarted me in this matter with my daughter."

"I can always use a healthy dose of forgiveness," I admitted.

"But be forewarned, McGill. If you do anything else, if you deviate, if you fail, then you will end up in the Vault of the Forgotten. I will see that you are placed in a jar directly adjacent to Drusus himself. Perhaps the two of you can reminisce about old times together. Wouldn't that be nice?"

For the first time during this entire interview, he smiled at me. I did not return the expression.

-16-

The very next day, I found myself fired out of Central's Gray Deck with a teleport harness wrapped around my gut. The straps chafed against the various bug-bite red spots I had on my neck and back. I ignored the pain and itching, and I quietly cursed Dickson's name.

Arriving on board *Scorpio*, I was greeted with squinting eyes and shaking heads. Every tech aboard my legion's ship seemed disgruntled at me for coming to the party late. I didn't care. They could all screw themselves, as far as I was concerned.

Before I could stretch, yawn, and take a piss, my tapper began buzzing. These messages were serious, and they were coming from every officer in my chain of command, all the way up to Tribune Winslade. I decided to answer his call first, since he was the most highly ranked on the list.

"Is this really the infamous Centurion James McGill?" Winslade asked.

"It sure as hell is, sir. And I'm mighty glad to be here at last!"

"Fancy that… Welcome aboard, McGill. I hope your vacation, wherever you took it, was worth all that you've lost over the last couple of days."

I blinked a couple of times as my slow brain digested his words. I had no earthly idea what he was talking about as far as "losing" anything went. I kind of figured I didn't want to know, either. But, after sucking in a deep breath of air, I went ahead and asked anyway.

"Uh, what's this all about, Tribune, sir? What might I have lost?"

"The 3rd Unit of my 3rd Cohort in Legion Varus, for starters," Winslade said. I could hear a tiny sliver of joy in his voice as he told me this news.

"Whoa..." I said. "Uh... Have I been demoted again?"

"No, no, no. Far from it. You've retained your rank of centurion, but you've lost your active command for dereliction of duty—for refusing to answer the mustering call."

"Wait, hold on a minute, Tribune. I didn't refuse to do anything. I simply wasn't reachable for a... couple of days."

Winslade rolled his eye. "Come now, McGill. Surely you must realize how many times all of us have heard excuses from truants such as yourself?"

"Truants, sir?"

"Yes. As in a no-show, one who fails to appear. You are a serial miscreant, McGill."

"But if I'd only known, sir—"

"Oh, I'm sure you've been off somewhere, enjoying some bit of tail on a beach, perhaps. That does not excuse you. That level of disconnection and remoteness from an official summons from Legion Varus is unacceptable. Graves and I have discussed the matter, and we concluded that an individual such as yourself is not worthy of operating a combat unit in this outfit."

My heart did sink a little when I heard these words. "Well, sir," I said, "I was distracted, and I—"

I broke off as there was a flashing, shimmering light appearing next to me. I took a sidestep, and what appeared on the deck was none other than Raash. He was instantly surrounded by a gaggle of arm-flapping technicians. Apparently, he'd teleported after me. He was using the power of Old Alexander's name to the fullest to follow me around. Say what you will, he was a dedicated lizard.

Raash struggled to get his harness off and began choking. A moment later, he barfed an unpleasant mess onto the deck.

"Who is this alien, Centurion?" one tech demanded. She looked red-faced and red-assed. "Is he with you?"

"Sort of…" I admitted.

"Fine. He's your problem. Keep him on a leash." The techs backed off, cursing.

I turned back to Winslade's face on my tapper. He was frowning sternly. "Distracted again?" he asked. "Another pretty face, perhaps?"

I showed him Raash's ugly, vomit-dripping snout, and he winced.

"Tribune?" I asked. "What might my new assignment be?" There was a strong bit of hesitancy in my heart as I spoke these words, but I knew I had to ask.

Winslade smiled for the first time. It was a wicked thing to behold. "Ah, yes. It's only natural you should be curious. You'll be happy to know that many people would consider it a promotion of sorts."

"Yeah? A promotion doing what, exactly?"

Winslade grinned. He outright grinned. He was an expert at coming up with shit-work. He'd learned it from Galina, I figured. She'd once assigned the two of us to manning the booth in the Mustering Hall of Newark.

"You've been added to the Gold Deck secretarial pool," Winslade informed me brightly.

My jaw dropped open, and it stayed there. I couldn't even speak.

"You'll be working for my staffers, Primus Collins and Primus Gilbert."

"Gilbert? Are you talking about that undertaker-looking dude?"

"Have a care, McGill. Keep a civil tongue in your head. You're talking about your new Lord and Master. You're to report to the Gold Deck immediately."

Winslade signed off, and I lowered my arm in shock.

I ripped my harness off and threw it on the deck. The techs around me squawked and complained, but I didn't listen to any of them.

I was angry, really angry. Hell, it was one thing to demote a man, and it was another to get him killed—but to kick a Legion

Varus man out of the combat arms...? Especially a man like me who wasn't much good for anything else? Well, sir, that was an outright crime against humanity.

I marched out of the place toward Gold Deck. Moments later, I noticed there was an excitable lizard in my wake.

A half-dozen pissed techs flipped us off as we went by, but we ignored all that.

"Do not attempt to escape me, McGill," Raash said. "I will not be evaded."

"Don't worry, Raash," I told him. "I can't get too far. This isn't that big of a ship."

Grumbling, the lizard dragged his tail after me in poor grace. He, too, had left his teleport harness in a tangled heap of wires back on Gray Deck.

We took the elevators up to Gold Deck. When I arrived at Winslade's outer office, the staffers there tried to shoo me away at first. You would have thought two stray dogs had come into their domain to lick fingers and sniff hinnies.

After I assured them that I was now an official part of their cohort, their attitudes shifted from disgust to dismay. They seemed especially horrified at the prospect of Raash joining them.

"Centurion?" Primus Collins asked me seriously, "what exactly is this?" She flicked a finger towards Raash, who was breathing deeply and rather noisily about a half-meter off my six.

Raash had never quite understood the concept of personal space, and he tended to linger a little too near humans. In fact, if you weren't used to it, having a nearly seven-foot-tall reptile blowing and snorting on your back was disconcerting. Raash was obviously a full-blown predator with a mouth full of snaggled teeth, but by this time, I was rather used to him.

"This is my *valet*," I told her. "My personal body-servant."

"Nonsense!" Raash exclaimed loudly. "I'm an agent of the Hegemony. My authority supersedes that of everyone here."

Primus Collins flicked her eyes from Raash and back to me again. I could tell she wasn't quite sure what to make of the pair of us. She shook her head slowly. "There are no pets allowed in this office, James," she told me sternly.

"I am no pet," Raash said. "The mere suggestion is absurd. There has never been a pet with a tail as long and glorious as mine."

I jabbed a thumb over my shoulder. "Don't worry. He's more or less house-trained. He does like to feed on the occasional enlisted man or woman," I said, glancing around at the staffers who were encircling us. They took a sudden step back in fear.

"Here," Raash said before Collins could say anything else, "I will present you with my credentials."

And he did so. He was officially an agent who worked for House Turov. To be precise, he worked for Alexander Turov, a famous Public Servant. At some point along the way, Old Alexander had seen fit to give Raash the status of a Government Observer.

Observers were usually accountants, spies, or sometimes lawyers. Raash fit the bill as a spy, I supposed. In any case, he was a government official representing Hegemony, charged with performing oversight in military matters.

"It says here," Collins said, "he's an official attaché. He's supposed to track the whereabouts and activities of one Centurion McGill." She looked at me in alarm. "James," she said, "what have you done to invite this level of scrutiny? Again?"

"Absolutely nothing," I said, throwing one hand high and crossing my heart with the other. "I'll swear that on my grandma's grave, a stack of bibles and my mama's wedding ring to boot. I did nothing to deserve this persecution. It was all Alexander Turov's idea."

Primus Collins threw up her hands. "Okay, whatever." She turned to her frowning pack of subordinates. "Find him a desk. And I guess you have to find one for that lizard, too."

The group reminded me of a pack of Nairbs. With ill grace, they did as they'd been commanded to do. There were lots of muttered comments and countless sidelong glances, but I didn't care.

Something like an hour later, I was bored. I was playing with my tapper, trying to catch a good ballgame from Earth. Every one of them I could find was a week or two old and uninteresting. I hated reruns, but oftentimes on a ship in the middle of an interstellar flight, that was all you could get.

Then Graves walked into the office. He took three steps toward the main doors where there was a conference room with a lot of high-level primus officers having a meeting, but then he stopped when he caught sight of me and Raash.

Turning on his heel, he marched over and stared at us. He slowly began to smile. Finally, he gave us a rumbling laugh. A laugh from Graves… that was a damn rare thing to hear.

But the sound wasn't a happy one to my ears. It didn't bring a smile to my face, either. I didn't join in his joke, and neither did Raash.

"I find your behavior insulting, human," Raash told him.

Graves ignored him and looked at me, grinning now. "What kind of a goat-roping is this, McGill?" he asked. "Did you take any good memos today?"

Then he laughed some more. I frowned at my tapper and glared angrily at him. I was supposed to have a rifle on my back and a plasma grenade on my belt. And all I had was a half-charged pistol. They hadn't even issued me a combat dagger. It was humiliating.

Winslade came out of the conference room then. He joined in Graves' humorous moment, with hands on his hips. "They do look like a pair of gorillas trying to smoke the same cigar, don't they?"

"I've always heard," Raash said, "that your kind likes to sit in trees and throw excrement. But today it's coming from your facial orifices instead."

Neither Graves nor Winslade cared about Raash and his complaints. They were mostly looking at me and greatly enjoying themselves.

"We should have thought of this years ago," Graves said. "You're an honorary hog today, McGill. Enjoy yourself."

He turned away and walked into the conference room. Winslade did the same. Graves paused at the entrance, however, and turned back toward me.

"Well?" he said.

"What is it, Primus, sir?" I asked.

"One of you two has to come in here and take notes."

"Oh, no... you've got to be kidding me."

He crooked a finger, and I followed him.

"I will remain here," Raash said. "Do not attempt to escape me, McGill."

I slammed the door behind me and went to find a seat behind Graves. The important officers were circling a conference table. I had to sit quietly behind Graves, taking notes, and possibly jumping up to help him with the display systems if the briefing required. I felt like I was being gelded with a butterknife.

The meeting began, but it immediately droned on and dragged horribly. It was all about the long journey we were taking, flying in a big arc around Rigel. We were trying to avoid violating their home space. We were to come no closer than a hundred lightyears from Rigel itself.

Other ships moved along different trajectories toward the same destination, a star system on the far side of Rigel. One was Armel's ship, apparently transporting his Saurian legion. Another was full of Rigellian troops. They also were bringing the main naval task force that was coming to defeat any warships the enemy might use to stop our invasion attempt.

Last to the party was a big, clunky bathtub of a ship. It was made hastily with puff-crete and poor geometry—a big, cheap freighter. Apparently, this last vessel was chock-full of ape-aliens and dog-man clones from Jungle World. This was the contribution provided by the Clavers.

Despite the humiliating circumstances that had led me to this meeting, I was actually impressed and beginning to be a bit interested. It was nice to be on the attacking side for once. We'd been running from the Crystals for years now. This looked like quite a showdown. We were making a blind attack against an enemy we barely understood. It was time for some payback—or possibly—time for a vast military disaster.

"Our gear will be different this time," Graves was saying. "For example, we will not be issuing any metal armor, and certainly none of the star dust suits that people like McGill over there have been so fond of in recent campaigns."

My hand flew up. I just couldn't help myself.

"McGill, you're not here to ask questions," Graves admonished. "You're here to take notes. I hope you've tracked down every word we've said and summarized them appropriately."

"I'm on it, sir," I lied. I hadn't even turned on my tapper to record anything, but I did so now surreptitiously. I figured I'd use my AI, the basic stuff on my tapper, to summarize whatever was said later on and submit it as notes. No one ever read those damn things anyway. At least, I never did…

"But Primus, sir, could I ask a question?" I said, waving a hand in the air.

Graves snarled a little, but then finally he nodded and relented. "What is it?"

"Why are we going without armor, sir? That sounds frigging crazy."

"Because that's our new policy," Graves said. "After reviewing the results of our battles on Jungle World with these Crystals, we've determined they manipulate gravitational forces."

This, of course, I already knew, but I forced myself not to get bored and tune out. It wouldn't do to stop listening now. There might be some actual information in this speech.

Graves shifted his gaze. "Primus Collins can probably tell you the technical details better than I can."

Everyone's eyes swung away from Graves and his craggy, old face to the pretty little primus who had been my girlfriend off and on in the past. I gave her an encouraging smile as she took the stage.

"Yes, well," she began, "I've been working with our techs and our bios. We came up with this new anti-armor plan after performing an analysis of damaged tissues. We took samples from the ape-aliens on Jungle World and our fallen human soldiers. The results were the same, either way."

"And what did you discover?" Winslade asked her, echoing my own thoughts.

"We found that the more metallic, high-weight materials a given soldier had on their body at the moment of being struck by the crystalline aliens, the more tissue damage there was."

"What?" I squawked. "Are you telling me we should fight these things naked?"

She cocked her head to one side as if thinking about it. She nodded appreciatively. "Actually, that would probably be the most effective. I don't think this planet's temperate conditions will allow it, but honestly, a pure organic form would be the least responsive to their weaponry."

"Huh..." I grunted, and I sat back down again.

It was weird and counterintuitive, but it did make a kind of sense. What kind of weapon would a rock-alien make, after all? Probably one that affected rocks. So, a straight-out piece of meat was probably not as easily affected as a titanium plasma rifle or a stardust chest plate.

"You see," Collins continued, "a gravity weapon has to have something to work with—something dense, which can be made denser momentarily in order to warp the gravitational field and cause damage to whatever matter is around it. So, while the bare body of a man might actually be crushed up against the bone when hit by one of these weapons, it wouldn't be that bad of an injury. Such a strike might only result in contusions and bruising instead of death from high-compression."

Winslade was nodding and squinting. "I get it," he said. "If there's nothing more solid than meat nearby, the enemy weapons are relatively ineffectual. Heavy, dense objects are more dangerous to be around when struck by one of these gravity beams."

I had my big hand up, waving it around again. At last, Primus Collins pointed to me.

"So," I said, "we shouldn't even wear helmets? Is that what you're saying?"

She frowned, thinking that over. "During actual combat, probably not."

"Damnation," I said, "if that isn't turning all of our training on its head."

"That's enough, McGill. Thank you, Primus Collins," Graves said. He stood up then and continued the briefing.

He talked about the various arcing trajectories of the four ships that were all converging on this distant unnamed star system. He talked about it being a high-metallicity world with more heavy elements in the dirt than there were naturally occurring back home on Earth. He also talked about our expected arrival date, which was approximately three weeks away.

Three weeks, I thought to myself. That was going to be a painfully long time to be sitting at a desk next to Raash.

I'd thought I'd known what Hell felt like before, but now I knew the truth.

-17-

In the end, it was Raash who got me out of purgatory. His bad attitude, poor hygiene, and genuinely scary looks had caused everyone in Winslade's office to complain. No staffer was happy with his strange, stinky meals, his tendency to drool, and his odd belligerent comments. He threatened people with regularity and made a huge mess whenever he went to the bathroom.

I think this last one was the clincher. The female staffers simply couldn't handle it.

"Whoa, Raash!" I said, walking out of the bathroom, waving both my hands at my face. My eyes were almost watering. "You have *outdone* yourself in there this time! There's never been a Blood-Worlder born who could drop a deuce like you can."

Raash actually seemed pleased by my words. "It has to do with the girth and the power of my tail," he said. "I'm experiencing a hormonal imbalance right now due to the lack of appropriate females on this ship."

That was just too much for the secretary leaders. Primus Collins herself led a revolt, demanding that he be removed from the office. Winslade finally relented and came out to do the honors, but Raash checkmated him immediately.

"I am going nowhere," he said. "I am under the direct orders of Alexander Turov."

Winslade raised a bored hand. "Yes, yes. I've heard it all before. You must go wherever McGill goes. I've seen your credentials and your Hegemony mandates. You bore me, Raash, and you're annoying everyone on my staff." He turned to me. "McGill, you're returning to your unit, and you're taking this reeking lizard with you."

I smiled at Raash. He was turning out to be my best buddy. In three days flat, he had gotten me kicked off Gold Deck, and I hadn't even had to stage something like a murder or anything like that.

"I'm just as tired," Winslade said, "of hearing all the bleating from your adjuncts. Harris and Leeson seem to be at each other's throats, and even Clane has been asking for a transfer since you abandoned your unit."

"Abandoned, sir? I was only gone a week. In fact, only four or five days of that were under the mustering call."

"Yes, yes, whatever," he said. "But this cannot be labeled as justice. You must suffer more punishment. All you've done is irritate my staff for days."

Winslade thought for a while, rubbing his chin. I wondered exactly what he was going to do to me.

"There should be a ritual slaying," Raash suggested. "When a member of our villages is found intolerable by everyone, we make a public example of him."

Winslade squinted at the lizard and nodded thoughtfully. "You know," he said, "someone made a suggestion to that effect recently... I'd not thought the idea was really feasible, but I think Raash might have struck upon something."

"Uh..." I said, gawking at both of them. Two evil minds were both working up some deviltry with my name on it, and I wasn't enjoying the process.

"Yes, yes..." Winslade continued, "McGill, you'll return to 3rd Unit and resume command. Tomorrow, we're going to have our first major exercise on *Scorpio* for this campaign. It's going to be a different type of competition this time, one that we've never done before."

"And what," I asked, "might be the heinous nature of this contest?"

"I'll give you a hint," Winslade said. "You're going to be playing 'King of the Hill'. We'll see just how long you can hold on to that title." He gave me a grim smile, spun on his heel, and walked back into his office.

I shrugged. I didn't know what he meant, and I really didn't care. I cleared out my desk as fast as I could, before anyone could change his mind. Minutes later, I was marching through the passageways down to the bowels of the ship where my module resided.

Raash followed after me, bitterly complaining the entire time about a loss of status. He made countless veiled insults concerning my ancestors, who, according to Raash, were all hairless monkeys.

I didn't care. I was a free man. "Raash, old buddy," I said, "I've got to tell you, you helped me out today. I'm really glad that you lay out the stinkiest, tarriest goo when you pass waste. Worse than anyone aboard this ship's ever seen."

"You admire my health," Raash said, "even as I find yours pathetic. The key is to eliminate all vegetation from your diet, and then to increase your grease and fat intake to much higher levels—triple the intake by volume, at least."

"Thanks for the tip, Raash."

We arrived at my module and were greeted like kings. Leeson looked like he was near tears—tears of relief. Harris seemed to be in the same mood—and Clane? Well, he was unpacking and ripping up his transfer request not two minutes after I showed up.

"Were you really going to transfer out?" I asked him.

He hung his head. "Sir, I'm just an adjunct in this outfit, and I'm the junior man. Without your leadership, I'd have to leave."

"Good to know," I told him.

Then I slammed my big hands together, signaling to everyone that the show was over. They were to get some sleep, polish their weapons and their boots. In the morning, we were heading to Green Deck for a major exercise.

They all inquired about the nature of this exercise, but I kept them in the dark, not even giving them the 'King of the Hill' hint Winslade had given me. I decided it was best to keep them totally surprised. Let them feel good about things for one solitary evening.

The next day at 0500 in the morning, we were jolted out of our beds by a ship-wide call to arise. We showered, dressed, and marched down for a hearty meal. I became somewhat concerned when I saw there was plenty of fresh fruit and even breakfast steaks to be had.

"They're fattening us up," Leeson said. "Mark my words. This is going to be a doozy."

Harris was poking at his eggs, hardly able to eat for worry. "Leeson's right," he said to me. "The brass seems to be feeling sorry for us. Are you sure you didn't do anything bad, sir?"

"Like what?"

He shrugged. "Something that would put us on a shit-list? Something that might leave Winslade and the other primus-level folks in a vengeful mood?"

I shook my head vigorously, denying everything. "Absolutely not," I told him. "Now, Raash over there," I said, pointing to where the lizard was heartily munching on what looked like a bowl of mashed insects. He preferred that sort of thing to straight-out beef. "His reputation upstairs isn't the best."

Leeson and Harris glared at Raash after that, muttering dark words. I figured they weren't talking about short-sheeting the reptile's rack, either.

It was pretty easy for me to shift all blame to Raash, so I did it freely. No one seemed to catch on, including Raash himself. He didn't really care what we humans thought of him.

After breakfast and a few quick exercises on the drill field, we were marched to Green Deck and positioned in the middle of it.

I was glad to have a decent-sized Green Deck on this battleship. *Scorpio* was well-armed with heavy cannons, but she hadn't originally been designed as a transport vehicle. To our good fortune, deep in her guts she had an extremely large, open, cylindrical cargo hold. They'd decided to convert this space into a novel form of Green Deck.

Unlike the old design for transport ships, this ship's largest open area was inside her belly. Instead of having nothing but a glass dome or a force field to shield the occupants of the Green

Deck from the harsh radiation and the cold vacuum of space, the hold was well-sheltered.

"This is really weird," Harris said, checking the place out. "The floor curves everywhere you look. See that up there!"

He pointed, and I stared up above us. Weirdly enough, there was a lagoon on what looked to be the ceiling.

"I'll be damned…" I breathed.

The entire deck curved in every direction, and it was all overgrown with jungle-like growths. Once the doors were sealed, you could essentially run forever in any one single direction of the compass, traveling around the rounded interior of the cylinder. If you ran long enough, you'd eventually come back to the point where you had started. We were essentially on the inside of a bubble-like surface, the walls of which formed the floor in every direction.

"I feel like if I jumped," Harris said, "I'd fly right up there and fall into that lake."

"Why don't you try it?" Leeson suggested.

Harris glared at him, and the two began an argument.

"We're going to have to fight this one differently," I told them. "Tactically, I mean. What would you say that range is?" I asked, pointing up toward the ceiling.

"I don't know. Something like six hundred meters or so."

"Yeah," I said, "something like that. Between six hundred and a thousand, well within snap-rifle range."

"That must be the reason why we didn't get any rifles," Leeson complained.

That brought my attention back down to the ground around me. A weapons rack had rolled up and landed in front of us. We examined the armaments with dismay.

We'd expected to find maybe plasma rifles, or at least snap rifles—but no, neither one was to be found. We were issued a combat dagger and a spear each—an honest-to-God spear.

We checked the points and found the tips were at least molecularly-aligned. They were quite capable of punching through a breastbone or an intervening tree if we threw it hard enough. But still, these were not encouraging weapons.

"No guns, huh?" Sargon said, going through the racks and eyeing each one carefully.

He chose one he found to be perhaps more balanced than the rest. I had respect for Sargon. He was probably my most athletic and capable fighter when it came to primitive melee weapons like these. He was also deadly with a javelin. I pointed up at the lake above us on the ceiling of the vast cylinder. "Do you think you could throw a javelin all the way up there?"

Sargon looked up seriously and eyeballed the distance.

"Nope," he said. "I don't think so. I know what you mean. The gravitational pull in here is light, and if I threw it with enough force and it got to the halfway point, it would be grabbed by the gravity pull of the opposite side and drawn down to ground over there. But I don't think I could do it. Just given the heft of this spear and the distance, I'm thinking I could maybe manage a two-hundred-meter cast. But reach the far side? No way. Even with the low grav, it's just not going to happen."

I nodded, and I passed on that tactical idea. I'd kind of hoped to spot enemies on the opposite side of the cylinder and shower them with spears from range.

"Okay," I said, "everybody take a spear and a knife and follow me."

"Where are we going, sir?" Harris asked.

I pointed with my javelin directly toward the region near the lagoon we could see up on the roof. "That hill, gentlemen, is our new kingdom. Right above where the waterfall gushes out into the lagoon."

"Ah, I get it," Leeson said in disgust. "So, we're the kings of that hill, is that it?"

"That's right."

"And the other fuckers will be another unit coming in here, trying to chase us off the high ground. Right?"

"That's it, Adjunct," I told him.

I began walking, but Leeson kept standing there and squinting at our destination. "Wait a minute," he said, "this all sounds way too good to be true."

"What are you talking about?" Harris demanded. "It sounds totally fair to me."

Leeson ignored him. "Graves isn't going to let us squat up on those rocks, throwing darts down at a pack of losers charging up after us. There's no way Winslade and the rest of those bastards would give us a setup like that."

"You're right, Adjunct," I admitted, deciding it was time to come clean and hear the whining. I'd read just the beginning paragraph of the morning brief, which had contained the rules and details of this exercise. "It's not quite that simple. It's going to be us up against everyone else."

They all squawked in dismay. "Everyone else? You mean the whole legion?"

"No, not the whole damn legion," I said, "just our cohort."

This was still met with groans and howls. There were ten units in our cohort. We were to play King of the Hill against a total of nine other units, each consisting of about a hundred and twenty men. It was going to be their job to knock us off and take on the role of King themselves. The winner would be, of course, the last unit to hold the hill and defend it against all others.

"We're starting off *first?*" Harris demanded, enraged. "That's a frigging death sentence! Why can't everyone start at the base of the hill or something and charge up, fighting each other for the top? That would be way more fair."

"It would be," I told him, "but Graves knows we're the best. 3rd Unit is unbeatable in any normal exercise. For that reason," I lied, "he's decided to give all his other pathetic losers a fighting chance. We're starting at the top, and if any of them can eject us, well, then I guess we're not as good as he thinks we are."

This mollified some of the cowardly, and most of my men seemed to buy my bullshit more or less. But still, they grumbled and lamented the fact that we were almost assuredly going to be left face down on those bloody rocks before this day was done.

-18-

The new scenario on Green Deck was utterly unfair. We were given a twenty-minute head start and a kick in the pants. We hustled toward our new kingdom, a big pile of boulders in the center of the vibrant, leafy space.

Essentially, we were sitting ducks parked next to a big lagoon. The only positive was the lagoon itself, which formed a body of water that curved in a crescent around our hill, giving us pretty good coverage on one flank.

My troops hiked up onto the pile of boulders, which were mostly fake puffcrete shells. They served the purpose nonetheless, and we squatted up there, lamenting our fate. I silenced all the complaints by banging my hands together and demanding my officers attend me.

The non-coms automatically gathered as well, and within a few seconds, I had pretty much everybody who mattered in the legion listening closely.

"Okay, okay," I said, "you can stop crying for your mamas now. We've got ourselves a situation, and—"

"No shit…" Harris muttered.

I glared at him until he looked down, then I continued. "Here's how this is going to kick off. Every other door all the way around Green Deck is going to open in about ten more minutes."

A general groan rose up. The biggest complainers in the unit, such as Carlos and Leeson, were especially loud.

"This is so typical," Leeson complained. "Absolutely typical. Again, we're singled out and punished."

"What I want to know," Carlos said, "is just what our illustrious centurion did to earn us this horrific fate today?"

"Yeah…" a few people muttered.

"What about that, Centurion?" Carlos called up to me.

I glared at them until they shut the hell up. "If anyone else wants to mouth off, let me know right now," I told them. "All the crybabies are going to find themselves standing in front of one of those doorways when the enemy emerges, lusting for your blood."

That threat shut them down right-quick.

"All right then, here's my plan," I began. "We don't have to worry about the units coming in on our six, where the lagoon protects us. It'll take them longer to get here, and with any luck, they'll run into each other and fight each other. The ones we've got to concern ourselves with are the ones that are directly ahead."

I pointed toward the nearest portals. From the rocky hilltop, you could see them. The gray, metal, round doors stood out as barren spots in the foliage.

"Here's my idea. I'm going to send out our ghosts, who I've noticed were issued their stealth gear. We're going to place them between the nearest doors, right out there," I pointed to a spot a half kilometer or so away.

"We're to deploy right in the path of the enemy?" Della said. She was invisible, but she was here, and she was listening. "What exactly did we do to deserve this fate?"

"At least it'll be quick," Cooper remarked.

"Yeah, yeah," Carlos chimed in, lighting up. "Throw the ghosts out there, *way* out there. Distract, delay, skirmish. Just throw rocks at their butts, or something. Give us a little more time."

I shook my head. "That's not exactly how it's going to go," I clarified. "What the ghosts are going to do is try to get two of the units to fight."

"The way I recommend doing it," Harris chimed in, suddenly catching onto my idea and liking it, "is you don't hit them from the front, see. What you do is you trail the fastest unit that enters the zone and then make an attack on their rear."

Everybody was listening to him now, because Harris was well known as the unit's master of dirty play. His eyes lit up as he described it.

"You see, you've got to be into the psychology of this," he explained. "That front group, they're going to be thinking, 'I'm heading right for that rock, and I'm going to nail McGill.' But very unfairly, they'll get hit in the ass. Now, they'll naturally assume, since you're going to be kissing the dirt as fast as you can after casting that one spear, that it wasn't *us* that did it. It had to be those dirty guys behind them."

"I like it," I said, pointing a big finger his way and waving it around. "There are a lot of units out there. They'll all be converging on us at the center. Just get between two of them, and bam! Nail one straggler. When he goes down, that unit will assume they're getting attacked from behind…"

"You've got it," Harris said, nodding vigorously. "They'll turn around, all pissed off. It'll be beautiful."

We thought about his idea, and all of us liked it. I gave the orders to capitalize on Harris's plan. My two scouts were muttering curses to themselves, but they hustled back toward the entrances. Della and Cooper soon disappeared from sight. I couldn't even see any leaves moving as their stealth-suited bodies glided through the ferns, rocks and fake banana trees.

"What about the rest of us, Centurion?" Leeson asked.

"The rest of us want to be as invisible as possible," I said. "Find cover. Any kind of cover. The most important thing is that no one should be able to see you except possibly from directly above," I pointed. "We don't have much to hide under, but we're going to try. Cut up some ferns and big palm fronds. Drag them over here and cover us. We're going to get in between these puffcrete boulders, lay on our bellies and be as quiet and invisible as possible."

People grumbled, but they didn't argue much. At least they had something to do. Using the monofilament blades we'd been equipped with, we hacked branches from all the nearby trees, dragged dozens of big palm fronds and even whole saplings over to decorate our pile of rocks.

The rocks themselves afforded a lot of cover. They were arranged with tunnels and pockets between them. They weren't real rocks lying on real dirt. Instead, they were essentially a fake pile of rounded, hollow puff-crete shells. Puff-crete was much lighter than any such boulder had any right to be, but harder than granite. It was kind of like hiding in a pile of giant petrified meatballs.

Once we'd all gotten hunkered down in the shade, hiding in every crack between our fake rocks, a voice rolled out over the vastness of Green Deck.

"Legion Varus," Graves announced. "I'm officiating today as all the participants are members of my cohort. Note the timer in the center of the chamber. You don't have all day."

A big set of blue digital numbers glowed into existence. It was a hologram of a clock, and it said 59:59, a timer that was frozen. The digits shimmered in the air unnaturally.

"As a reward for being the last unit to fully muster out in this cohort," Graves continued, "3rd Unit, being led by Centurion James McGill, has earned the honor of being our first King of the Hill. It's the job of all the other centurions to pull him down from his throne. Open the doors and let the games begin! May the last man alive be King of the Hill!"

Resounding clangs echoed across the massive chamber. We looked around wildly, craning our necks and gawking. The timer overhead began ticking away the seconds. A whole hour… how could we hold out for that long? It seemed impossible.

Every round, gray, metal doorway had slammed open all at once. We felt surrounded, hunted and hated simultaneously. I immediately wished I had a sniper rifle in my hand. We could have put some fire down on some of those doorways from here.

But alas, it was not to be. It was probably a good thing as well, as they would have been able to shoot back, and there were many more of them than there were of us.

Each of the great doors was ten meters across. They rolled open and then closed again about thirty seconds later.

Varus troops knew nothing if not how to hustle. They raced into the exercise zone and immediately spread out. Once they were inside, however, they became paranoid.

Watching them, I had to note with a touch of pride that every other centurion had ordered their troops to proceed with some level of caution. Nobody charged at us too terribly fast. No, they were looking around everywhere, expecting an ambush behind every rock and tree.

In the past, when similar games had been played and 3rd Unit was involved, I'd frequently staged vicious surprise strikes on my attackers the moment they entered the field.

Everyone was paranoid—scared of each other and scared of me. It was a delight to behold.

I wondered if my decision to camouflage my men and hide them among the rocks was helping. Since the unit commanders could see the hill they were supposed to take the moment they entered the chamber, it might be freaking them out that they couldn't see any movement. They couldn't see any troops here. We weren't taunting them, shaking fists and spears. No, this time we kept quiet.

A worried commander might even think we weren't on the hill at all, that we were hiding somewhere out in the jungle. Honestly, that wouldn't have been a bad move. We could have found another hiding spot out in the jungle somewhere, waiting for an ambitious group to claim the hill, only to charge out at the end and finish off the survivors.

I'd considered but rejected the idea. Graves had wisely set up his clock, and that simple fact had made me decide to ditch that tactic.

Glancing upward, I saw the large blue digits ticking away. They now read 56 minutes, 12 seconds. I'd decided I couldn't afford to try anything tricky. I had to hold on for the hour and hope for the best.

The attackers came from every possible angle. It was unnerving to watch them move stealthily through the trees and grassy fields. Around me, my officers, non-coms, and especially the troops themselves, whispered, pointed, and lamented their fate.

"Enough whimpering and whining," I called out. "If you all don't shut up, I'm going to drown Carlos here in the lagoon."

There was some laughter, but they quieted. I wasn't a man given to idle threats, and they all knew it.

We waited. Surprisingly, the first fight broke out not between the units that we had targeted with Cooper and Della, but between the two units that were the farthest from us on the opposite side of the lagoon. Perhaps they'd realized they were both going to have to circle around somehow to reach us. That put each in the other's path. Their commanders decided to preemptively strike one another, and an all-out melee began. Within a few minutes, there were fifty dead, maybe more. My troops hooted and jeered from cover.

"We didn't go down first!" Carlos kept saying. "Not first! We probably won't be the last to breathe today, but we're going to outlive those losers!"

Maybe he thought he was encouraging the others, so I didn't tell him to shut up.

"Lookie-there!" Harris shouted. He'd been carefully watching the zone where I'd sent Della and Cooper to confront other units. "See the 9th? They've got to be more than halfway to us, but they just halted."

I wished I'd had better optics so I could zoom in, or a drone from my techs, but nothing that complex had been issued to us for this exercise. Instead, we had to squint, stare, and point.

But what Harris had noticed was true. The unit that had moved the closest to us, the most rapidly advancing group, had suddenly halted. Now they turned around and cautiously stepped back the way they'd come. I winced, hoping that Della or Cooper weren't in their path, or if they were, that they could evade detection.

Not long after that, another unit coming from the portals came into view, facing the 9th. They were moving slowly, cautiously, obviously not planning to be the first to get to the hill—but they'd found trouble anyway.

The men around me hooted and cheered as two units turned on one another. The fight was savage, probably because it was out in the open. Whoever had tricked the 9th had done so masterfully. I hope they'd managed to crawl away and live.

"I bet it was Cooper," Harris said with glee. "I bet he's right in the middle of that shit-storm, dodging feet and pissing his drawers."

He was pointing at an outcropping of fake boulders in the middle of the field where the two units clashed. "You see that stack of rocks? I bet he threw from right there. He's hiding in those boulders. Look what one spear can do!"

"Isn't that Jenny Mills' unit?" Leeson asked.

"I think it is," I said. "Yeah... and she's got a vicious temper when she's feeling vengeful."

"You oughta know, sir."

I glanced at Leeson, but I didn't admonish him. Everyone was in a good mood.

"That's right," Harris said. "She's not one to let somebody come up and peck one of her boys in the ass. She turned right around, and she's going for it."

The two units threw down, and there couldn't have been more than thirty or forty survivors left before it was over. Both sides broke and ran off to hide in the jungle.

"With any luck, they lost their officers," Leeson was saying. "Without leadership, they'll never come and take us out."

I nodded. I was feeling better and better. So far, four out of the nine units approaching us had been seriously damaged.

But now, it was about to be our turn. Approaching our flanks from the left and the right, each alongside the shoreline of the lagoon to our rear, were the 6th and the 4th Units.

"Uh-oh," Harris said. "Those boys hate you, don't they, Centurion?"

"Yeah," I nodded, unable to deny it. "Hate. Pure hate."

Last year at Jungle World, the two centurions in question had somehow been blamed for a disaster that I'd caused with a bit of illicit drone-flying and a lot of large, angry apes. Graves had dressed them down for it, but they'd maintained throughout the campaign that the disaster had not been their fault.

They'd never been able to prove their innocence. Now, mysteriously, they'd both flanked me. They were coming around from opposite angles toward my stack of puffcrete rocks.

"This is it, kids," Sargon shouted. "Get ready!"

As if responding to his words, the approaching units emerged from the trees and charged at our hill, abandoning the shelter of the jungle.

The battle was on.

-19-

When one hundred men are being charged by two hundred guys from two different directions—well, that's a bad situation, period.

We only had one real advantage, and that was the rocks that we'd hidden ourselves within. The enemy didn't know exactly where we were—or even if we really were in those rocks at all.

Regardless of their thinking, they seemed to be dead-set on killing us, no matter where we were hiding. They were advancing in a very decisive and determined way. I could almost feel the hate coming from those two centurions, who were clearly in cahoots against me.

To my mind, they were making a mistake. They were taking unnecessary risks to knock me out of the game early—but so be it.

When they got down to the last hundred meters, they charged. They held their spears in the air, puffing and leaping from bush to bush. No cover higher than a man's waist could be seen for quite a distance around our rock pile, so they'd decided to get to us as fast as they could.

I thought about ordering my men to cast their spears. Surely, in an exchange of fire, we would have been able to kill more of them than they could have killed of us, just because our rocks would have gotten in the way of the return fire.

But I didn't give the order. The enemy might simply ignore our shower of spears and then rush in close. If my men were down to knives, we'd be at a disadvantage despite our covering boulders. With longer weapons and superior numbers, I felt pretty certain the enemy could root us out of our stronghold.

I decided on a different tactic as I watched them approach.

"Sargon!" I shouted. "I want all weaponeers to throw. Clane! Have your lights tease them!"

Clane and his light troops shook the palm fronds and other cover that we'd set up on top of the rocks. They bounced up like frisky gophers to look around. Showing themselves momentarily, they poked up heads, hands and spears. But none of them threw anything.

At the top of the hill was a circle of my weaponeers. These were the men with the strongest arms and the greatest training with throwing things.

As one, the seven men stood and cast their spears. Six of the seven each pierced a man in the chest and took him down, but the seventh, Sargon's cast, took down no less than two of the enemy. Sargon himself was a master. He'd nailed one through the guts, but the spear continued on with such force that it stuck in the leg of an unfortunate light trooper girl that was running in the shadow of the dead man.

The enemy had thus taken casualties before they'd even reached us. That sort of thing always caused a shock. A few of their charging lights even tripped over those who had fallen.

Most of them, however, kept on coming. Our quick, deadly strike had created the hoped-for effect. It had both pissed them off and freaked them out.

When they were only about thirty meters out, the approaching centurions on both sides ordered their troops to pause and return fire. They cast a hail of spears at our tower of fake rocks.

I'd been expecting this. My troops were lying low, hiding in crevices and twisty little tunnels that ran between the puff-crete stones.

Spears came flying at us all over our makeshift mountain. They sparked when their tips struck the artificial stone and fell clattering into the cracks among us. One or two of my men were injured, but since we were taking shelter, the attack was pretty fruitless.

After their sweeping cast from both sides, they continued their headlong charge. At that point, I ordered all my troops to stand and cast point-blank.

The enemy had essentially wasted their spears. Their casts had only given us more ammunition.

Sargon was still heaving spears from the crown of the hill. My heavy troopers stood in the middle-zone heaving down rocks and spears as well. Our numerous light troops were all around the lowest ring of rocks. Their job was to keep the enemy from climbing to the crown of our hill.

As the enemy got close, there was nowhere for them to hide. A few crouched or even crawled, but this mostly caused them to be tripped over. Some ducked, some dodged, but I had to guess that at least a dozen were struck down on each side of the hill.

"They're eating shit down there!" Harris shouted, his face split apart in a broad grin. He liked nothing better than to take advantage of a weak enemy.

"Stand and cast!" I ordered. "Don't miss, boys!"

My heavies and the weaponeers had soon thrown all their own weapons, so we were reduced to scrambling to gather the spears that had been thrown at us by the enemy. These were strewn all over between the rocks. Our shower of projectiles slowed, but it didn't stop.

The two approaching armies, what was left of them, now formed ragged lines. They hit our bottom rank of stones. They crawled in-between the rocks and were greeted by Clane's light troopers. A vicious series of knife-fights broke out all around the base of the hill.

"Throw rocks when you run out of spears!" I ordered Sargon. "Harris, advance with the heavies. Push back anybody who breaks our line."

Here and there, when my light troopers were faced by superior veterans on the other side, they fell back. I hissed to see my lines folding.

You would think Clanes men could have done better. After all, their flanks and rear were protected. The enemy was taking fire from above, and we had the psychological advantage. But still, there were many cases where Clane's men simply couldn't hold. They weren't, after all, the best.

Harris and his heavy fighters operated as my tactical reserve. They pushed back wherever there was a penetration. As soon as the enemy crawled on top of the first tier of the rocks, he charged them and drove them back into the field.

Sargon's heavy weaponeers had run out of spears by now, of course. They'd gathered a lot of head-sized puff-crete stones in preparation for this moment. While not as heavy as actual granite, these rocks were plenty hard and heavy enough to crush a man's skull.

They threw them with great accuracy, and with the added force of gravity, they nailed any group of the enemy that dared gather. The effects were devastating.

When any army approaches a fortified position, the individual soldiers will naturally focus on their own knife and the knife of the enemy who is jabbing at him just inches away. Rarely do they look up.

Crawling over the rocks, they made easy targets. They were caught unaware, with careful casts from above by my most powerful troops. Those who did make it, who were able to gain a foothold here and there, killed pockets of Clane's men. Sometimes they reclaimed a spear or two when they took over one of the enclaves that honeycombed the stack of rocks.

But then Harris's heavies would arrive. Survivors were rooted out and destroyed. Here and there, a man ran off in fear.

In the end, the enemy broke on both sides and routed. Beaten and broken, they ran off back toward the distant line of trees. Some dove into the lagoon and swam away, bloody and fearful.

My men cast spears after them, but I told them to hold back. Every spear was precious. Taking a quick glance upward at the hologram clock, I saw we hadn't even reached the twenty-minute mark yet. We had a long way to go.

The first round was over, and my troops were panting. They began the grim business of stabbing at wounded enemies who wouldn't die easily. We wanted no surprises when the next attackers arrived.

We gathered up more rocks, loads of spears, and stacked more knives than we could use. We stockpiled them inside of our fortress.

Forming a bucket-brigade, I had a great deal of this weaponry handed up to the top of our pyramid of stones. From there, it could be cast down with greater force when the next attempt was made to take our hill from us.

"All right," I shouted. "Clane, how many did you lose? Sound off!"

"Twelve dead, sir. Five more wounded. A few of those are still worth their salt. A few aren't. Should I dispatch the wounded, sir?"

"Negative," I said. "Patch them up as best you can. Give a spear to the injured, and stick them in a hole with their back to the dirt. Tell them to jab at anyone that comes at them. A rat in a hole can be mean enough to hold off a dog."

"Good enough, sir," Clane answered.

"What about you, Harris?"

"I lost exactly one heavy, sir. Just one."

"Well done. Well done," I said. I was beginning to hope that we might get through this, but I couldn't let it go to my head.

We patched ourselves up, sorted through the dead, threw extra bodies out in the lagoon, and gathered up a significant stockpile of spears, knives, and heavy stones.

I went to talk to Leeson, who'd been spending all this time keeping an eye on the other forces moving around out there on Green Deck.

"What have you got for recon, Leeson?" I asked.

"They're being tricky out there now," he said. "I think they've caught Della and Cooper—unless they've managed to escape. Doesn't matter. They're pretty much out of the fight."

I nodded. My ghosts had managed to tangle up two units, lowering their numbers by half. Now we only had to face fifty men each in those divided groups, rather than two units, fresh and uninjured, of one hundred men apiece. I'd call that a good trade for two scouts any day.

"Where's our trouble spot?" I asked Leeson.

"I'd say out there where the thickest trees are. There's at least three units somewhere in those trees, and I haven't heard a peep out of any of them."

I thought about that, and I didn't like it. Three hundred-plus fresh troops? They were either fighting to the death inside those palms, or they were parlaying—plotting our demise in the shade.

Taking careful stock of things, I felt a burst of pride. We'd pretty much shattered four units already. Two others had gotten into an altercation on their own.

But that left the three who were quietly lounging under those trees… Leeson was right. They were our only problem now. They were fresh, and they probably had four times our numbers now. What were they doing out there, in the thickest, most heavily forested region of Green Deck?

"All right, everybody," I said, "get back into your hiding spots, pull all the palm fronds back into position. Let's not let the enemy count heads. I want everybody to have two spears, and I want three or four with the weaponeers at the top. And get that bucket-brigade going again, passing the big stones all the way up to the crown."

I joined this last group, sweating and heaving, as rock by rock was dragged up to the top of the hill and stacked into cairns at strategic locations all around the top of my soon-to-be bloody hill. The stones weren't as effective as the spears, but they still did the job when the thrower's aim was good.

We hunkered down and waited.

"Maybe…" Leeson said, sidling up to me on his haunches.

"What?" I asked.

"Just maybe we could consider…" Harris said, coming up from the other side of me, also on his haunches.

Immediately, I was on guard. These two were either going to assassinate me or perform some kind of chicanery.

Harris smiled. It was a fake smile, a hopeful one. The kind that showed his teeth but not any form of happiness in his heart.

Leeson gave me a similar expression, but it was a bit more apologetic.

"Maybe what?" I asked him.

"Maybe, sir," Leeson said, "we could consider a different strategic position?"

"What are you boys talking about? Spit it out."

Leeson pointed toward the lagoon. It was bright and azure, something like ten meters deep and at least an acre or so in size.

"Refuge is right that way, sir," he said. "We know there's not much out there on the other side of the lagoon. What if—and I'm just spit-balling this—we were to fool the enemy?"

"All we'd have to do is jump into that pond over there," Harris said from the other side of me. "We'd swim away to the opposite shore and wait there. Maybe there's a few nice caves and grottos, you know?"

I was frowning at him. Actually, I was glaring.

"Just look at that beautiful waterfall," Harris said. "Isn't it lovely?"

"That's right, Centurion," Leeson said. "I've been thinking we could fool them—instead of facing these next three units alone. I mean... it's frigging obvious they're in cahoots."

I nodded slowly because I couldn't really deny that obvious fact. There had been no bloodshed in that forest. No one had come running out of it. No one was making a peep in that thick, forested area. When three hundred plus men fought to the death less than a kilometer away, believe me, you could hear a ruckus.

Sensing they might be making headway, the two pressed their plans upon me. "You see," Harris said, "here's the deal. They can't see what we're doing from there. Even with the curvature of this fish-tank Green Deck."

"So," Leeson said, picking up where Harris left off, "we'll retreat unseen. We'll cross the lake and wait over there, keeping all of our strength. Most of our boys are still alive, see, and we've got extra spears, at least two each. I bet we can carry them all the way over there."

"Keep talking," I said, even though I was still glowering angrily.

"Yeah, well... that's really the whole thing," Leeson said. "The point of this exercise is to be the King of the Hill at the one-hour mark. See those blue numbers up there?" He pointed.

"Nineteen minutes left. Nineteen minutes is an awfully long time. At some point, we're going to get hit by those three units, and—"

"But what if we're not here?" Harris said, suddenly and loudly. "If we're not here when they all come for this pile of rocks—who are they going to fight?"

I looked from Leeson to Harris and back again.

"*Each other*," Leeson said, smacking a fist into his open palm. "You get it? That alliance they've just formed will crumble instantly. The moment they see that we aren't here, they'll know the team effort is over with. Only one unit can hold this hill and win. That means you'll have three sides, all grinding on each other. Nobody with any advantages. I bet you they suffer losses of fifty each—easy."

"That's right," Harris said. "That's when we come sneaking back around the lake. As soon as we see their fight winding down, we'll come right around on their flank and knock off whoever is sitting here. At that point we'll be the only unit in this fishbowl that still has most of our troops intact."

I nodded, actually considering their plan. Sure, it was a chicken-shit idea. It was exactly the kind of thing I would expect from Harris, who hated dying. He loved taking advantage of anything he could come up with to keep drawing breath.

But honestly, I'd pulled similar maneuvers in the past.

"That's not as half-assed of an idea as I expected you to come up with," I told the two of them. "I can't reject it out of hand. However, there's just one problem."

Both of their faces fell a bit, but they still looked somewhat hopeful.

"Uh..." Harris said. "What would that problem be, sir?"

I didn't even need to point. Right then, Sargon shouted. His voice rolled over the rocks down to us from on high. "Here they come!"

We all stood up and craned our necks out toward the deepest forest. Three lines of troops were marching toward us. They weren't shoulder-to-shoulder, not exactly. There had to be at least fifty meters between each of the three units, but they were obviously a united, combined army. Worse, they weren't running, shouting, or disorganized. They were marching steadily. They each held a spear in one hand, but what was in the other hand—?

"I'll be goddamned," Harris said. "They've got shields."

Leeson slapped a hand to his forehead, which was sweaty, and the sound was loud.

"Holy shit," he said. "That's what they've been doing out there in those trees."

"They were plotting our deaths and cheating," Harris said in a rage, "flat-out cheating. They aren't supposed to ally up against us, and they took the time to make fricking shields. I can't believe it."

"What horseshit," Leeson said, marveling. "They took twenty minutes just to make frigging *shields*."

The shields were only wood, as far as I could tell—but that didn't matter. They would be at least somewhat effective to stop the barrage of missiles we would surely throw at them.

"That army," I said, "that's the problem. We don't have time now to perform a retreat. If we jump into the lagoon, they'll surely see us. They'll be here in a minute. We don't have time for an orderly withdrawal."

"How about a disorderly one, then?" Harris suggested.

I twisted my lips and shook my head. Then I got to my feet and raised my voice to a roar. "Adjuncts, take your positions. This is it. We're going to be the kings of this hill, or we're going to be buried on it!"

"Shit," said Leeson. "Shit, shit, shit."

-20-

Three units marched on us. They spread out a bit as they came, with one unit flanking to the left, another to the right.

"They're out in the open," I shouted, trying to spread courage among my weary, despairing army. "We have the higher ground, and we're going to be able to hit them with spears before they can hit us."

As if the enemy had heard my tiny pep speech, they stopped marching.

"They're halting," Leeson said. "Just out of range. Goddamn it."

At something like a hundred meters distance, the enemy army halted. Each of the units stood four ranks deep. The front two ranks were light troopers, the second was all heavies, and the rear was made up of auxiliaries. It was obvious they meant for their light troopers to take most of the punishment up front, with the second rank doing the real damage after the front had fallen. The auxiliaries in the rear were there to clean up the pieces and drive us off the hill completely.

"Sargon!" I shouted.

"Here, sir."

"If you stand up at the top of this hill, do you think you can hit one from here?" I asked.

Sargon hesitated. "I can try, sir."

"Go for it. The rest of you boys, keep feeding him spears."

They were psyching out my men, standing out there in the open, looking like an organized army, not a mob. It's hard to watch yourself being stalked by a superior force—especially men that are better-equipped and outnumber you three to one.

But our lone champion, Sargon, had the strongest arm on this battlefield. He also had the best aim and a serious height advantage.

We craned our necks and watched as he climbed up on top of the highest rock. There, at the very peak, the pinnacle of our pyramid of stones, he stood tall.

He lifted a spear, rolled it in his hands, and measured its weight. Then he switched it for another one he thought was more balanced.

Suddenly, he cast. He let loose a war whoop as he did so. Even before that one landed, he snatched up another, grunted, and heaved it right behind the first.

He cast for the center group, aiming for the middle of their organized ranks.

The enemy troops lifted their shields—but some of them shuffled around, wavering. They already wanted to break, to scatter, to throw themselves on the ground. Unlike ancient armies, modern troops aren't trained to stand there and take it like the ancients would have.

But they did stand their ground. I'm sure they had been ordered by the centurion to do so.

The first spear punched through a splintery, soft wooden shield that had been held high in vain. It chunked right through the hand and the shoulder behind it, and I think even protruded from the back of the man's neck.

He fell, scrabbling in the dirt like a gigged rat. Blood sprayed everywhere.

Moments later, the second spear landed, lancing a light trooper in the front lines. This time, the cast was not quite so perfect, but it wrecked his shield and sunk deeply into his hip. He pulled it out with gouts of blood, squalling like a stuck pig. He unnerved the men around him.

But Sargon was not yet finished. Every few seconds he threw another spear, always towards the center unit. Those men were already breaking ranks, already backing away. They'd been lifting their shields up, but now realized that they were essentially useless.

The trees that grew on the Green Deck weren't entirely artificial, but they were more akin to giant grass stalks than oak trees. This was because the flora had to take damage and be quickly regrown. The genetically engineered plants grew a foot or two every night. They looked good, but they could never withstand punishment like a denser, older form of wood.

Those shields had only served to give the enemy a false sense of personal protection. This was now being shattered.

Worse, Sargon was effectively breaking their morale by continuously pelting one group, a strategy he'd wisely chosen. I nodded in appreciation. I'd not given him any orders in that regard. He'd come up with this tactic on his own, and it was extremely effective.

A roar went up from three hundred throats. They'd had enough. They'd attempted to intimidate us. They'd marched up, formed ranks, and looked tough—but it had all blown up in their faces.

Their centurions, sensing that their troops' morale was crumbling—and maybe even the alliance between the three units was falling apart as well—ordered their army to attack. They now had suffered no less than seven dead and injured, all from the middle unit of the three. They had to make good on their assault before they suffered any more long-range losses.

The army spread out further, and they trotted forward, none of them casting spears. Not yet.

Sargon threw down a few more mighty spears from his mountaintop, but then I ordered him to duck low under cover. I didn't want him to be taken out. He was too valuable, and it would have reversed the surge in morale my men were feeling. I felt like a company commander who owned a single cannon, and I didn't want it knocked out.

When they got close enough, I had all of my troops stand and cast a single spear, all at once. Then they ducked back into the rocks again.

The enemy absorbed this shower of projectiles and faltered. They wavered as the spears landed among them. A dozen more attackers screamed and fell, writhing in the dirt, their blood churning into mud.

"Charge!"

A roar went up from perhaps now something like two-hundred and fifty raw throats. Still too many. Still more than double our number.

They came on fast and hard. Not one of them had yet to throw a spear.

"Wise," I thought to myself.

"These guys are smarter," Leeson said. "Those shields of theirs are shit. But a spear's deadly when you're jabbing at a fox in a hole."

I had to agree. Previous attacks had been far more fruitless. They'd given up their weapons with reach and been forced to use nothing but knives. When you're fighting a man hiding in a hole, believe me, the guy poking at you with a spear is at a great advantage compared to the guy crawling in with a knife.

This attack was going to be different. This time, it was going to hurt.

Still, we had numerous advantages. As they crashed into our bottom rank of rocks, Clane's men were essentially surrounded and being assaulted from every direction. But they still had their flanks covered by the rocks. They also had an element of surprise when they appeared out of a dark crevice to attack the men scrambling up the rocks.

But these advantages were short-lived. Our real power, our real strength, was once again my heavies and weaponeers that were up high on the pyramid of stones. They threw a continuous hail of spears and rocks from above. They smashed skulls, pierced limbs, broke ribs. Enemy spearmen howled and reeled back, stricken and dying much faster than we were. Only their sense of their own superior numbers, their fury at having been abused thus far, and possibly their centurions' raw hatred for 'yours truly', kept the army together.

Sargon stood on the very peak of the hill, casting spears down like lightning bolts from heaven. But now I noticed that a weaponeer or two from each of the three units that were assaulting my hill were playing the same game as Sargon himself. They stood back, grabbed spears—usually ones cast down by us, whether it had missed or succeeded in piercing the breast of some hapless light trooper bleeding in the grass. They heaved these spears back up at Sargon himself. Most missed wildly, sailing off harmlessly into the lake on the far side.

A few, however, struck near his feet, sending up sparks and sprays of chipped puff-crete. Finally, one got him in the shin. He went down to one knee, but he kept on throwing. Leeson's men huddled at his feet, unworthy of our champion. They kept passing up one spear after the other.

Among those supporters were people like Carlos, Kivi and Natasha. They were more or less useless techs and bios. They weren't much better fighters than your average light trooper—sometimes worse. I'd turned them into couriers, fetching ammunition for those who could do the serious fighting.

Sargon, by the end, must have thrown fifty spears and killed perhaps thirty to forty men before his luck ran out. Almost at the same time, a spear lanced through his upper chest and a second one caught him in the back. The shock of the first blow had left him unable to dodge the second.

He tumbled from his perch, falling over backwards. His body rolled, flopped, and slid into the lagoon. There, he sank like a stone.

"Harris," I shouted, "take Sargon's place."

"Goddamn it," I heard Harris grumble, but he scrambled to obey.

The shower went on from above, but we were running out of ammunition. The first rank of boulders, those at the bottom where Clane's men had stood, were pretty much abandoned and taken over by the enemy.

Now the fighting became vicious. Most of us were wounded. Most of the enemy were too, but they still outnumbered us, probably by two to one now.

"We have to break one of their units," I said.

"How the fuck are we going to do that?" Leeson asked.

"Leeson, if I fall, you're in command."

"Oh, crap…"

I turned away, ignoring him. "Heavy platoon, gather around me. Arm yourselves. We're going to charge right down the middle."

Panting, bloody men, pouring with sweat, soon surrounded me. There couldn't have been more than fifteen of them left. I didn't bother to count.

We moved out, scrambling down over the top of the rocks. We had spears held like lances. We jabbed, and we leapt from stone to stone. We pushed hard against the middle unit.

All along, that group had taken the worst of the punishment. It had started with Sargon, who had cast his very first spears in their direction.

We hadn't let up on that strategy, not from the first moment until now. They had to have lost fifty percent of their troops by this point.

My heavies came down from above, relatively fresh, and we began a quick, powerful blow—a slaughter, really—against that middle unit. I myself managed to find the enemy's centurion.

It was Johnson, and his eyes were wide. I came for him remorselessly, thrusting with my spear directly toward his heart. He backed away, gave ground, and dodged from side-to-side.

He was good, but I could see that one of his legs had been crushed, probably by a rock that we'd rolled down earlier. It was all he could do to evade my thrusts.

But then he reacted to a feint I made. Aiming to the left, I switched directions at the last instant and plunged the spear through his heart. With a look of shock on his face, he managed to flip me off, and then toppled over backwards. He rolled and slid into the bloody mess that was the lowest of the stones. He landed at the very bottom of the pyramid of rounded rocks.

That was too much for his unit. They'd taken heavy, heavy losses. They'd seen their commander die right in their midst. They turned, and they fled.

This was the critical moment in any primitive battle in history. In the olden days, battles were fought eyeball-to-eyeball, nuts-to-guts. This was like one of those ancient conflicts. When you saw your own side throwing down weapons, turning tail and running—that was hard to take.

At that point, your fear grew exponentially. Since we'd chosen to break the center of the three units, this caused even greater psychological pressure on the other two units. They couldn't see each other. For all they knew, the other flanking team had already retreated. Maybe they were the last chumps left standing against these crazy, vicious psychopaths that were holding this hill, every stone of which was slick with blood by this time.

A retreat was called by both flanks.

"Give them hell," I shouted at my remaining weary troops.

We cast spears after the running men. It was a rout. I let my men chase them for a bit, but then I called them back. I didn't want them to wear themselves out, racing after the enemy. We killed a few more as they fled, then we slaughtered all the wounded in the field.

"Now," I said, "throw all their bodies off our hill. Form a massive ring of death all the way around the base of our mountain."

It was a grim order, and it was an even grimmer spectacle when we were finished. Bodies lay, in some cases, three or four deep all around the base of our hill.

Then we wearily gathered our spears and stones. We dragged our tired, injured, bloody selves back into the rocks. There, we hid in our shady bolt-holes and disappeared from view.

-21-

The great game of "King of the Hill" ended with more of a whimper than a bang. In the end, no one else dared assail our position.

I think the effect was more psychological than practical. There were several groups of fifty or more running around out there, biding their time—but none of them quite had the guts for an assault against us.

They didn't know that we were down to nothing more than thirty-nine exhausted survivors. All they knew for sure was that we'd turtled up again, hiding among the rocks. We'd covered ourselves once again with leaves and sticks.

Around the base of our hill was a mass of strewn bodies. They'd watched us repel five full units making determined assaults. On top of that, they had to know we were armed to the teeth with countless spears to shower down upon any new attacker.

No one felt like climbing over that shifting pile of dead bodies, only to catch a spear or a rock in the face from some psycho who couldn't be dislodged from that infamous pile of stones.

So, they let the time run out, and none of them attacked us again for those last eleven minutes.

"Time!" Graves shouted. "3rd Unit wins the game. In my opinion, the other nine centurions should consider themselves shamed. Seriously? Nine hundred of you couldn't kick McGill off those rocks? It's absolutely disgusting…"

People hung their heads and threw down their spears in anger all over Green Deck—except for my boys. We waggled our dicks and our tongues at the distant chickens, laughing and hooting.

"I'm ordering double PT for everyone who died," Graves continued, "starting the minute they come out of a revival machine. That policy will continue until the day we land on our target planet."

Graves dropped the mic after that, and everyone on Green Deck breathed a sigh of relief. The time read 00:00 in big blue digits.

"I can't believe it," Leeson said. "It's friggin' over."

"I'm kind of surprised you survived this long," I told him.

"Maybe it was because he never came out from under one of those rocks at the top," Harris complained.

"What about Clane?" I asked.

Leeson answered me. "Oh, him? He died, like, half an hour ago."

I nodded, unsurprised. "Good work, people," I said, clapping hands and giving everybody I could a bloody grin of congratulations. "Excellent work. I'm proud of each and every one of you."

Those of us who could still walk dragged ourselves back to our module and stretched out on our bunks. Blood oozed into our blankets, along with sweat and dirt. We took showers in shifts, laughed, drank booze, and swapped funny stories about when we'd taken out one or another of the enemy.

Sometime later, I heard a shout from the front door.

"Attention! Primus on the deck!"

Harris had given the warning call, and I staggered out of my centurion's quarters, wearing a crusty grin. My head was dripping from the shower, but I hadn't gone through a revival machine. Even the bio people had declared my injuries superficial. They'd patched me up and sent me back to my bunk.

"Well, Primus Graves," I said, "I've got to thank you for that opportunity."

"How's that, McGill?" he asked.

"Well, sir, that was the most fun I've had since Jungle World. That's what I'm saying. Whoever came up with that idea, they are to be commended."

Graves smiled at me with half his mouth. "I'll take that as a compliment. The idea was mine."

"Good going, Primus."

Graves paused for a moment, then spoke again. "You know why I'm here, McGill?"

"I surely do," I said. "You're here to congratulate the winners of the great contest."

"No, I'm afraid that's not so. I'm here to ask what the hell you're doing in this module. These are no longer your quarters. You've been reassigned to Gold Deck. Did you forget?"

I stood there dumbfounded, my mouth gaping. In a way, yes, I had sort of forgotten. It seemed so natural to return to the module with my troops, the men who I'd fought with all day. I rotated my head this way and that, looking like an owl with a broken beak.

My shoulders slumped in defeat.

"But Primus, sir, I thought Raash was so stinky no one wanted him up there with the Gold Deckers?"

"You're not going back to Winslade's office, if that's what you mean. You're still part of the secretarial pool, however. I thought you might want to serve as a personal valet."

"To Primus Collins?" I asked, perking up a little.

"Hell no," Graves said, glaring at me again. He didn't like it when I got fresh with ladies he figured were outside my zone. "Maybe they'll put you on laundry duty, or something…"

"Aw, come on, sir!"

Raash appeared then. He loomed behind Graves. "So!" he boomed, pointing a nasty claw in my direction. "This is where he hides. Do you see this? McGill has made yet another attempt to evade me. He will not be successful. I will follow him to the ends of the cosmos."

"Shut up, Raash," Primus Graves said.

Around me, my soldiers walked up one at a time and clapped me on the back. I winced from one injury or another, but they all shook my hand and bid me farewell.

Leeson, my last fully whole and hale officer, seemed almost ready to burst into tears. "Does this mean, sir," he asked Graves, "that I'm acting centurion again?"

"Yes, it certainly does. You're the senior."

"Holy hell," Leeson said, turning and walking away.

Graves frowned after him. He seemed indecisive. "McGill," he said, "I'm going to go talk to Winslade. You stay right here."

We all perked up and watched as he marched out without saying another word.

Harris approached me a moment later. "Do you think he's going to try to get you out of purgatory?"

"I hope so," I said. "I truly hope so."

"Hey, Graves!" Harris shouted down the hall after him. "Tell him that Raash is coming with McGill if they want him back."

Graves waved dismissively over his shoulder, not turning to give Harris any special recognition.

We all waited for the next hour or so. It was a tense time, and my men slowly trickled back to the module from the revival machines. Each of them congratulated me in turn. They hooted with pleasure when they learned that we'd lasted the entire time and held the hill from minute one to minute sixty.

But then they got the message that possibly old McGill was going back to Gold Deck, that the matter hadn't yet been decided. Universally, their spirits were dampened.

It was about an hour later when word finally came back. Winslade himself lit up my tapper.

I answered the call wearily. "Hello, Tribune, sir. I'm sure you're calling to congratulate me."

"Oh, stuff it, McGill," he said. "How did you convince Grayes to wheedle and whine so much? I've never seen such a spectacle from him."

"Well, sir..." I said, "I don't rightly know what you're talking about. I didn't say a damn thing to him."

He squinted at me for a moment, then he heaved a sigh. "All right," he said, "you've been reinstated with your combat unit, back to combat arms. But there's one condition."

"What's that?" I asked, while men cheered behind and around me.

"You must take that lizard with you. Keep him in your module—in your barracks. He's never to return to Gold Deck again."

"Request granted, sir!"

Raash grunted and complained about this result, but we all ignored him. The rest of the evening fell into a celebration. The night ended when Kivi, Natasha, and a freshly revived Della, all vied for my attention.

I chose Della, oddly enough. She'd been the one who'd died early and hard—caught between two angry units she had tricked into fighting each other.

We spent a fine night together, and I told her many quiet secrets in my cabin about Etta and her new boyfriend, Derek.

She was not entirely thrilled with the idea that our daughter was considering marriage with a hog.

"I'm shocked you didn't kill him outright," she fumed.

"Well, it's not that I didn't think about it…"

"And you're saying my father's putting up with all this? That he's fine with having an Earth Gov stooge as a son-in-law?"

"A grandson-in-law," I reminded her. "But yes, it's got to be devastating news." I shook my head. "Things have gone a little strange out there on Dust World. Della, how long has it been since you've been out there?"

"I don't know…" she said. "Probably a decade."

"Right," I said. "Well, maybe you should visit. Try not to freak out when you see what's become of your father and his people."

I described a few of the things, like the strange guys in leather pants with knives who could barely speak, and Boudica, plus a few other details. When I got to the vats of stinking liquids used for illicit revives, she became alarmed.

Della seemed aghast. "I've heard of a few of these things before, of course, but I hadn't realized it had gone this far. Next time we've demobilized, I'll make it a point to visit and see this for myself."

"Good deal. Now… where were we?"

We stopped talking about upsetting things and tried to recapture our moment. We made love again, but it wasn't quite the same.

We were both worried about our relatives and all the strange things happenings in the cosmos. We slept together for the night, but by morning, Della was gone.

She was one of the few girls I knew who could sneak out of my bed without waking me up.

-22-

It was only a few days later when a major alert sounded all through *Scorpio*'s echoing passageways.

"James McGill to the bridge. Centurion James McGill, proceed to the bridge immediately."

I was taking a shower when this rang out across the ship. I gawked at the ceiling, wondering what the hell was going on.

"Didn't you hear that, Centurion?" Harris asked behind me. "You gotta go, man."

"Yeah, yeah," I said, spraying off suds as fast as I could, trotting out of the place buck-naked through the passages. I took just long enough to grab a uniform, pulling it over myself as I trotted, still dripping wet. The smart cloth stretched and cinched itself all around me. I was still barefoot, barehanded, and had suds in my hair when I arrived at Gold Deck.

If it hadn't been for my summons, the hog-like guards wouldn't have let me through. As it was, they shook their heads and waved for me to trot on by. I was still leaving wet footprints when I stepped onto the bridge proper.

"There he is... Centurion? What the hell?" It was Graves, and he was in shock.

"What's going on, Primus?" I asked.

"Why are you so inappropriately dressed, McGill?"

"Well, sir, I was taking a shower, see, and then—"

"Never mind, never mind. Get into the conference room."

I was chased off into the conference room that was immediately adjacent to the bridge. There was a big holo-table in there surrounded by high-level officers. Tribune Winslade, Gilbert, Collins, and Graves were all there. The last man to waddle in the door was Captain Merton.

Damn, that boy hadn't died for a few long years, now...

"McGill is barefoot on my bridge?" Merton said with disgust. "Tribune Winslade! Can't you even get your men to dress appropriately?"

"I apologize, but we did summon him with all haste."

All the officers looked at me as if they smelled shit, but to my surprise, they didn't order me to run off and get myself all the way dressed. That had been, to be fully honest, my greatest hope. A man sent off to get dressed... well... that could take a long time. By the time I wandered back, the meeting might even have been over and done with.

But my dodge did not bear fruit. Instead of shooing me out, they waved me toward the circular holo-table. Even now, it was flickering into life.

"What's the big emergency?" I asked.

"A Mogwa ship has been detected," Winslade said. "Several of them have been, in fact. They've been identified in our wake. We're slowing down and allowing them to catch up. We're coming out of warp now."

The flickering ended as the ship itself transitioned from hyperspace into normal space, which made it a lot easier to have a conversation with other starships.

A view of space appeared. It was pretty much empty: interstellar dust, a little bit of gas, maybe, and an occasional frozen comet. Nothing else was on track.

Then a large blip appeared—then three more.

"Holy hell," I said. "Those *are* Mogwa ships. Battlecruisers, I'd say."

The rest of the officers said nothing. They looked grim. It was Primus Gilbert who finally spoke up. He was a sallow-faced skinny man who reminded me of a cold-handed undertaker.

"This has got to have something to do with McGill," he said. "The first message they sent to us indicates that much"

"It was only a text," Winslade told him. "We don't know what's happening. Stay calm."

170

Captain Merton pointed a shaking, fat finger at the ships, which kept popping into view. "Four now! Four battlecruisers, all from the Core Worlds. Mark my words, they're here to arrest McGill. We'll be lucky to escape with our lives."

"Wait a second," I said, leaning close and squinting at the high-resolution holograms. "Isn't that... yeah, I'm sure of it! That's Admiral Sateekas's flagship, as I live and breathe! Remember? We flew with him out to the Mid-Zone."

For once, it wasn't me who was slack-jawed in astonishment. Everyone else around that table stared aghast and amazed.

It was true. The flagship was well-known to us, and she wasn't a standard Mogwa ship from the Core Worlds. Her class was built by the Mogwa of Segin, a breed apart from those who lived on Trantor, the Mogwa home system.

The distance this fleet must therefore have flown to catch up to us was vast. It was thousands of lightyears to the Mid-Zone. Our fringe of stars along the Perseus arm was a veritable desert of stars in comparison.

The Core Worlds were something else again. It never grew dark there, where the Galactics lived at the hot core of our galaxy.

The ships were impressive—a full squadron of battlecruisers now paraded on our tails. They were more advanced than our best and larger as well. Even *Scorpio*, which was massive, probably couldn't take down even one of these Mogwa warships. This was especially true since we'd converted *Scorpio* to carry troops and had disabled some of her armament in order to do so.

"Where are the rest of the ships in our flotilla?" Winslade asked.

Captain Merton worked his fingers and a sub-box appeared in the upper left region of the holo-display. "They're converging on our position, but they aren't yet at the rendezvous point. We've got perhaps a day before they all meet up with us."

"How poorly timed can we be?" Winslade complained. "Here we are, caught alone with our pants down."

"I feel like we've been caught speeding in an aircar," Primus Collins said.

"In that case," I said, grinning, "it might be time for you to turn on some of that feminine charm."

They all looked at me as if I'd made an inappropriate comment. Perhaps I had, but I didn't really care.

Finally, the screen flickered again, and we got a transmission that was directly from the lead battlecruiser. It was none other than Admiral Sateekas himself.

I couldn't help but recognize him. He was younger these days, no longer the ancient wattled Mogwa of the past. He'd died back during the City World campaign at Segin, and I'd helped get him a revive. He was still going on that lifetime as far as I could tell.

So, while he was older now—perhaps middle-aged for a Mogwa—he was by no means ancient. His eye-groups moved from one of us to the next, taking us all into account. I felt like he was measuring us up. The final person his eyes landed upon was me.

"The McGill…" he said. "It has been a long time."

"It sure has, Admiral Sateekas, sir." I saluted him, and he slapped one of his hand-foot things up near his own forehead in response. He had, of course, learned many of our gestures.

I was proud to get possibly the first human-type salute out of this Mogwa admiral that anyone had ever seen. It was proof-positive that the old spidery bastard of an alien still liked me.

Normally, when he and I met, I made a huge point of referring to him as an admiral or grand admiral, which had been his original title. In his heyday, he'd commanded a Mogwa fleet from the Core Worlds, Battlefleet 921. It had been a long time since he'd had the official title of grand admiral, but he had always considered it his greatest achievement.

It was best to flatter those who are powerful, especially when they deserve the flattery. Grand Admiral Sateekas was not the best navy commander I'd ever met—in fact, he was probably one of the worst. But he was a loyal creature, and he'd fought and died and sacrificed many Mogwa ships on Earth's behalf over the decades.

"McGill?" he said, "for once, you have given me the correct title. I am indeed an admiral again. Behold my small flotilla. My consort, Vox, and I have been rebuilding our fleet from Segin. This force is nowhere near as grand as the armadas that Trantor can field, but it is fully half our total naval strength."

"Wow," I said, pretending to be stunned and amazed.

In truth, I was disappointed. Only six ships? Was that it? That was a sheer disappointment, even if they all were large, capable capital vessels.

"Hold on," Sateekas said, turning toward a subordinate. "Nairb? You have failed me."

"How could that possibly be, Admiral?" The Nairb asked.

"You have kept most of my vessels hidden."

"Oh, that... Well, I thought we should check on the human status before we..."

Sateekas took a swing at him, but he ducked. I could tell by that interaction that it was not the first time, probably not the last, that this Nairb had faced instant death at the hands of his Mogwa overlord.

"Make them all appear, fool! What kind of grand entrance can I perform to impress these lowly humans if they can't see all my ships at once?"

The Nairb humped away, his green baggy body rising and falling. He reminded me of a slug, or a worm—or maybe a humping caterpillar. Most people thought Nairbs looked like green seals, but to me, they were even more disgusting than that.

Within thirty seconds, dozens more vessels appeared. They were all smaller than the grand battlecruisers, but they were numerous. They were heavy cruisers, light cruisers, destroyers—something like a hundred ships surrounded the six monstrous battle wagons at the center of the formation.

"Ah..." I said, finally impressed, "now that's a fleet, sir! You're not just an admiral, you're a grand admiral once again."

Sateekas puffed up with pride.

What was this? The fourth fleet I'd seen him guide through space? I wondered vaguely if he was going to get them all destroyed somehow before the day was done. That seemed to be his singular master-class skill. His most impressive resume item was the ability to get fleets destroyed in terrific battles.

"Why, may I ask, Grand Admiral," I said, "are you out here? Are you here to help us out? Are you here to make a strike against the Crystals?"

"Indeed, I am here to pay an old debt of service. A marker has been called in."

I blinked, as did the others around me. I noticed then that Collins, Gilbert, even Winslade had all been remarkably quiet since this conversation had begun. Was that because they simply didn't have the balls to talk to a Mogwa? Especially not one guiding a hundred-plus warships? The Galactic fleet could easily destroy all our ships without suffering any losses. Hell, the Mogwa were sporting enough firepower to wreck Earth if they'd really wanted to, despite all her defenses.

Yes, that probably had to be it. They were fearful. It was a crying shame to behold humans trembling in terror before any of the Galactics, but I guess it just came with the territory. They'd been trained to be subservient since youth. I'd been trained the same way, but it just hadn't stuck in my case.

"Soooo…" I said, "who called you? They sure didn't tell us about it."

"We were summoned here by your Public Servant. An extremely unpleasant human. What was his name?"

I thought about it for a moment. "Not… Alexander Turov?"

"Yes, yes, that's the moniker I'm thinking of. A balding, decrepit member of your species who exhibits an alarming degree of cunning. He claimed that we'd agreed upon a mutual defense contract long ago. While this is technically true, I'd never imagined Earth would summon us to their aid. I'd envisioned the treaty working entirely the other way around."

I nodded to myself. The thought processes he was describing were perfectly natural for any Mogwa. They saw everything as a completely one-sided affair. Any agreement you made with them, you could be certain, was designed to be self-serving.

But in this case, Sateekas was in character. He'd felt compelled to honor the deal he'd made. After all, Earth had been under attack by these crystalline creatures. We'd raced out to help the Mogwa of Segin when they'd been attacked by the Rigellians. Today, the tables were reversed.

"So, you're here to help us smash the Crystals?" I said. "Is that it?"

"Yes. We've analyzed your fleet strength and the capabilities of the enemy with their gravity weapons. As far as I can tell, you have no defense against this technology. But rest assured, Mogwa engineers have faced enemies with this sort of weaponry in the past. We can, and will, destroy the enemy fleet that is already approaching this very position."

It was time for all of us to gawk now. Winslade dared to ask the question on everyone's mind.

"Sateekas," he said, "um… Grand Admiral Sateekas, may we ask how far away this enemy fleet is? We cannot detect it."

"Naturally, you wouldn't be able to. There are no obvious energy releases that a normal fleet would use for propulsion. Using gravimetrics, however, we've been able to pinpoint the Silicoid fleet. They're at least one day's travel distant, possibly two. They're not traveling in hyperspace right now, but rather stalking you, with stealth as their primary defense."

"Ah," Captain Merton said, "so that's why you hailed us? That's why you demanded we come out of warp? You were trying to help?"

"Obviously."

"Then we are in your debt, Grand Admiral."

"Indeed, you are. But the situation goes far beyond such a circumstance. There is no comparable nature between our species. You're far more than 'in debt' to us. Consider yourselves to be an asset on my battlefield. A fleet of primitive ships filled with useful servants."

"Uh…" I said, not liking the sound of this. "Is there something we can do for you, Admiral?"

"We came here to ensure you weren't wiped out immediately. This foolish crusade of yours, as it stands, is doomed to failure. But the Mogwa have need of ships like yours—in particular your troopships. On City World long ago, you proved to us that while your warships are vastly inferior to Mogwa technology, your ground troops are, at least, comparable."

This, of course, was a flat-out lie. Our ships were a lot less powerful than Mogwa vessels of the line, that much was true. But our troops were vastly superior. The Mogwa as a species were innately cowardly. It took many years of training just to get them to stand up and take a hit. Even their best-trained Mogwa marines were inferior fighters in virtually every way to an average legionnaire.

Still, despite all of his bluster, I could understand where Sateekas was coming from. He didn't want to see us lose these transports with their vital ground forces. He was going to need them if we were going to take out these mother-loving Crystals—or, what had Sateekas called them? The Silicoids? Whatever.

The Mogwa were always thinking of number one. Why had they come out here with a fleet to help us? Just because they were honoring a past agreement?

No, definitely not. They'd come so we couldn't be easily destroyed in a space battle with a fleet we hadn't even detected yet. Sateekas was essentially protecting his investment in humanity.

-23-

Sateekas abruptly disconnected, and the meeting broke up entirely soon after. Captain Merton contacted the other transports that were going to help us with this invasion of Crystal World.

Seeing my opportunity, I snuck away off Gold Deck and hurried back downstairs toward my module.

That's when Raash caught up with me. He found me in a passageway and thumped along, complaining in my wake.

"I have discovered your deception," he said. "Again, you attempt to evade me, and again you fail. You are doomed to such failures, human. You should stop these relentless attempts. You are embarrassing yourself."

"Look, Raash," I said, "I got summoned to the bridge, so I went with all haste. I wasn't even thinking about you."

"Ah, so this is how you plan to save face? I was wondering how the attempt would be made."

I rolled my eyes and ignored Raash, trudging down the passages back toward my module. He followed along, dragging his raspy tail over the deck.

He continued to complain bitterly until I explained to him what the meeting had been about. Then he became alarmed.

"The Mogwa are here?" he demanded. "How is it I'm saddled with such fools?"

"What are you talking about now, Raash?"

"Why would you grunting humans trust the Galactics? How could you be so unintelligent you would take their motives at face value? I do not believe they are telling the truth."

"Well, we're trusting you Saurians, aren't we? You've got a ship and a legion out here with this fleet."

"No," he said, "It is we, the Saurians, who are trusting you to lead the way. As it turns out, we were following fools."

He ranted like that for a while, and I couldn't really blame him. After all, what have the Mogwa ever done for the Saurians? Even less than for humans, that's what.

"You should be happy the Mogwa are here, Raash," I said. "We were flying into an ambush. We were probably all going to be destroyed, anyways."

I tried to explain more to him about the gravity weapons, the kind of alien tech we were up against. Raash had never directly fought with the Crystals. He'd only heard secondhand about their dangerous nature back during the Jungle World campaign.

He became increasingly concerned as I explained things to him. "Normally, I would not believe a word you say, human," he said. "For you are an impaired creature when it comes to being honest."

I couldn't really argue with this, so I didn't try.

"But I've heard such things from other, more trustworthy throats," he went on. "You are, therefore, only confirming the dangerous nature of our adversary. I do not like the sound of this gravimetric weaponry. To crush a warrior's tail up against his own bones—it seems unfair, wrong—and dishonorable."

"It's all of those things and more, Raash," I told him. "You better hope the Mogwa ships can win this battle."

"Why should I hope for such a thing? If the Mogwa are so powerful, we are nothing. What is left to keep despair from consuming my mind?"

"The Mogwa have advanced tech of their own," I said. "You've probably never seen Battlefleet 921 in combat—but I have. If anybody can beat these freaks, they can."

"What I hope, human, is that you are as wrong about the power of this enemy as you are usually wrong about everything. That you have exaggerated the threat in your fear—or perhaps you do so knowingly."

"Why would I do that?"

"Perhaps you seek to spread discord and dishonor amongst this fleet."

"Nah. I'm just trying to warn you about the coming battle, that's all."

Raash grumbled and hissed and dragged his tail around for a bit. At last, he made one more cryptic announcement. "If you are correct... we are in for a difficult time. I must alert my brothers. The idiocy of the prey animal walking into slaughter, that is your strength. I will have none of it!"

With that strange statement stacked up on top of all the others, Raash left. It was a sheer relief for me.

He made haste to the deep-link machines. Like Merton, he made a call to the other ships. He contacted Armel himself and reported in.

I guess that was a good thing, in a way. Having a spy aboard was much like having a diplomat or an envoy. I was sure his own people would believe him sooner than they would believe us.

Our combined fleets gathered and organized themselves. Up front, the Mogwa fleet led the way. Just behind them were Rigellian warships. Lastly, there were a few human warships, the escort force we'd brought from Earth.

In the rear, *Scorpio* was joined by three other transport ships. They'd converged upon our position. All of them came out of hyperspace and began braking hard. We formed a broad, loose formation.

I tried to count all the ships and lost track somewhere around two hundred. I hoped it would be enough.

I recalled that the largest Skay I'd ever seen had been cracked wide open by just one of these Crystal bases. What would one of their fleets be like?

A few more hours crept by, and then we were treated to a front-row seat of a new and desperate battle. From the very start, there was little for troops like me and my unit to do. There wasn't even any guard duty assigned, as we didn't expect boarders.

"We're canned meat," Leeson complained. "That's what we are."

"Speak for yourself, cowardly human," Raash admonished him. "I'm a proud killer, a predator, a creature that is feared by all others."

Everybody rolled their eyes at Raash. We were getting pretty sick of him by this point. Even those who had first found it rather novel and interesting to have a Saurian in our midst were now more than tired of him.

"Shut up, Raash," Leeson shouted back.

Raash went on about the glorious nature of his tail for a while before he finally quieted.

Then, as if on cue, *Scorpio* lurched first to the port side—then back starboard. These were violent motions, and we were tossed around. We hadn't been braced for it.

A second or two after this initial lurching evasion action, all the alarms lit up. The floors glowed orange, the sign of a general ship-wide alarm.

Harris climbed back to his feet, cursing. There were bloody noses, sprained limbs, and a rising storm of profanity all around me.

I couldn't blame them for all the bad words they heaped upon the heads of those Gold Deck sopranos upstairs. It was unusual for *Scorpio* or any large ship to begin evasive actions without a moment's warning for the crew.

Captain Merton's voice rang out on the public address system.

"Crew and passengers," he said, "objects have been detected in our path. We believe they might be mines or possibly crystalline boarders of some kind. In either case, stand ready. Everyone should suit-up and prepare for further evasive action."

"Oh, Lord," Leeson said, "I hate space battles."

It was a sentiment that all of us could get behind. Never had there been a marine or any soldier aboard a transport who liked to hear secondhand of a battle going on outside the hull in space. There was nothing we could do to affect such a battle, but it could affect us, usually with sudden, violent death.

"Natasha?" I said, turning to face her. I lowered my voice when I caught her eye. "Hack into something. Let's see what's going on out there."

She looked at me furtively, and I realized that she'd already done it. I smiled. "Come on, hand me the feed."

She made a surreptitious flicking motion over her tapper. All of a sudden, I could see outside the ship. There was our squadron of transports, gliding through the endless darkness. Up ahead, a wild swirl of vessels was in motion.

"Holy hell, what are they doing out there?" I asked.

"I don't really know," Natasha said. "It seems insane, but it reminds me of when Battlefleet 921 fought at Rogue World. Do you remember that?"

I did, vaguely. The Rogue World tech-smiths had had a vessel of their own, a very high-tech ship, which had been able to stand toe-to-toe with the Mogwa vessels at the time. It had flitted about like this, teleporting from location to location in a seemingly random sequence.

"Dodging, that must be what they're doing," I said. "You think they're evading teleportation bombs?"

"Maybe," she said, "or maybe just the gravity beams of the enemy ships. I can't even see any enemy ships. There are some blips out there, some points of gravity, contacts on radar, but I'm not *seeing* anything."

It was true. Whatever we were fighting against, we couldn't actually see it. Could it be we were at too great a distance?

Pretty quickly, I surmised that's what it was. That's what it had to be.

"Look," I said, "none of our ships are firing anything. We're just jumping around."

"Oh, no…" Natasha said. "That means the enemy range must be greater than ours. Those gravity weapons, they must have quite a reach."

We both stared at our tappers, highly concerned. Pretty soon, Harris, Leeson, and even Clane sidled close. They'd heard that we had the feed. They exclaimed and commented. Soon after that, loads of people hot-spotted in and my entire module was full of gawkers.

"Did you share it with everybody?" I asked Natasha and Kivi, my two techs.

"Only a few people..." Kivi said.

The effect kept spreading, and it was electric. Everyone was blabbing. The techs were talking to other techs. The feed was spreading throughout the ship.

"Shut it down," I told Natasha. "Shut it down. The people on the bridge are going to figure out where it's coming from!"

But it was already too late. My tapper suddenly filled with another image, one that was much less interesting than the exterior view of the battle.

It was Graves. His craggy face was clearly unhappy.

"McGill," he said, "we've detected your hacking. Did you order Natasha to share this with half the fleet?"

"Hell no, sir. I can't even figure out what people are squawking about. I was trying to watch a ball game from Earth, see—"

"Shut up," he said. "You just volunteered yourself for a special operation, McGill. Report to Gray Deck with your combat personnel."

I sighed, stood up, and ordered my men to gather their gear. I didn't even bother to ask Graves what our mission was going to be. I was sure it was going to be something heinous and possibly even unnatural.

It seemed like Graves really had it in for me on this campaign. Ever since I'd been late answering the mustering call, even though I'd been off-planet, he'd been leaning on me. That tendency had continued right through that hellacious exercise on Green Deck, and now this.

Just because of a little hacking, just because my techs had done a bit of information-spreading when it wasn't ours to spread, we'd been volunteered. Volunteered for what? I had no idea, but it would doubtlessly be suicidal.

With grunts of dismay and flagging spirits, we reported to Gray Deck. To my surprise, we weren't greeted by a group of regular techs with teleport harnesses, or lifter pilots, or even capsules with drop-pods.

No, instead, there were Nairbs waiting for us. A whole herd of them.

"What the hell is this?" Harris asked.

The chief Nairb turned to eye us. I thought I recognized him. He was Sateekas' sidekick, who we'd caught sight of on the Mogwa ship.

"Ah, you're the humans I requisitioned, yes?" he said. He consulted a piece of computer paper. Squiggles crawled all over it, and I couldn't make heads or tails of it. "According to this document, your performance parameters are woefully substandard. Any proper Core World drone would do better—but I suppose we'll have to make do."

"Uh… what are we going to be doing for you, Mr. Nairb, sir?" I asked.

"We have need of couriers."

"Couriers, huh? What exactly are we delivering? Some kind of message?"

He laughed. He had to be the most laugh-happy Nairb I'd yet to meet. "Yes, in a way, that's accurate. A message is contained for these Silicoid monstrosities. We're transmitting it in the form of antimatter bombs."

"Oh…"

A general groan went up from my troops.

"Uh…" I said. "Can't you guys just teleport them out there by themselves? What do you need us for?"

"That's exactly what we've been doing. But the enemy has disabled all of our T-bombs thus far. They have an EMP field, you see, a very effective one. All electronics, such as detonators," he waved towards a stack of things that looked like metal watermelons, "have been disabled. As of this moment, our teleportation bombs have simply bounced off the enemy hulls without exploding."

"Oh, I get it," I said. "You figure flesh and bone is immune to EMPs. Is there some kind of timer on these things or something?"

The Nairb laughed again. "Certainly not. In fact, we don't want you to delay in any way, shape, or form. The enemy ships are moving so fast, you will have no ability to perceive the nearness of the vessel. They will be invisible to you, and then one nanosecond later, will strike you. Your corpse will be destroyed by a quadrillion joules of released energy."

I didn't know much about joules, but it sure sounded like a lot to me.

"A nanosecond, huh?" I said. "How quick do you think a man's thumb is? We can't possibly push a button on one of these Easter eggs that fast."

The Nairb frowned, and he argued with a few of his techs. "We shall make adjustments," he said. "You'll be given one second. Is that sufficient time?"

"Yeah," I said. "That should do it. All right, boys," I said, "Everybody grab a harness and pick up one of these here bombs. When the nice Nairb fires you out into space, and you arrive, just push that one button, and you'll come on home again. It's an instant retrieval button, see?"

I explained that we were on a scouting mission of sorts. A few of my soldiers actually seemed to believe me, but not the more experienced types. Some of them just flat knew better, like Leeson and Carlos. They knew bullshit when they smelled it, and they weren't fooled for a second. They did accept their fates with dignity, however.

"At least it'll be quick," Clane said, picking up his bomb and shuffling with the rest of them to line up.

I flashed out with the second squad. I'd wanted to go with the first, but the Nairb simply began firing men off without even giving us a warning. After I complained, they allowed me to make a little speech.

"Now listen, boys," I said, "I want everybody to have their thumbs right there on the trigger. Don't push it now, fool!" I roared at Carlos, who was playing with it. "So, here's the sequence. A Nairb is going to push that big button over there. We're going to all flash out, going blue. When we arrive, as soon as you're aware you've stopped moving through time and space, hit that switch and hope for the best. See you in the revival chamber. Let's do this."

I tried to get them to engage in a quick, rousing cheer, shouting "Varus." It came out badly. The men released a single, mumbled, groaning sound. I regretted having even asked.

And then the moment came, and I was gone from the confines of *Scorpio*. Less than a second later, I reappeared again out in open space.

There was nothing here but stars. I couldn't see the enemy fleet. I couldn't see the Mogwa ships, either. I knew the Crystals had to be out here somewhere, but where?

What I did see distantly, I believed, was a flash off to my left. That had to be where the fleet was. Perhaps that was a hit, a glow from the previous wave. The first squadron had already been fired out here to perform the job of suicide bombers. Yes, that had to be it.

Then I realized that a whole second had already passed, and I hadn't pushed the button. So, I did it.

And then I knew no more.

-24-

I hadn't come out of a revival machine lately, but I was very familiar with the process.

"What have we got?"

"Centurion. One James McGill."

"Oh, he must be one of the suicide bombers."

"Gotcha. What's the score?"

"Not bad. 9.5. Almost perfect."

I mumbled to both of them that I *was* actually perfect, but they ignored me. After they poked, prodded, and shined lights into everything they could open, they finally let me stagger out of there.

My first hint that the battle wasn't yet over came when *Scorpio* shifted violently to the left—to the port side, as the Navy pukes like to say.

Then she heeled over, and I fell on my head on the roof. Sometimes, the inertial dampeners that were supposed to switch the gravitational direction circumstantially didn't always catch up in time. You could get a nasty knock on the noggin that way.

Scorpio's passages, in particular, tended to be cramped for me. They'd originally been built for Rigellian bears. I felt like a frigging mouse in a shoebox, banging around on the walls.

Finally reduced to crawling, I pulled myself using loops of metal on the walls. I wouldn't stoop to call them ladders. They were less than that, just handholds. I found that method to be the fastest way to make progress.

Somewhere up on Gold Deck, a genius finally turned down the artificial gravity and cranked up the dampeners. All that violent lateral motion was reduced. It was now survivable by the crew and ground troops like myself.

Able to walk with a staggering gait, I finally reached my module. My troops, at least the noobs among them, were puking on the deck.

I yelled at them, kicked at them, and cuffed them until they stopped embarrassing themselves and me.

After about five full minutes of violent evasion maneuvers, the ship went quiet. A lot of the lights were off, a lot of systems were blinking, but it didn't seem like we'd taken a direct hit.

"You see now?" I said, standing up and putting my hands on my hips. "That was just a false alarm. Get to your feet, ladies, and stop crying."

More and more of my troops kept returning from the revival chambers. Lord only knew how those Blue Deck people could keep working under these conditions.

More than a few of my men claimed that they'd been badly injured the first time they came out of the machines, and that the bio people had decided to reroll. They rudely shoved my boys into the grinders and started over again. That sort of thing always left a sour feeling in a man's innards.

I asked Natasha and Kivi what had happened in our absence. Before they could answer, Harris came staggering through the door, slamming it behind him.

"You two," he said, pointing at the two tech girls. "You got us into that in the first place. You and your goddamn hacking. Don't tell me you're doing more of it now!"

"McGill told us to," Natasha said defensively.

I understood why Harris was pissed off. It did seem unfair. After all, the combat wing of my unit had just been thrown overboard to do teleport-bombing, while the people who'd caused us to be volunteered for this mission had been left behind. Our techs Natasha and Kivi had been deemed unworthy of the exercise and had stayed here safely in the module. They were uninjured except for a few bumps and scrapes as *Scorpio* slewed from side-to-side.

"Rigel's lost some ships," Natasha said. "With your permission, sir?" She looked at me, and I nodded.

She cast the stream she was intercepting onto our biggest wall. The troops gathered around, rubbing their heads, their eyes, and their busted lips from having been tossed against the walls. What unfolded on the screen was quite remarkable.

We saw the enemy vessels—if you could even call them that. They were more like large stalagmites—pointy-tipped, conical machines that appeared to be made out of rock or some other kind of silicate. There were about a hundred of them, all knobby and mottled gray, with surfaces that reminded me of melted candlewax.

At first, they seemed invincible. They were immune to most normal weaponry, and possessed longer-range cannons than we had.

"This feed is a few minutes old now," Natasha said. "Watch as their line absorbs our massive wave of teleport-bombs."

As the flashes began to go off, I cheered. I shook my fist, and I pointed to the screen.

"You see that? That's us. That's us right there. You boys did that! All of you."

There were weak smiles. Some spines straightened.

Anti-matter bomb after anti-matter bomb showered the front line of approaching ships. Half the strange vessels were destroyed or hopelessly ruptured. These stricken rocks fell out of the formation—but the others continued ahead. I got the feeling that if you were a rock person, you didn't turn tail and run easily.

Natasha rolled the stream up to the current time. "This is real-time, now. It's all quiet… but not for long if my sources are to be believed."

We watched, we stared. Nothing happened for about two minutes, but then, finally, our front line of ships came onto the battlefield. These were all Mogwa vessels. They were serious warships from Segin led by Admiral Sateekas himself.

They'd been taking fire for a long time, but now they'd finally gotten into effective range. It was time for some payback. A massive barrage was launched.

"Are those missiles? T-bombs?" Leeson asked.

Natasha shook her head. "No, some kind of beams. The video feed is enhanced to reveal them, but they really are invisible."

Then, the Mogwa ships began to dance. They teleported, essentially, from position to position in a random sequence.

They got closer every second to the enemy. You could see the front tips of those stalagmite-type ships. The enemy Crystals glowed and fired salvo after salvo at the Mogwa. Possibly, they'd never fought a fleet so advanced as this.

It was an interesting battle to watch. We were witnessing alien technology from the outer limits of our galaxy facing up against the old, ancient, but highly effective know-how of the Galactics.

It soon became apparent that the Galactics had the advantage, now that they were in range. The Crystals were simply unable to retarget their long-range gravity weapons fast enough and accurately enough to catch the blinking Mogwa ships. Oh, they got in a few licks, probably by happenstance, but they were losing and losing fast.

"I count seven!" I shouted. "I think they nailed seven of ours!"

Natasha nodded, confirming my count. "Seven light cruisers," she said. "There were about a dozen smaller ships destroyed. Destroyers and escorts, that sort of thing. They were running screen maneuvers on the front line to cover the battlecruisers."

Now the big Mogwa ships waded in. The battlecruisers could fire an astounding amount of heavy weaponry. Stalagmite after stalagmite broke apart, blew up, or flashed into an incandescent flame.

When they were down to about thirty vessels out of the original hundred, the Crystals tried to break off. They went in random directions. Some attempted to do U-turns, others flew up, down, and sideways—but it was all for naught.

Sateekas had excellent control of his fleet. He set a trio of ships to chase down and destroy every one of the Crystals. In the end, the big, strange alien ships turned upon their harassers.

At close range, they managed to destroy a few more Mogwa vessels before the last of them was annihilated.

The cheering in our unit quarters was deafening.

A few moments later, a big, booming announcement rolled across the ship. It was the voice of Captain Merton, and he sounded like the Almighty himself.

"Crew and legionnaires," he said, "today is a good day, a fantastic day. We have completely destroyed the enemy fleet. They are no more."

The cheers were amazing.

"I'll be damned…" I said.

We could hear voices from all over the ship. You could hear people screaming themselves hoarse right through the walls of our module. The men in the large bunk room next door had gone bananas with glee.

"All right," Graves said, coming on the screen a moment later. "This battle was to the finish. It was kill or be killed—and we did the killing today."

There were more cheers, then we hushed our neighbors as Tribune Winslade spoke next.

"Celebrations are in order," he said, "but let's keep them brief—and no one is to become intoxicated."

This statement was met by general groans throughout my unit. There were already a few canteens and flasks out. I sent my non-coms, Sargon, Moller, and the others, to cuff recruits and force them to put away their beverages. That kind of thing would come later—if we lived.

"Listen up, listen up!" I shouted, throwing my hands wide and booming for quiet. "The tribune's not done talking yet!"

Winslade's face—gigantic, craggy, and sharp-nosed—was still on our screen. He had overridden the battle replay we'd been watching.

"We aren't in the clear yet," he said. "Yes, we've brushed aside their fleet. Their defensive formation of ships has been shattered, and now we are on a steady approach. Within a day's time, we'll be able to make planetfall over our target world," he said. "But there is yet another problem. We've detected ground batteries—quite a number of them."

Harris and I, along with others who'd experienced these ground batteries before, winced in concern. Just one of them had destroyed multiple lifters when we'd landed on Jungle World.

"Yes, that's right," Winslade said. "The enemy has been rebuffed, but they are far from helpless. Naturally, in order to assault the planet, we must attack with a ground force. Either that, or at least be in range to stand off and bombard. One of these two approaches will be required to win this battle decisively."

The mood in our module had taken a turn for the worst. We were still smiling, but the cheers and hoots had died down. He was talking about *us* now—ground troops against Crystals on one of their own worlds. It had never sounded fun, and right now it sounded even worse than it had during the briefings.

"Unfortunately," Winslade continued, "I've been informed by Captain Merton and others that it's simply too dangerous for our ships to get into range for bombardment. We shall have to discuss this with Admiral Sateekas and see how he wishes to proceed. All my troops in Legion Varus are to stand by. Winslade out."

The screen went dark, and my men immediately went back into a celebratory mood. A few, like Harris, shouted with glee.

"That's it," he said. "That's it. We're gonna have to do a U-turn right here, right now. For once, boys, the fleet took all the hits—and it wasn't even a human fleet. Can you believe that?"

"He's right," Leeson said. "This is the best piece of luck I've seen in probably seventy years."

That statement made me wonder just how old Leeson was, and how long he'd hung onto working in Legion Varus. I supposed the alternative would have been pushing up daisies by now at his age.

I shrugged. One day, I might find I'd put in as many years myself.

"Don't you see?" Leeson said. "Here's how this is going to play out. Just listen to me for a minute."

And we did listen, all of us did. Because Leeson was the most senior man in this unit, and he'd seen a lot of shit in his time.

"These fleet-boys are sissies. There ain't no way they're going to risk all of our lifters by flying them in from long-range. At the same time, there's no way Merton is going to come in under fire from a whole bunch of those crystalline gun batteries. He's going to balk right there. That's what's going to save our balls. He knows it's his ship on the line. If there's anything a captain from a human fleet doesn't want to see, it's a wreck with his name on it."

"So… what's going to happen next?" Sargon asked.

Leeson pointed a finger at him. "That's undetermined, but I'll tell you what it's all about. It's all about Sateekas now. He's half-crazy, and he might actually go bat-shit and opt for a full assault on their ground batteries."

The crowd broke up, talking among themselves.

"What do you say, McGill?" Leeson said, turning to me. "Is Sateekas going to turn tail, or is he going to plow on and possibly lose yet another fleet?"

I thought about that for perhaps half a second. Then I sighed. "I know Sateekas. I know him better than anyone, or at least better than any human alive. He's going to attack. Even if it means the destruction of the entire Mogwa fleet, with us all dying on top for gravy."

Leeson's face fell. Not because he was worried about the Mogwa fleet, but because he'd realized I was probably right. This battle was far from over.

-25-

Shortly after our victory in space, our entire fleet hit the brakes. The big ships shuddered against the inertia, with our reverse thrusters doing their best to slow down our advance toward the target world.

To me, this seemed crazy on the face of it. When you're flying to battle, it's kind of like being a knight charging on a horse. You wanted all the speed and impact you could get. You wanted to make yourself the smallest target you could for the enemy's missiles.

But noooo, that wasn't what we were doing. We were slowing down. We were slowing down almost to a crawl, at least in terms of space travel. We were flying no more than a thousand kilometers a second and still reducing speed.

"The Mogwa is chickening out," Leeson said. "I'm sure of it. There's not going to be any space battle today!"

There were scattered cheers around our module, but some of us were still worried.

Then, as if the word had come down from the mount with Moses, a call blared over the PA system. "James McGill. Centurion James McGill, report to Gold Deck immediately."

I looked up, staring at the ceiling for a second in befuddlement. They hadn't even announced it on my tapper yet.

Oh, wait a second. There it was. Red text was all over the place on my poor forearm. I guess it was for real.

"What did you do now?" I heard Harris ask, but I pretended not to notice his rudeness.

Gathering my kit and shaking a few extra greasy droplets of amniotic fluid out of my hair, I spit-polished myself for about thirty seconds, straightening my uniform, and marched out of the module.

A few minutes later, I arrived on Gold Deck. Graves was on hand to greet me in person.

"About time you showed up, McGill," he said.

"Sir, I was only just banned from Gold Deck a couple of days ago. What's the cause for this reversal?"

"That's all changed now. The Mogwa commander has demanded your presence for this conference."

"What?" I said, baffled. "You mean Grand Animal Sateekas?"

"That's him."

"What the hell does he want with me?"

"I don't know—and I don't care. Just try not to say anything inflammatory for the sake of Earth, will you?"

"Absolutely won't happen, sir. It *can't* happen. You know you can count on me."

I brushed past Graves, who was shaking his head and looking highly concerned. When I arrived at the conference room, I immediately noticed only the most important members from this coalition force were on hand—plus me. That meant I was about two ranks lower than the guy who was serving up drinks.

Fortunately, I'd never been a man who was overly impressed and overawed by members of the brass. I swaggered in, found myself a chair, and made myself comfortable. Looking around, I took stock of the group.

Tribune Winslade was there, as was Captain Merton. Normally, I would expect someone like Galina Turov to be here, but she was still dead and on ice back out at Dust World. Knowing her, I kind of figured she preferred it that way.

A group of techs showed up with, of all things, a set of gateway posts. They set them up at one end of the room, and they immediately began buzzing and spitting out more people. The first man through was a person I knew too well.

It was Maurice Armel, tribune of a mercenary group of ornery lizards. Essentially, he worked for the Saurians—or at least he led a legion that was made up entirely of Saurians. In recent years, he'd been hiring out to Rigel most of the time.

The next man through was a fuzzy little fellow known as Squantus. When I say fuzzy, I don't want anyone to picture anything cute. He was more like the kind of fuzzy a man saw in the mirror when he looked at his privates on Saturday morning.

Squantus liked to refer to himself as the lord and governor of our beloved Province 921. Even though he'd been losing battle after battle out in the frontier zone lately, he still frequently claimed it was inevitable that he would enslave all of humanity. But despite all of that smack-talk, he'd found the audacity in his soul to ask for our help against the Crystals. To me, he seemed to be talking out of both sides of his little snaggle-toothed snout.

I had to think to myself that maybe Alexander Turov was right. Maybe we should rid ourselves of these bears forever…

Next up was another unexpected member of the coalition. He was a Claver Prime, a copy of the original. He, just like all his brothers, was as crafty, heartless, and double-dealing as anyone in the clan.

Claver swaggered into the room and looked around, seemingly unimpressed. He hitched up his pants and laughed at the crowd. "This is what it must look like when they have a powwow of Galactics in the Core Worlds," he mused. "Like a frigging zoo."

The others either ignored him or snarled at him, depending on how they felt towards Clavers in general.

The last arrival at the party was definitely the most important personage at the meeting that day. It was none other than Grand Admiral Sateekas. His weird spider monkey-type body with a shiny black carapace waddled through the gateway posts. He took the spot at the head of the table without asking.

A lone Nairb followed in his wake, slapping his floppy body over the deck. His nose swiveled this way and that as he sniffed the air. He looked for all the world like a big, green, snot-filled seal.

"And that's it," Tribune Winslade said, "that's everyone." He stood up and began clapping for Grand Admiral Sateekas. "Let us all lift our voices in a rousing cheer," he said. "Admiral Sateekas, let me be the first to congratulate you on a battle that was fought masterfully. Never have I seen better—never!"

He then proceeded to slam his skinny hands together until I thought blood might shoot out of his fingernails. That was Winslade for you. A worse brown-noser had never been born.

Sateekas took this moment to stand up again. He did so on top of his chair in order to appear taller.

I could see that he was basking in the glory. I, for one, couldn't fault him for that. After all, his fleet battles usually ended in disaster. The reports were usually all about countless shipwrecks, thousands of dead—a horrific tale of destruction and woe. Even in the few battles he'd won, he'd always done so at a tremendous loss.

This was, to my knowledge, the first battle that he'd ever participated in that had resulted in complete and utter victory with relatively few casualties on his own side. I could also see this proud moment had gone completely to his head.

"This is most appropriate," he said at last. "Your slave love is well-deserved, and it will not be forgotten. Gratitude overwhelms your hearts, not just for the victory that I've secured for you today, but also for the opportunity I've given you to go down in history as winners."

The humans in the crowd winced at his arrogant and insulting words. I thought that showed how ignorant they were. The Mogwa always talked like this, like we humans were lower than the stuff a farmer scrapes from his boots.

"Be it known," Sateekas continued, "that since we are out past Rigel, we're past the Imperial Frontier. We're now in an unknown zone. These stars are unexplored and full of wild threats. Long ago, the Empire faltered in her initial drive to conquer the entire galaxy at this very border line."

That did sink in, and it had a few of the officers glancing around in concern. We hadn't really thought about it, but it made sense. We were, after all, venturing out past the limits that the Galactics had ever managed to reach. It was as if Rome had discovered the feisty natives of the Americas, for example.

"Today," he speeched onward, "I've done more than beaten a few rocks from the darkest fringe of the fringe. I have—with your pathetic support—actually expanded the glory of the Empire. I've taught these savage monstrosities to fear us—if they're capable of such a wholesome emotion. These strange aliens have met the eternal might of the Empire and her servants—and they have fallen hard!"

There was some cheering then, and some hand-slapping. I saw Tribune Winslade was goading everyone to clap—even though some of them had foul expressions on their faces. Armel's mustache, for example, was squirming like a caterpillar on his lip. I knew he was a proud fop, and he didn't like how Sateekas was taking credit for pretty much everything.

"In essence, we've expanded the reach of the Mogwa and the Empire itself to new heights. You can all thank me for this by observing whatever slavish rituals you find customary. I would recommend that you should all name your next male heir, 'Sateekas', in memory of this fine day."

This was a bit much, even for Merton and Winslade, who exchanged glances and shrugged. The Mogwa was plainly delusional—but we didn't let on.

When Sateekas finally finished his odd, gushing speech, Winslade stood up again. He began slamming his hands together until they must have stung. I did the same, and then, with evident reluctance, Armel, Captain Merton, and a few others followed suit.

Only Claver stayed seated. The Rigellian bear stood, but he looked around, bewildered. It was as if he couldn't believe what he was witnessing. For once, I commiserated with the little bastard, because this was indeed a strange spectacle.

When the cheering and the clapping finally halted, Sateekas cleared his throat tubes noisily and spoke again. "Now," he said, "let us move on to the next phase of this amazing triumph."

That was when Claver spoke up at last. "The next phase?" he said. "And what exactly might that be, Admiral?"

Sateekas eyed him with a certain level of irritation. "That is in question," he said. "That is what we're here to discuss. The enemy fleet has been destroyed, yes, but the planet—the source of these invasion ships that plague the border of our provinces—those incursions have yet to be put down."

Claver couldn't argue with that, so he finally shut up.

Armel stood up. He didn't lower himself to waggling a hand like I would have. The Mogwa finally pointed at him.

There was a certain light in Armel's eye, a light that I didn't like. "Grand Admiral Sateekas," he said, "the answer to your query seems clear. We must forge ahead. We must devastate this planet just as you destroyed the enemy fleet. We should not delay another hour, in my opinion. Drive forward your fleet like a vast wedge! Pound the enemy ground installations into submission! And, as a final solution, drop hell-burners on every inch of the surface of that offending world, turning it into a permanently lifeless wasteland."

Sateekas worked his mouthparts for a few moments, as if chewing on this suggestion. It was a disgusting sight to behold, but I was used to it, so I winced less than the other humans did.

"There is merit in that approach," he admitted, "but it will result, most likely, in a devastating amount of loss—chiefly among my own vessels. I was thinking more along the lines of casting forward the Rigellian and Earth ships at this point. Up until this juncture, you've participated little in this struggle. You've done nothing, in fact, but trail behind me, as bunder-scuttles might attach themselves by their oral suckers and glide along with a larger predatory leviathan. I think perhaps it's time for your vessels to serve their most obvious purpose."

"And what might that be?" Captain Merton asked, speaking up for the first time. He still maintained a polite, affable tone, but I could tell that he didn't like the direction the conversation was going in.

Sateekas shuffled his bulky body around and regarded him with multiple eye groups. "That would be the role of a distraction, of course," he announced. "You will launch all of your lifters and all your missiles at once. Fly every ship you have in a wide formation, scattered ahead of my own fleet. We will follow, and after you have been destroyed and swept aside, we'll be close enough to bombard the surface. In that manner, we'll take out these diabolical Crystals and their gravity weapons. If we get close enough, we'll be able to land those hellburners you were talking about." He said this last part with a nod toward Armel.

Winslade, Claver, and Armel all looked like they'd swallowed beetles. Their spirits were crushed.

Even the Rigellian bear, Squantus, pulled back his black lips and displayed a mouthful of curved teeth. He then joined the conversation for the first time.

"Insanity!" he said. "These others you might consider slaves, Galactic, but not Rigel. We exist entirely outside your decadent Empire. We are allied only as a matter of convenience. We will not accept the role of cannon fodder, wasting our ships and our troops to no purpose."

"Who is this incalculably rude creature?" Sateekas asked, pointing a wobbly foot-hand toward the Rigellian.

"He is a frontier barbarian, sir," his Nairb assistant said. He'd been squatting quietly at Sateekas' side like a well-behaved dog this whole time. "A resistant primitive. His kind have never been dominated by the Empire—at least not yet."

"What?" Sateekas boomed, staring at the bear. "Why is he here, then? I do not like to be surrounded by those who are not conditioned to obedience."

The Nairb shuffled a bit and looked around at the group. "I dare say that none of these primitives from the fringe of the Empire are so-conditioned, no matter how they may behave or what they may say."

I nodded appreciatively. This Nairb knew who he was talking to. Even Winslade, who might clap his hands until they bled, wasn't genuine. He would turn on Sateekas in a heartbeat if he thought that would serve his purposes.

Sateekas shuffled his limbs around, grumbling in his own language and releasing some pungent, unsettling noises.

"Disgusting..." he said, "absolutely disgusting and degrading that I should have to deal with such creatures. But so be it."

He puffed himself up and addressed us again.

"Winslade," he said, throwing a foot-hand in the direction of Squantus, "slay this irritating creature, destroy his vessel, and cast him out of my fleet. I will not have this kind of nonsense besmirching my finest hour!"

Claver cackled at this, but no one else seemed amused.

"Hold on!" Winslade said, throwing his skinny fingers high. "Let us all relax. Emotions are running high today!"

Both Sateekas and the Rigellian bear glowered at him. Neither was accustomed to anything like diplomacy. Both aliens were arrogant in the extreme and prone to violent outbursts.

I didn't envy Winslade. I'd probably have gone off by now if I were him.

"I can see there is a new enemy afoot," Winslade said. "It stalks us even today, like a predator in our midst."

"What are you grunting about?" Sateekas demanded. "Ejectus flies from your mouthparts! Where is that speaking ape, McGill? He would know how to handle this."

"Right here, your Overlordship, sir," I said, throwing a big hand high and waggling my fingers.

Both Squantus and Sateekas looked at me.

"Oh, yes, of course," Squantus said in his warbly underwater voice. "The human of mutated size and girth. Why is he even here? Do you not know, Winslade, that this treacherous beast nearly broke our alliance? He launched a bombing attack on our planetary shield."

Sateekas boomed with laughter at that. "You did this, McGill?"

"I surely did, sir," I admitted.

"Excellent. Well done. You should have wrecked the entire thing—and his planet, too."

Squantus stood then, standing on his chair to appear taller. In response, Sateekas immediately did the same.

Both of these aliens were kind of dinky, if the truth were to be told. But they were having a serious dick-measuring contest right now.

They stared one another down for a moment. Then Winslade stepped between them, lowering his head and putting up his skinny hands for peace.

"Hold on, great sirs, hold on! Don't you want to hear about the new, third enemy we are clearly facing?"

Finally, he caught their attention again.

"I don't know what you're prattling about," Sateekas said. "Nothing of the kind could be further from the truth. Our sensors show no approaching fleets—and our technology is infinitely superior to your own detection gear."

"In this one instance," Squantus said, "the foppish Galactic is correct. You are a fool, Winslade. No enemy approaches us. There is nothing out here in this desert of stars other than our coalition fleet and these miserable rocks."

"Ah…" Winslade said, daring to lift his head up a bit. He'd finally gotten the two of them to focus on him, rather than each other. That was sheer genius if you asked me. I couldn't have done it better.

"But that's where you're both wrong," he said. "The third enemy is right here in this room. It persists in the form of rancor between members of a coalition that is winning this war. The only way we're going to lose now is if we break apart and do not cooperate. The third enemy is discord—that's the monster I speak of."

Sateekas and Squantus both stared at him and paused for a moment. They grumbled. They groused. They made foul noises and smells.

But then, at last, the Rigellian bear sat down. I thought that was a good first move on his part. His people needed this coalition to succeed more than anyone else. The Crystals were, after all, knocking on the gates of Rigel. They'd already thrown invasion ships at every world these nasty bears had ever colonized.

Sateekas, seeing Squantus back down first, sat down as well. "All right," he said, "let us hear what you propose, Winslade. What is your solution if mine is so foul that it drives you into paroxysms of cowardice?"

Winslade was on the spot. He'd always been a man who was good at diplomacy, good at schmoozing. He could kiss an ass that was forty yards out, easy. I'd always said it, and I always would.

But Sateekas had called his bluff. He wanted to know what Winslade had in mind. When it came down to actual tactical ideas, actual military solutions, he always came up short.

His rat-like eyes searched the room for help.

Claver smirked at him, shaking his head. He'd clearly checked out, and it was obvious to me that he was considering bailing on the entire coalition.

Armel shrugged when Winslade ran his eyes over to him. He was either out of ideas or unwilling to say whatever was on his mind.

Sateekas and Squantus, of course, were in no mood for coming up with a cooperative plan.

Then Winslade glided his eyes to Captain Merton, who was as still as a stone. Merton had learned long ago that offering nothing was much better than offering something which might somehow turn into a failure.

Last but not least, Winslade's eyes came reluctantly to land upon me.

Me, who was standing taller than any of the others, even when they were standing on top of their chairs.

I was up, and I didn't have just one hand waggling in the air for attention, but two.

With a deep sigh of regret, he finally nodded. "Let's hear it, McGill. What do you have in mind?"

-26-

"To me, sirs," I said, "it's high time we charged right to the unspoken meat of this overly long meeting. We must destroy these mother-effing Crystals once and for all."

"We all know that, McGill. Do you have a plan or not?" Winslade demanded.

"I do. The answer seems frigging obvious to me."

Winslade made a 'hurry up' spinning motion with his fingers, but I ignored him.

"It's going to take all of us," I said, building it up. "Not just with one fleet leading and taking all the hits while the others come in late."

"Come, come, McGill," Winslade said, not trusting me at all. "Let's not waste everyone's time, please."

"I'm getting to the point, sir. I'm getting there. Our big problem is range. The enemy Crystals outrange us. We're going to have to be mighty close-in to drop troops or bombs, for example."

"That is self-evident, McGill."

"Not entirely, sir. Not entirely... What I propose is that we use the power of hyperspace."

They stared at me questioningly, but a few of them were already beginning to catch on. They were starting to frown, wrinkling up their noses as might anyone confronted with a new and unpleasant stench.

"That's right," I said. "We have to hyperjump from here to our destination in one-go. We have to squat right on top of their planet, with no warning. Then we'll begin the bombardment and the troop deployment from—I don't know, maybe two thousand kilometers out?"

"Two thousand kilometers is absurd!" Captain Merton shouted. He'd jumped to his feet like I'd stung his big ass. He hammered a big fist on the table, making the holograms dance. "It's unthinkable! You know our hyperspace engines aren't that precise. Next to a gravitational source like a planet, we can't be sure where we'll come out. If we try to come out within a few thousand kilometers... half of the *Scorpio* will appear in the atmosphere or in the ground itself!"

"Okay, okay," I said. "How about ten thousand kilometers out? Still close enough to launch a quick assault, but ninety-percent plus safe for every ship in the fleet."

"Let me hear and understand your concept, McGill," Sateekas said. "You're proposing a grand and brave opening. We'll hyperspace-jump right on top of the planet, close enough to launch an immediate surprise attack. That will, as your cowardly captain suggests, cost perhaps ten percent of our forces at the outset. That's apart from every bit of damage that those crystalline ground batteries will no doubt wreak upon us immediately afterward."

"That's right, Grand Admiral. You've got the gist of it. As far as I can see, it's the only way. If we're going to drop bombs, we've got to get in close enough to do it. Jumping in close is dangerous, but it's the only way to beat their range advantage. If we just fly at them in normal space, they'll be able to shoot at us for hours before we can reach them. I'd say we'll lose ninety percent of our fleet if we go that route."

"And what about after we fire off all of our ordnance?" Winslade asked. "What then? Do you think we'll be able to knock out all those ground batteries?"

I shook my head. "Probably not. That's going to take ground forces—which is what I'd recommend."

"Hmm..." Winslade said, tapping a stick-like finger on his narrow chin. "If we dare entertain this tactic... I'd add a detail. All our capital ships that survive the jump should immediately hyperspace out again."

Armel looked happy about that idea. He wanted to cut and run as soon as possible. "We'll cycle-up our warp engines and leave enemy orbit just as fast as we came in."

"What do you think, unworthy servant?" Sateekas asked his Nairb sidekick.

"The solution is suboptimal," the Nairb said. "Without detailed numeric data, I can make no analysis of these wild claims and generalities."

Winslade turned toward me. "Any more details for our number-crunching friend, McGill?"

"Well, sirs," I said, laughing, "I'm no math-surgeon. You guys have to tell your nerds to figure out the numbers. I don't know exactly how many more ships we'd lose with the traditional approach, or what the optimal target warp-in point would be."

This caused a great deal of babbling to erupt. Everyone began to work calculations on the battle table that was between us—everyone except for me, that is.

I leaned back in my chair and knit my fingers behind my head. As far as I was concerned, my job was done—except for the part about dying hard during the attack, of course.

Even the Mogwa could be seen scratching away in a strange alien script. Finally, the Nairb's voice piped up.

"It is feasible," he said. "My estimates are that we'll lose no more than twenty to twenty-five percent of our fleet using this unorthodox tactic. That's assuming, of course, that every vessel goes back into hyperspace again to escape enemy defensive fire."

"Does that include," Sateekas asked, "the previous ten of my force, which you erased just for having transported themselves so close to the target world in the first place?"

"Yes," the Nairb said, "that number is included in the estimate."

There was a lot of frowning, a lot of complaining. A general hubbub rose up in the room.

Arguments broke out. Some said twenty-five percent was insane. Others said it was better than turning around and going home right now, because that was essentially the alternative.

I was prideful and puffing myself up as I leaned back in my chair, confident that I had once again cut to the chase. Anyone who spent five minutes on this tactical problem had to realize my approach was ballsy, but it was the only viable move. The only one that could succeed. When the enemy outranged you, you had to get in close. The only way to get in close in a spaceship was to use a hyperjump.

Now, we could have done something else. We could have attempted to teleport troops or bombs directly to their surface, for instance, from way out here.

But every report said the enemy had shielded themselves against such assaults. Hell, bombs like that hadn't even worked against their spacecraft until human troops had gone with the bombs to serve as organic detonators.

The officers argued and carried on, but at last the Mogwa waved his limbs for attention. They would have probably ignored anyone else, but they did listen to the Grand Admiral. This was his big day, after all.

"I think McGill is right," he said. "I've even looked at the possibility of teleport bombing with suiciders, the way we did against their ships. Unfortunately, while we have plenty of organic guidance systems," here I realized he was referring to me and my men in a rather impersonal way, "we are in short supply of bombs. We simply don't have enough—we used the vast majority to destroy the enemy fleet."

That unknotted my guts a notch. I hadn't much enjoyed playing detonator the last time around.

"I would recommend, McGill," Sateekas went on, "that when you land your troops upon this world, you go naked, as nature intended. Warriors such as yourself have no need of clothing or weaponry. This will render their gravity beams ineffectual."

I knew, of course, that no Mogwa would be caught dead or alive anywhere near a battle unless said alien was tucked inside one of their mini-tank battle suits—but that's just the way the Mogwas thought. We were like sheep or cattle to them—perhaps even less important than that. We could be thrown against enemy walls to dash our brains out as needed, to die and to kill until their enemies were overwhelmed. In their eyes, we were like a herd of rabbits wearing suicide vests.

"There are many details to work out," Armel objected. "This might take days to perfect. We need to refer the task to our most qualified technicians."

There was some general agreement with this notion. Although I don't think a single one of the important brass members there liked my idea, they were all coming around to the acceptance that nothing else was going to actually do the job.

I almost nodded off to sleep as the meeting dragged on. I had my hands folded over my belly, and my head was lolling around over the back of my overly comfy conference chair.

Then a loud bang sounded, and I jerked awake. Sateekas had slammed a limb down on the table painfully hard.

"Let us adjourn," he said. "We will seek refreshment. We will discuss this further. Our technicians, our battle computers, they will all work together to come up with an optimized version of this plan to see if it is workable."

"Rigel will not commit to such a plan without being forewarned and made privy to every number and every detail of analysis that is available," Squantus said loudly.

"I will grant your cowardly request in this case," Sateekas responded.

This set off a fresh bout of quarreling. I came to think that perhaps Claver had been right in the first place. This was probably exactly what a council meeting with all the top Galactics looked like.

A lot of petty infighting, jockeying for position, hatred for past wrongs, and an overwhelming cloud of self-interest and arrogance were obvious in the positions taken by every member there. No wonder the Empire was falling apart.

There was no Emperor ruling the Core Worlds these days. The Imperial forces were reeling back in every known frontier province. Earth academics had done predictive models that showed within a few millennia the Empire would either be reduced to the Core Worlds alone—or utterly destroyed by internal strife and warfare.

When no one was looking at me, I stood up, yawned, stretched, and headed for the refreshment table. To my utter shock and dismay, it had been removed.

"Where's the food?" I asked.

One of the waitresses spoke up in reply, "I'm so sorry, sir. It's been moved to the dining hall."

That made me smile broadly. "And where, exactly, is that?" I asked.

She turned away and led me down a passageway that went deep into the guts of Gold Deck. I followed her and found the banquet room. A sumptuous repast was being laid out for all, me included.

Even if no one else wanted me to attend this banquet, I knew that Sateekas would. So, I stubbornly refused to be dislodged. Like a tick in a dog's ear, I planted myself in front of the buffet and, as fast as they brought food out from the kitchens, I began scooping up two plates for my own personal consumption.

It was moments like these that made up for everything else. Sure, I was kicked around during these high-level meetings. It generally didn't pay to be an infamous loudmouth who liked to hobnob with the brass.

But being constantly dragged into nonsense meetings did have a positive side. This kind of food, that was the twist. That's what made it all worthwhile to me.

-27-

"McGill?!" squawked a female voice. Like so many others before her, her tone was strident, shrill, and flat-out angry.

I turned my head with a guilty start. Primus Collins marched toward me, but she wasn't giving me her pursed-lip stare of disapproval. Nope. Instead, she was showing me some teeth with an outright snarl.

"Hi there, Cherish," I said in a cheery tone, "I got you a plate right here."

This was, of course, a sheer lie. I'd stacked up two plates, and then I'd noticed this really big, tall lobster-cream-pie thing. It looked mighty good. The third plate I'd reserved for this special item. I didn't quite know what the heck it was, but I planned to enjoy it to the fullest. I'd scooped the crown off it, in fact, and slapped a dollop down on the biggest plate I could find.

"McGill…" she said between those tightly clenched white teeth, "that cake isn't for humans. It's for the Mogwa. We had it imported as a specialty for him—for his tastes."

"Oh…" I said, eyeballing the pie. I stuck my finger into the creamy sauce, gave it a little swirl, and tasted it. Cherish glared at me the entire time I went through this process. "The sauce isn't too bad…" I said. "Is this meat here safe to eat?" Using the serving spoon, which I had purloined from the buffet, I tapped at the lobster-like meat.

"I'm curious too. You should try it," she said. "Maybe it will poison you."

I frowned at this idea, thinking it over. I finally shrugged and took a bite.

"It's pretty good," I said. "Not exactly like it looks. It's not lobster, I'd say. It's more nutty-flavored, you know? Like escargot or something."

"You took the crown off the pie, McGill?" a gravelly voice asked. Graves was here now, and he was almost as pissed off as Cherish herself. "Get away from that food, you gluttonous moron."

It was my turn to pout a bit as he snagged one of my plates, and Cherish snagged another. I was left with a big pile of Mogwa sauce with some unknown mollusk swimming in it. Shrugging, I took the plate to the nearest table, sat down, and began to chow.

"Primus Collins," Winslade said as he entered the room, "I'm giving you an assignment."

He pointed at me where I sat at a separated and lonely looking table. "You are to keep an eye on the biggest variable in this room."

They both looked at me. Cherish didn't look terribly happy. With a sigh, she came over and sat next to me.

"How's that food, huh?" I asked her. "This is a great spread. Earth has gone all-out. There's squab, too, over there. Did you know Mogwa love squab?"

She wasn't talking to me. She was staring at her plate, poking at it, and chewing in a rather deflated manner. I was trying to cheer her up, but it surely wasn't working.

"Uh..." I said, "is something wrong, Cherish?"

She aimed her fork at me and jabbed it in my direction. She didn't actually poke me and puncture the skin or anything, but I certainly didn't think it was a friendly gesture.

"That's it, right there," she said, "that's the sort of thing you keep doing."

"Huh?"

"You keep calling me Cherish," she said, lowering her voice.

"Well, uh... that is your name," I whispered back.

We were both hunkering forward, hissing at each other at this point.

"No, it's not, McGill. Not as far as you're concerned. I'm a primus. I'm your superior officer."

"Yeah, yeah. But you're my ex-girlfriend too," I said. "I let a lot of my subordinates call me James. You know, after a couple of decades of knowing each other, I kind of figured..."

"Well, you figured wrong," she said, interrupting. "It's inappropriate. We no longer have any kind of informal relationship, and I want you to use my appropriate rank and last name, please."

"Okay, okay," I said, "geez, what's gotten into your bonnet?"

She showed me her teeth again, but her eyes were cast down. She was poking at her food. She wasn't really eating anything, and I was beginning to get ideas about cleaning up her plate after she gave up.

All too soon, I polished off the Mogwa sauce and whatever the hell that lobster-like thing was. I was thinking about going to the buffet for another platter, but I restrained myself. I was getting a strange vibe from Cherish, like she was about to say something. Something she figured was important.

"James," she said at last, "I think your behavior is tying the two of us together in the minds of other officers—like Winslade."

I looked over toward Winslade, who was indeed guiding the most important personages to a separate table. He was playing *maître d'* seating them at the largest table at the front of the room. He placed Captain Merton and himself there, along with Tribune Armel. They were the highest-ranked people in the place right now, so I guess it made sense.

Cherish and I didn't rate, apparently. We were kind of the weenies at this shindig, but that didn't bother me one bit. I'd never wanted a lot of rank, and I'd learned during my lengthy time with the legions that standing out and getting the attention of important people simply made them give you more work to do. Rank was all about stress, responsibility, and kissing ass. I wanted nothing to do with any of that stuff.

"James, are you even listening to me?" Cherish asked.

I glanced back at her and grinned. She'd been talking, I realized that now. "I sure am!"

She shook her head and huffed a bit.

Now, right there, I thought that she was being unfair. Here she was, calling me James all the time. Yes, sure, sometimes she said "McGill," but now that we were in private, now that it was just the two of us at this table, she couldn't be bothered to follow the formal rules she'd laid out for me.

I shrugged my shoulders. I'd never been able to figure out the motivations of women like her. Over time I'd learned through sheer persistence and repeated harsh lessons when to shut up and when to go with the flow. So, while my natural behavior tended to piss off just about every female I'd met in my life, I still managed to be successful with them.

"What I'm saying is," she continued, "you keep on giving off signals to everyone around us that you and I are an item—when we most definitely are not."

"Got it. I hear you loud and clear," I said. "You needn't worry your pretty little head about it any further. I'll call you Primus. In fact, maybe I'll even call you 'sir' from now on. Would that make you happy?"

Cherish poked at her food some more and shrugged.

All of a sudden, right then, I got a shocker of a message from her. Maybe it was a message I was supposed to be getting all along.

Cherish wasn't really angry because I was calling her by her name. She was upset because I'd pretty much ignored her on this entire campaign. I'd pestered a number of other women, mind you—but not her.

With this sudden realization, I decided to attempt a tactical shift in our conversation. "You know what?" I said, "I really think I have to explain myself."

Her face was still tilted down toward her food, but her eyes flipped up, boring into me. She was listening, and she was listening intently. "How's that?"

"I—well, I just don't know how to go about things sometimes, you know? People think I'm some kind of Romeo, but I'm really not. I'm more of a ham-handed character when it comes to women."

She made a piffing sound and blew her bangs up in the air. Her eyes were cast down again, but she was chewing again, starting to eat. That had to be a good sign.

"Well, anyways," I said, "what I'm trying to say is I just didn't know quite how to get around to… you know… asking you out on a date again."

Her fork clattered on her plate. She looked up, and her face did register what I imagined was astonishment. She stared right at me for a minute, but then she glanced off, sliding her eyes all the way to the right, then to the left.

That meant, I knew after countless years of study, she was considering my offer. She wasn't rejecting it outright.

"Are you trying to tell me," she said, looking back my way again, "that you keep calling me 'Cherish' and making these overly-familiar comments in the presence of others… because you're still interested in me?"

"Yeah," I said, looking down at my food. I tried to look glum. I imitated a big, dumb hound-dog as best I could.

To my surprise, she seemed to be buying it. She heaved a big sigh, and she fell quiet for a second.

Realizing this was an opportune moment to get on with the banquet, I got up and moved to the buffet. There, I loaded-up big-time. I contemplated stealing another one of those big, weird lobster-like things out of the big Mogwa-sauce dish. It looked like a banana cream pie with lobsters shoved into it, to be honest.

Looking around, I made sure no one was looking, and I reached for it. But at that exact moment, everybody in the room stopped talking.

"Attention!" Graves boomed out. "Admiral on the deck!"

Everyone got to their feet in a hurry. I plopped my overly full plates down. Crumbs fell away from my face, and I wiped my mouth with the back of my hand.

Admiral Sateekas waddled into the room, as proud as a six-legged peacock. In his wake was his Nairb sidekick, that nasty green blob of an alien that seemed to be his chief of staff.

Once he was in the room, Sateekas scanned the place carefully. His eye groups landed on all the important people. At last, they came to rest upon me.

I lifted a hand and waved it at him in greeting. No one else in the room moved a muscle. They were all standing with ramrod stiffness.

As I'd expected, Sateekas turned in my direction and began waddling forward.

Winslade rapidly moved to intervene. He'd seen this interaction, and he'd realized that the Mogwa was about to sit at my table. In his mind, that was an unacceptable choice.

"Dear Grand Admiral," Winslade said, sucking up hard right from the start, "we have prepared some of your favorite dishes, and we'd love you to sit at the most prestigious and status-filled table in our banquet hall."

He waved a set of stick-like fingers in the direction of his table where all the biggest brass in the room had already set up camp.

Sateekas glanced back at me and then sort of sighed. He looked a bit deflated. I knew from experience that he considered me the most entertaining human he'd ever met, and that he generally preferred my company—although he'd probably never admit it.

That was largely because we had such a history together. We'd shared a lot of battles and spilled blood over the years, and I think he appreciated the company of another true warrior who didn't simp and kiss his ass all the time.

Now, to be fair, I did that some of the time, just not *all* the time, like Winslade and his ilk.

As Sateekas followed Winslade toward the head table, his Nairb followed him like a floppy green dog. But Sateekas turned on the Nairb and made a sweeping gesture with one of his foot-hands.

The poor Nairb ducked with practiced precision, avoiding a blow that might well have shattered his jaw. Nairbs were very thin-boned and weak-skinned, since they came from a low-gravity world.

"No," Sateekas boomed so loudly I could hear it all the way over at my table, "not you. Make yourself useful for once. Go to the McGill's table. Squat there and see if you can absorb anything useful from him. Perhaps you'll learn something of honor or bravery—although I doubt that's possible."

Rebuffed, the Nairb cringed and cowered away. He humped over toward my table, found the seat which I'd offered him, and slimed his way up onto it.

"Hey there, Mr. Nairb," I said, "I can see you're a bit too short to dish up some of the fine food from the buffet. Perhaps you want me to get you a platter? Maybe some of this Mogwa sauce and, uh, I don't know, what are these things floating in it? Mollusks?"

"Yes," he said, "they are indeed mollusks. A variety of flying mollusks that was originally native to Trantor. They're now entirely domesticated and bred only for consumption. I'm surprised you have them here."

"Uh... I think we must have imported them from the Mid-Zone."

The Nairb nodded. "That's a logical conclusion. Segin does maintain a flock, as I understand it."

That was a Nairb for you. They were the kind of guys who functioned like walking encyclopedias. You hardly needed a tapper when you had a Nairb around. He was always there to either correct you or to spout facts that you had little or no interest in.

I forced a smile, headed over to the buffet, and found a few items he might want to nibble on. Most notably, these consisted of herring, mustard sauces, and fungi—truffles, lots of truffles. I knew from experience that Nairbs liked fish and fungi the best.

I brought this back to him, and he poked at it for a while—sniffing suspiciously like a housecat. After sampling a few items, he found he liked the flavors and dug in noisily.

He pretty much just shoved his face into the plate like a dog at dinnertime and chowed. He never touched his silverware because he didn't really have hands in the first place, just flippers with articulated points. I wouldn't call them fingers, not exactly, but he could wrap his flipper around things and manipulate them. There must be some bones in there, or something. I shuddered just thinking about a Nairb's internals...

Cherish was doing her best not to look completely horrified. She kept casting glances over at the Nairb. These looks would have been considered rude if the Nairb was capable of interpreting the expression on her face. Fortunately, he wasn't.

After having consumed half his plate, he came up for air. He turned toward Cherish. There were lots of grimy little bits around his face, things like scales and bones from the herring, I think it was. That kind of food tended to make little black specks all around one's mouth if you really went to town on it.

"Primus Collins," he said, "you are known to me."

"I am?" she said, in honest surprise.

"Yes, humans in command of an important unit, such as Legion Varus, are now tracked and cataloged by my office. This is a departure from previous Nairb thinking. We have decided that some of you—especially the military types—are worthy of classification as individuals."

"Um… thanks, I think…"

The Nairb then pointed a flipper at me. Unfortunately, this gesture caused a small spray of mustard sauce to fly in my direction. A few yellow specks appeared on my uniform, but I pretended like I didn't even notice.

Cherish was squinching up her eyes but still forcing her face to smile. She reminded me a bit of Galina Turov in that way. She knew when she should control her natural responses toward repugnance. But she wasn't as good at it as Galina was, not as practiced and smooth.

I kind of liked that about Cherish. She was more honest, in a sense. You always knew where she stood. Galina, on the other hand, was fanatically devious by nature.

"Take this one here, for example," the Nairb said, still pointing at me. "A Chief Inspector of my ilk has long kept a detailed file upon this creature known as the McGill Mysteries."

I hooted. "Yeah, that's right," I said. "I remember that guy from the Moon. I met him during the Edge World campaign. He came and he tried to prosecute me for—"

"James?" Cherish interrupted. "Perhaps we should let the Nairb finish."

She gave me a meaningful glance and I realized I was mouthing off. She was right, of course. Why bring up my own persecution and prosecution by some other Nairb while I had one standing right in front of me?

The Nairb slid his eyes from Cherish to me and back again. "Do not fear, humans. While it is true, there's an active investigation file still open regarding this oversized speaking ape, it's not my responsibility. I am now servicing the Mogwa of Segin."

"Oh..." I said. "You know, I've heard that your kind act as bureaucrats for all the Galactics. Is that true?"

"No," he said. "Not all of them. The artificially intelligent beings, such as the Skay, generally refuse to contract with us. They do not see any advantage to an organic species that is somewhat robotic in nature."

"Ah. I guess that makes sense, them being robots themselves already."

"Correct. As I said, I'm not here to forward the agenda of any Nairb from the Core Systems. I'm working for the mid-zone Mogwa, who are a splinter group."

"Outcasts," I said. "That's what they are."

The Nairb looked at me seriously. "That is an unfortunate moniker, but accurate," he said. "Please do not mention that term in front of Sateekas himself. He may take violent action against either you or me upon simply hearing the word."

"I get it. I get it. I've had some tough bosses, too."

The Nairb studied me for a while. "A remembered incident has emerged in my mind," he said. "Many years ago, we were at a banquet similar to this one. You introduced me to a substance which I have long had a craving for since that date."

"Really? What's that?"

"I believe you call it *alcohol*."

I stared at him and blinked, and so did Cherish. Then a grin began to rise up on my face. It was like a full moon coming out from behind a cloud. I grinned so hard it made my cheeks hurt.

"You're in luck, Mr. Nairb," I said, "because I've got just the thing."

I stood up so fast my chair flopped back on the deck. Several officers glanced my way, wrinkling their noses, but I took no notice.

"James," Cherish said, "don't go and get drunk now."

"Come on, girl," I said. "This is a night of celebration. We'll probably all die fighting rock-people tomorrow. Let's party with this nice Nairb and make him happy. That's what we're supposed to be doing, isn't it?"

She sighed and nodded vaguely. We were, after all, sitting at the kids' table at this banquet. All three of us had been shunned. It only made sense that we should entertain our disgusting guest, as unimportant as he might be.

I went and found the biggest bottle of wine I could. It wasn't good wine, mind you. It wasn't even old wine, but it was powerful and there was plenty of it.

I brought back three big glasses as well. The kind that formed a force field when you poured something into them. You just held onto the stem, started pouring in the air, and the goblet automatically formed a force field that captured the liquid. It even chilled it a bit if you adjusted the settings on the bottom of the stem right.

Placing one of these goblets in front of each of us, I began to pour. Soon, a waiter came by. He looked upset. Maybe that was because I'd stolen the wine bottle from a carton beneath the buffet tablecloth.

"Can I open that for you, sir?" he asked.

"Nope," I laughed. "It's already open."

I'd ripped the cork out with my teeth, and I showed him this by spitting it out onto his hand. The waiter retreated, looking annoyed.

I doled out the wine in healthy pours. I gave Cherish and my new Nairb buddy a half-glass and myself a full one. This was only to be fair due to our varied size and tolerance levels. I was pretty sure I could drink both of them under the table and hardly have a buzz on.

While Cherish was still lifting up the glass and marveling at the force field encapsulating the liquid, the Nairb was sniffing at his wine glass, like a pet with a new dish of food in front of it.

I raised mine high. Some of the liquid sloshed out and splashed down onto the tablecloth, but I took no notice. After all, to my mind, if there weren't some purple stains on your white tablecloth at the end of a fine dining experience, you'd truly missed out.

"A toast," I said. "A toast to the kid's table and all low-ranking officials like us. We may not be in charge, but we actually do all the work."

Both of the others seemed pleased by this toast. Cherish had a faint smile and the Nairb made a couple of hissing sounds.

Laughter? Was that a Nairb laughing? I didn't think I'd ever heard the sound before.

I tapped my glass to each of theirs and then began to guzzle.

Finally, at long last, the evening was going in a direction that I understood and approved of.

-28-

For the second time in my life, I'd gotten a Nairb seriously drunk. What made this extra remarkable was the simple fact this was the same Nairb I'd gotten drunk the first time.

He behaved in a very similar fashion this time around. He became somewhat of a smart-aleck and put his head down on the table with his eyes closed in between drinks. As soon as he did that, I remembered him distinctly.

"Hey, buddy," I told him. "We're blood brothers, remember?"

"Blood brothers..." the Nairb said.

"You know what that means, don't you?"

"James," Cherish said, "leave the poor creature alone."

I waggled my fingers at her, trying to get her to be quiet. She didn't seem to understand this was the precise moment we could pump serious information out of this Nairb—or just about anybody.

"You know what blood brothers always do?" I asked him.

"What, ape-creature?"

"They tell each other the *truth*. They share *secrets*."

Cherish cocked her head and folded up her lips. I don't think she approved of my tactics, but I didn't care. After all, this Nairb knew every secret intention the Mogwa ships might have.

Sure, Sateekas was all grand and overbearing and arrogant today, talking about how much he enjoyed our slave-love. He was practically buttering us up, from his point of view. But what exactly was the heinous fate he had in mind for my precious Legion Varus? That's what I wanted to know.

I put my head down low with my left cheek touching the table. That way, I could look right into the Nairb's half-closed eyes.

"Hey, buddy?" I said. "What's your name? I don't think you ever told me."

"Yes, actually, I did." He then proceeded to rattle off a series of odd noises. My tapper began to pop up a long set of symbols and hieroglyphics. That was its best guess at interpreting the beeps and farts coming out of the alien.

"What the hell?" I asked. "What kind of a name is that?"

"That's my serial number," the Nairb replied.

"Serial number? You poor bastards don't even have names?"

"We are assigned a unique identity at our spawn-points."

"Oh... okay, yeah, yeah... That's really cool. Sure... Tell you what, that last digit in there, what was that? A seven? I'm going to call you Seven."

"Seven..." the Nairb said, "that is a pleasant and easy-to-remember moniker. However, it occurs to me that if you meet too many Nairbs, you are going to know a lot of them named Seven."

"I only care about just one Nairb, Seven," I said, "and that's you." I reached over very gently, patting him on the back. It was little more than finger-drumming, actually. These Nairbs were so delicate, you had to be careful. You could pop one like a water balloon if you weren't very soft when you touched them. I'd done it more than once.

"Now, Seven, do you know what this blood brother needs to know?"

"What?"

"I need to know what Sateekas has in mind for the ground troops in this invasion."

The Nairb made a little humping motion. I figured it was a shrug.

"That depends on various factors," Seven said.

"Like what?"

"Like how close I'm going to be able to get to the target world with the insertion ship."

I sat up and stared at him, squinting. I had no idea what he was talking about, but I was recording it all in my tapper, just in case. "Insertion ship? Huh? You are going to fly this thing?"

"That's correct. I am destined to have my atoms scattered all over this unpleasant planet, just as you are, McGill-creature. We are both equally doomed. Possibly, you will last longer than I will—but I doubt it."

Totally befuddled now, I looked at Cherish. She also shrugged her shoulders, spreading her hands wide. The Nairb was talking in riddles. Maybe he was too drunk to make sense anymore.

"You know what, buddy?" I said. "I don't think we're quite getting the message, here. How is this going to play out, exactly?"

Seven lifted one flappy finger. "I will tell you, ape-brother."

I leaned closer, and so did Cherish. Then he burped up something wet and fishy, which made us both recoil a bit. "But first, you must impart something to me. Something I've been dreaming of for many years now."

"What's that? Just name it. Cherish and I are like two genies in a bottle, waiting for your commands." I was looking at Cherish questioningly, thinking that maybe old Seven had taken a sudden interest in human females. She pinched up her face and shook her head a bit, letting me know in no uncertain terms there was zero chance of such an interlude ever taking place.

"I need the formula for making these beverages," Seven said at last.

"Drinks? What, you mean like... wine?"

"Yes," he said. "Ever since the last time we consumed alcohol together, I've been fantasizing about this state of inebriation. I've never experienced such mental euphoria."

"What?" I said, "Don't you Nairbs take any recreational mind-altering substances?"

"Never," he said. "It never even occurs to us to do so. It is actually a great fear for many of us that we shall lose control in such a moment. Control is everything, after all."

"Yeah, yeah, that's right. Sure it is."

"Seven," Cherish said, leaning close again, "if we gave you the formula to make alcohol, what would you do with it?" She looked concerned and somewhat motherly. I was beginning to think it had been a mistake to let her sit at my table.

"I shall make great quantities of it," Seven said, his head rising from the table where it rested, "and I shall enlighten the lives of countless members of my dull species."

I pushed out my lower lip and nodded. It seemed like a solid plan to me.

Working on my tapper, I didn't listen to Cherish. She'd started giving the Nairb a lecture about alcoholism and the dangers of chemical substances when they were introduced to aliens. All about how they might react in unpredictable ways to the chemical. All kinds of horseshit like that.

What I did in the meantime was stew up a whole raft of different alcoholic recipes. There were whole textbooks on fermentation, distillation—all that kind of stuff. Then I touched my tapper to his, which was of course embedded in his left flipper. In an instant, the data was transferred.

"James!" Cherish admonished me. "You can't just give him—!"

"Don't worry," I said. "It was just an article about margarita mixes, and how to grow the right kinds of grapes to make wine, that sort of crap. He doesn't even have yeast or anything. Don't worry about it."

She still seemed huffy and concerned, but she bought my lies.

Seven lifted his head slowly from the table again. He glanced down at his tapper, and his bleary eyes read through the data I'd given him. It was quite a thorough analysis of the process of creating alcohol.

"Some of these methodologies, I believe, will be adaptable," he said.

He looked at me then, peering with his two strange eyes. I don't think I'd ever had a Nairb look at me like that—like he was really seeing me as a person.

"McGill," he said, "blood-brother... There is no chance Sateekas will risk losing his battlecruisers from Segin by attacking the Silicoid planet directly. For this purpose, he is producing an assault capsule in the great hold of his flagship."

"A what?" I asked.

"An invasion ship," he answered. "Your plan was to teleport the fleet close to the enemy planet and bombard it from space, quickly dispatching troops, bombs—whatever we could send down at close range. That approach would undoubtedly cause the enemy serious injury, but it would also damage our fleet irreparably. Sateekas doesn't want that. He wants another nice, clean victory. Such a result as was achieved today."

Cherish shook her pretty head doubtfully. "That result is a rare and special circumstance for him."

"Don't I know it," I said, thinking of all the Pyrrhic victories that Sateekas had delivered to the Galactics over the decades.

In almost every battle the old buzzard fought, he lost all or most of his ships, whether he won or not. That sort of performance had gotten him reduced to the rank of governor—and even worse, he'd recently become an official serving a lost colony of outcasts.

"Tell me more about this assault capsule," I said.

"It is built of puff-crete. It's not uniform in shape. It looks like a bulbous version of one of those stalagmite ships that attacked us."

"Ooh..." I said, unhappy about what the Nairb was describing. "So... it's kind of a big ball of puff-crete? Blown up like a balloon with a couple of engines welded onto the ass-end?"

"Yes, that's accurate."

"And you're going to pilot this death-trap?" I asked.

"Correct."

I was beginning to understand why old Seven was so keen on getting drunk tonight. "Why you? Are you an especially good pilot?"

"No. I'm dismally unqualified for this task. However, I do have one distinct quality that has caused Sateekas to choose me."

"What's that, buddy?"

"I am completely, one hundred percent expendable in his eyes."

"Ugh..." I said, thinking about that one. It made perfect sense to me, but it was kind of sad for the little Nairb guy.

"That's awful, James," Cherish said to me. "He's basically a civilian."

"Well, listen-up, Seven," I said, "I'm fixing to go over and have a word with old Sateekas. Maybe I can talk him out of this crazy plan."

The Nairb reached out his flipper, and he grabbed at my wrist. Of course, his finger-things were almost helpless. They were even weaker than what Cherish might have slapped upon me.

But I stopped anyway, and I turned back to him.

Seven seemed truly desperate. "Don't speak to Sateekas about this. He will know that I told you of the plan."

"Oh..." I said. "I guess he would at that. He's a clever one."

"You can't say anything, James," Cherish said. "He'll perm Seven for sure."

"Yeah... Yeah... He'd perm him. Well, okay. The admiral is going to send this funky invasion ship at the planet. How's it going to get there? It's going to get blown out of the sky."

"No," he said, "it's not. It's going to be hyper-jumped—one brief jump. Then from there, the commandos will teleport down to the surface, set up gateway posts, and form a beachhead."

"Huh..." I said, thinking that over. "Just who are these commandos supposed to be?"

The Nairb squinted at me again. "Even in my current mental state," he said, "the answer seems obvious."

I thought that over, slack-jawed. Then I looked at Cherish, who had her face in her hands. That's when I got it.

We were going to be the commandos. We were going to be aboard this bathtub of a ship that Seven was describing. Now I

understood why he'd said I might survive longer than he did—
but he doubted it.

-29-

The next day went about as badly as we'd all expected.
"3rd Unit, report to Gray Deck."
My troops got up, assembled their gear, and began marching out the door. We'd already been warned that we would be deployed early and in advance of the main column today.

Was this because Graves was still leaning on me? Maybe.

Instead, I spouted the cover-story that our early deployment was due to the fact my unit was the most experienced teleportation-based commando team in the entire legion. It only made sense we'd be chosen as a frontline spearhead. It was our job, regardless of the reasons, to establish the legion's beachhead.

The troops grumbled, but they lined up and jumped to their feet when the arrows in the deck plates began to flash, leading the way.

When we reached Gray Deck, however, I was somewhat surprised to see Primus Cherish Collins was already there. I'd just spent the night with her, of course, as the Nairb named Seven wasn't the only individual who'd gotten drunk and a little bit out of control the evening before.

Cherish seemed somewhat embarrassed and chagrined to be facing me this morning.

"Centurion McGill…" she said as formally as she was able.

I knew right off this was a signal from her. She didn't want to hear any informalities come out of my mouth or give me any goodbye kisses at the start of this mission. I could understand that, as we were standing in front of about a hundred and twenty of my troops, most of whom knew that Cherish and I had once been an item.

"Yessir, Primus Collins," I responded, saluting crisply.

"Your group has been designated as the tip of our spear on this mission. That's an honor."

I already knew all this and so did she, but we had to go through the motions. I hadn't explained to anyone that I'd worked hard to get a Nairb drunk and pumped him for information about today's events—not that it had done me much good in the end.

To be sure, I complained a little to Graves and tried to get hold of Sateekas. No one had been interested. So, here we were.

"First off," she said, "you've got to strip off that armor."

I looked down at my black combat armor, the stardust suit that I'd been wearing for nigh on a decade now.

"Really? Not even this stuff is any good, huh?"

"No. Ditch it."

"All right, all right…"

Everybody began shucking off their armor: breastplates, stardust, regular titanium greaves, exoskeletal frameworks—everything that served to protect us. This was an especially big shock for the weaponeers who normally walked around like robot tanks in inch-thick plate.

"I feel frigging naked here," Sargon said. "Are we literally going to use spears on the enemy, too?"

Cherish folded her lips in disgust, but she didn't even glance at him. He was out of line, but I knew how he felt, so I didn't tell him to shut up.

Sargon wandered off and marshaled his team of weaponeers. They were relieved of the weight of their armor, which of course made things easier, but they also had removed their exoskeletal help, which made the large weapon systems they had to carry all the heavier.

"I don't think we can carry an 88 like this, sir," he told me.

I thought about it and shook my head. "Nope. We're leaving them behind. Belchers, we'll take. Belchers, mini-missile swarms, and morph-rifles. That's all we get this deployment."

Of all of us, the light troopers seemed the least affected. They pretty much were running around naked in tough fabric spacesuits anyway, and snap-rifles didn't have all that much metal in them.

"Wait a frigging minute," Harris said, walking up to me and waving for attention. Primus Collins glared at him, but he didn't wilt under her stare.

"Sirs?" he said. "What about our force blades?"

I frowned at that. He had a point. Normally, force blades were part of every man's kit as heavy troopers.

"We've got nothing but morph-rifles," Harris complained. "We're not going to be much better than the lights themselves."

I had to agree with him.

"It's true," I said, turning to Cherish. "How can we get some of this kit to be more manageable?"

"I don't know," she said. "Ask the techs."

She walked away with her clipboard-computer, shouting instructions. Already, the gateway posts had been set up. They were glowing a bluish-purple today. It was an evil color, which I didn't like the look of.

I talked to the techs about what we could do in order to allow our heavy troopers to use force-blades. Natasha and Kivi teamed up on the problem with some of the Gray Deck pukes. Together, they came up with a solution.

"If you just remove most of your armor," Natasha explained, "and the exoskeleton, you're left with these bracers."

"Those are pretty beefy bracers…" I complained.

And they were. They were essentially the entire disconnected piece of metallic tubing that normally covered the forearm, plus the gauntlet.

"You want one of these on each man or two?" she asked.

"One is safer," Harris said. "I mean, if you're going to get hit by one of those gravity beams…"

I thought about it and finally agreed. "All right, let's go minimal metal. We're going to have one gauntlet on each heavy trooper. It'll be capable of extending a single force beam. That'll reduce the power pack drain we have anyway."

They worked quickly to create a loadout. Fortunately, our gear was fairly modular in nature these days. It had been built to work for many different species and in many different configurations. Some planets were hot, after all. Some were cold. This was a critical variability that we had built into our uniform design.

"Okay," I said. "Every heavy trooper can choose—your right or left arm. Choose your dominant one, obviously, to wear the gauntlet. You'll still have to carry your morph-rifle and your basic breathing gear."

After the heavies were organized, I turned to my specialists. "What are the atmospheric conditions of this planet?"

One of the techs spoke up. "You can breathe there, Centurion. It'll probably smell rather sulfurous. The oxygen content might be a little low, carbon dioxide a little high. That's because the plant life on this world is sparser than it would be on Earth. There are no oceans, either. No moon, no tides, but the water bodies that exist are going to be universally brackish and probably impure."

"Sounds like a real Garden of Eden," I said.

"At least the temperature is relatively stable for Earth-human normal. You're not going to need air conditioners or heaters. Your basic spacesuits will do."

"Okay then," I said, "everybody, remove helmets."

There was a general broad groan across the entire deck.

Cherish glared at everyone. The response seemed inappropriate to her, but she hadn't spent that much time with my unit. After all, we were facing a suicide mission with a solid chance for a perming as our just reward at the end of it.

So again, I did not tell my men to shut up and stop complaining. If they got on this planet and set up a beachhead successfully, they were heroes, one and all. Hell, they hadn't even seen or heard about the Nairb-driven invasion puff-crete balloon yet.

Carlos got bored and began pecking at the gateway posts, which flared with an evil light if you tapped at the top of one of them.

"Does that go to the planet?" he asked me.

"No," I said, "it goes to our invasion ship."

"What invasion ship?"

Naturally, he knew nothing about what the Nairb had told me the day before. I decided that today there wasn't time to enlighten him. He would figure it out soon enough. "Never mind, Specialist. Okay, people, let's try the new heavy gear."

It took us about forty-five minutes to sort everything out, gear ourselves up, and be ready for the jump. Graves had shown up by then, complaining that we were taking too damned long.

"Sateekas is chewing my ear off. I want you boys to launch in the next five minutes."

Say what you will about Graves and his gruff nature, he was always able to get people to move faster than they might otherwise have done. Once he arrived on deck, everybody began to speed up and hustle.

About four minutes and thirty seconds after he first set foot on the deck, the exodus began. My nervous light troopers, led by Adjunct Clane himself—lucky him—walked through the gateway posts and disappeared.

Harris was standing nearby to watch. He turned to me. "You never did say where these posts led to, McGill. If not the planet, then where?"

"You'll see," I said. My tone was flat, and I didn't even look at him, so he knew the answer was grim.

"Oh, Lord…" he said.

I still didn't meet his stare. "Heavies, you're going through next. Harris, lead them."

That was Harris's cue. He marched through, following Clane and the lights.

Each of his men looked strange to me. They were carrying big guns, small packs, no helmets, and one silvery gauntlet each that was rigged to extend a deadly force blade in a pinch.

Many of them did at least have one of the shotguns we'd used to crack Crystals on Jungle World. We'd also issued no less than three plasma grenades for each man. Those grenades were known to disrupt and stun the enemy, giving us a chance against them in close combat.

"The last group," I announced, not even waiting for Graves to give the order. "Will be led by me. Circle up, specialists!"

As soon as Harris and his men disappeared, I marched at the head of the auxiliary platoon. This was made up of Leeson as my adjunct officer and all of our techs, bios, and weaponeers.

We all marched through the portal together and vanished.

-30-

What seemed like a moment later, we reappeared. We were not in a happy place. Men stood around everywhere, complaining bitterly.

"What the fuck kind of a cluster is this?" Leeson asked.

"The air stinks in here," Carlos complained. "It *really* stinks."

He was right. There was a nasty fishy odor that was overpoweringly pungent.

I knew the smell in an instant. It was the raw odor of Nairbs in their natural habitat. They liked to live in soupy green water—if you could call it water. The liquid mostly seemed to consist of Nairb waste. They slept in that, lived in it, and slapped around in it, as happy as pigs in their sty.

The weird, curving, bulbous interior surface of the ship we were in went upward in every direction. It was indeed in a balloon shape. I could tell it was over a hundred meters across. It was somewhat cylindrical, but not entirely. The deck was uneven, to be honest.

"Is this ship organic?" Carlos asked me.

"No," I said, "it's puff-crete."

"Puff-crete?" Carlos was baffled. He tapped the deck with his foot. The curvature of it extended in both directions as far as the eye could see.

A creature then came slapping toward us. It was none other than Seven. I could tell it was him because he was leading a team of identical Nairbs, and he was making a beeline for me. I doubted that any other Nairb, except possibly the Chief Inspector who was still researching the McGill Mysteries, would recognize me on sight and come humping in my direction without a moment's hesitation.

"Hey, Seven," I said, greeting him.

He stopped, stared, and sniffed for a moment. "Yes…" he said, "I remember that moniker now. You call me Seven."

"Yep, that's right. That's your new name, as far as I'm concerned."

My various adjuncts were all giving us quizzical looks. They were somewhat used to me greeting aliens in a familiar fashion—but a Nairb? No one had ever made friends with a Nairb before. Not that we knew of, at least. I had to wonder if I was the first human in history to accomplish the feat.

"How you doing today, Seven?" I asked him, wondering if he had a hangover or not.

"I am depressed on this dismal day," the Nairb responded.

"Depressed? Why? You're the one flying this bathtub. We're the ones that have to jump out and invade some planet. We'll get shot up by crystal aliens, not you."

"You are incorrect about that, McGill. Although it's true you will be landing on the planet as quickly as we can deploy you, I am doubtlessly going to experience the sensation of being lanced by gravity beams. We expect the enemy planetary defense stations to strike this ship with great frequency and intensity immediately upon exiting hyperspace."

"Whoa, whoa, whoa, whoa!" Harris said, throwing up his hands. He was starting to catch on as to what the real plan was for today's invasion attempt. "Are you telling me this big, bloated pig of a ship is going to take us to Crystal World?"

"That's right, Adjunct. Today is your lucky day. None of that riding down in a drop pod nonsense. You'd probably just splat from inexperience, anyways."

He glared at me when I said this, but I kept right on.

"No, sir. No riding in a lifter to be chased down a ramp and ditched, either. Hell, no. We're doing this the fast and easy way. This amazing ship is going to pop into hyperspace, then pop right out again. We'll appear on top of the atmosphere, and then we're all porting down to the LZ. Bam!"

Harris looked horrified.

Leeson shook his head and tsked. "We're the monkey's football today, that's for sure…"

"By the way," I said, "where is the new set of posts we're taking down with us?"

The Nairb flapped dismally at the posts we'd just exited from. "Those are the ones you'll be using."

"Huh? Really?"

"Yes. The Admiralty has decided not to waste equipment. You will take these harnesses." Here, he indicated a cart loaded with harnesses that his Nairbs were rolling toward us. "Distribute these to your troops. You will take the same gateway posts you used to get here and set them up on the planet."

"Oh, I get it… they don't want the gateway to get blown up when this pig of a ship… uh… pops…"

"Precisely."

"Uh, okay," I said. "But what about you guys, Seven?"

"What do you mean 'what about us'?"

"You and your Nairb buddies have to get off this death-wagon somehow."

The Nairb shook his head sadly. "There are no facilities set up for that purpose."

"You're just going to die aboard this pot-bellied pig?"

"Yes, quite probably."

I frowned at that, putting my hands on my hips. I didn't like the taste of it. Here, once again, the brass was more worried about a little bit of hardware than they were about flesh and blood. That was so typical of any high official.

I knew from long experience there'd be no way Sateekas or Winslade would put up with such disregard for his own sacred carcass. Hell, there'd be six extra backup harnesses ready to beam him home at a moment's notice if he'd been in this situation.

"Hmm… This all seems just plain unfair, Seven. You know what? I'm going to fix it."

The Nairb stared at me, not understanding what I was saying. He began making some of those farts and whistles, but before the translator could interpret those words, I took off my own harness and slipped it over the Nairb's weird pointy noggin.

"There," I said.

He looked at the harness, baffled. "But... what are you going to wear, McGill-creature? How are you going to get down to the surface?"

"Don't you worry about me," I said. I turned around and walked back through the gateway posts. A fraction of a second later, I reappeared on the Gray Deck. Immediately, the techs there began squawking.

"McGill? What the hell are you doing here?" Primus Collins marched toward me. Her step was quick, light, and angry.

"Hey, Cherish," I said.

"Don't call me that on this deck! Not just because of last night, but—"

"Oh yeah, sorry, sorry, I just forgot. Listen... uh... sir," I said, "I have a favor to ask."

She glared at me. "A favor? You've got to be kidding."

"No, I really mean it. I need one extra teleport harness."

She stared at me. "What for? They've been issued, and carefully accounted for. You don't need another harness to complete this mission, McGill."

"I surely do. Just trust me. Can you get me one? I know you can order these techs to get one out of the lockers." I pointed towards rows of lockers, which I knew were simply brimming with extra equipment of this kind.

Cherish thought about it, glared a bit, then finally shook her head. "I can't do it."

Now it was my turn to be angry. I leaned close and lowered my voice. "Come on, girl. Do it right now, or I'm going to give you a kiss and a pat on the bottom—right in front of everybody. Look, they're all staring already."

She showed me her lower pearly whites in an angry line. "If you do something like that, James, I will have your balls on a platter."

"You can do that, Primus," I told her, "but not today. Because I'm kind of busy teleporting into a death trap."

She seethed for a bit. "What the hell do you need it for?"

"I made a deal with Seven," I told her.

That made her face soften. "Well, why didn't you say so in the first place? All right. We screwed that Nairb. I guess we can cut him a break."

Stalking away, she went to the lockers. She had to brush away some squawking techs. They swarmed her like park-pigeons until she shooed them away. She opened a locker with her command override on her tapper, and she pulled out a harness.

Complaining technicians circled and buzzed, but they didn't dare refuse her orders. They set the coordinates on the harness to the appropriate lottery-winning numbers.

I was all smiles by this time. When Cherish came into range, I leaned in for a kiss, but she ducked me.

"Damn it, James…" she said.

A few of the techs twittered.

Then I turned around and walked out through the posts. The bug-zapper noise buzzed loudly, and I was gone. A moment later, I was standing on uneven puff-crete again. The saddest looking Nairb in the cosmos faced me.

"Are you quite finished with these delays?" he asked.

"I sure am, Seven. Let's do this."

The Nairbs, operating as technicians, disconnected the gateway posts. They handed them over to my techs, Natasha and Kivi. All these ladies had been doing was screwing around hacking into the alien ship's networks, anyway.

I had each of the girls take up one of the big posts, which was quite a heavy load for a small woman. They grunted under the weight, but they accepted their new burdens. The Nairb posse humped away.

We did a double-check on everybody's harnesses. But then, before we'd even finished the process, the big bulbous ship flashed into hyperspace.

The invasion of Crystal World had finally begun.

-31-

I don't mind telling you, when we came back out of hyperspace about ninety seconds later, my balls were crawling in my thin spacesuit.

All of us were looking around at the walls, just waiting for some big gravity beam to come and lance right through us, crushing everybody into pulp.

One of the reasons the brass had chosen to use a puff-crete ship was precisely for this maneuver. Puff-crete ships were usually used as a final resort of planetary defense or desperation shipbuilding in general. When you wanted to be quick and dirty, nothing beat this substance when it came to building just about anything.

Vessels of this kind couldn't take a serious hit, of course, not compared to a real sophisticated, multi-layered reactive-stardust hull. But they were airtight and almost instantaneous to create, even in space. They could even absorb minor damage—stuff like pebble-sized meteor strikes and radiation.

In this particular case, the puff-crete hull was optimal because it didn't weigh that much, and it was non-metallic. Therefore, the gravity weapons employed by our crystalline enemies shouldn't be able to maximize damage on the organic bodies inside the ship.

"Okay, okay," I said, "spread out until Seven gives us the signal to teleport down."

This operation was really rather simple for my soldiers. It was going to be hard for even Carlos to screw this up. The coordinates had been pre-programmed into the harnesses that rode on everyone's chest. All we had to do was press a single button.

The battery would discharge, and we would immediately teleport to the destination that had been pre-programmed into the harnesses. You held down one button for about three seconds, and that was it. It was as simple as a plasma grenade to operate, possibly even simpler because you didn't even have to throw it at the enemy.

We stood around, waiting for the signal—but it didn't come right away.

"What the hell is going on?" I demanded. "Why haven't we ported yet?"

"I'm hearing nothing from the pilot pod up front," Harris said, pointing in the direction the Nairbs had gone. "You think maybe the whole crew is dead already?"

"Oh, shit..." Leeson said. "That would be just our luck, wouldn't it?"

Even Clane added his two cents. He wasn't usually part of the bitching crew, but this time, well, maybe he was feeling nervous. "What would you do if you were a Crystal?" he asked. "You'd strike at the bridge, right? That's what I'd do."

"Dear God," Harris said, gawking at the puff-crete walls around us. "They're all dead up there. Maybe they've taken out the engines, too. What if they plan to capture us?"

"Shut up, Harris," I said.

"Yeah, shut up," Leeson said, agreeing with my sentiment. "You're just freaking out our troops for no reason."

"Natasha, I know you were doing some hacking earlier," I said. "Show me what the hell's going on outside."

She immediately cast me her tapper feed. Apparently, there were a few cameras on the outside of this puff-crete clay jug we were sitting inside of, and she'd already hacked into them.

The view was spectacular. The planet was close, and it filled my tiny screen.

The world below us was a weird-looking one. Most life-bearing planets were either green or sometimes purple, depending on the nature of the vegetation.

This one was different. Instead of blue water, the seas were pink and the land appeared to be almost uniformly gray. Some sections were a darker slate gray, others a lighter stone gray. Nothing looked green.

"Huh…" I said. "What a weird-looking planet. You can see the atmosphere with hazy clouds hanging above it. So, there was some level of precipitation. But Earth would be much more overcast on a typical day."

"You want to see freaky?" Harris said. "Look at that pink water over there."

"That's due to the nature of the organics here," Carlos said, saying something useful for the first time I could remember.

I looked up and gestured for him to explain. He was, after all, our most senior bio specialist. That made him the closest thing we had to a xenologist. He certainly knew more about biology than anyone else in the unit.

Normally, that was fairly useless knowledge. But we were invading a new planet today. Everyone wanted to know if something was poisonous, if the air could be breathed, or what the nature of the natives might be. For all that kind of information, he was my man.

"Pink oceans…" he said. "That indicates the bacteria here use retinol, rather than chlorophyll."

"What the hell…?"

Carlos shrugged. "Retinol is a simpler organic compound than chlorophyll. It's pink. It lets plants and stuff absorb sunlight and convert it into energy. So, you've got pink oceans on some planets… or purple, like Dark World."

"They aren't technically oceans," Natasha corrected him. "They aren't—"

Sensing there was about to be a nerd-fight, I put up two big hands between them. "I don't care. They're big. They're pink. They're bigger than the Great Lakes of Earth. Even if they're freshwater and not seawater, I'd call them oceans. Carlos is right."

Natasha pouted a bit and crossed her arms. "You want to know something else?"

As we were waiting for death of one kind or another, I figured it couldn't hurt to indulge her, so I gestured for her to keep talking.

"Well," she said, uncrossing her arms again, "back on Earth, we once had pink oceans. That was about two billion years ago. For hundreds of millions of years, the oceans were pink."

"That's frigging weird," Harris said.

"Yeah, and you know what else—?"

She broke off because right then, a booming message hit all of our tappers at once. It was audio, and it was Seven's voice.

"Humans, now is the moment to teleport yourselves. We have been detected by the enemy defense systems. We can provide no closer approach, no safer launch conditions than this moment. Teleport out."

"Everybody hit it!" I ordered, and we did.

Every trooper in my unit mashed our buttons. Blue lights began flashing.

We were supposed to wink out by squads, but the urgency of Seven's call had thrown all that out the window. We began winking out one after another.

I realized some people had vanished ahead of me. That meant they must have pushed the button even as the Nairb had been talking, before he'd finished giving the order.

A few of them were *really* early. Like they'd had a thumb on that button the whole time. Probably a man like Harris, who I believed was the first man I saw disappear, had pushed his button the moment the Nairb had said "humans" and he'd never looked back.

That would be like Harris. He usually wasn't the first man to jump blindly into danger—but he was frequently the first man to bug-out.

A moment later, I stepped onto the crunchy, unpleasant surface of Crystal World. The alien soil sent a tiny flurry of dust up around my boot, dissipating quickly in the arid breeze.

The horizon seemed to stretch to infinity and back again. It was saw-toothed, with rough, jagged hills that looked as though they'd been torn from the mouth of some great beast.

The ground was uneven, every step making me grateful for the reinforced soles of my boots. The rocks were sharp, hard, and in some places, gleaming with minerals. As I walked, I could see streaks of what looked like metal in every boulder. Those were rich veins of unknown materials that would no doubt make a miner's heart skip a beat.

But what caught my attention, as it would any traveler's, was the pink hue that occasionally glistened between these rocky outcrops. Those had to be bodies of water, and they were the most alien thing in sight to my eyes.

Instead of the soothing blues of Earth, they glowed an otherworldly pink. Vegetation was scarce, and what little there was clung fiercely to the rocks, stubbornly adapted to this harsh environment.

There was nothing as grand as a tree. Even the shrubs seemed to be all rough bristles and thorns that reached out, as if seeking something to latch onto.

Looking up, I was met with an empty sky. There were only a few clouds, and the unforgiving glare of a distant, hot, white star. Its heat was undeniable, yet it seemed so far away. Its light filtered through the hazy atmosphere, casting an almost dreamlike glow over everything.

I took my first deep breath then—and it was a mistake. The air, while breathable, held a sulfurous stench that hit the back of my throat. Every inhale came with a tinge of unpleasantness. The disgusting taste it left behind reminded me how far I was from home.

I adjusted the grip on my rifle. This strange place, with all its beauty and menace, was about to become a blood-soaked battleground.

"Carlos?" I shouted. "Where's my bio?"

He came trotting over to me, wheezing and coughing.

"Give me your analysis, Specialist," I said.

"My analysis? This place sucks. That's my analysis," he replied.

"It stinks too," Harris shouted over his shoulder.

I couldn't honestly deny what either of these men had to say, as unprofessional as it seemed. "Any more than that? Are we being poisoned, or what?"

"No, no. As far as I can tell, I'm not registering any pathogens. The toxic level of the atmosphere is tolerable long-term. It's just unpleasant."

"Right... Okay... Techs? Kivi? Set up those gateway posts. Natasha, you're on drone duty. Scout the area—let me know what we can see."

"What we'll see?" Leeson said, marching over to me. "I'll tell you what we'll see: a bunch of frigging rocks, and not much else."

I scanned the horizon closely. Carlos walked up and stood beside me. He was using the extreme range optics afforded by a pair of modern-day binoculars. I used the reticle on my rifle.

"What's that over there?" I said, pointing.

"I was just about to ask that myself," Carlos said. "You know what? That looks like... well, it's sure not natural."

We both stared.

In a rough valley between two of the towering stacks of boulders, we spotted something I hadn't expected: a village. Not just any village, but one that appeared to be crafted from the very rocks that surrounded it.

Cautiously, I brought my rifle up. The high-tech scope operated by increasing the density of the air above the barrel into a lens. This allowed me to zoom into the intricate details from my vantage point over two kilometers away.

At first glance, the structures seemed to be just a natural part of the landscape. But as I focused, the organized patterns became evident. These weren't just randomly placed boulders. They were masterfully crafted homes, shaped and smoothed with artistry. The buildings were symmetrical, with arching doorways and clear pathways between them. Some even had what appeared to be windows, albeit not transparent, but rather thin slits through which the inhabitants might peer out.

What struck me most was the way they seemed to blend into their surroundings. From a distance, without the scope, one might not even notice them. The village was an extension of the planet itself, seamlessly integrated into its rugged environment.

But where were its builders?

I adjusted the focus on my scope, scanning slowly from one end of the village to the other. At first, all was still. But then, there it was — movement.

At the far end of the village, near what appeared to be a central plaza, I saw them. Rock creatures, their bodies mimicking the rocky terrain around them, moved with surprising grace. Their forms flowed like liquid stone, and they shimmered slightly under the bright white sun. Some were taller and more jagged, like rough statues, while others were smoother, almost polished.

They communicated with each other, though from this distance, I couldn't decipher how. There were no audible sounds, but they moved in patterns, sometimes coming close together, other times forming circles. It was like a dance, a choreographed routine that only they understood.

"What the hell are they doing?" Carlos asked me.

"I don't know, and I don't care," I said. "I think they're civvies. As long as they stay out there and don't mess with us, we don't have to mess with them."

"What kind of rocks are civilians?" Carlos asked. "I'm no geologist. If one of these things comes at me, I'm going to blast it."

I frowned at him, but I couldn't argue with his logic. I set up some snipers and deployed Harris with his heavies on the ridgeline overlooking the village. I sent some of my weaponeers to accompany them with belchers. Everyone was aiming in the general direction of the village.

"Kivi, how about those posts?" I said over my shoulder.

"You should have put me on drones," she said. "Natasha is better at this stuff."

I didn't respond. The truth was that Natasha was better at both drones and gateway posts—and just about anything else you might want to throw at a tech in your unit.

But that didn't matter. I wanted Kivi to feel a bit of stress. She needed to step-up her game. It was one of those little charming moments that officers in the legions live for—to stretch the horizons of their troops.

I kept checking on the village every few minutes. I couldn't help myself. Within about ten minutes after we had landed, Natasha had drones over the site.

"I've got some video of that native habitation," she told me.

She passed the feed over to me when I waved for it, flicking her tapper toward mine. I caught the stream and watched with fascination.

Carlos was close enough that he caught the stream as well. "Whoa," he said. Without asking, he'd hopped onto the direct drone output. I didn't complain, as he was essentially our xenologist—or at least the closest thing we had to one in this unit.

"What do you think?" I asked him.

"They're weird... really weird... but they don't seem dangerous. At least, not yet."

I nodded and pulled back from my rifle scope.

"Are you done with those posts yet, Kivi?" I demanded.

"Almost!"

I shook my head, thinking I'd made a mistake. "Go help her," I told Natasha.

"But the village—"

"Go help her!"

She trotted away, dropping the drone controls. I knew they'd circle for a time, then fly back home automatically.

As the sun cast elongated shadows over the village, I realized there was no way the enemy didn't already know our invading force had landed. That simple fact put us on a timer. At some point, they'd counterattack.

Everything was taking too long. But didn't it always when reality struck an operation in the face?

Still, it made me edgy. The clock was ticking fast.

-32-

"Those things are so weird…" Carlos said for like the tenth time. He was fascinated by the villagers we were observing. "They're kind of like slugs or something. Slugs made out of rocks and dirt."

He was right. The aliens, when they moved, humped around on the ground like fast-moving slugs. But when they stopped to do something—like open a door to one of their weird huts, or to operate one of the strange metal pieces of equipment that were in their village, the purposes of which we had yet to determine—they would transform. They'd rear up into a taller, stationary shape. Their upper bodies became swollen, almost balloon-like—but they were still made of dirt and stone.

Arms—or maybe pods was a better word—extended from their bodies. Then they could manipulate whatever they were working with. It was really strange to watch.

"I saw one with three frigging arms!" Carlos shouted, waving for me to check it out. I switched to drone four, which was the feed Carlos was watching.

To my surprise, I saw he was right. One of these creatures had extended no less than three pods to operate some kind of device.

"That's really weird," I admitted.

"They don't really have arms," Carlos said. "They kind of make them from their bodies whenever they need one. We're really making history here, McGill. This lifeform is so different. I'm taking lots of video, and I'm going to take samples, too, as soon as I get the chance. I bet I win some kind of science prize back on Earth."

I studied the aliens, frowning. "These things are nothing like those many-sided dice that they threw at us on Jungle World. I don't see any of those rock soldiers we fought around here."

"You're right," Carlos said. "I think this might be their regular-life, civvy form."

"That makes perfect sense," Leeson said, joining the conversation. He had somehow latched onto the feed as well. In my unit, intel was passed around pretty freely—and even if you didn't pass it, everybody just stole it anyway.

"What do you mean?" I asked.

"Those Crystal soldiers on Jungle World didn't make any sense. I mean, I couldn't imagine they were really alive and able to have a town or a community or anything like that. I bet you they were just a form of robot that these freaks like to make."

I thought about that and indeed it did make sense. "So," I said, "we've actually found one of their home worlds. A place they're native to. Or, maybe they've colonized this planet? It's hard to tell."

When we'd first come here, arriving in a flash and falling into orbit around this strange world, we'd had a brief chance to check the place out. I hadn't seen anything like a large city. Nothing indicated a heavily advanced world that was populated by billions.

Instead, we'd found a rather small village. The population down there couldn't be more than a thousand. That alone made the place seem more like a colony than a home world.

"Leeson!" I said. "I don't want you to shoot anybody, but I want you to line up some artillery on that village, just in case."

"Already on it, sir," he told me. "I've got plasma mortars set up and ready to go."

Our mortars didn't drop traditional explosives, but rather energy-bursting pods. We knew from experience that this particular type of alien was fairly vulnerable to plasma charges. It stunned them, threw them for a loop, and sometimes blasted pieces off them. Of course, we'd only fought their drones in the past. Maybe these living rock-creatures would respond differently. I hoped we wouldn't have to find out.

For right now, I was content to not drop any bombs on the populace, as they weren't directly threatening us. I hoped it was going to stay that way.

"Got it!" Kivi yelled suddenly.

I turned and crunched across the gravel to her. The two gateway posts were standing a meter apart. They were glowing, and I could tell they'd been activated.

"We synced up, sir," she said, getting up off her knees. "It only took me eleven minutes."

I knew from long experience that Natasha could have done it in half that time, but I praised her anyway. "Good job. Now test it."

She looked at me, startled. "Me, sir?"

"Yep. It's your gateway. You go through first."

Kivi squinted her eyes up tightly, nodded, and marched through.

A worrisome twenty seconds passed.

"She fried herself," Carlos said. "Mark my words, she frigging fried herself."

"She better not have," Sargon said, standing and coming near.

Sargon had been Kivi's long-time boyfriend, and although she did occasionally have dalliances, they seemed to have a pretty stable relationship over the years.

Carlos was probably somewhat embittered by this, as he'd been an earlier conquest of hers. The truth be told, just about everybody in the unit who'd been around long enough had known the gentle touch of Kivi.

"She set up the posts, Sargon," I told him. "If she turned herself into a hamburger by walking through… well… she's only got herself to blame."

But then Kivi stepped back onto our side of the posts. Behind her was an individual I'd hoped I'd evaded by invading this strange planet. It was none other than Raash. His blue scales glinted in the distant sunlight, making him the single most conspicuous thing in the pink and gray landscape.

"I am here," Raash stated, as if this was the most significant fact anyone had heard today. "These gateway posts must now be recalibrated to a new destination."

"What?" I asked. "Raash, first of all, what the hell are you doing here on an unsafe beachhead? Technically, you're a civilian in this legion. Secondly, what are you talking about?"

"Your orders have changed. It has been decided that you're not to drain the monkey house you call *Scorpio* of all her irritating apes. At least, not yet."

"What are you talking about, you overgrown lizard?" Harris demanded.

Raash turned and glowered at him. "It has been determined by the coalition commanders that Armel's legion of Saurians will arrive first."

"Why?" Harris demanded.

Raash stood tall, and his blue tail lifted up higher as he spoke. I could tell he was feeling prideful. "The superior performance of my species is obvious. Once this beachhead has been secured, the lesser beings will deploy in our proud wake."

I hadn't been informed of any such changes to our plans, but Raash had brought receipts. His tapper had official orders emblazoned on it.

Skimming the overly-long read, I found that Admiral Sateekas had made the call. Armel's group was coming through next.

Shrugging, I decided I didn't care. I set both Kivi and Natasha on the job of changing to the new coordinates. This took only a minute or so.

Immediately, a long column of lizards began to march through. Walking one at a time, a new soldier set foot on Crystal World about once a second. The troops were pouring onto my hilltop area very quickly.

Even at this pace, I realized it would take something like three hours to march the entirety of Armel's legion through these posts. I rubbed at my face. That seemed like too long to wait for real strength to arrive.

"We need more gateway posts," I told my techs. "And all you Saurians, stop crowding my camp. March down that hill! Everybody! Head down to the bottom, into that rocky valley."

There were some bitter-sounding hisses in response. "Who is this prey-creature who dares give us commands?" asked a lizard centurion.

Raash interposed himself between us. "He is in charge of this transport facility. You are to obey."

Making bad sounds and smells, the surly centurion led his brood downhill. After that, every lizard that appeared was directed to follow the conga-line of tails and scales downslope, off my hilltop.

Raash confronted me after this was moving smoothly. "Your solutions are substandard," he said. "Soon, the valley below will fill with Saurians. They are poorly placed."

"That's true. When your commanding officer shows up, he can deploy them as he wishes. But for now, this hilltop is my command post. Everybody is going to march in here and form a line down the slope."

Raash showed me some long, curved fangs, but the rest of his kind didn't argue. That was one good thing about Saurians. When they were of a lower rank, they were generally rather obedient.

Pissy Saurians like Raash were relatively rare, in my experience. I supposed that meant among his kind, he was a high-ranking individual. Maybe that's why he was so arrogant and constantly talking about the size of his tail.

I didn't really understand Saurian society—but then I really didn't care much about it, either. I just wanted them out of my hair. They kept marching through, and then in a winding single-file line, made their way down to the bottom of a nearby valley.

My techs had been busy while the lizard-march became smoother. They'd set up an encrypted radio connection, linking through some satellites that had been dropped into orbit by Sevens' invasion ship. Those satellites had deep-link capability, and I was soon able to contact someone back on *Scorpio*. It turned out to be Graves himself.

"McGill..." he said, "about time you reported in. What's your status?"

"Things are going pretty well, sir. We've set up the beachhead. We've got the gateway posts operating, and we've brought in about five percent of Armel's legion so far."

"Armel's legion?" he asked. "Oh... I see here a change of orders. Why didn't anyone inform me?"

I shrugged. "Mogwa command didn't tell me anything either, sir."

"Arrogant bastards... Well, that's not your fault. Give me your report. Have you encountered any resistance? Any enemy contact at all?"

"No, sir," I described the village, and I showed him a few of the streams.

He eyeballed all this sternly.

"There is one other thing, sir," I told him. "We did see a flash up in the sky above. I'm not sure if that was one of their defensive ships or not."

"That was your Nairb-driven transport," Graves told me. "They caught a blast from the enemy ground cannons and blew up shortly after you arrived."

I nodded, unsurprised. Seven had probably died when the defensive beams had locked in and nailed them. But there was some hope that he had managed to use the teleporting harness that I'd given him to escape.

I shrugged to myself. Either way, it was no longer my problem. I was in the middle of an invasion of a hostile enemy world. The most critical moment for any invading force was the first few hours. We were at our weakest right now. If the enemy could hit us before we could get organized and deployed in force onto their world, they might destroy us all.

So many things might hit us before we were set up: a simple A-bomb explosion directly overhead, for example—or they could send an aerial strike by fighter craft of some kind. There were dozens of ways the enemy could take us out before we were truly prepared to defend ourselves.

"Primus," I said, "I think we need a second set of gateway posts down here. We need to get troops deployed faster. It's going to take hours to deploy just a single legion. It'll take twelve to fifteen hours to get all of our troops onto the surface at this rate, and we'll all be bunched up."

"You're right about that. I don't like them all being in the same spot, either," Graves said. "I'm going to talk to these techs on Gray Deck. We'll send you a fresh set of gateway posts. That will double the speed with which we can deploy. Now that we know it's safe, no one's going to argue about the possible loss of some good equipment."

"Thank you, sir," I said.

"Graves out."

True to his word, less than ten minutes later, a pair of gateway posts sizzled into existence inside a cargo pod right in the middle of us.

The shipment set off squawks of alarm. A lot of light troopers were feeling jumpy, and they threw themselves down on the ground and crawled away. But when they saw that the cargo pod didn't explode—and in fact, it had the emblem of Legion Varus on the side of it, they settled down. We opened it up, and the techs began setting up a new deployment site.

Leeson whooped when he opened one of the bigger crates. "We got our first 88, boys!"

He and his weaponeers began to drag away the light field artillery.

The two tech girls went to work on the new gateway posts, but I interrupted them. "Not here," I told them. "Over there." I pointed to the next hill over.

"That's pretty far away, Centurion," Harris complained. "We don't even have enough troops to cover this hill much less two."

"Then the Saurians will defend it. You two techs," I said, speaking to Natasha and Kivi. "You're going to climb the next hill and set this rig up. I'll get Armel's group here to send a couple of Saurian units to protect you. In the meantime, I want some real eyes out there on that village. Della, Cooper—I know you're around here somewhere."

"Yes, sir—and we're way ahead of you," Cooper spoke, his voice raspy in my headset.

"That's right," Della said. "We're only about three hundred meters out from the village right now. And James, I've got to tell you something."

"What's up?" I asked her.

"Centurion... there's no one in the village anymore. All the aliens have disappeared."

Squinting, I turned back toward the village. I hadn't really checked on it for quite a while. I walked over, set my scope up, and aimed my rifle carefully, scanning the village.

"Natasha, Kivi, what about those drones?"

"We're over here setting up the posts you told us to, sir."

"Right, right. Carlos, can you operate those damned drones?"

"I can try," he said. "Oops, just crashed one."

I cursed, but I waited. Soon, I got a wobbly feed from Carlos's tapper. It was true. The village was just as weird-looking as ever. It continued to hum and operate with its strange machinery. There was some kind of bubbling metal in the center of the place. It looked almost like a mercury pool or something. It didn't seem hot, but it was definitely liquid, a shiny, molten metal.

"What the hell...?" I said. "Do these guys drink mercury?"

But although the village looked normal, exactly as it had when we first arrived, I could no longer see a single alien. The place was completely empty.

"Centurion McGill? James?" It was Della's voice in my headset, but there was a certain note of fear and worry that made me tune into her immediately.

"What's wrong, Della? Talk to me."

"It's Cooper, sir. He's... he's gone."

Frowning, I checked my tapper. I examined all my unit personnel. Sure enough, Cooper's status light was flat red. That meant he was either dead, out of range, or in some way completely removed from this operational area.

"Della," I told her, "I want you to retreat. Withdraw from that village and get back here. Circle around to our position if you can."

"Roger that." Her voice and her connection were gone. I knew she was stealthing. I hoped it worked against these aliens. I seemed to remember the Crystals weren't really concerned about our stealth tech when we were fighting their drones. I wondered if the alien civilians themselves had similar abilities to detect humans that weren't visible by normal human standards.

"Okay, unit," I said, making an announcement over the tactical chart. "We've had our first casualty. I want everybody on alert. Keep your eyes open and your weapons hot. Check your six every five seconds. We have no idea what happened to Cooper—he's just plain gone."

-33-

Suddenly, I sensed a large stinky presence on my own six. "You should destroy that village, McGill," Raash said. "I do not understand why you hesitate. Any rational predator would have struck the moment the enemy was spotted."

"Because they're civilians, Raash," I told him. "Not all aliens are combatants, and they haven't shown any hostile intent. By the Legion's standard rules of engagement, I have no cause to harm them."

Raash pointed a long-clawed finger downslope to the west. "Is that sufficient cause?" he asked.

Following his gesture, I saw strange humping shapes. It was almost as if the ground itself were boiling up, then flattening out again. I knew in an instant what it had to be. The enemy slug-creatures were coming toward us, upslope. They'd probably encircled this entire hill by now.

"Your foolishness will get us all killed! What crime did I commit in my egg to deserve such a monkey-brained leader!"

Alarmed and worried that Raash might be right, I contacted Kivi and Natasha. I messaged them directly and asked if they'd gotten the second gateway posts going yet. They were about a kilometer away, on another hilltop. They informed me they were having trouble with it. The coordinate settings seemed to go to a destination point they were unfamiliar with, rather than *Scorpio's* Gray Deck.

"Don't worry about that," I said. "They've been changing things on us all along at the high end of this command chain.

Just align them, turn them on, and let's see what the hell walks through."

"Having a little trouble, McGill?" asked an unwelcome voice.

Another man stood to my side. It was none other than Tribune Maurice Armel. He was a tough-minded but foppish sort, with a whispery mustache and a permanently engraved sneer on his face. He was so French in both looks and attitude, it was kind of cringe-worthy.

"Ah," I said, spotting him, "about time you showed up. I noticed you didn't come through the gateway at the head of your legion."

Armel snorted at me. "The very concept is absurd. I sent a full cohort of these lizards through first to see if it was safe. Just like your Primus Graves—I don't see him here yet."

I had to concede the point, so I moved on. "Armel, we've got enemies coming up this hill. At least, I don't think they're part of the neighborhood welcome-wagon."

"And you, of course, want my Saurian troops to intercede?"

There was gunfire going off now. My troops hadn't yet been ordered to fire upon the advancing horde of slug-creatures, but I found it difficult to fault their presumption.

"Permission to fire belchers, sir?" Leeson asked.

"All right, fire off your belchers, but not at the village. No mortaring that village, either."

Leeson cursed a bit, but he didn't argue. A lot of heavy beaming noises began to come from the front line, the top of the ridge, which was less than a hundred meters distance from the gateway posts where Armel and I stood having our conversation.

Armel checked his tapper. "According to my drone feed," he said, "there are better than a thousand of the enemy. You will soon be overwhelmed, even if they don't have ranged weaponry."

"All right, all right," I said. "Get your lizards up here. We could use some help."

"Ah! There, that's it! The fearful request for aid that I've been expecting. Could you possibly put a 'please' on top of that?"

I gritted my teeth. This guy just couldn't make anything easy for anyone.

"*Please...*" I said in a growling voice.

He beamed a big smile at me as if he'd scored some kind of point. Then he made a sweeping gesture with his arm.

Almost instantly, something like two hundred Saurian troops rushed up from the valley where I'd been sending them this entire time. Two full units appeared, and there was no way he hadn't set them all up for this dramatic shithead moment.

The lizards took up flanking positions around my own troops, and everybody squeezed in together on the hilltop. The firing soon intensified. The Saurian troops seemed to have brought mostly short-range shotgun-type weaponry, something suitable for fighting enemies in stardust armor like the Rigellians—or possibly crystalline drones.

I had to figure, though, that their guns should work well on these dirt-creatures.

"There you go," Armel said. "You have your reinforcements."

I nodded and trotted to the front lines.

At first, the battle was something of a turkey shoot. The enemy seemed to lack ranged weaponry entirely. This made sense, as the village they'd come from seemed to be a civilian settlement. Our attackers clearly weren't military in nature. Hopefully, that meant they wouldn't be as difficult to injure as the crystal drones had been back on Jungle World.

Still, watching plasma bolts pop small chunks of rock and dirt off them, I had to admit they were still tougher than any human that had ever lived. They also moved quickly, and they seemed very determined.

"You see this bullshit right here?" Harris began telling me. "If one ant from another colony walks into a colony full of ants that are hostile to him, why, they'd all go berserk and tear his ass apart, right? Sure, you've got your soldier ants, but that doesn't mean the workers won't attack just as fiercely."

"What's your point, Harris?"

"This enemy... they don't have civvies. Not really. No more than an ant colony has civvies."

I turned away from him and watched the battle going on downslope. If you could call it a battle. We were gunning them down as fast as we could, but still, they kept humping forward. There were broken-off chunks of the creatures that looked like gemstones or lumps of dirty quartz. Every time we shot one, bits like that flew away from the enemy aliens. Their bodies dribbled dirt the way ours leaked blood, too.

In order to stop one completely, it seemed like you had to blow about half of its mass away from the rest of its body. At that point, it was no longer capable of locomotion.

The slaughter seemed like a sickening waste, but there wasn't anything in the hearts of these aliens other than a fierce desire to reach our lines and destroy us.

Harris himself moved up to the ridgeline, and he aimed his heavy morph-rifle. He began firing off shots rapidly into the approaching forms. He laughed as he did so, clearly enjoying himself. There was nothing more delightful than a helpless enemy to Adjunct Harris. He liked winning—especially if he was winning easily.

But then, just as I began to think we had matters cleanly in hand, the situation changed. The gateway posts in the midst of our encampment were undergoing some kind of adjustment by Kivi. I had to think that Natasha had probably ordered her here to get her out of her hair on that second hill.

Whatever the case, the posts which we'd so carefully set up upon our arrival were suddenly disrupted. There was a loud buzz and a snapping sound. The post on the right ceased functioning.

One of the posts suddenly jumped into the frigging air. An electrical arc jolted up between the post and the rocky ground, startling everyone. It burned like a lightning bolt.

This electrical arc went right through Kivi, who was right there, kneeling on the hilltop with her tools out. She was blown to a smoldering heap by the discharge.

"Holy shit..." I said, stunned.

How had the enemy...?

A Saurian trooper had been traversing between the posts at that very moment. He was just one of thousands who were lined up to march through the gateway—but it wasn't his lucky day.

The poor lizard's body was sheared in half when the posts were disrupted. Half of his body was left back on his transport ship, and half was here. That was the kind of thing that happened when the connection between two sets of posts failed unexpectedly.

There was a splattering sound, and gore flew everywhere. It was as if a bucket of paint had exploded. It was enough to make a grown man wince.

"What the hell happened?" Harris demanded. He was at my side, gaping at the scene. "How'd they get all the way up here to our posts?"

"Foolish humans," Raash admonished us, pointing at the ground. "See that hump in the dirt? They dig. They've dug up into our midst!"

It was true. There was a hump now, a hump of earth that was at least a half meter higher than the flat ground the posts had been sitting upon. One of those posts had been lifted up into the air, which had disconnected it from its brother. The resulting discharge had killed two of our troops within less than a second's time.

The sinister hump transformed into one of the alien Silicoids. It reared up to confront the hundreds of troops that surrounded it. More humps were here and there.

"Over there, you see that?" Raash pointed. "There's another one!"

There were at least six, seven… no, eight of them now.

"Heavies!" I shouted. "Pull back from the walls. Move to the center. Form a reserve. Kill every hump you see. Lance it with your force blades. No shooting, no grenades. We don't want any blue-on-blue, here."

Well-disciplined, Harris's group pulled back from the ridgeline where they'd been firing and cackling at the approaching enemy hordes. They gathered in the middle and began stabbing at the growing humps of earth.

Somehow, the Silicoid creatures were capable of moving themselves through loose ground. It seemed like they weren't appearing where there was a hard, rocky slab, but only in areas with loose gravel and dirt.

Fortunately, their sneak attacks weren't a super-fast process. When they moved underground, they seemed to move with much less speed than when they humped over the surface. That gave us time to spot one, run over to the spot, and stab and hack at it with force blades, tearing chunks off the beast before it could break through and attack.

Occasionally, one of these invaders sank back down again with a hissing, foul stench. Then the ground would revert to being nothing but simple dirt again. But in most cases, they forced themselves upward, seeming only to accelerate. Our attacks only goaded them into faster action—or even a berserker rage.

The men squared-off, fighting with the Silicoids. The aliens reached out with pods, smashing at my troops and forming rocky fangs at the top of their bodies. I supposed these openings in the monsters might be considered a mouth—or perhaps better termed would be a maw.

They attempted to lunge and bite. Occasionally, this was successful. If a troop was unable to dodge, or if he tripped and fell and was caught, he was often doomed. They latched onto legs—or worse, heads.

I watched as a light trooper, taken by surprise on the ridge, was swallowed, squalling until he disappeared into one of those maws. Such attacks were almost always fatal, even though other troops gathered around trying to help. They cursed and stabbed and tore at the monsters. But they were rarely able to kill it before limbs were severed from the victim. This left troops to die, screaming in a churning puddle of mud and gore.

"You see this?" Harris said to me. "I told you we should have bombed that village first thing!"

I frowned and did not respond. I had to admit, Raash and Harris might have been right in the end. This wasn't the kind of enemy I was used to. It was the furthest thing from a mammal, and not even along the same evolutionary path as a reptile. No, even an insect would have been more relatable.

These Silicoids, as the Nairb Seven called them, weren't even carbon-based. They didn't drink water, and I doubted they felt pain. The Wur seemed normal by comparison.

They had to be the most alien enemy I'd yet to encounter.

-34-

The Saurians really had to flood in to help us before the battle was finished. Armel had ordered his first cohort, which was finely organized and ready to participate functionally in the battle, to sweep around and flank east. Once in position, they charged and went into close combat with the numerous, dirt-humping slugs that were rolling uphill at us. Surprised by our determined resistance, the last of the villagers broke and fled.

Armel and I surveyed the damage when the battle was over. He was walking around executing the last living, flopping villagers by setting off plasma grenades on their bodies.

I didn't like this much, and I rushed up to him, shouting and waving my hands. "Hey, hey, hey!" I yelled. "What are you doing?"

"Finishing the job that they started, McGill."

"Hey, Tribune, I know you don't want me to tell you your business—"

"Finally, you speak words I agree with. You are highly intuitive in this particular instance."

"Well, sir... I just gotta say, these are technically civvies. At least they're what passes for a civvy on this strange planet. We really shouldn't—"

He held up a gloved hand in my face. "Cease speaking, Centurion. I'm already sick of your sniveling. I've heard it all before, and I refuse to hear it again. These aliens aren't a harmless species of rodent, or sweet birds of paradise. Nor are they even as unlovely as a Nairb, or as disgusting as the spider-like Mogwa. No, they are further from us than even the Wur. At least plant-creatures have multicellular body structures. They may not have brains, most of them, but you can talk to them after a fashion. Not so with these beasts!"

He kicked the squirming pile of ash and dirt at his feet. A tendril of smoke came up from the dead alien. It had finally given up the ghost. "Your sympathies are completely misplaced with this strange Silicoid being. If it is alive at all, in even a technical sense, I assure you it feels no pain. It has no anguish. It probably doesn't even have any young to speak of."

"You don't know any of that, sir," I said, getting angry. "We don't know enough about these aliens to write them off as devils."

"Surely you jest! Must I demonstrate?"

"Uh…"

He didn't wait for an answer. He walked over to another alien that was flopping about. "Here, here's another one. It's not dead yet, McGill. Have a fruitful discussion with it. I will watch."

"Uh…"

"Well? Go on! I have already prepared myself to be astounded."

I scratched a bit, having no clue as to how to proceed. He threw his hands high and walked away, grumbling.

I knelt by the flopping, mortally wounded alien. I did have to admit I had no idea how to talk to it. I tried the Imperial translator buried in my tapper, an app that was generally successful in allowing me to converse with any alien species in the Empire. That covered most of the galaxy at large—but this thing was an exception.

My tapper didn't even recognize whatever rasping sounds it was making. It sounded like two stones grating on one another. Were those words? I had no idea.

Nor could I detect any radio transmissions, organized releases of gas… nothing. I tried scanning for patterns of stinks. I tried drawing a few symbols on the ground with sticks. I tried it all.

These guys were even harder to talk to than the Machine World aliens had been. I'd attempted to communicate with those guys, and I'd eventually succeeded—but that was long ago. The Machine World aliens were essentially sentient robots of a primitive sort. You could scratch pictograms into the ground to get some kind of conversation going with them. But with this thing, a pile of moving dirt, I wasn't sure how to even begin.

I remembered the Wur. I'd spoken to them, too. You essentially had to set up a blood transfusion to talk to those guys.

With my hands on my hips, I sensed—and then smelled—a foul presence behind me. "Hey Raash," I said, "you got any ideas?"

"Yes," Raash said, "I always have excellent ideas. In this instance, I recommend that you humans retire and return to Earth."

"Yeah? Why's that?"

"It has become obvious to me from today's battle that you are an inefficient and ineffective force against these aliens."

"What are you talking about? We whooped their asses good enough from what I can see."

"Is it not obvious? Even someone such as yourself, who possesses the brain of a lemur, should have come to certain realizations by now."

"Spell it out for me, Raash."

He helpfully lifted up a fist full of claws. He began flicking up one claw at a time, flipping his long, curved talons in my direction as he spoke. "Firstly, I have heard great tell of how dangerous these Crystal aliens were on Jungle World. How you were nearly defeated by them. Now, we have met them in battle, and we have brushed them all aside."

I opened my mouth to object, but he had already flicked out a second talon. This was effectively his middle finger, and it was up in my face as he spoke. "Secondly, you have been told not to wear metal, and yet you all have metal weapons. Our Saurian troops are much more effective. We employ simple beam tubes, with barely any metal content at all. Our harnesses are leather. And with our diamond-reinforced talons, we were able to rip apart the enemy. We can fight them almost on an equal basis. Two Saurians in hand-to-hand are always enough to destroy a single Silicoid."

He was bragging, of course. I knew this to be false. I'd seen five, six, even eight Saurians at a time, all tearing at the same Silicoid. Frequently, they'd lost one of their own in the process, too.

I put my hands on my hips and glared at him.

"Lastly," Raash said, flipping up his third finger, "you have been whimpering nonstop about the natural butchery of battle. Who would not finish off an enemy such as this? Something so alien it deserves not even my urine!"

Here he went over and whizzed on the dying creature we were standing over. The urine stream steamed and formed mud in the creature's massive wounds. Sure, those rips just looked like cracks in the stony body. But still, I figured this was pretty damn disrespectful to a dying soldier.

I couldn't help myself. I got a bit angry and kicked him right in the tailfeathers. Actually, my boot went up under his tail, because he had no feathers.

Raash gave a strange snorting sound and hopped forward, almost sprawling upon the alien and the piss-mud he'd made.

"Oh no!" I said. "I'm so sorry about that, Raash. My foot must have slipped. The gravity's all different here, you know?"

Raash leapt up, whirled around, and went into a fighting stance. He flung wide those talons he'd been lecturing me with.

Raash was angry, and I honestly couldn't blame him. "So," he said, "you assault an ally while his back is turned? Is that the state of dishonor in—?"

"All right, all right, Raash," I said. "I shouldn't have kicked you. But you don't have to piss on that dying alien. Have a little respect."

The alien finally stopped squirming and flopping about. His crumbling dirt transformed into a lifeless ash heap. I wondered about that death-drama. Raash stared at it as well.

"Did you see that?" I asked. "As this thing died, it seemed to lose its form..."

"It was the power of my urine," Raash declared. "The monster was overcome and welcomed the final sleep."

I wrinkled my nose because Raash's piss did indeed always put up a nasty odor. Combined with the alien's remains, it was pretty overpowering. It had to be that sulfurous soil mixed with the ultimate unpleasantness of Raash's body wastes.

"I'm saying that we just saw it crumble as it died," I said. "Whatever holds these things together, whatever makes this dirt seem like it's alive, must also keep their bodies in one piece."

"As I said, the monster was overcome by my bodily essence."

I shook my head. Raash was pretty hopeless in situations like this. He was less understanding than even your average alien when it came to compassion. He never seemed to worry about retribution, either.

"Humans have a concept known as karma, Raash," I told him. "Evil deeds result in evil events befalling the perpetrator."

"What does that mean, McGill? Are you cursing me? Are you casting a monkey-curse upon me?"

"Yeah… well…" I said. "If you want to think about it that way. What goes around comes around. You've abused these creatures, and mark my words, before this campaign is over, they will abuse you in a similar fashion."

Raash looked troubled. He stared down at the smoking, crumbling corpse. He hissed and displayed his teeth. When a Saurian did something that looked like a grin, it wasn't because he was happy. It was a show of long curved fangs—the very picture of anger and threat.

I didn't care. I left him out there to ponder what I'd said and marched back up the hill to our encampment.

"What's Raash doing to that alien?" Carlos asked me.

"I don't know," I said. "Maybe he's going to make mud pies or something."

"That's just sick. Hey, McGill—you've got to come see this."

"What?"

"I've caught one."

"One what?"

"I've got one of the *aliens*, dude!"

I stared at him and followed in his wake. He led me over to what wasn't an entire alien—or maybe it was only a baby one, I wasn't sure.

"You see this?" he said. "What happened was it squirmed out of one of these holes they were drilling, see. Then it wormed its way onto that big slate slab over there."

He pointed and I looked at a large flat stone. "Yeah, so?"

"And then some of the heavies slashed the shit out of it. This part became separated from the rest of it—the main part got off the slab and got away."

I nodded, getting the picture. "Weird that it can live while in pieces…"

"Yeah, freaky huh? So, the part that stayed right here on top of the slate slab, I trapped with this box. It's a puff-crete crate, there's no way it can dig through that."

I looked at the box, which was indeed shivering. We opened the lid of the crate and looked inside. A strange, slug-like creature was squirming around in there. It was about a meter long with perhaps the total mass of a large dog. It wormed its way around in circles inside the crate.

"It seems dumber than the other ones," Carlos said, poking at it with a stick.

"Leave it alone, Carlos. It might be a baby."

"It's not a baby. It's part of one of these adults. They left it behind, like I said."

"So strange…"

Natasha, Kivi, and some other bios soon gathered around and were discussing it. They filmed the alien and transmitted the information up to *Scorpio* for analysis.

"It is odd," Natasha said to me, "that part of these creatures can be severed from the rest of its body and still retain some level of functionality. I'm starting to wonder if these creatures that we've been battling are really separate beings at all."

"What?"

"I'm saying," she said patiently, "that they seem more like a colony—a reef of living individuals functioning as parts of a single unit."

"A colony… like how?"

"Yes. They might even be organic. With cells, like we have."

"What are you talking about? It's frigging dirt."

"Maybe..." she said, "but do you see how it's behaving? It's definitely less intelligent than one of the other aliens. The full-size ones have more brains and more capabilities."

"That's true," Carlos said. "This thing can't even crawl out of a box."

"Right. What I'm thinking, James, is these things may not be entirely abiotic."

"I'm still not getting it," I said, because I wasn't.

"Well, it's like this. What if some kind of bacteria evolved to grow in dirt? Something that wrapped itself into soil, rocks—whatever."

"Okay, that's pretty normal."

"Right. But what if colonies of these bacteria were able to cooperate? To act together? Think about our own bodies. We're multicellular, right?"

"Uh... sure," I said, barely knowing what she was talking about.

"But how do your brain cells tell your hand how to move? Well, they've got to talk to other cells, right? So, even we are just interconnected masses of cells. What if you had a creature that was built of many more independent cells that were somehow bonded together with earth?"

I stared at the squirming alien. It didn't look too bright. "So, if we cut into this thing, we're going to find like a brain stem, or a spine, or something?"

"I don't think so. I think the cells are encrusted in the earth. They're like one with the earth. Maybe they're even silicon-based multicellular organisms. We really have to get out microscopes and other serious gear to study these things."

I raised a finger. "You know, I've got just the person that should be in on this. I'll call her on the deep-link."

And I did so. I gathered all the information we'd put together and sent it off to Centurion Evelyn Thompson, who was my long-time-ago ex-girlfriend. I just knew she'd get big eyes over this weird alien species.

Evelyn was the one who'd done all the bioanalysis on the ape-aliens of Jungle World. She'd figured out that they were related to the dogmen, and that the Clavers were in fact breeding both and using them as foot soldiers.

If there was some kind of weird life driving these Silicoid beasties, well, Evelyn was my go-to gal. She would figure it out if anyone could. She was the most senior biologist we had in Legion Varus.

Besides, she and I had gotten kind of close during the Jungle World campaign… and I wouldn't mind having an excuse to see her again.

-35-

"Well, McGill?" Carlos asked me.

"Well, what?"

"Can I keep him?"

"Keep what? You mean this alien? No way. He's not a pet, Carlos."

"Oh, come on... Can I at least have a souvenir or two?"

"A souvenir? What are you talking about?"

Carlos knelt and dug out a sharp-looking chisel from a tech toolkit. Natasha immediately squawked about that, but he ignored her.

He reached into the puff-crete crate and, using the butt of his laser pistol as a tap hammer, he began chiseling at the back of the squirming crystalline alien.

"What in the nine hells are you doing, Specialist?" I asked.

"Just a second, almost done."

Suspecting the worst, I plucked him up into the air, taking away the chisel and his laser pistol. I looked at the alien and realized that a small shiny chunk had been broken off it.

"Can I have my new souvenir back, sir?"

"No! What is that you chipped off him?"

"Well... I think it might be diamond," Carlos admitted. "That's gotta be around two hundred carats, McGill. I could cut you in for part of it."

"Goddamn it."

I turned him around, gave him a kick in the ass, and threw his laser pistol after him. He got back to his feet and walked away, grumbling.

Carlos had always been a man easily swayed by possible wealth gathered on the battlefield. He was willing to do the gathering by any illicit means possible.

Natasha was incensed when she learned of this latest depredation by my chief bio specialist.

"That's just awful," she said. "You've got to keep him away from the poor thing, James. No creature deserves that sort of treatment. Technically, it's a prisoner of war. In fact, it looks kind of like an *infant* prisoner of war."

"Okay, whatever. We'll get Evelyn down here, and she'll classify it as soon as she's able."

While all this excitement was going on, the entirety of Armel's Saurian legion had finally been completely deployed to the battlefield. Accordingly, Graves contacted me again with new orders as to how to change the gateway posts.

Each time we got a legion off the invasion ships, I was charged with connecting them to a different transport. The key was to keep the troops flowing. We needed every soldier we could get down here, disgorging them from the ships as quickly as possible.

The cool part was our ships weren't in danger as they unloaded. Staying a safe distance from Crystal World and using the gateways was quite a neat trick. Blood World had once used the same technique to invade Earth long ago.

"It's gotta be time for Legion Varus to deploy, right Primus Graves, sir?" I said. "We're more than ready. I'll have Natasha adjust the coordinates, and—"

"Belay that, McGill. You are to connect to the Claver ship next."

"What?" I squawked. "The frigging Clavers? Are you serious? This place stinks to high heaven as it is, sir. We've got sulfur-holes, some kind of weird dirt-aliens, stinking lizards—"

"Shut up, McGill. Winslade and Admiral Sateekas have made the decision. It's their call. I didn't make these decisions, but I'm going to follow the orders my commanders have given me. We're putting the ape-aliens and the dogmen into the field next. Make it happen."

"But sir," I complained, "they've got to be the worst troops in this entire coalition. How are they going to fight these dirt aliens? If they throw spears at them, they're just going to ignore it."

"They won't be using spears. Not this time, anyway. Don't worry about it. That's all been planned out by your superiors. Have Natasha connect to the Claver ship and stand aside. These troops have orders to come through hard and fast."

I thought about that, and I realized these instructions were concerning. After all, the ape-aliens and the dogmen were capable of running on all fours at speeds that were at least double that of a human…

They also lacked any awareness they were being disintegrated when they went through the gateway posts. I had no doubt that they would come through, maybe two—or even three a second. If they kept up that flow rate, the whole legion might be able to form in an hour or so.

"All right, we're doing it," I told Graves, and he signed off.

Natasha grumbled as she worked again on the gateway posts, assigning them to new coordinates. She soon had them connected and syncing-up. On the distant Claver transporter, another set of gateway posts were glowing into life.

I figured Natasha was complaining because she wanted to play with the captured baby alien we had in our puff-crete crate. She'd been working like a dog ever since we got to this planet.

Meanwhile, our combat soldiers were lounging, laughing, taking pisses off the side of the mountaintop, and generally goofing off as there were no aliens in sight.

My tapper buzzed again. After several minutes had gone by, the girls still had not gotten the link to the Claver ship operating yet.

"McGill?" Graves said, "What's your defensive status?"

"I'd say we're doing pretty well, sir. There was an assault by the locals, but they failed to take us out. Now that Armel's full legion is here, I'm feeling pretty secure. We've got two sets of gateway posts going, and—"

"Listen McGill, we've got bad reports coming in. Some eyes were placed in the sky by the Nairb ship before it was destroyed. Many of those satellites have been located and destroyed—but a few are still functional. One of those units is relaying a shocking signal to me right now."

"Uh…"

"Check your tapper, Centurion. The feed should be coming in live about now."

"Oh… right, sir," I said, "and I'm very thankful for that."

"Shut up and listen. After reviewing the previous battle you had with the locals, we began scanning for other settlements. There's a rather large one directly to the north of your beachhead."

"A large settlement? Uh… how far away are we talking?"

"Maybe twenty kilometers."

I nodded. The first one had been only two kilometers away. That meant we should have some time—but we'd been out here for hours. "Okay… and what's the headcount in this 'large settlement?'"

"Guesstimating, my techs say the civilian population should number no more than a hundred thousand."

"Whoa!" I whistled, "that's a whole lot of dirt clods they're fixing to throw our way!"

Graves gave me his disappointed-dad look. "Dirt clods? You've already created a pejorative for this new enemy, McGill? That's simply unprofessional, especially in a mid-ranking officer."

"I'm sorry, sir. These things just come natural to me."

"All right, whatever. I just wanted to alert you that the enemy to your north may be on the move."

"Uh, hold on, sir," I said, before he could sign off. "What makes you think they might be on the move?"

"Well, shortly after doing a rough count on the alien population and the general size of the city…"

He kept on talking after that, but I'd stopped listening. All of a sudden, I'd come to realize they were calling it a *city* now, not a village. That by itself was alarming.

"— and the city now seems to be entirely empty of inhabitants."

I blinked once, then I blinked twice.

"Oh shit," I said, "Sir, we need more troops down here! Right now!"

Right then, Natasha shouted out good news. "I've got the sequence! Troops incoming!"

Once again, the gateway posts flared into life. Three seconds later, dark furry shapes began racing out of it. There were ape-aliens at first, then a dogman. About one of every ten was a dogman, I soon realized.

The dogmen were clearly in charge. Some even wore clothes and shouted orders at the ape-aliens—orders that sounded like barks and grunts to me. The dogmen were actually operating as officers and non-coms for the ape-aliens.

I shook my head. I knew that your typical dogman had a lower level of intelligence than your average human—and the ape-aliens were even below that. But they were capable enough. I'd seen dogmen fly helicopters, that sort of thing.

The ape-aliens... well... they were pretty much gorillas with a few extra brain cells—but not a huge number of them. Smart enough to ambush you, smart enough to fight tactically as a group, but they'd never developed technologically past the invention of a grass hut, a fishhook, or maybe a net. As far as I knew, they didn't even have boats. They just swam across rivers when they had to.

Still, they were big, they were strong, and there was a hell of a lot of them. They were flowing between the posts without any direction until they got here. The dogmen took over, directing the troops downslope to a pre-designated position that I had nothing to do with. There was a veritable river of furred, round-shouldered, squatty aliens rushing by.

They went right over the top of my men if they got in the way. Harris was shooing away his heavies so they wouldn't become injured.

"Stay the hell out the way of these crazy apes!" he kept shouting at his men, waving big hands. "They'll run your ass right over as soon as look at you."

"Sooner, I'd say," Veteran Moller complained. She was climbing back to her feet, complaining because the onrush of furry shapes had essentially chosen to run right over her, trampling her until she got out of the way by rolling. Cursing and brushing herself off, she went the long way around the gateway posts and came to my position.

Moller marveled at the flood of furry figures. "This rate of deployment is pretty impressive."

"Yeah, they hit like linebackers too, don't they?"

"I didn't mean that, sir," she said. "I mean the rate at which these guys are taking the field—that has to mean they're seriously organized upstairs. They must be lined up in a queue all the way through the guts of their transport ship. The Clavers sure know how to make their boys move out."

She had a glint in her eye as she said this, and I knew she was admiring Claver's style. Her own lights and heavies were a surly lot. They'd never throw caution to the wind and race into an unknown environment like that—at least, not without a lot of rump-kicking and complaining.

"Oh…" I said, "I guess you're right about that. Legion Varus men would never go this fast. We'd come through at a jog, maybe…"

Moller watched the unbroken stream and shook her thick-necked head. "You think the Clavers are standing behind these guys with electric lashes, Centurion? I mean… like cracking whips on any red-assed alien who doesn't move fast enough for their tastes?"

I nodded. "That's quite possible, Veteran. Quite possible."

Thinking about what Graves had told me, I decided to contact Armel. He was, in fact, in charge of the largest organized force on Crystal World at the moment. I warned him that it was possible about a hundred thousand of the enemy were on the march toward our position.

"That's very alarming news, McGill," Armel said. "I got a report from Graves, but I wasn't given details on the numbers. I shall configure my troops on the southern flank. I want you to redirect Claver's apes to the north. Place them directly in the enemy's path."

"Hold on, sir," I said. "You're going to make us take point with a few hundred apes?"

"May I remind you, McGill, that I'm currently the highest-ranking officer on this planet? That places me in charge of the distribution of forces."

"No arguments there, sir, but we're the ones on this hilltop with the gateway posts. Sure, we're pouring out ape-aliens and dogmen at a terrific pace, but we need at least an hour to get them all through. Then they'll need another hour after that to get organized."

"I see your point... It is well taken, and it is my unwelcome duty to protect your position until Claver's animals are completely deployed. *Merde...*" he said, and I could pretty much figure out what that must mean in French.

He disconnected, and I sweated for a few minutes, but then he called me back. "All right, I had intended to retreat to a highly rocky area so the aliens wouldn't be able to dig up in the midst of my troops by swimming through the earth. But instead, I am swinging my forces to the north. They will deploy in front of your position."

"I'll remember you in my prayers for this, Armel!" I told him.

He made an unhappy face and signed off without so much as a thank-you.

The next half-hour was tense. The ape-aliens kept coming through with their occasional dogmen taskmasters sprinkled among their ranks. I hadn't seen a damned Claver yet—but then, when about four thousand of the primitives were milling around in a valley to the south, the flow stopped. A man came walking through the posts alone.

He was a Prime, and he looked bored. He immediately walked over to me and pointed a big finger in my direction.

"As I live and breathe!" Claver said, "it's the biggest moron in the sky, James McGill! I haven't seen you for ages."

I blinked and squinted at this Claver. "Uh..." I said, "didn't we just talk up on the transport ship? At that meeting, remember?"

He laughed at me, putting his thumbs into his belt loops and leaning back so he could bray louder.

"You big dummy," he said. "I'm not a Claver Prime. I'm Claver-X."

Then I got it. Claver-X was a special type of Claver. A man who, unlike his brothers and his sole sister, had a mind of his own, so to speak. He was slightly more pleasant, slightly more agreeable, and less treacherous than the majority of his kind.

He was also a known horn-dog. He had, in fact, created Abigail Claver, the only female among his countless brothers. Among his own family members, he was persona non grata. They had it in for him, and most of them wanted him dead.

I smiled, walked forward, and clapped a hand into his. We shook, and we grinned at each other.

"Claver-X!" I said, shaking my head. "I thought you must have died the final death by now. I haven't seen you for a decade."

"It's been a long time, all right," he said. "But I'm still around."

"Ice World," I said, shaking a finger at him. "I think that's the last time I met up with you."

He nodded. "Yeah, that's right."

"You got waxed on Ice World. They figured out who you were, and they nailed you."

He nodded grimly. "Yeah. Not this time, though. No Claver Prime is going to come along to shoot me in the back. Not today."

"How are you so sure, X?"

He smiled again. "Because I'm the only Claver on this planet, and that's not changing. This is *my* legion. This whole show is mine to command as I will. No one else from my family is coming to this party."

"Oh..." I said, impressed.

Old X was right. If his brothers weren't here, they sure as hell couldn't shoot him in the back. I watched as he went off to marshal his troops. He was a smart one, all right.

Later, the sun began to sink in what we'd decided to call the West. I was happy to see it go. We had night-vision gear, after all, and the sun on this planet was one of those glaring, painful, headache-inducing types of suns.

It was an F-class, a white star. It was distant, sure, but those stars were always a bit more intense. It was like the difference between looking at some tram's high beams and the soft, flickering yellow glow of a lantern. On Earth, the mornings were blue, while the afternoons were dominated by reddish tones. Here on Crystal World, the light was blue all the time.

My timer went off on my tapper, and I glanced toward the gateway posts. To my surprise, they were still spitting out ever more dark-furred shapes. They never seemed to stop coming.

"There's no end to these furry bastards," I commented. "We must have seen ten thousand or more so far."

Natasha came near, and she gave me a more detailed count.

"I set up a counter," she said. "It's been counting feet and shapes since they began coming through. Actually... I'm seeing twelve thousand eight-hundred eighty-two... make that about twelve thousand nine hundred, now."

"Okay, I get it," I said. "That's a damned big number. There are more apes south of us now than all Legion Varus, I think."

"Yes, that's correct, and they're still coming through at the same pace."

"I think we'll go have a talk with Claver."

Claver-X, naturally, was quite busy. Being the only human riding herd on no less than thirteen thousand aliens—a number that was growing by the minute—he had quite a lot of talking to do. Ordering dogmen this way and that, he had taken up a position to the rear of our hill.

Using my rifle scope, I swept the field, full-circle. We were now completely encircled by friendly troops. That was a nice change. Armel had pulled back his cohorts of lizards to the north again. I couldn't fault him. I wanted coverage on every flank. After all, we couldn't be sure where the next alien attack would come from.

"Hey, X," I called out.

"What is it, dummy?" he said back in a not-unfriendly tone.

"How damned many of these furballs do you have on that ship of yours?"

He laughed. "About twenty thousand of the apes and fifteen hundred of the dogmen."

"Oh, wow," I said. "That's insane. That's really a big group."

He shrugged. "They tend to die fast."

I couldn't argue that point. It felt strange to me that he should have only one top officer—one Claver, trying to ride herd on something like twenty-two thousand alien troops. I shrugged. It seemed crazy, but it wasn't my problem.

"Any sign of the clod-hoppers yet?" I asked.

"Nope," he said. "Every time a pebble falls off one of these boulders, all my apes jump around and tell me about it—but so far, I don't think a single one of them has died."

"That's a frigging miracle."

I went on and checked on Armel next. I asked him about the status of his gateway posts and asked if we could rewire them to get more troops.

"Absolutely not, McGill," he said. "We're using that set of posts purely for supplies now."

Again, I could not fault his logic. We had to feed this army. We had to give them the ammo, explosives—everything they needed. They couldn't just sleep on the rocks. We needed tents, all kinds of stuff. Even medical gear.

That's what was flowing out of the second set of posts even now. We had troops coming out of the one on my hilltop, while the other hilltop was overflowing with equipment.

"In fact," Armel said, "I think it only makes sense that Claver should use his stinking brutes to gather and transport the gear I'm providing."

I thought about telling him that his sorry-assed lizards stank as well, at least as badly as the apes, but I passed on the idea. Instead, I relayed the request to Claver-X. To my surprise, he agreed.

Soon, whole companies of ape-aliens were transporting massive loads on their backs. They carried countless puff-crete crates to supply the growing army we had placed here.

Heavy equipment was coming through now as well. I was glad to see force-dome equipment, anti-air mini missiles, automated defensive cannons, and all kinds of sophisticated technological gear being brought out and set up. Mostly, the setup was being done by the Saurians and the dogmen, but the apes were doing the carrying, transporting, and placement. The whole thing was working pretty smoothly.

Soon, it would be difficult to take us out with a single bomb dropped from above. I was, in fact, somewhat surprised the aliens hadn't tried something like that. Or maybe something more sophisticated, like an air attack or gravity beam system, but I shrugged. It was best not to look a gift horse in the mouth.

When the second alien attack on our hilltop position finally did come, it was dark out. Some of my men had set up tents. They were cooking their rations, using bubbling pots on artificially heated stone.

The oldest trick in the true starman's book was to take your laser pistol out, burn it for five seconds on the right kind of stone, then put your pot on top. That would bring water to a boil within a minute. Every now and then, of course, you had to lift the pot and give the rock a couple more zaps. Then you'd put it back down again when the stone was glowing hot.

-36-

Night fell hard on Crystal World. It was moonless and dark. People settled down in tents under the stars.

We Legion Varus types felt relatively secure. After all, we were in the middle of a growing formation of troops. We had the high ground, and the outer perimeter of our beachhead reached for a kilometer or more in every direction.

More importantly, my unit held the most protected position. We had literally twenty thousand apes to the south and ten thousand Saurians to the north. No one expected any trouble.

The two gateway posts were still buzzing continuously. Instead of churning out troops now, they were both flowing supplies and heavy equipment. Tons of complex gear, munitions, and food arrived every minute. The transport ships were unloading everything we'd need for an extended campaign on this desolate planet.

Right now, the Claver ships were sending down masses of strange fruits. Most of these consisted of big, brown, spiky gourds. There were also some green, bulbous melons. These looked like grapes the size of cantaloupes and grew strung along something that resembled the branches of a tree. I guessed that was how the ape-aliens liked to package things. The food looked exotic and tasty. Just the kind of thing a jungle creature might eat.

Despite this relatively peaceful scene, all was not well. As soon as we dared to relax and hope for the best, the minute we weren't filled with paranoia and fear—things went wrong.

Maybe the enemy sensed our calm. Who knows? But the long and short of it was—we were attacked.

"My crate just tipped over!" shouted Carlos. "They're back!"

It was true. His puff-crete crate had spilled over. At first, I thought perhaps his captured little alien was escaping.

Then I heard Carlos squealing like a stuck pig. "They're back! They're back!"

I saw the humps growing in the dirt all around us, everywhere on our hilltop. My immediate thought was to draw force-blades and fight. After less than two seconds, I ditched that idea. There were too many of them. There had to be a hump swelling up out of the ground every meter or two all over the hilltop. How many was that? A hundred?

More were coming into sight every second. They were popping up like a tidal wave of gophers.

"Abandon the hilltop!" I shouted. "3rd Unit! Get off the hilltop and climb the rocks around the fringe. They can't get under you if you get up on top of those rocks."

It was the opposite of what troops are normally trained to do. In ninety-nine percent of our drills, we hunkered down in a trench behind something solid like a boulder. But today we all jumped up on top of those boulders like housewives evading mice.

Beams began to sing. Force blades were extended, lighting up the night. Here and there, a tent or a pot of bubbling liquid was spilled and dumped over. Countless were the cries and curses of surprised soldiers. A few of them were grabbed by pods or opening maws. Their boots were eaten, with the foot inside crushed to pulp.

So much for worrying about gravity weapons, I thought. I was beginning to wish we'd come down here in full armor. After all, these aliens hadn't shown a single Crystal drone to us yet. All of our planning seemed to be pointless on this mission.

It seemed to us that we'd discovered more about this enemy. We'd always called them the Crystals, but that wasn't the only form their military took. They had these less organized, ugly types, too. It seemed clear to me that these dirt-clod-looking guys were the originals. That they'd manufactured the Crystals… somehow.

It was kind of weird having to do battle with creatures so alien. Creatures you didn't even understand. Something like a Nairb or a Mogwa seemed almost homey after dealing with these freaks. Even the Wur weren't as bizarre.

We had to have a new name for these dirt-clod civilians, so we began calling them "Silicoids"—that's what the Mogwa and the Nairbs had been calling them all along. The name stuck.

Most of us managed to escape the initial Silicoid assault, but unfortunately, our gateway posts did not. No less than six of the Silicoids emerged right there where our posts were still firing out a continuous stream of furballs bearing foodstuffs and the like. I realized this could not possibly be an accident. The enemy had pinpointed the position of our posts, and they'd struck in a coordinated fashion.

They literally devoured the gateway posts. There were electrical discharges. One of the beasts blew apart when a jolt of power tore through his body, transforming him to ash.

The Silicoids still kept coming up in the center of our position. They bit and chewed, even as we killed them. The gateway posts were transformed to smoking stumps of metal and wire.

The last of the ape-aliens to make it through was carrying a large satchel of what appeared to be plasma grenades. I noticed there were quite a few of those—thousands, in fact, had come through from Jungle World's transport. The Clavers obviously knew what was effective against these aliens, or at least against the crystalline drones they'd deployed in the past.

Trapped by a Silicoid's maw, one bawling ape had his foot stuck in its mouth. He howled and beat his fists on the rocky monster, sending up showers of dust and blood. We tried to help him, shooting at the creature that held onto him, but it was a losing battle.

Realizing he was about to be dragged into the earth and consumed, the ape took a noble stand. He pulled out a grenade and worked to set it off.

"Hit the deck!" the shout rang out.

Even as several Silicoids devoured him, the ape managed to execute his savage plan. The pods were reaching for his limbs, chewing on them, tearing him apart. Then a blue glimmer grew to a brilliant light. They were all consumed together.

It was a dramatic sacrifice, one I wouldn't soon forget. Whatever you might say about these ape-aliens, they were more than willing to sacrifice themselves to destroy an enemy. That was a good thing for us, because the Silicoids seemed to possess the same mindset.

I called Claver-X, and he sent several hundred more of his apes to support us. Together we counterattacked the hundred or so Silicoids that had taken our hilltop. We destroyed them—but they'd already succeeded in their goal. The gateway posts had been wrecked.

Unsurprisingly, after taking perhaps fifty percent casualties, the Crystal World aliens sank down into the dirt from where they'd come and disappeared.

"They got what they wanted," Harris told me. "They came for our gateway posts, and they ate them up."

"It was a surgical strike of sorts," I agreed. "They must have been digging for an hour or two. They came all the way from beyond Armel's line—under the ground that entire time."

Sure, they didn't move all that fast while digging—but I was still impressed. They'd unerringly made their way across the landscape, worming their way through the earth. How had they navigated between all the rocks, to come up here and destroy our posts?

Another idea struck me right then, and I immediately whirled around and looked to the east. Using my tapper, I shouted at Armel, screaming at my blinking forearm.

But it was already too late. I could see on the second hilltop where Armel's men had set up a similar encampment, the Silicoids had also struck there. Gunfire played brightly in the night.

Both sets of our gateway posts were soon gone. We were now officially cut off from our supply chain.

My heart sank. This attack was obviously a good first step for anyone attempting to counter something like an invasion beachhead. I reviewed the Silicoid responses, and they seemed clearly motivated.

First, they'd tried to overwhelm us with their initial attack. They'd driven at us in waves, making a suicidal assault on our position. From the moment they'd detected our presence, they'd been trying to destroy us.

This second assault had been much more successful. They'd used a smaller, more thoughtful force. They'd targeted our most critical vulnerability: the gateway posts.

Now we would get no more food, no more ammo, no more reinforcements. Whether the other commanders knew it or not, our situation was grim.

"James?" a familiar feminine voice said behind me. I turned and saw the flickering blue light of a teleport harness glimmering with the afterglow of a recent arrival.

A small, slight woman stood at the center of that glow. She was known to me. It was Evelyn Thompson.

She was a centurion and a bio—the highest-ranked bio in Legion Varus. "James…?" she said, "you sure know how to put on a party. Have I arrived in the middle of a battle?"

"Actually," I told her, "that was the tail end of it. It's all over now."

She nodded, looking at our wrecked gateway posts. "I came here to check out that fragment of an alien you said you had."

I directed her to the tipped-over puff-crete crate.

"Here it is," I said, "if he's still in there."

Evelyn moved to it, and we found that Carlos had wisely sealed the top. The thing was still rattling around inside. There were big gouges all over the outside of the crate. Apparently, the Silicoids had been aware that one of their members was trapped inside, and they'd attempted to bite their way in—but failed.

Righting the crate, we opened the lid and looked inside.

The creature instantly stopped squirming around, almost as if it was aware of our presence. Perhaps it was.

The Silicoids had to have some sort of sensory apparatus, didn't they? How else could they have found our gateway posts? How else could they have unerringly seized upon limbs and chewed on them?

I didn't understand if they were using sight, sound, radar—hell, I didn't know. But they were in some fashion sensing our presence, if only to know what they should attack.

The creature had stopped moving and essentially stared at us, studying us, even as we studied it.

Evelyn immediately crouched, fascinated. She shone a light inside and ran her tapper and various wands over the thing. It suddenly lashed out with a pod, whipping the wand from her grasp.

She squealed and fell back. I caught her and kept her from landing hard on the rocks.

The alien dirt-slug was chewing on her sensory wand, and we could hear the thin metal crunching as it worked to devour it.

"It's vicious..." she said.

"Yep. He's a frisky devil, all right."

I gently stood her up on her feet again. She let me do this without complaint.

My big hands lingered on her upper arms. They felt like they belonged there. Evelyn didn't even seem to notice.

We used to be an item, Evelyn and I. Holding onto her in the face of a strange, nasty alien—well, that felt kind of natural to both of us, I guess.

Carlos appeared right then, spoiling the mood. He began to claim that the alien was his property. He'd captured it, and he was owed some kind of special credit.

"Rank, a cash reward—anything," he said. He had a million such ideas, most of which Evelyn and I ignored.

He was helpful, however, in presenting the ideas which he'd stolen from Natasha about the little monster's possible origins. He talked about its potential nature as a multicellular creature held together with earth.

Evelyn took several samples of the twisting, squirming thing. She put them in different tubes and began to set up a small lab to examine the specimens. She conducted a chemical analysis upon what she found.

Natasha showed up soon after that. She was like a hound dog sniffing a pork chop when it came to unusual research. Natasha began to help Evelyn automatically. She loved things like this, things that allowed her to plumb the new, unknown mysteries of the universe.

I got bored real fast. I turned away, letting the two women work.

Walking to the edge of the hilltop, I stood atop the rocks and gazed to the north.

The Silicoids had already hit us with a commando team of sorts. They'd plotted an assault and carried it off without a hitch.

How long would it be before the enemy came in real force and attempted to wipe us out?

Using my tapper, I conveyed these misgivings to Claver-X and Armel. They both echoed back that they agreed the risk was real.

All of us figured that before dawn—probably long before dawn—the Silicoids would make an all-out assault on our position.

-37-

By the time dawn did finally come, we were beginning to relax again. We dared to feel good about ourselves. After all, we'd been hit a couple of times, but we'd driven off all the attacks we'd seen thus far.

"Hell," Leeson went as far as to say, "if that's all the fight these dirt worms have got in them, I don't care if they throw the entire population of their best city at our fortifications. We're going to wreck them. Wreck them good."

Harris seconded the motion, but I wasn't so sure. Yes, we had two full legions on the surface of this world now. We had all the apes, all the Saurians, and lots of gear.

The Silicoids had made a couple of determined attacks, which had dismally failed to drive us from their planet. But I knew there were a hell of a lot more aliens out there. I could just feel it.

They had a city, it was said, a hundred thousand strong to the north. Killing a thousand dirt-worms was nothing like killing a hundred thousand, no matter what Leeson said. On top of that, we'd yet to encounter any of their big, jewel-like crystalline drones. Those had to be out there somewhere, didn't they?

The long Crystal World night finally ended. The day-night cycle on this planet was about thirty hours long. That felt weird, but not intolerable.

We were well-rested but expectant. We'd been more than half-expecting a pre-dawn raid. After all, when human militaries attacked one another, they almost always chose the time of around four or five in the morning to make an assault. That's because human beings were at their most groggy and unready to fight at that time.

But it hadn't happened. The night passed by peacefully.

Was that because the Silicoids didn't even know about stuff like circadian rhythms? Did they understand that we meat-based creatures more or less shut down in the middle of the night? Did they even know there was a day and a night at all? Hell, I didn't even know if they used vision as a sense.

There was so little we knew about these creatures: whether or not they were affected much by heat and cold, whether or not they went to sleep, or if they just kept on moving and squirming around forever.

Regardless, our natural expectations weren't realized. When the dawn attack didn't come, we all started to relax, yawn, stretch, and make breakfast.

We even got the stingy transport ship captains to send us fresh gateway posts. We needed supplies, and although they were still complaining about us losing two sets of these valuable technological wonders, there was no better option. Our techs set them up quickly and supplies began to flow again.

The Silicoids finally struck around midmorning. This time, it was a completely different form of assault. I had to think that previously, when the villagers had thrown themselves against us, they'd been in emergency mode. They'd dashed their bodies against our defenses like waves crashing on a stony beach. They'd done so without planning or forethought.

"They're like ants!" Harris kept saying over breakfast, "frigging ants! They charged out in a frenzy to assault the invaders—and they all died."

But this time was different. The enemy had been planning. They were organized. They were coordinating against us, in their thousands.

Our drones detected movement out to the south. Our northern flank was rockier, and that rough terrain continued out past the village we'd pretty much depopulated. Out there, too, movement was detected. Strange humps and trails in the sand appeared in the regions beyond our perimeter.

"There they are!" Sargon shouted, pointing south. We all rushed to that side of the hilltop and stared through whatever vision enhancement devices we had.

He was right. At long last, the crystalline drones had made their appearance. Floating, jewel-like contraptions glided toward us over the rocky ground. Some had twelve sides, others had twenty or more. They came flying low over the boulders, using gravity manipulation. They approached our outer ranks, where Claver-X had deployed his twenty thousand-odd ape-aliens and their dogmen masters. This time, they were coming in serious numbers.

"There has to be better than a thousand of those crystal drones," Claver complained in my earpiece. "Have we got artillery yet from Legion Varus?"

"No," I said, "just defensive systems—force domes, repellers, things like that. We do have a lot of plasma grenades."

Claver-X cursed in my ear, and I couldn't blame him. It would have been nice to have some supporting artillery right now. But Winslade, in his infinite wisdom, had decided to defensively protect his investment, his beachhead on the ground, before he started adding more large, expensive, offensive gear.

In practice, that meant we had domes of force over our heads to prevent an air attack. We had reams of sensors and patrolling drones of our own to use for scouting. We also used pigs to scratch out big trenches even in the deepest, roughest soil.

But star-falls to bombard the enemy? No, we had none of those. Leeson had deployed exactly two 88s, which he had set up right in front of the gateway posts. The best thing we'd built up in the way of ground defenses were puff-crete barriers. We'd protected our hilltop by pouring puff-crete all over the area. This essentially formed an impenetrable layer against underground attacks. A zone under which the Silicoids could dig, but they couldn't surface. We only had a few thousand square meters of puff-crete so far, but at least it was something—a zone where we knew we were safe from attacks that came up from below.

"Let's watch the fun," Carlos said, coming up and standing next to me. He had those binoculars out again. I used the scope on my rifle to zoom in to the zone he was pointing at.

The crystalline Silicoid drones were performing a sweeping advance. They moved at a pace that was something like thirty kilometers an hour at maximum speed—a little faster than a man can run, but no faster than a man can easily ride on a bike. So, I wouldn't call it a lightning attack.

What was powerful about the crystal drones was their ability to glide over any kind of terrain with equal speed and alacrity. It didn't matter to them if they were crossing a river, a lake, or a rocky ridge. Even a forest didn't really slow them down. They came on with a uniform pace because they didn't actually touch the ground.

They had no feet, no beating hearts. They didn't get tired, and they didn't show fear—not unless you destroyed a hell of a lot of them. Even then, I doubt it was fear that they felt. I think whenever they turned tail and withdrew, they'd simply been recalled by their masters, who had deemed they were becoming too damaged to be serviceable.

"How the hell," Leeson began, coming up and standing next to me with his hands on his hips, "do those freaking apes plan to destroy the Silicoids? I remember back on Jungle World, they pretty much got their red asses handed to them."

I nodded. "We'll see," I said. "Claver wouldn't have come out here all this way without having a plan of some kind."

I tilted down my scope so that I could see the actual lines that Claver-X had formed. They were two ranks deep, and you could see the dark-furred ape-aliens deployed in ragged ranks. Among them, the dogmen were marching. Each dragged a large satchel. Big bags of something. Then I saw they were handing out objects from these sacks, giving one to each of the ape-aliens. I thought I had it figured out.

"Plasma grenades," I said, "or explosives bigger than that."

"What?" Leeson exclaimed, grabbing the binoculars right out of Carlos's hands and ripping them off his neck. Carlos squawked and complained, but we paid him no heed. After all, that was one of the privileges of being an officer on the battlefield. We didn't much care what a specialist thought about anything.

"Holy jumping Jesus," Leeson exclaimed, "those are explosives. What the hell are they going to do with those? Set them up as mines or something? Seems a little bit late in the game for that..."

I nodded. I was getting a grim feeling in my gut.

The crystalline drones, at least a thousand of them, swept forward. Then, suddenly, when they were about a hundred or so meters out from our lines, they began to beam the ape-aliens who were facing them. The apes predictably threw a volley of plasma grenades in return.

Now, this was one thing these ape-aliens were good at, and I knew it from personal experience. They were good at throwing something and nailing whatever they threw it at.

Due to their Olympian shot-putter arms, they could heave a heavy object at least a hundred meters and strike it unerringly. Some of the crystals dodged, but most of them were nailed. Plasma grenades went off all along the line.

Now, as we'd learned during the Jungle World campaign, plasma grenades caused these crystal drones to lose control. They spun and dipped, scraping against rocks. They twirled away in random directions.

All along their advancing front line, the enemy halted their assault and began to spin, wandering drunkenly. The effect was temporary, but it was quite pronounced. Essentially, any drone struck by a plasma grenade wasn't necessarily destroyed but was definitely discombobulated and unable to function for something like twenty to thirty seconds.

I heard a screaming whistling sound a moment later. The noise echoed again and again. Looking around with my scope, I saw the dogmen weren't howling, they weren't lifting their muzzles at the moon, but rather putting metal whistles to their black lips. They blew on these shrilly and persistently.

Apparently, that was a prearranged signal. Hundreds of dark furry shapes raced forward in response. At the last moment, before the drones could come back to life again and begin beaming them down, the apes leapt and flew the last ten meters or more in a wild, savage, snarling fury.

They landed with their arms spread wide. They clung to the crystals and rode them as they came back to life. Some of our hairy boys were obviously being beamed as the enemy woke up and attempted to crush their flesh to their bones. I could only imagine the din of howling and squalling that was going on down there as the ape-aliens were being gravity-beamed to death.

That's when the first explosion ripped through the air. A great blast of light and an orange fireball rose high. Smoke shot upward an instant later.

Like a glass jar with a stick of dynamite shoved in it, the first of the crystalline drones was blown apart into shards.

More ape-aliens popped off, about one every second. It was like popcorn in the microwave, and the intensity and frequency of these blasts escalated.

The slower apes charged into this mess fearlessly. Many of them were struck by flying shards—but after tumbling down in a heap, they usually got back up and pressed forward. A good number reached a drone and latched on for their final ride.

"Hot damn," Leeson said. "Those boys know how to die hard."

"They sure do…"

The apes petered out after about a minute. Those who hadn't managed to blow themselves up were struck by beams and injured. They fell and flopped about, unable to press ahead with the attack.

But then the dogmen whistled again. Another fast wave of ape-aliens raced forward. They were expending, with each wave, perhaps a thousand of Claver's troops. Many of these raced forward to grab up unexploded ordnance from their fallen brothers.

"They're frigging suicide bombers," I said. "They're killing themselves to take out these drone-soldiers."

"The best-trained monkeys I've ever laid eyes on," Leeson marveled. "If only we could get Clane's light troopers to act like that, the enemy wouldn't stand a chance."

At the last moment, the second wave launched themselves. They landed on the crystals and rode in an embrace that could only result in death for everyone involved.

After the second wave petered out, the enemy advance had halted. It had turned into a milling confusion. When the third and fourth waves struck, the enemy had had enough. They turned and ran. Reeling from the shocking ferocity of our Jungle World brothers, they'd been driven off.

All along our hilltop, my men whooped and hollered in support. We'd been impressed, one and all.

We watched, fascinated, as the battle died down. The crystalline drones had taken their toll on the ape-aliens, that was for sure. By the end of it, at least five thousand of our furballs had been slain, possibly more. But the drones had lost a thousand or more of their number as well.

The enemy fell back, more than half of them destroyed. Many had large, jagged, slagged holes in their sides. Some of them were throwing off sparks as they dragged their shiny asses over the rocky land, unable to lift themselves completely into the air and fly at full speed.

The dogmen whistled again, releasing a new, lower note. A massive wave of ape-aliens charged forward. They'd sent in all their reserves.

This time, they didn't throw grenades or blow themselves up. Instead, they raced after the wounded enemy bearing puff-crete hammers. I'd seen them do this before, and when they caught up with the damaged drones, they went to town on them. With a few more losses, they managed to chip, crack, and finally bring down the damaged drones that lagged behind.

Leeson laughed and grabbed his belly, thoroughly amused. "Those frigging crystals got the shock of their lives right there, didn't they? I've got to admit, that Claver-X friend of yours, he knows how to ride herd on his apes."

"I have to second the motion," Harris said, coming near. Everyone was grinning hard. "That was a great use of the most primitive force imaginable. It gets me to thinking... what if we did something like that?"

"What?" Leeson asked him. "You want to strap on a bomb and go commando?"

"I was thinking about Clane's lights…"

"That's crazy-talk," Leeson complained. "Men can't run and jump like those apes. Clane and all his men would be face down in the dust. They wouldn't be worth a damn."

Clane walked over then, having probably heard his name mentioned several times. He surveyed the battle.

Harris made his suggestion, but Clane didn't take to the idea. I couldn't blame him for being skeptical.

Clane shook his head. "Well, I think that Adjunct Leeson has got the right idea. My boys couldn't have done as well as those apes. First of all, they're not that suicidal. And secondly, they can't leap that far and hang on that tightly."

"Well," Leeson said, laughing, "at least it looks like my 88s aren't even going to get a trial today. The enemy has been driven back again. This has got to be the easiest campaign on record so far. What do you say, McGill?"

I opened my mouth to express my doubts and misgivings, but I wasn't even given the time to do so. A new squalling sound filled my headset. This time it was from Armel.

"McGill! We're under attack from the north! Send whatever help you can!"

I rushed with my officers to the opposite side of our command post.

"Damnation," Leeson said, "you've got to give it to these rocks. They certainly are persistent."

The enemy attacked Armel's lines differently than they'd hit us in the south. Instead of using crystalline drones, they used a massive wave of Silicoids—so many, in fact, that they were beyond counting.

"Oh, shit…" Leeson said as we watched Silicoids rush toward our lines.

The enemy were bubbling up into the midst of the Saurian army. They'd dug right up into their defensive trenches. There was no chance to use guns. They couldn't organize themselves into a different formation other than the simple, long, ragged line that Armel had thrown up to deploy his troops.

We watched with sagging spirits. This was the real attack. The big one. Maybe the drones hitting us in the south had been a distraction…

It was almost as if every Silicoid had targeted a specific lizard of his own to molest. And who knew? Maybe that's exactly what they'd decided to do.

Dirt began to rise up in humps all along Armel's long, uneven trench-line. It was absolute chaos.

-38-

"McGill!" Armel screamed in my headset. "We need help!"

I called Claver-X and asked if he could send a cohort or two to support Armel. This suggestion was met with a snarl.

"Why can't you humans do it? Or better yet, those cowardly bears?" Claver-X asked. "Where the hell are they at?"

"We've set up the new posts, but—"

"McGill, my fuzzballs just suffered—I don't know—something like four or five thousand casualties over here."

"Yes," I said, "we watched that. It was a tremendous sacrifice… but the important thing is you drove off your attackers! Now, Armel needs help, and he needs it badly."

Cursing, Claver signed off by simply disconnecting the channel. For a few minutes, nothing seemed to be happening. But then I noticed that two large groups of furry shapes were on the move. Probably two thousand strong in each instance, these forces had detached themselves from Claver's lines. One group swept around on the east side of my hilltop and the second moved by on the west.

The ape-aliens raced across the rocks, no doubt carrying hammers and explosives. It was impressive how fast they charged to battle.

When they arrived at the Saurian trenches, a desperate, savage melee broke out. The Silicoid tactics of digging up into the midst of the Saurians had been highly effective—but then the apes arrived to even the score.

Explosions boomed and body parts flew. It was enough to make even a hardened soul like mine wince.

I stood on the northern ridge of our hilltop stronghold, gazing down at the struggling forms. Harris and his men had moved up to surround me. Leeson had come to stand there, too.

"We can't even use my 88s," he kept saying. "All we'd do is burn Saurians. I don't think it would have much of an effect on these Silicoid monsters, anyways."

I agreed and told him to stand down with his antipersonnel artillery. We had brought them along to see if they might be effective against the enemy. So far, the Silicoids hadn't done much more than steam and smoke a bit when hit by an 88.

"Damnation," Harris said. "I sure wish we could go down there and help out."

I glanced at him, noticing he hadn't moved a muscle in that direction. Would they win this battle and overwhelm us despite all our preparations? It all depended on how many of these Silicoids they had flowing in to attack us even now.

It was always frightening to face a large, unknown alien force on a planet that hadn't been explored. What if another hundred thousand of these Silicoids showed up—or a million? We would be overrun.

I thought about ordering an advance to contact, I really did… but I held off. We didn't have enough men to change the outcome of this battle. So, we stood on our hill and watched with our thumbs up our butts.

The Silicoids hadn't all dug under the ground. A lot of them were humping in close, choosing to use the faster overland approach now that the Saurians were engaged.

The two lines merged, and then the supporting apes added their weight to the struggle. The battle was fierce and raged on for several minutes.

Finally, to my surprise, Armel's troops broke. The Saurians had apparently had enough. Those that still survived turned and raced uphill toward us. Armel called me, and I gritted my teeth as I listened to his report.

"McGill, we're pulling back to your position. Provide us firing support, if you would."

Grimacing and showing all my teeth at once, I put every soldier I had on the northern flank. I lined them up on the ridgeline, and the various loopholes we'd carefully molded into the puff-crete walls proved their worth. I'd assigned Leeson to that detail, and he'd kept his specialists working long into the night.

We began peppering the Silicoids as they chased the fleeing Saurians. The apes broke too, a moment later. I'm not sure if Claver-X had ordered them to retreat, or if they'd also taken too many losses to stomach. Either way, a disaster seemed imminent.

Feeling it was my duty to report in, I contacted Primus Graves.

"What do you mean, Armel's falling back to your position?" he shouted in my ear, as if it was my fault. "You tell him to stand firm!"

"Sir, I think it's too late for that. We've lost thousands upon thousands of the ape-aliens. Maybe five to eight thousand. And Armel's force? He had ten thousand Saurians. Now, I don't think he has more than three thousand left."

"Damn it!" Primus Graves shouted. I could hear him banging one fist into the other. "Stop sending supplies," he ordered the Gray Deck lackeys. "McGill, we're connecting *Scorpio*'s gateway post to yours. Get your techs on it. I'm sending reinforcements down to your position immediately."

My heart surged. Finally, Legion Varus was taking the field in force.

I cleared everyone away from the posts, which were surrounded with a warehouse's worth of supplies. Within a few minutes, troops began racing through at a steady jogging pace.

Jenny Mills led the 7th and Manfred the 9th. They were both from my own cohort, and I was relieved to see them.

"Harris?" I shouted. "Advance your heavies down the hill. Take up firing positions on the hillside and shoot anything that humps and dribbles dirt."

Harris was already cursing, but I ignored him. I turned toward my other adjuncts. "Clane! Support Harris with your lights. We're going to let these new troops man our loopholes here at the top of the hill. Leeson… warm up the 88s. Just in case."

"Just in case, Centurion!" he said, and he hustled away happily. He really liked blowing apart aliens from a safe distance.

So far, we had two fresh units deployed on the battlefield, and the posts were already burping up a third. By the time the thundering wave of routing Saurians and apes arrived, they simply overran our position.

They were in full panic, many were wounded, and all of them were dirty and afraid. I really couldn't blame them. Almost no force in history could endure over fifty percent losses and still keep fighting.

Fortunately, the Silicoids were now in the position they'd carefully avoided until now. They were going to either have to dig down into the earth and come up in our midst—which was virtually impossible with all the puff-crete we'd poured over the hilltop—or hump their way uphill pursuing their enemies. They chose the latter option.

Once the routing apes and lizards had raced through our ranks, we began to fire on the slower, worm-like enemy. More and more Varus troops poured out of the gateway posts to join us. They were also emerging from a fresh set of gateway posts on the secondary hill, which had been similarly fortified during the night. All told, by the time the Silicoids hit our lines, we had about a thousand men—real humans with real guns—all blasting away at the freakish aliens.

Armel had managed to regain control of his Saurians by this time. Claver's dogmen officers had managed to rein in the apes as well. They were returning to the front lines, puffing, wheezing, and dragging their weapons rather than marching in an organized fashion.

Still, I was glad to have their support—an extra few thousand fighters who were skilled in close combat would be invaluable. That's what a ranged force like Legion Varus needed most to help bolster our defense.

I think what saved us in the end was the fact that the enemy Silicoids had already suffered grievous losses. Sure, they'd inflicted many casualties, but they'd sustained thousands of their own in the process.

It had been a very bloody, and dare I say, dirty battle. There was as much mud smeared on the puff-crete walls as there was actual blood. The stench and roar of battle continued for about half an hour, but finally, the enemy retreated to the softest areas of soil they could find and burrowed their way down.

We chased after them, shouting hoarsely. We ran them down and killed all those we could catch.

I had to admit, I no longer saw any of the Silicoids as civilians. They might have been that at first, when we'd arrived and scared them in their village, but after fighting a determined foe that had killed literally thousands on our side, at some point, you just stopped caring about the nuances distinguishing soldier from civilian.

Maybe it was as Harris had suggested. Perhaps these Silicoids operated like an ant colony, with every member willing to fight to the death for their side. If that wasn't the definition of a soldier, then what was?

The aftermath of the battle was quite grim. We had won—sort of. We'd driven them back on all fronts, and our gateway posts were still functional. Overhead, our shields still protected us from aerial bombardment.

But for all of that, we'd lost a hell of a lot of men. Well... not only men.

Armel was the first and loudest to point this out. Of course, he had survived, because he'd never moved his precious carcass too close to the front lines.

After having dealt with him on many worlds, I'd had the opportunity to learn his style in numerous campaigns. He often built himself a secure puff-crete bunker a significant distance back from where his troops sat in trenches, whether they were lizards with shotguns and harnesses, or humans from a legion such as Germanica. His mode of operation was always consistent.

He shouted as he limped up the mountaintop to my position. "MCGILL!"

He was a mess, I had to admit. He wore a black suit of stardust armor this time, which, considering we were facing

Silicoids rather than crystal drones, made sense. Perhaps it had saved his life when one of them tried to bite his leg off. I regretted not bringing my best suit of armor to this battlefield.

But now was not the time for regrets. That is, unless you were Maurice Armel.

"This was all planned, wasn't it?" he demanded angrily.

He barged into my command center, shoving anyone who got in his way. Saurian and human alike were shunted aside.

"You! You planned this!" he accused, pointing a finger into my startled face.

"Planned what, Armel?" I replied.

"This utter destruction, this demolition of my Saurian legion. Recruiting new reptiles will be hard after this. News travels fast in their community."

"False!" Another voice boomed out. It was Raash, who had been shadowing me here on this hilltop for days. He approached, dragging his raspy tail across the puff-crete deck that covered the entire hilltop. "You speak false words, honorless cur," Raash said.

Armel turned to him. "Shut up, foppish lizard. Do you know how many of my men mock you for being blue-scaled and cowardly? You call yourself a spy purely for self-preservation!"

"Tell them about his tail, Maurice," I suggested. I was beginning to grin. It wasn't often that I got to watch two ornery polecats have a squabble over me. I felt like I was a princess or something.

"Yes! Yes!" Armel shouted, overcome with emotion. "I'll personally shorten your tail, lizard. It's among your greatest embarrassments." As he spoke, Armel extended a meter-long blade of force from his gauntlet.

Raash hissed, hands wide and talons grasping the air. They looked like they were about to throw-down, and every human on the hilltop was nudging one another and forming a circle.

"You have called my people cowards," Raash said.

"Watch out, Raash," I warned.

My officers gathered at my elbows, and they were grinning. Grinning big. They enjoyed a good duel, especially between two unpopular figures.

"Yeah," Harris added, "he's skilled with that blade!" He had to shout to be heard over the growing, noisy crowd.

Soon, a few of Armel's Saurians joined the crowd of Legion Varus soldiers. They showed no love for their tribune. We all began clapping and chanting, "Fight, fight, fight!"

Raash and Armel snarled at each other, lunging occasionally but never landing a serious blow. I suspected that while both were angry, neither had anticipated things escalating to this point.

"McGill!" a voice from my tapper interrupted the fun. It was Graves.

"Yes, sir?" I responded, turning on my camera, so he could see the action. "Check this out. Armel and Raash are going at it."

"Stop those idiots," Graves exclaimed.

"How, sir?"

"I don't care, just do it. We won't be able to properly revive Raash, given his unique body. And Armel? He's technically a wanted fugitive. If we have to revive him here, he'll be arrested rather than returned to the battlefield."

I watched the two with growing concern. Raash was irreplaceable? Well, that wouldn't be such a big loss… But Armel?

Huh… I really didn't like the idea of losing him. Who the hell was going to give commands to his lizard army after he was gone?

Sure, they'd lost thousands, but they were still a significant force. Hell, they might even go berserk and try to kill all of us if Armel was cut down.

With an unhappy grunt, I realized I was going to have to get involved.

-39-

"Okay, okay!" I shouted, slamming my hands together to make booming reports. Other people might call them claps, but to me, they sounded like I was beating shoe soles together. "That's enough! That's enough! Settle down! Save it for the enemy."

Armel and Raash both shot me surprised looks.

"What is amiss with you humans?" Raash exclaimed. "One minute you counsel us to slaughter one another, and the next you recommend cowardice!"

"The lizard is right," Armel said. "This is a matter of honor that should be settled with a duel."

They continued to grumble and complain about my stopping their possibly deadly duel. But I persisted. Judging by their behavior, I could tell they were probably happy to turn the heat down a notch.

Armel, after all, was wounded and winded. Sure, he had a force blade, and he was a master with it—but the Saurian was twice his weight or more. I knew from experience that Raash was no slouch in close combat. I wasn't even sure who I'd put my money on if it came down to it.

Shaking my head, I realized I needed to stop thinking about betting on duels.

"Okay, okay," I repeated. "You two should arm wrestle or something. That'll give you some kind of closure. You both lost a lot of men today, Armel—and Raash here has seen thousands of his brothers with their tails stuck straight up in the air."

"You mock our classic pose of death?"

"No, no. No offense meant, Raash. What I'm saying is there's no good reason for you two to go after each other. I suggest we keep our eyes on the real enemy: the Silicoids. They're going to keep coming at us until all of them are dead—or we are."

"Ah," Armel said, retracting his force blade into his gauntlet and placing his hands on his hips. "Suddenly, you've twisted your point of view until it matches my own."

"Huh? I've performed no kinds of perversion, Armel."

"No, idiot. I'm talking about these dirt-creatures. Are you now willing to confess that the Silicoids are the enemy, one and all of them?"

"Well…"

Now that Raash and Armel were no longer fighting to the death, the two of them moved on to a whole new level of complaining.

"I understand all of the trickery now," Raash said. "This ape is wiser than you, Armel."

"Bite your forked tongue, reptile," Armel retorted.

"No, no, it's true. You see now how Legion Varus is finally taking the field through their gateway posts?"

Raash gestured to the continuous marching lines of human troops. Varus was on the 4th Cohort and the flow was steady. The two gateway posts disgorged more armed men rapidly every second.

"Yes…?" Armel said, watching the march of Earthmen and frowning.

"Don't you understand what's happened?" Raash demanded. "You've been fooled. The humans have wasted the lives of my brothers. They could have had a strong force up here on this mountaintop with guns all aimed down to support you. But no, instead they waited."

"Now, wait a second, Raash," I said, trying to shut him down.

He ignored me. "They waited until your troops were broken and mostly dead. Now, when you have no strength and are of no consequence, they march fresh troops onto the field. Face reality, mercenary warlord. The earthmen blunted the enemy's army with the bodies of your troops."

"And with mine too," Claver-X said.

I hadn't even noticed him walking up the slope, what with all the excitement. He had his thumbs in his belt loops, and he looked as pissed as everybody else did.

He was also dirty and disheveled. He must have run from the front lines, down where his apes had fought crystal drones to a standstill.

"My troops fought the crystal drones down there on that pile of rocks," he said, pointing to the south, "and then I was called upon to send four thousand more of my apes over here to save Armel's worthless mustache..."

Armel bristled at this, but he said nothing.

"Now," Claver continued, "I've lost over half of my apes. Ten thousand dead, easy! Some of my dogmen noncoms are growling about mutiny."

It soon became a three-way bitching session. Raash was egging the other two on, and both the commanders of major portions of this coalition force were leaning close and grousing fiercely. Every now and then, they threw me a dark glance, like this was all somehow my fault.

After a time, the trio broke up. Raash walked away into the shadowy area of high-stacked supply crates, while Claver went to marshal the apes he still had left.

But Armel came directly to voice his opinions into my face. I wondered if he actually thought I cared or could do anything about it.

"McGill! This is entirely unacceptable. I will not be treated—" he went on, but I tuned him out by about the tenth word. It was a sheer relief.

With a sigh, I decided to go ahead and pretend to listen to him. Even my dim brain understood that now was not the time to grin, or even to smirk. Now was the time to pull down the corners of my mouth and look as sad and contrite as possible.

I frequently shook my head and made tsking sounds whenever I felt the moment must be right. In essence, I let

Armel rage at me, hoping he would get all of that piss and vinegar out of his system.

He bitched about Graves with special vehemence and told me how, in the Unification Wars, he'd performed similar disservices. That was halfway interesting, but he soon moved on to other topics, slapping a gloved fist into a gloved palm.

When I sensed he was winding down a notch, I finally cut in. "Are you about done, Maurice?" I asked.

"Yes. I have said my words. I will go now."

"Good. It's time to put some starch back into your pecker. Marshal your troops and hold that northern flank."

"I cannot, McGill," he said, shaking his head. "We don't have enough troops. It's now Graves' problem."

Still grumping, he limped back out to the north. No doubt he would gather what was left of his Saurian army, patch them up, and prepare them for battle once more. But he was truly being a bitter dick about it.

Something like fifteen minutes later, there was yet another surprise on our ill-fated battlefield. An explosion went off right near the gateway posts. The bodies of legionnaires—my own human brothers and sisters—were blown apart. There was a lot of shouting, and a large group gathered. Primus Collins walked up to me, injured and dragging her foot.

"Cherish?" I said, lifting her up. "Are you okay?"

She shook her head, which was both bloody and scorched. "It was a landmine, McGill," she said. "Who the hell would put a landmine right in front of the gateway posts?"

I stared and gaped. The posts were still there. They were still operating. In fact, Legion Varus' troops were still jogging through, although there were looks of concern on the faces of every new man who had to walk onto a pile of burnt corpses and body fragments.

"A landmine? Here? Who set it?"

"The tribune is dead," a voice pealed out. It seemed to be Primus Graves. He came walking over to me, glowering.

He pulled a pistol out and pressed it against my face. My jaw sagged low, and it wasn't even an act. "Uh… hello there, Primus Graves, sir," I said. "Good to see you make it down to the battlefield at last."

"Let's cut to the shit, McGill," he said. "Who did this?"

After gaping for a second, I clamped my jaws closed and stood at attention. I knew that when Graves put a gun in your face, he meant business. He'd executed me probably more times than anyone else, living or dead.

"Now," he said, "you're going to tell me why this happened. Our command staff came directly from *Scorpio* to deploy onto the field—and at that exact moment—a frigging landmine went off."

"Did someone say something about the tribune, sir?" I asked.

"He blew up. Along with Primus Gilbert—and I think you did it."

"Whoa, whoa, whoa," I said, lifting my hands.

Graves twitched, but he didn't fire. Not yet.

"Are you telling me Tribune Winslade is dead?"

"Yes, that's exactly what I'm telling you. He was in the middle of that sycophantic little group of primuses he likes to travel with." Here he glanced over toward Cherish, who was frowning and crossing her arms. Apparently, she didn't like being called a simp, even if it was true most of the time.

"Uh…" I said, "I'm pretty sure we don't have any landmines down here…" I dared to reach up and scratch the top of my head with a couple of stray fingers. "Just check the manifests, could you? Primus Graves, sir?"

He showed me a lot of teeth, but then he lowered his pistol. He looked down, lifted his tapper, and began paging through it.

"You're right…" he said after a minute or so. His pistol drooped to his side. "I'm not seeing a single landmine here. We haven't deployed anything like that yet." He looked back toward the gateway posts. "Okay… Who do you think set that mine there, McGill?"

"I don't rightly know, sir," I said. "But I'm dead certain it wasn't a Legion Varus man. Hell, we didn't know you were coming down until a few minutes ago."

"Right, right…"

His face took on a new cast. I could tell a darker, even more suspicious line of reasoning was forming in his mind.

He slid his eyes to the north of the hilltop and then to the south. "We've got Armel out there with his legion of stinking lizards. He's a turncoat if we ever saw one. We're only operating this coalition under a temporary truce—you know about that?"

"I sure do—and you're right about Armel. He's a snake with bells on."

"Hmm... What about this new flavor of Claver? The one you call X?"

"Oh yeah, he's more trustworthy than most."

Graves shook his head. "All Clavers are the same, McGill. You need to get this idea out of your head that there's one nice Santa Claus Claver—because there isn't."

"Yessir, Primus Graves, sir. Whatever you say."

But he wasn't listening to me. He was looking around and asking more questions. "Where's that lizard?"

"Which one, sir? We got millions of them around here."

"The blue one."

"Oh, you mean Raash? I'm not sure. He was here not too long ago…"

Graves glared at me. "All right," he said, nodding and putting his pistol away in his holster again. I was relieved to see it go. "All right... I know what's going on here."

"I sure wish you'd let me in on it."

"Haven't you caught on by now, McGill?" Cherish asked, she'd been listening in, and she sounded as angry as Graves. "One of these three—either that Saurian agent friend of yours, Raash, or maybe Armel, or maybe Claver-X—decided to blow up Winslade."

I frowned, put my hand on my chin, rubbed it a bit, and thought that over.

"Well," I said, "you know, they were a bit upset about how we left them down here all by their lonesome to face the Silicoids. Tribune Winslade waited to deploy his men until their forces were broken on the battlefield."

"Is that what they said?"

"Yes, I do remember distinctly hearing them talk about the possibility of such actions being deliberate on Winslade's part."

Graves nodded at me. "I think you've got it now, McGill."

And I did get it. Could they be right? I wasn't sure. But knowing those three—Raash, Armel, and Claver-X—well, any one of them might have set up a booby trap like that. They all three hated Winslade just on principle. They didn't even need a good reason to hate him and want him dead.

-40-

Since the very beginning, our coalition army had been on thin ice. Now, it appeared that one of the groups—or possibly more than one of them—had decided to take out the leadership of Legion Varus.

Even I knew this spelled big trouble.

Graves called a meeting, which Armel and Claver-X attended. Graves insisted that I be brought in as well, because I'd been present during the entire battle up to this point. I'd also witnessed the actual snuffing of Winslade in person.

Raash, of course, managed to tag along. His claim was that he represented the Saurians and the legions of Steel World. He'd also been ordered by Alexander Turov to follow me to the ends of the universe.

Graves rolled his eyes at the big, blue lizard, but he allowed it. "But Raash, you have to stand in the back and stay quiet."

Raash did this with poor grace. His tail rasped on the puff-crete floor of the tent, and his labored breathing sounded more hissy than usual to me.

"Gentlemen," Graves said, turning to the other two, "it has come to my attention that there has been a serious breach in decorum and behavior in this coalition force." He looked at the two men sternly.

Neither one of them looked too impressed with his accusatory stare.

"Let's discuss the chain of command as it now stands," Graves said.

"Yes, let's," Armel interrupted. "I am in charge."

Graves bristled at this and so did Claver. I felt a bit angry myself. I opened my mouth to speak, but Graves put a hand up in my face, so I kept quiet.

"That is false," Graves said. "You are not in charge. Admiral Sateekas is in charge of this task force."

"That's true," Armel said with a shrug, "but Admiral Sateekas is not here. Should he dare to set his frightened, churning feet upon this planet's unpleasant surface, I will immediately concede he is our rightful leader."

By this time, I was frowning big time. I could smell a gigantic, mustachioed, French rat. I could also tell, just by looking at them, that Graves and Claver felt the same way.

"So," Raash said, stepping forward, dragging his scaly tail over the puff-crete we used to keep the Silicoids out, "this human confesses immediately. The matter of guilt is thus resolved."

"I declare no such thing, rebellious lizard," Armel said. "Back, back into your hole! You are not to speak here!"

Graves made brushing away motions at Raash, and Raash retreated, making angry, nasty sounds and smells.

"How do you figure you're in charge of jack-squat?" Claver-X asked, speaking up for the first time.

Armel turned to him, raising his eyebrows as if surprised. "Is it not obvious? Sateekas is not here, so it cannot be him. Legion Varus has no commander—therefore, they are set aside by default. There are no forces from Rigel present, either. Obviously, the responsibility falls upon my shoulders."

"What about me?" Claver-X asked. "Am I chopped liver?"

Armel laughed rudely. "You, with your wild pack of genetic mutants? You are, I dare say, less than chopped liver. Your army is illegitimate. You have no officers or command staff. Yours is a bizarre vanity project. You have no rank or legitimacy in the eyes of the other coalition members."

Claver-X stood up suddenly. "Perhaps then, I should just pull out."

Armel made a brushing-off gesture with his fingers. "Possibly, that would be for the best. All you have to do is walk back through the gateway posts and—oh, oh my. The gateway is connected to *Scorpio* at the moment. Could it be that you are cut off from that form of retreat? Perhaps your cowardice will have to wait for a better day!"

The two fell to arguing. Finally, Graves had had enough. He stood up and barked at them both to shut up.

Oddly, despite the fact they technically outranked him, they both listened. Graves always had carried a weight that was above his actual rank.

"What about me, Armel?" Graves asked. "If Winslade's down and out for the moment, I will command Legion Varus, and I will command this beachhead."

"Nonsense," Armel said. "You have never even held the rank of tribune, Graves. Great though your contributions have been, you know as well as I do that if Earth were to learn that you'd somehow inherited the rank of acting tribune, they would wish to take action. They would probably remove you from command entirely."

Graves stood there in stony silence for several long seconds. It gave me time for my slow brain to catch up with what was being said. I'd spent a lot of time being tormented to death on behalf of Graves. He'd done questionable things in the distant past, before my birth—before I was even a twinkle in my father's eye.

Back at Central, the brass took a very dim view of allowing Graves to ever achieve a serious command. They feared him, I figured. It was a wonder they even allowed him to keep breathing.

Finally, Graves sat down. "What do you propose then, exactly, Armel?"

Armel smiled. It was a wicked thing to behold. He had all the cards at this moment. He was, after all, a tribune in full charge of a legion that was not only intact and had a regular command structure, but which also gave him technical representation of the Rigellian forces. Unless Squantas himself came down here with his bears—which wasn't in the cards right now—he was next in line to command this hodgepodge force.

He nodded graciously. "I accept your acquiescence, Graves," he said, although none had actually been offered. "A wise man once said that loyalty is an affliction of dogs—but in your case, he was incorrect!"

This didn't go over too well with Graves, who continued to stare at Armel like he wanted to squash him. I had no doubt that if the two ever came to blows, Graves would be the victor. Hell, I could hardly take the guy, and I'd tried a few times.

"What about revival machines?" I blurted out suddenly. "Why haven't we got any down here on Crystal World?"

The others glanced at me as if I'd farted, but I didn't care. Everybody else was talking out of turn. Why not me?

"Because, my simple friend," Armel said, "the gateway posts we have set up thus far have only been the smallest kind. They're incapable of transporting such a large piece of equipment down here. Notice we don't have tanks, starfalls, Blood World giants—none of these amenities."

"The gateway posts," Graves said, "are technically wide enough to allow a starfall to be deployed."

"Yes, yes—but Winslade didn't see fit to do so, did he?" Armel pointed out.

Graves shook his head.

It was true. Earth was being stingy. I knew that one of the last things they wanted to lose during any campaign was a first-class revival machine. Plus, they were actually too large and bulky to be brought through a simple set of gateway posts.

However, I also knew there were options...

"We could do it another way," I said. "Hell, Claver here is an expert. He once set up big gateway posts that allowed giants from Blood World to march right onto our green mother Earth."

Armel pursed his lips and nodded. "The trouble, I believe, is all entirely budgetary at this point. I've asked for such equipment from *Scorpio*. I have been denied at every step of the way. It is your leadership who is preventing us from properly being equipped. They've allowed us a few pigs, a few posts, but keep in mind, we've already lost a couple of sets of posts. It is their firm belief that we may be wiped out at any moment. Therefore, they want to see more progress, more headway here on the planet's surface before they provide us superior equipment."

Everyone moaned and shuffled a bit. It was a difficult situation for all of us. Our top commanders were acting like a bunch of prissy accountants.

Sure, giving us gear was a risk. We might lose it. We might all die. Everyone here knew that, but denying us the gear we required to be successful? That was the surest way to make us all lose in the end, to make us lose everything in the end.

"All right, then, head-honcho," Claver-X said, "you're in command—however temporarily—so tell us what to do. Are we just going to sit here, squatting on these rocks until the Silicoids bring up enough force to wipe us out once and for all?"

"No," Armel said, lifting a finger high. "That is the one thing we must not do. After examining the battle which we just fought with the enemy, we have discovered an effective means to destroy their crystalline drones. When we fight out in the open against the Silicoids, however, we are at a serious disadvantage. If they manage to tunnel up underneath us and surprise us in close combat, all could be lost."

"But we can destroy them easily at range," Graves pointed out. "They don't appear to have any ballistic weaponry."

Everyone nodded. We were eyeballing the battle computer now, which was replaying a hologram of the day's events. The bloody, semi-disastrous battle wasn't pretty to watch.

"Therefore," Armel said, "we must not squat here waiting for them to gather their forces, waiting for them to burrow up into our midst and kill us all in our beds. No," he said, "we must march. We must move faster than they can dig. Therefore, if they want to come at us, they'll have to do so on the surface."

"What if they send drones?" Claver asked. "Thousands and thousands of them?"

Armel shrugged. "It's a possibility," he said, "but I would assume that if they had such a force readily available, they would have already thrown it against us. No, I think they have lost a great number of their drones."

"Hmm..." Claver said. "Maybe they just completed one of their great ships, launching it into the sky to assault one of our colonies. In that case, it means we've surprised them by attacking this advanced base."

Armel nodded. "All the more reason to strike hard and fast." Here, he slapped his fist into his palm.

We all looked at him. We all listened. I had to admit, what he was saying made a certain degree of strategic sense.

Then Graves leaned forward, putting his elbows on the hologram. The battle computer's screen glimmered around his forearms and his gauntleted hands.

"I agree with Tribune Armel," he said. "In my estimate, we do not have enough manpower, material—and certainly not enough will from our own leadership to take this planet in a traditional fashion. That would require a mass invasion force and a slow, grinding battle. If we apply such an approach, using attrition and the slow expansion of held territory, we will lose this war. Instead, a small but highly effective force, used boldly, might succeed…"

"It is decided, then," Armel said. "Our best move is to attack the enemy and deliver a crippling blow as quickly as possible."

Claver grumbled a bit, but finally, he agreed as well.

I sat back, seriously impressed. These three men all pretty much hated each other, but now, here we were, forced to work together. It had to be the highly hostile nature of this alien planet that had performed such a miracle.

Armel was right. The only alternative to cooperation was to suffer and die in the maw of something resembling living stone. A gruesome death waited for all of us down here on Crystal World. When a horde of the enemy was at your gates, people tended to see reason and give up on petty arguments.

The truth was, all three of these men were excellent at tactics. Winslade, on the other hand, would have been the weakest link in the chain.

Thinking about that, I had to wonder if that was the reason someone had engineered his death. Winslade would have attempted to assert his authority, and then he would have come up with some cockamamie idea of his own.

Starmen like these three were a mean, tough lot. If they thought you were a fuck-up, they'd sooner stab you in the ass than listen to you give an order. Much sooner, in fact.

The only one among them who wasn't like that was Graves. He probably would have followed Winslade on some disastrous mission, turtling up here on this hilltop until we were wiped out. But with Winslade out of the picture, he'd taken to the new thinking quickly enough.

After an hour or so, I was yawning. The three men decided to break the meeting up. Graves left first to organize his forces. Legion Varus was the newest group to set foot on this planet. Graves commanded the freshest troops with essentially no wounded and nothing to hold them back. It was decided they should take the lead and begin the march.

And where were we headed? Toward the big red crystal— the biggest, baddest, reddest crystal that we'd seen when we first arrived aboard the Nairb invasion ship. It was essentially a giant cannon-like machine, something which flung other crystals up into space after they were assembled or forged—or whatever the hell they did on the surface of Crystal World.

Instead of waiting for them to strike us, we were going to strike them, and we were going to do it first. I approved of the idea. Not that anybody cared...

There was just one thing that puzzled me. After Graves left, I turned to Claver-X, who was the closest thing in the group to a friend of mine.

"Hey," I said, "who waxed Winslade?"

Claver-X laughed and cackled at me. "What? Haven't you figured it out yet, boy? Not even you can be that dumb."

"Don't underestimate him," Raash said. "His ignorance is boundless. He has astounded heads of state with his inabilities."

I pointed a big finger at Raash and wagged it. "He's right about that, you know."

Claver, shaking his head, leaned closer. "It was *all of us* who cleaned Winslade's clock."

I stared, blinked, and looked up at Raash. The lizard was looking at me with that expressionless reptilian face of his. I pointed. "What? Even him?"

"Yes, of course."

"And Armel?" I said, pointing across the room to where Armel was shrugging on a cloak. He had been listening without seeming to.

"Of course, McGill," he said. "Don't be a child. We all decided that Winslade could never be allowed to lead this army. It would be a disaster if he assumed command."

"Uh…" I said, thinking it over, "well… yeah, but it still doesn't seem right."

They made various snorting noises. A bit of snot even flew from Raash's overly large, blue-scaled nostrils.

"I told you he was a fool," he said. "He will run now. He'll run and tell Graves. He will bleat as a pup does to its egg-mother."

"No…" I said, thinking it over, "I'm not going to say anything—because you guys are probably right."

-41-

We did not wait for dawn to begin marching. To rouse 3rd Unit, I began clapping my overly large hands together. This made loud popping sounds that couldn't be ignored. My adjuncts and noncoms automatically seconded the motion. The troops groaned as we ordered them to break camp. They were crying for their mamas, let me tell you, but we just kept kicking butts until everyone was on their feet.

Graves was kicking ass up and down the rest of Legion Varus, demanding everybody load something up on a pig—or their own backs—and begin to walk.

In the distance, echoing up to our hilltop, we could hear similar efforts underway all across our ragtag coalition army. Claver-X was beating on his dogmen, who in turn beat on the ape-aliens. It was much the same with Armel and his banged-up lizards. Working together, we got everyone moving within half an hour's time.

It occurred to me that this decision to march against the largest enemy stronghold on the planet was an insane move. After all, we couldn't even carry all of our gear—not even all the food we'd brought with us. Some of it had to be abandoned.

But what else could we do? Just sit here and wait for every Silicoid on the planet to mass-up and overrun us?

When asked, I dodged the question as to who had come up with this cockamamie plan.

"When the brass says it's time to move out—we move out!" I told a couple of griping adjuncts. "That's how it is when you're a starman with no permanent home. When we get back to Earth, you can all resign if you want to."

This idea was met with disdain by all my troops, but at least they more or less shut up.

The man who had the easiest time of it had to be Claver-X. His apes could drag a hundred kilogram sack behind each of them without breaking a sweat. Running along on one fist and two leathery feet, they set the pace.

The army marched for hours until the sun blazed hotly. At around mid-afternoon—which was about ten hours after dawn on this long-daylight rock, we reached a pink lake. Before sunset, we set up camp on the shores of the strange water and filtered what we could from it. It was infected with weird bacteria—that's what had turned it pink—but it was drinkable.

We'd covered a goodly twenty kilometers so far, and we hadn't been attacked. That was a bigger distance than you'd think, especially when the terrain was rough and we were carrying heavy loads. You'd think that much progress would make even a man like Graves happy—but you'd have thought wrong.

"We're lagging," he complained when he met with all the centurions in his cohort. "At this pace, we'll never reach the enemy stronghold in time to surprise them."

"Maybe we should bring down a lifter, sir," I suggested. "Or maybe one of those hovercraft. We'd be there in an hour!"

He glared at me. "No such vehicles are going to be deployed on this planet. You know that, McGill. What I'm trying to point out is that Legion Varus is the hold-up."

"Huh?"

"That's right, you heard me. Human feet are too slow. The apes and dogmen are outpacing us, waiting every kilometer or so for us to catch up. Armel's lizards aren't as fast as that, but they never seem to get tired. They march until their commanders tell them to stop, without making any comments or slowing down."

"You want we should break out the whips, Primus?" Manfred asked him, only half-joking.

"Nah... that will damage morale. Just urge your men to walk faster. Point out how they're being humiliated by the likes of a zoo's worth of physically superior aliens."

Manfred and I exchanged glances, shaking our heads. Neither one of us believed such a tactic was going to get people to pick up their heels any faster.

We made camp on the shoreline, but we only had enough spare puff-crete available to make a small slab underneath our command tents. Everyone else bedded down on the cold beach of rocks and sand.

None of us slept easily. We all knew that something vicious and evil could come swarming up out of the earth at any moment.

Talk about a nightmare waiting to happen. On this planet, the earth actually *could* come alive and tear your foot off if it felt like it.

But the night passed, and nothing attacked us. I woke up around midnight to the fake call of trumpets.

The sound was emanating from our tappers, telling us our beauty rest had come to an abrupt and premature end.

I was openly surprised to still be breathing. I expressed this idea to Harris, who yawned and stretched out his back under the stars.

"Possibly," he suggested, "our unexpected advance has foiled the enemy's plans."

"Yeah, maybe... Or maybe they're still recovering from that last battle we fought with them. There's no way of knowing."

After spending half the overly long night in camp, we arose to march again long before dawn broke. That might sound like a difficult regimen, but we'd just enjoyed a solid seven hours of rest. That wasn't as much as a man might want, but when your nights are fifteen hours long, you don't really need to sleep the entire time.

Running our suits on batteries, we walked in the starry night. We circled the pink lake, which had turned inky black in the darkness, and made our way around it to some spiky mountains on the far side.

"I have a theory," Raash said, trudging along at my side.

"Another theory, Raash? Say it's not so!"

"Do you insult me again? Even now?"

"Uh..." I said, thinking that over, "Nah, not really. Just making a joke."

"Your jokes are forever without humor," he told me. "You should avoid making those pointless noises with your face."

I couldn't believe I had to endure this from the world's ultimate straight man, but I let it go. I shrugged it off, not caring. "What do you want to tell me, Raash? What's your theory?"

"It is this," he said, pointing to the inky lake we were passing by. "This strange body of water has aided us. I do not believe the aliens can come close to it."

I blinked a couple of times, staring at him. "Why not? Don't all creatures require water to survive?"

"No," Raash said, putting a single clawed finger up between us. "Not these creatures. Not the Silicoids. There's very little moisture in them. I heard that female of yours, Evelyn, speaking about it. She marveled at the lack of moisture, at the lack of traditional water-based solvents in their physical makeup. She said there are indeed cells in these things, but they are not like the cells that make up our bodies."

"Oh yeah? How's that?"

"They're bizarre, she said. They possess different chemicals making up the membranes between these cells. They're nowhere near as dependent on moisture as we are."

"Huh..." I said, not knowing what to make of that idea. "These Silicoids are freaks, all right."

"But there's something more important than that. Imagine if you were essentially a piece of sentient mud. What if you were to come digging up into a lake bottom?"

I thought about that and stopped walking. "You'd probably dissolve..." I said, "like a dirt clod thrown into water."

Raash bent down, picked up a chunk of dirt, and threw it into the lake. There, it did indeed disintegrate.

"You see that?" he crowed. "That is what would happen if the Silicoids dared attack us this close to water!"

I stared open-mouthed and then began to walk again—this soon transformed into a trot. I moved past all the other figures trudging sadly in the dark. I brushed past them, ignoring their curses, until I finally found Evelyn.

Raash thundered after me, puffing his stinky breath on my back. Evelyn looked at the two of us, concerned.

"What is this about, Centurion?" she asked.

All of a sudden, it was "Centurion" again? Maybe that was because Raash was there, listening. The last time we talked, she referred to me as James every time.

"Hey," I said, catching her elbow and smiling at her. "You see this big, foul-smelling lizard right here?" I tossed a thumb over my shoulder at Raash. "He's got an interesting theory."

I relayed to her what he'd said, and she nodded slowly.

"It does make a kind of sense... Yes, I do believe he's correct. I hadn't thought about what a large body of moisture would do to one of these creatures, should they encounter it. It would melt them—like a human putting his foot into lava."

Together, the three of us went to tell Graves the news. Graves would almost certainly have waved me away in disgust if he hadn't seen Evelyn and Raash in my wake. Finally, reluctantly, he allowed us to speak to him.

I began to explain the concept when suddenly Raash erupted.

"It is my idea! These two seek to thieve it. They are egg-stealers. They raid my private nest of concepts!"

We all looked at him quizzically for a moment. "All right then, Raash," Evelyn said, "you explain it to Primus Graves."

Raash did so, emphatically. Graves listened to him and then turned to Evelyn. He completely ignored me.

"Is this theory a possibility, Centurion Thompson?" he asked.

"I think it is," she said. "Notice how they didn't attack us last night? I think it might've been that body of water we were next to. To us, of course, it was simply a means to refresh ourselves, but for a Silicoid—why, it might well be deadly. At least it would have been very difficult for them to swim up under the earth and attack us by surprise."

Graves ordered the entire column of Legion Varus to halt and demanded that we take a short fifteen-minute rest. Then he ordered a battle computer to be brought up. Within a few minutes, a tent was thrown over it, and we encircled the device.

"We still have a few satellites operating in orbit," Graves said. "Let's just take a look at the regional terrain."

We eyeballed our planned path of attack, which was essentially a straight line toward the red crystal stronghold. There was still something like a hundred and fifty more kilometers to go—several days' march.

"What we'll do," he said, drawing a few lines, "is take an alternate route."

He worked to bend the lines on the map away from a straight and narrow path to one that took us to low points. It wouldn't be the easiest, as we had to cross high mountains, low valleys, and circle the occasional pink lake. Essentially, he drew lines between each of the lakes, chaining them together, like connecting dots or hopping from one lily pad to another. There were six daily marches identified.

I whistled long and low. "There's going to be some sore feet when we get there.

"Yes," Graves agreed. "The worst day will be the last one. We'll have to take one long, final march. Nearly twenty kilometers on open rocks. There are no water sources near the red crystal."

"I betcha that's no coincidence, sir," I said, speaking with a certainty that I didn't feel in any way, shape, or form.

But Graves took my input seriously and nodded. "We need to have a test," he said, "before we put everything on the line."

"A test?" Evelyn asked.

"Yes…" Graves squinted at me and Evelyn. "I hear you two have a specimen. A captive, as it were."

We gawked at him, and he made a disgusted sound. He brushed past us, walking out of the tent. We followed him, feeling a certain sense of concern.

"Primus Graves, sir?" Evelyn said, "if you're talking about that one segment of a Silicoid, the specimen I've been keeping for study, I—"

He waved her off. "This is too important, Thompson. Set aside your misplaced motherly instincts. We need to know for sure."

So saying, despite a lot of squawking from Evelyn and a bit of hissing and grunting from Raash, which I thought might be an expression of laughter from the scaly bastard, Graves finally found the puff-crete crate.

He ripped it open and plunged a gauntlet inside. Evelyn squawked, but he didn't even look at her.

Graves pulled the Silicoid beastie out of the crate. The squirming little monster immediately attempted to attack his glove.

Walking to the edge of a pond of pink liquid, he hurled the Silicoid far out into the water. It splashed down, and Evelyn trotted out several steps into the water until she was knee-deep.

She stood there, like a child crying over a lost pet.

"Look, he's swimming back to us," she said.

It was true. The rock-like creature, although it couldn't really *swim*, was definitely creating a ripple in the shallow and otherwise motionless pond. The ripple was headed in her direction.

"Hold on, Evelyn," I said, taking a few splashy steps after her. "He might be in an ornery mood. After all, we just threw him in there."

The creature was indeed homing in precisely on her position. Could it hear her voice? Was it coming to her like a dog?

I wasn't actually sure, but I didn't like it. I had a laser pistol out in my hand, just in case.

Evelyn had no such qualms. Had she actually bonded with this nasty thing? She was clapping her hands, practically whistling with her fingers in her mouth for the beast to come home to mama.

The little monster made a valiant effort. When it finally reached us, the water around our feet became frothy.

"Hey..." Evelyn said, with ripples and bubbles near her boots. "Something... I think he's biting me!"

That was it for me. I put a big looping arm around her waist, hoisted her up, and marched her out of the pond.

Sure as shit, there was a flipping, flapping, half-melted rock-and-mud alien attached to her boot. It was chewing ferociously. To me, it looked like an ornery turd that had come to life to assault its maker.

I grabbed the thing, ripped it away from her, and threw it onto the shore. Then I lasered it until it stopped moving.

Evelyn sat on the side of a big flat rock. She worked on her boots, checking them for damage.

They were scuffed up, but space boots are made of extremely tough material. Even the gear that light troopers wore was difficult to cut in any way. Possibly the creature could have done it, though, if it hadn't been in its death throes.

Graves marched over, ignoring us, and knelt beside the creature, which was steaming, stinking, and squirming very lightly.

"It's dead," he said, "or nearly dead."

He looked up at Evelyn and me, then turned to Raash. "Congratulations, Saurian. Your theories have held water." He smiled and walked away.

"Was that supposed to be a joke?" Evelyn asked.

"Yeah," I said, "that's the kind of joke he makes."

"The not-funny kind," Raash said.

I aimed a finger in his direction. "Yep. That's the kind of joke Graves' *always* makes."

-42-

The following days were long and difficult. On the fifth morning, Winslade came back to rejoin the legion using a teleport harness.

He was hopping mad at first, but after the situation had been explained to him, he finally decided that our strategic decisions were the right ones. No one said it, but even he was thinking that he would have been too chicken to have set off marching toward the biggest enemy base on this planet. Only by doing so had we figured out that the Silicoids were vulnerable to the bodies of water on this planet, and that it was essentially deadly to them.

So, he eventually shut his face, took command of Legion Varus again, and marched with us on the sixth and final day.

As the white star rose and dawn broke over the harsh landscape, we approached the massive red edifice. This was the Great Crystal Launcher. The strange super-weapon that had sent so many invasion pods into space, assaulting numerous worlds. It was, in fact, the very reason this shaky coalition of alien species had come together. We simply couldn't tolerate this scourge any longer.

Now, if it'd been a defensive weapon, it would have beamed us to death long ago. But this thing wasn't built for that purpose. Instead, the Silicoids had constructed it to project their power deep into our territory. It seemed to me that they'd long ago made the decision that this world would be protected by a fleet in space—which the Mogwa battlecruisers had wiped out—and then by large gravity beam installations dotted here and there over the surface of the planet.

At the outset, the plan had worked. Those big gravity guns had a devastating punch and a vast reach. They'd kept our warships at bay. But we'd slipped past their defenses with Seven's invasion ship. That brave little Nairb had allowed us to sneak in an invasion force, and now, at long last, we'd reached our final goal.

We were marching across the surface of their planet, instead of them smashing us all the time. It felt good to reverse the game on them.

As the crystal cannon grew bigger on the horizon, I thought to myself that Raash's contribution to our effort had been significant. I didn't think we'd have made it this far if we hadn't come up with the idea of hugging wet areas of ground each night as we camped. Ours was indeed a coalition that was greater than the sum of its parts.

With the cannon growing ever taller as we got near it, Evelyn and I took to sleeping together in the same sleeping bag. One thing that Legion Varus had very helpfully designed into our gear was the ability to unzip any given sleeping bag and transform it into something like a cloak, or a long-hanging coat—or, if you married it with a second sleeping bag—into a comfy double bed. This was the option she and I had chosen to adopt.

Why had she suddenly turned sweet on me? I wasn't completely sure, but I think it might have been that moment when I'd plucked her ass out of the lake and saved her from the beast that was trying to eat her boot. Women tended to fall for guys who physically rescued them from danger—I guess that must have been it.

In any case, we'd spent the better part of a week sharing a bed as we hadn't done for many years. We'd flirted with the idea back on Jungle World, but it had never happened.

Unfortunately, others in my unit weren't blind to this new reality. With great regularity, I received eyerolls, folded-lip stares, and angry mutterings from other females all across the encampment.

Della was miffed. Natasha was miffed.

And Primus Cherish Collins? She was outright pissed off.

"Centurion McGill," Cherish snarled at me.

I turned around and saw Cherish standing there with a nasty little frown on her face and two small fists planted on her hips.

"Uh..." I said. "What's the problem, Cherish?"

She showed me her teeth. That was a bad sign. It was always a bad sign.

"Don't call me that, McGill," she said.

I knew in an instant what had happened. Someone had told her about Evelyn and me. Damn it. Was there a girl in this entire legion that could keep her mouth shut?

"You," she said, pointing at my nose in an accusatory fashion, "are coming with me."

She turned around and marched off, and I had no choice but to follow in her wake. She led me to Winslade's command tent, which was, naturally, the most audacious one in the entire campsite.

It was planted atop a nice spread of puff-crete, too. This was damn near a crime, as we didn't have much puff-crete material left. But old Winslade thought nothing of wasting a big slab of it to protect his personal quarters every night when we camped.

I walked into the tent with Cherish's small form leading the way. Hulking in the doorway behind her, I hesitated.

"Here he is, Tribune," she said.

"Ah, McGill!" Winslade said, "I'm only slightly surprised."

"Uh..." I said, "surprised about what exactly, Tribune, sir?"

"I asked Primus Collins to locate the individual responsible for this *theory* about the Silicoids being water-averse."

"It's more than a theory, Tribune," I said.

Winslade lifted one skinny finger. "That is exactly what the propagator of such dangerous talk would say. Did you know that scientists who lead us astray throughout history nearly always do so with unbridled enthusiasm?"

"No, sir... I guess I didn't know that."

"Well, it's true."

"Yeah, but... um... I'm not sure how that makes much difference," I said. "I mean, after all, we're getting past the region where we have any water sources. We're about to make the big push across a wide-open plain."

Winslade aimed his finger at me again, as if it were a gun in a child's hand. "There, you've struck upon my next point," he said, "surely by accident, I imagine."

"I'm sure that's so," I said, as I was utterly baffled by whatever the hell he was getting at.

"McGill, are you aware that the Silicoids haven't hit us a single time since we left our original beachhead?"

"Yessir, I'm well aware of that—unless you count that one that was chewing on Evelyn's boot over at—"

"I do not, as that event was self-inflicted," he said, and I fell silent.

He stood up from behind his fold-out battle computer and began walking around the tent in circles. It wasn't a very large space, just large enough for him to pace.

"Just listen," he said. "Why do you think the enemy hasn't attempted to stop us during this obvious march toward their stronghold?"

"Well, I don't rightly know..." I said. "Maybe because of the lakes we keep camping next to?"

Winslade nodded indulgently. "That is a possibility, as we've already discussed. Can you give me another?"

"Well..." I said, giving myself a long scratch.

My finger worked along my chin line and up to my ear on the left side. Winslade looked increasingly impatient.

"Uh..." I said, "how about—?"

"How about you listen, for a moment?" he said, interrupting me before I could get another fool idea out of my mouth. "My concept is that the enemy has decided to take advantage of our aggressive approach. Rather than continuing to try to take us out at the beachhead, I believe they're gathering up all their strength to meet us here at their stronghold."

He slapped at his map, which shimmered. The 3D hologram danced over his battle computer. In the center of the depicted scene was the rather bulky mass that formed the vast red crystalline cannon.

I could see it on the horizon quite easily now, and here on the map, it took up a lot of real estate. It resembled something like the Matterhorn back on Earth, but it came up at more of a slant—a leaning tower effect. That's what it was, canted perhaps 20 degrees off-center. The mountainous structure was aimed up into the skies, the deadliest and largest cannon we'd ever encountered in all of our travels.

"Here," Winslade said, "that's where they planned to meet us if they couldn't take us out where we landed. And then, when we started to move, why, the most obvious counter-option would be to mass your forces at the point that we're clearly headed toward."

"Oh," I said, thinking that over, "so you think they aren't running scared? They're gathering up an offensive army instead?"

"Obviously, McGill. How is it that no one has thought of this possibility before?"

I'd started scratching again. I stared at the table. The shivering hologram of that gigantic red space cannon stood damn near a foot tall. It came right off the battle map at you.

I nodded my head. "It's a possibility, sir. I have to admit."

Winslade threw both his skinny fists high and waved them around. "Even you can see it!" he said. "This is going to be a disaster! An unmitigated disaster! I finally get down here to the planet—for the second time, mind you, having been blown apart within seconds after my initial arrival. And now, here I am, saddled with the task of command. My charge is to follow a plan of action I didn't authorize, but for which I'll most certainly be held responsible if it all transforms into shit."

He paced around for a while, fuming and complaining. I tuned him out and stared at the Matterhorn-looking thing on the hologram. I frowned and thought hard, and then I came up with an idea.

"Hey, sir?" I said, "how about we do this a little differently?"

Winslade spun around on one heel and looked at me, putting his tirade on hold. "Another idea, McGill? Dare you offer so much?"

"Yes, sir, I think I do. How about we just blow it up?"

"Blow it up?" he said. "How? It's well-shielded, it's made of rock essentially, and none of the cowardly captains in this fleet are willing to come near to aid in this assault."

"Yeah…" I said, "I get that. But a thing like this… it's got to have a command center of some kind, doesn't it? What if we were to knock that out?"

Winslade blinked, then he stared at his map. He thought about it. Soon he was tapping at his own chin with those skinny, stick-like fingers of his.

"I like it," he announced, turning toward me. "What will your target area be?"

"Uh… my what?"

"Where would you insert yourself? I'm assuming you'd use a teleport harness for this?"

I was squinting now and beginning to look alarmed. My mouth sagged low. Had I just volunteered myself for something awful?

Winslade continued eyeing his map. He peered and brought his face down close to it, bending down almost to where his eyes sank into the folds of the mountain-like illusion.

He made stretching, spreading motions with his fingers, expanding one point, then another. "There are various porous structures," he said. "I'm not sure if these are vents where the flame comes out when they fire the thing, or what. It's unclear, but they most certainly provide points of entry."

Winslade was off and running, and I was starting to feel sick at heart. I realized that I'd somehow volunteered myself for a suicidal mission. I had to wonder if my big dumb brain was ever going to stop doing things like this. Honestly, I doubted it would.

Less than an hour later, I found myself being trussed up by a couple of techs. I was allowed to hand-pick my commando team. I asked for my entire unit—my entire cohort, in fact—but those requests were denied.

Instead, I was given Harris, Natasha, Carlos, Sargon, and a half-dozen other squalling heavies and specialists. Bringing up the tail end of things was Clane with a platoon of long-faced light troopers.

Every last one of them was in a sour mood, with the possible exception of Sargon. "At least we don't have to march all the way across that open plain to our deaths," he said, "not this time. Nope, McGill's arranged it so we can just pop on in there and get things over with."

"How very thoughtful..." Natasha said bitterly.

I brought one more man along for the ride. He was a fellow I hadn't seen for quite a while, as he had wisely kept himself in an invisible state. He was none other than our stealth-suited ghost, Cooper.

I could have brought Della instead, of course. But she was already pissed about Cherish and Evelyn. So, I decided to go with Cooper and saddle him with this duty.

Leading my ragtag, grumbling crew, we reported to a makeshift Gray Deck inside a tent that was luffing in the desert breezes of Crystal World.

-43-

We put on the teleport harnesses and gritted our teeth. Blue lights began flashing, and my troops winked out one by one.

Some of us were saying our prayers. Others were muttering curses. We all knew this was going to be a hard mission. This enemy was no pushover. Hell, even a Silicoid peasant could eat the boots off a man if they got in close enough.

When we reappeared a moment later, a dry, dusty wind struck us. It was like a dragon's hot breath, coming down from the north. That was nothing unusual for Crystal World, which was pretty much one giant, dusty, gritty land. It was the kind of place where even the rare plants were covered in spines and leathery skin.

We stood at the base of the crystalline space-cannon. It vaulted up at a sharp angle all the way into the clouds. You couldn't even see the top of it.

"Holy shit…" Harris said, gawking up at the thing. "We are *so* screwed. What are we going to do? Just set an A-bomb or two at the base of this monster and run for it?"

"I don't think so," Sargon said. "About the running part, I mean. We're not going anywhere. They didn't mention this during the briefing, but if you check our battery charges on our harnesses, they're all dead-empty."

Half-panicked and growling with rage, my troops checked their harnesses. It was true. The techs back at the encampment had—without mentioning it beforehand—preset our teleport harnesses with a minimum charge. They'd given us just enough juice to get out here to the target, but not enough to take us back to safety.

"Then this *is* a suicide mission!" Harris shouted. "Another frigging suicide mission!"

"It always was, you moron," Clane told him.

I was stunned by that. Clane had always been the most level-headed of my adjuncts. I didn't like to see him bitch and moan like Harris always did. Apparently, he'd had enough of Harris and his game-over routine, and he'd snapped.

The two officers snarled at one another, but I threw my hands up. "Listen, guys, this is most definitely *not* a suicide mission. Not if we don't light up any big explosives."

"That's right," Natasha said, backing me up. "And we're not going to be able to set off any big bombs."

We all looked at her.

She took out one of the devices they'd provided us with. It certainly looked dangerous. "These bombs they gave us, they aren't antimatter. They aren't fusion either."

"Well, then what the hell are they?" Harris demanded.

"They're EMPs," she said. "We're here to scramble the enemy communications—whatever it is that keeps their network of defensive cannons all over the planet functional."

"That's just grand," Harris said. "Do we even know if EMPs are going to have any effect on these guys?"

Natasha shrugged. "Electronics are electronics. Unless they're using mental powers to talk to each other over distance, it should work."

"What about our own gear?" Harris demanded. "It's going to knock out our force blades. It's going to knock out our comms."

Natasha chewed her lip for a moment, looking around. Everybody was squinting. The gritty winds stung our eyes just from the dryness. The actual flying bits of sand in the air were a bonus.

"I don't see any doors, Centurion," Clane reported in to me. "We've run halfway around the base—found nothing."

"All right, bring them all back here."

I squinted in the bright white sun, trying to think. "No doors? How do they get into the damned thing and run it?"

"Underground," Natasha said.

Our eyes met, and I knew she must be right. These rock-creatures didn't need doors on the surface. They might have tunnels... or hell, they might even have sandy channels under our feet that served them as entrances.

"What are we going to do?" I asked Natasha. I needed her brainpower now more than ever.

She thought for a few seconds more. The other adjuncts mouthed off, but I ignored them.

"There's no enemy in sight," she said at last. "If we move, we might find some—so let's just set the charges right here."

"Yeah... Yeah!" Harris said, glomming onto the idea. "This is as good a place as any. We'll set them all and move away to a safe distance."

I shook my head. "Not good enough. No, we're going to spread the charges all around the base of this cannon. Then we'll find some kind of shelter from the blasts."

"It's just an EMP blast you're talking about, right?" Harris said, still nervous about getting blown to bits.

I nodded, and he rolled his eyes around for a few seconds, thinking about it. "All right. Yeah, sure. Let's do that."

I gave a charge to every light trooper I had and ordered them all out in a crescent around the base of the big launcher.

"Cooper," I said, "you head around to the back of this thing. Find a way for us to hide, somewhere we can get into, somewhere we can hunker down before we set this off."

"Anybody seen any of those crystalline drones?" Harris demanded. "Any Silicoids? Anything?"

Everybody shook their head. The plateau we were on, which formed the vast base of the launcher, seemed to be empty. That could either be a very good sign or a very bad one, depending. It might be that the enemy was hiding, that we'd already pretty much won this war. Or... it might mean they were about to fire this monster space-cannon of theirs, and they'd retreated to a safe distance before the hellfire was released.

Naturally, I didn't mention these thoughts to my troops. They were already as nervous as cats in a room full of rocking chairs.

Clane and his men trotted away, setting charges as they went. The base of the great cannon was about a kilometer in circumference. That was a lot of territory to cover, but light troopers were the best at racing around performing suicidal tasks.

Cooper contacted me less than ten minutes later. "I think I found something, Centurion."

"What is it? A cave? An alcove? A secret passage?"

"No, none of those things. A slanting set of cut steps went up the back of the cannon itself."

I squinted at my tapper, pondering that, and I heaved a big sigh. It didn't sound all that promising. We wanted to get inside this thing, or under it—we didn't want to climb it.

Looking around at the desolate landscape surrounding us, I shook my head. It was our best option, as far as I could see. The only other thing I could think to do would be to simply trot out into the desert surrounding the massive machine. Who knew if that was going to be safe or not?

Nodding and coming to a sudden decision, I ordered all the men with me to start running to Cooper's position.

Clane's men were the last to catch up—and they were, in fact, too late. The blast went off on the opposite side of the cannon. Fortunately, it didn't harm them. It wasn't the kind of thing that would do much other than blow the circuitry out of a man's tapper.

The main thing it did to us was knock out our comms. We couldn't talk to the rest of Legion Varus now—not even if we wanted to.

We were left climbing up what amounted to a very steep stairway cut into the crystal itself. Actually, calling the treacherous series of handholds a ladder or a stairway was improper. It wasn't anything that any human would have built.

Each of the risers—or handholds, or whatever they are—came out only about half as far as a man's boot needed for a firm grip. Worse, the risers were about twice as tall as they were wide. Each of these precarious steps propelled you upward, but they left you feeling like a gust of wind might blow you off the stair to your death.

We all began to climb anyway. I realized that we were actually going up the back of the cannon at a very steep angle. It had to be about a sixty-degree tilt, jutting up into the sky and away from the surface of the planet.

On our hands and knees, grunting with the strain, we kept inching upward. Now and then, a man slipped and fell. Once, the guy who slipped took out another man below him on the way down.

The wisest threw themselves flat, letting the bodies tumble past them while they clung to the unforgiving surface. I was glad I wasn't down there at the rear of this long line of struggling men. The odds had to be the worst for Clane's guys, who were at the very end of the procession.

When we managed to make it to something like two hundred meters up the back of the great cannon, I noticed that Natasha, who was directly ahead of me, was slowing down.

All we could do was shout at one another, so I started shouting. "Natasha!"

The sight of her fine rump moving up the crystal ladder ahead of me would normally have given me something to smile about, but not today. All I could think of was that if she lost her grip and fell, it would be me next, and I didn't know if I could hold on.

The only thing that gave us a chance at all was the nanite grips built into our gloves. We had them in our kneepads and boots, too. These gave us a semi-adhesive effect, usually used in Null-G environments, but today we were using it for a very different purpose: to cling on to a slick, glass-like edifice that had very clearly never been designed for a man to climb.

"Natasha!" I shouted.

A face turned and looked down at me. The expression on that face was one of terror and strain.

"James," she said, "I don't know if I can hold on much longer."

I frowned. If there was one person in this entire unit that I thought we needed right now, it was probably Natasha. I would have gladly sacrificed every one of Clane's lights to keep her breathing. Hell, I'd put them on a spit and barbecue them all, if I thought it would help.

"What's the matter?" I said. "Why are you slowing down?"

"It's this wind. It's the strain," she said. "I'm in good shape, but I'm just not strong enough. I'm running out of gas, here."

I nodded, understanding. I thought about what I could do. Then automatically, I reached up with one of my long arms and pushed up against that fine rump of hers. She squawked just a little, but then I think she realized I wasn't attempting to cop a feel, but simply working to give her a boost. She let me push her forward and up the stairway.

"What if this thing doesn't even go anywhere, James," she said, as she began climbing again. She was mostly using her hands and legs to cling to the glass-like stone, while I used my own strength to propel her upward.

"We're going to find something," I told her. "An entranceway, a ledge, a balcony. I don't know, something."

About then, the whole base of the great space-cannon did something utterly unexpected. It began to move.

The world rumbled and shook. We all hung on for dear life.

There were lots of screams, mostly from below me. A few people fell, flying out into nothingness. They grasped wildly at the air, as if they could somehow catch onto something and stop the long trip to the ground.

To me, they resembled cats falling from trees, spinning around, desperate. Then they disappeared from view.

We all stopped progressing upward while the cannon was in motion. We simply clung to the spot we were at, praying that we wouldn't be shaken loose.

Heavy vibrations came to the great device as the base slowly rotated. These vibrations were painful to the fingers, to the toes. To me, it felt as if I was clinging onto a block of hardwood, perhaps a baseball bat, and beating it on concrete until my hands stung.

But still, I kept clinging, and Natasha did the same.

"What the hell is it doing?" A voice came up from below me.

I took a chance and glanced down.

It was Carlos. Somehow, Carlos was right behind me? There had been one or two others ahead of him... but apparently, they'd fallen.

Immediately, I felt a twinge of suspicion. Had Carlos perhaps sought to nudge an ankle out of the way? I wouldn't put it past him, but I couldn't prove it, so I didn't make the accusation.

"McGill!" he shouted up at me, his round face was full of fear, as were his even rounder eyes. The wind was whipping his hair around, and his mouth was wide open as if he was screaming. Perhaps he was. It was hard to hear with the massive, rumbling, screeching sound of the cannon in motion.

"What the hell is it doing?" he asked me.

"I don't know," I told him. "Why the hell do you think I know?"

"Because you're in charge," he shouted back.

I would have shrugged, but I didn't dare. Every limb I had, every finger, every nano-adhesive pad on my gloves and boots was clinging to that impossible stairway.

"It's obviously realigning itself," Natasha said crossly, shouting down at us from above.

"Why would it be doing that?" I said.

"Because it's going to fire soon!" Natasha said.

"Oh, no... dear, God no!" Carlos wailed.

I looked up at Natasha, and my mouth sagged open. I thought to myself, *of course. Why else would the damned thing be in motion?*

Why else would the space-cannon be realigning itself? The only thing I could think of is because it knew we were out here, and it knew we were climbing on its back like fleas, trying to find a way in.

But possibly, that wasn't what was happening at all. Possibly, it was just performing its primary function, and it knew no more of us than a horse knew about a fly on its rump. Possibly, it knew less about us than the horse, because we had caused it very little discomfort.

Sure, we'd set off our tiny EMP charges, and they'd crackled and possibly destroyed some of our own equipment. But this great machine, it seemed to be operating perfectly. It seemed to be one hundred percent functional, as far as I could tell.

"James?" Natasha shouted down at me. "I've been trying to contact headquarters, but I can't get through to them."

"Great," I said.

"All we managed to do was wreck our own gear," Carlos said. "All our comms are down."

This entire mission was a giant cluster. What was it the fleet pukes liked to say?

When everything went completely wrong, they would say it was like a monkey trying to fuck a football—and the football was winning.

-44-

The damned cannon we were climbing stopped moving after what had to be a full minute. By that time, no less than five of my men had been shaken loose of that evil stairway and fallen to their deaths. Two had lost their grip, while three others had been knocked off by the falling bodies.

Again, I thought of Natasha, of her weakness. She simply wasn't cut out for something like this, a true commando mission. She was all about brains, not brawn.

Why the hell did I put her up ahead of me? I should have strapped her onto my back. That would have been better. If I'd simply tied her wrists together and hung her around my neck like a rucksack, we'd probably both live to see the next hour. But it was too late for any of that kind of thing now.

When the cannon finally stopped twisting and rumbling, I reached up and pushed on her butt again. She'd been clinging and shivering, flat against the stair, not daring to do so much as move a finger.

But with my prodding, she got moving again. I wasn't quite sure if she felt like getting away from that hand of mine, or if it made her feel safe and secure—and I didn't much care either way. She was holding up the line, and none of the rest of us could climb over her. She moved her arms and legs, progressing higher up the impossible slope. I was following behind her with Carlos next in line behind me.

Daring to glance back down now and then, I spotted Sargon. He was about five men down the line from me. At least he hadn't lost his grip yet.

Looking upward and squinting into that harsh sunlight, I counted butts and boots. Who was that up ahead of Natasha? There was someone there, but it wasn't clear who…

Occasionally, I saw the flash of white metal glinting in the sunlight. Then I realized who it had to be: Cooper was up there.

He was in the lead still. He'd never fallen. It was just like him to wear a stealth suit, no matter what. When you were inside one of those things, you were half-blind yourself. Cooper was still wearing it, even while he climbed a nearly impossible edifice.

It made me smile to think about the day I'd introduced him to that rustling mesh of light-bending material. The moment he'd put that suit on, he'd fallen in love with it. Something about being invisible really appealed to some people.

The only reason I could see him at all was because now and then, in the whipping winds, the bag-like stealth-suit revealed a glimpse of his boot heel or perhaps the barrel of his laser pistol. There was often something left uncovered by the baggy suit as it flapped in the endless hot breezes coming off the desert.

"McGill!" he shouted down perhaps a minute later.

We were climbing blindly now, not knowing where we were going, not knowing if we could survive. We didn't know if there was anything up here other than the mouth of this gigantic cannon.

If that was all we found, maybe we'd all have to throw ourselves in. How else might we affect this monstrous device? Thinking about it, I figured I'd have to give the order to come up to my position, one by one. I'd demand each man came up into grabbing-range. Then, I'd give them all a healthy toss, dropping them like maidens into a volcano's maw.

Lastly, I'd jump in myself, whooping and hollering all the way to the black pit below. That would be easier and less pointless than attempting to make the impossible climb back down to the ground again.

"McGill!" Cooper shouted again.

"What do you want?" I shouted back.

My arms were stinging now and shivering a bit. We were reaching the limits of even my strength. It was Natasha that was the problem. It seemed as we went farther and higher up the crystalline ladder, the more she was slowing down. This caused me to push harder against that fine butt of hers to keep her going upward.

It no longer felt like any kind of thrill to be pushing on her hindquarters. It now seemed like a chore, a painful weight. Having to hold my arm up above my head for so long, the blood had drained from it. I'd begun to switch arms, using first my left, then my right for about a minute at a time. But they were both beginning to sting, the way your arms hurt when you painted a ceiling for an extended period of time.

"I found something!" Cooper shouted. "There's something up here!"

I called a halt then. Grateful, everybody relaxed. They were panting, hugging up against the great stairway. Everyone's muscles trembled with exertion.

"Well?" I shouted up to him. "What the hell did you find?"

He didn't answer immediately, and I began to fear the worst. Had he gone too far? Had he gone over the top and fallen into the mouth of the cannon? That was how I was thinking this was going to end.

But no. I looked ahead, and I could see the barrel went on for a long, long way. It plunged right up into the clouds. We couldn't be more than a third of the way up to the top.

So, what had Cooper found?

"Natasha, I'm gonna push you up a little higher. Try to figure out what Cooper was talking about."

"Oh God, James. Really?"

"It's that, or I'm giving your ankle a yank and sending you to the revival queue."

"Oh shit…"

I pushed her butt again. She grunted. She heaved. She strained. I could tell she was probably cramping up. When you stop moving, and your muscles were really tired, stopping was dangerous. They would cramp up, lock up, and prevent you from moving forward.

We inched upward another ten steps.

"It's a hole," she shouted down. "To my left. He must have gone inside of it."

"Follow him," I ordered her.

She did it. She went off to the left and disappeared.

Heaving myself higher, I saw a dark hole. It was perfectly circular. It bore deep into the cannon itself, just to the side of the stairway. Could this be the goal? Could this be the entire point of this insane climb?

Looking above us, I could see that the stairs kept going. But I was through with that. Whatever was up there, it couldn't be better than this.

If I was exhausted, my men had to be in even worse shape. There was no better refuge.

I crawled into the hole. It was about a meter in diameter. I quickly spun out a monofilament line. The others were grateful to latch it onto their belts.

I couldn't hold the weight of all of them by myself, of course. So I used nano adhesives and advanced climbing gear, which was never meant for something quite like this. It had to suffice.

I used every adhesive patch I had, attaching them to the inside of the round chamber we were now taking refuge within. I hoped it could support the weight of those who came after me.

They used the monofilament as a safety line. It looped through every belt loop, all the way down to the bottom of the struggling group.

One by one, they snaked their way into the dark chute. When they got to the top, I grabbed them and pulled them inside.

When Sargon reached me, I let him take over for me. After all, he hadn't had to push anyone's ass all the way up that ladder, and he was at least as strong and full of stamina as I was. So instead of worrying about getting everybody into this strange exhaust pipe or whatever the hell it was, I let him do it.

When we were all inside, I did a headcount. There were about twenty of us left alive. We all lay panting and groaning in that pipe—or whatever it was.

From a platoon strength of thirty-plus down to twenty... I tried not to think about it.

I made my way ahead to see what Cooper and Natasha were up to. Together, we came to an unhappy spot. About a hundred meters from the entrance, we found the end of the line.

My first guess about what this thing might be turned out to be true.

"It's an exhaust pipe," Cooper said, as if unable to believe our bad luck. "That's what it's got to be."

"He's right," Natasha said. "It flows from the inside of the cannon to the outside. There must be flares like this all around the giant barrel. They're pressure-release holes. Probably, when they fire this monster, a lot of gases are released. Maybe they bored some of these spiraling tubes to relieve the pressure, to keep the cannon itself from shattering when it fires the projectile all the way up into orbit."

"Orbit? Hell," I said. "It fires these things so hard they fly all the way out of the star system."

She nodded. "Yeah, that's right. But I don't think all of that power comes from here. This is just a launch system. They must use some kind of gravity manipulation to get up to relativistic speeds. It can't all come from here, you see, because—"

"It doesn't matter," I said, sensing a nerd-lecture was incoming. "They just turned and realigned this cannon. They just aimed it somewhere. If they're going to fire it off soon, well, we're all as good as torched."

The tube, channel, relief valve—whatever the hell it was, was long enough for all of us to take shelter. At least the hot winds and the pelting sands weren't hitting us anymore. At least there was no longer any danger of being knocked from that dreadful stairway.

We'd traded the hell of the treacherous stairs in for another form of certain death. What a deal...

"Okay, boss," Carlos said. "So... we're here. What a garden spot. I'm so glad we climbed up here for an hour. I've got dozens of pictures on my tapper now for my kids."

"You don't have any kids, Carlos," Natasha said.

"Shut up, Ortiz," I said tiredly.

Carlos was lying on his back in the middle of the exhaust channel, taking a break and complaining simultaneously. He'd always been a man who was quick to give in to the inevitable. I guess that came with the territory for some men after they'd died enough times as a legionnaire.

"What's the point?" he asked. "What's the damn point of all this? We're going to be incinerated next. Incinerated and probably permed."

"We're not gonna be permed," Harris argued. "They know exactly where we are. When they destroy this big cannon, they know they'll be killing us too. They'll revive us after that."

"Ah-ah-ah," Carlos said, waving one finger up in the air from where he still lay flat on his back. "Haven't you figured that out yet, my big-brained adjunct? These guys don't plan to blow this cannon up."

Harris growled, and he made scrabbling sounds. I figured he was trying to get to Carlos to strangle him or throw him out of one end of this pipe we were all lounging in. I couldn't blame him for that, and if he did it, I'd already decided I wasn't going to stop him.

"Shit's just coming out of your mouth, Ortiz!" Harris said.

"No," Natasha said. "I think he's right. They sent us out here with nothing but EMPs. That's a disabling system, not something for sabotage. The brass must want to take this installation intact. Maybe they want to study the technology. You've got to admit, it's pretty impressive."

"What the fuck?" Harris shouted, outraged. "You mean they're not gonna blow it up? After we came out here and did our job?!" With each of these phrases, he slammed a fist against the wall of the exhaust channel. "We busted our balls coming up that damn stairway, and now you're telling me we're out of communication? They don't know where we are?

"That's it, sir," Carlos said, putting a little extra insult into the "sir" just for good measure. "Hell, some of those losers who just fell, those guys who went twirling off into space past your nose? They're all permed already."

"Hold on, hold on," I said, trying to put the best possible face on things. "Don't talk crazy, guys. Carlos, you quit having Harris on."

Harris was glowering now, clearly blaming anyone and everyone around him for this dismal fate.

"We're not going to be incinerated. We set off the EMPs, and this big squirt gun is disabled. It's not going to fire, that's the whole point. The legion will come, and we'll capture it intact, just like Natasha said."

"Why did it rotate, then?" Harris shot back.

"That's just a big mechanism. That's not the electronics. That's not about communications, or some targeting computer. That's just giant gears or whatnot."

We argued about this for a while when suddenly another shout came from the front of our line. It was from Cooper, who was still at the end of the tunnel, perched inside the barrel of the giant cannon. He was staring up at the sky.

"Sir! Sir!" he shouted. "There's something up there!"

I squirmed toward him along with Natasha and Ortiz. Carlos followed us, putting his round face at the back of the group.

The four of us could barely look out of the hole at once, but we managed. We craned our necks and tried to figure out what Cooper was talking about.

It quickly became obvious. There was a shadow up there. You could only see it now and then when the clouds broke through. But it was unmistakable. A dark looming ship had appeared.

"What the hell?" Cooper said. "I think those are drop-pods."

It was true. Dark cylindrical specks were falling. They flared white when they got down to a low enough altitude. They were definitely drop-pods.

"Drop-pods?" Carlos said. "But the legion is already down here..."

"It's got to be the Rigellians," Natasha said, sucking in a breath. "They're the only ones left. The only ones who never did deploy. They're landing. They're landing right here on the cannon."

Everybody gaped. Everyone was baffled. But I was the one who figured things out first.

"That must mean that we did it," I said, grabbing Carlos and giving him a shake. He cowered, scared I was going to throw him off the ledge and down into the cannon's maw. I had half a mind to do it, too.

"What are you talking about, McGill?"

"Look, there's no way that transport ship would dare come down into orbit and drop those bears unless we'd disabled the planetary defense systems. We severed their connections. It's the only answer."

Everybody craned their necks and gaped, blinking in disbelief. But it did seem to be true. More and more ships began to appear, coming out of hyperspace and gliding into orbit.

"That's a battlecruiser," Carlos said, still lying on his back. He was kind of shoved in among the group of us. "That is a freaking Mogwa battlecruiser."

It was true. Sateekas and his flotilla of warships had arrived. They'd all come to Crystal World at last.

-45-

"Centurion?"

It was Clane this time. I was surprised he'd stayed alive this long. He was way at the back of his team, trailing behind the last of his lights—all the men he'd managed to get up the ladder alive.

Damn, I thought. He was one brave dude to go last.

When you were climbing a ladder out of Hell, you always wanted to be the *first* one in line, not the last. That way, you were that much less likely to get knocked off when the guy ahead of you fell.

"Centurion McGill, our troops are assaulting the cannon. They're coming in from every angle!"

I had to see this for myself. From inside the cannon, you could only see a slice of the sky—so I had to get to the far end of this chute.

I began shoving people out of the way, crawling over them, putting knees into guts. My hands and boots squashed legs. There was a lot of cursing and complaining. If I hadn't been their commanding officer, I'm sure they would have kicked me savagely—but they didn't dare. Sometimes, command did have its privileges.

I made my way all the way through that long, narrow pipe to the back of the group. It gently curved around the circumference of the great cannon as I went.

When I finally reached the opening where we'd come in from the steep stairway and looked outside, I couldn't believe what I was seeing.

It was true. Troops were marching—no, it was more than marching. They were frigging *charging* across the open plains at a ground-eating pace.

Thousands of legionnaires, Saurians and ape-aliens were out there, as far as the eye could see. They rapidly made their way across the arid landscape toward the base of the cannon. In response, we whooped, we hollered, and we cheered.

"We're saved!" Harris shouted, laughing. "There's not going to be a perming—not tonight, friends!"

Legion Varus and the other survivors were about to take this installation by force. Whatever the Silicoids had planned seemed doomed—but then, the battlefield we were observing changed dramatically.

The converging armies were about two kilometers from the base of the cannon. It looked like victory was assured. There were Rigellian bears coming up on the eastern flank, thousands of them. On the western flank were the ape-aliens. Due south was the main vanguard, Legion Varus marching fast, double-time. They'd all raced across hundreds of kilometers to reach the cannon and make this final, desperate assault.

But then the Silicoids finally made their move. They burst from the ground like landmines beneath the feet of man, ape, and Saurian. Even the Rigellians, who'd deployed on the other side of the cannon, weren't safe. The Silicoids had been hiding all around the cannon, in a full circle surrounding it.

As I watched, I realized that this had been their plan all along. Why had no one met us at the base of this cannon? Why had no one chased us, or climbed the stairs to attack? Why hadn't the enemy at least tried to knock us from the deadly stairs as we climbed them?

The answer was simple. The Silicoids weren't here—at least, not their main force. They'd deployed themselves underground, in a wide ring around the cannon.

Maybe they'd been lurking beneath the sands all along. Perhaps that was safe and comfortable for their kind until their full strength was achieved.

Whatever the reason, once marching men crossed their position in large numbers, they responded. They reared up, growing pods to grasp churning legs. They opened their slate-fanged maws wide. They clamped onto boots and chewed. When men tripped and fell, they crushed helmets and skulls.

It was horrible to watch that fine, rapidly marching mass of men recoil in shock. Approaching the cannon from every angle, what had been a stately, organized rush across open ground, was halted and cast into confusion.

The march immediately transformed into a battle. It wasn't a traditional battle, however. It was really thousands of individual struggles.

The enemy had gotten in close, taking advantage of our commanders' eagerness to reach their goal. The Silicoids had avoided our ranged combat power. They'd dodged our firepower entirely in the one simple way that they could do so: by ambushing us.

Jumping out of the sand to attack, they used their superior strength, weight, and toughness of body to defeat soldiers one at a time in close combat.

Harris was beside himself, shouting: "No, no, no!" over and over again.

He'd been full of doom and gloom, then given a glimmer of hope, and now that had been stripped away again.

"McGill!" Natasha cried out to me. "I've got comms again. Check your tapper."

She had been busily setting up her computer right there inside the barrel of the cannon itself. By aiming an antenna directly up toward space, she'd managed to connect with the ships that were drifting in the sky beyond the clouds.

With her superior receiver, we were able to link-up to the network. Apparently, the EMP effect was fading out. Did that mean that the defensive network we'd worked so hard to silence was now operational again? I had no idea.

"McGill?" said a voice coming out of my tapper. "McGill, it's Primus Graves." I knew that voice. It frequently haunted my dreams.

"Yessir, Primus," I said, answering the call. The reception was fuzzy, but functional. "We did it, sir. We laid our mines, we set them all off, and—"

"Why are you still alive, McGill? What are you doing? Are you fighting inside this cannon? Have you knocked it out yet?"

I blinked a few times. "Knocked it out, sir? That was never our mission. We—"

"Shut up! Just shut up right now. Listen to me, McGill. You're the only asset I have inside that facility. The enemy has realigned the gun."

"Yes sir, we know all about that."

"Shut up," he repeated. "Just listen. We've calculated the trajectory as best we can. The Silicoids are about to fire that weapon. As soon as it becomes active again—"

"Uh…" I said, thinking that over. If it fired in any way, shape, or form, we were all going to be burned to ash inside this exhaust pipe. There was no way around that. I couldn't imagine that even if we *did* manage to get out of this tube, climb down that long ladder, and start running across the desert, there would be time to get to a safe distance. Hell, with the power this thing must have, the legionnaires surrounding the launching device on foot might all perish as well.

"They're aiming for Earth, McGill. Are you listening? They're aiming for Earth!"

I finally heard what Graves was trying to tell me and realized the implications.

"Earth?" I said.

"Yes, that's right. We have to stop it. There's a dome, a force dome, directly above it. We would've laid waste to it by now, whether the brass wanted us to or not—but we can't. We can't bombard from above. You're the only asset I have in play that's closer to that cannon than two kilometers."

"What do you want me to do, Primus, sir?"

"Disable the damn thing," he said. "Make sure it doesn't fire. Do anything you have to. Break the frigger, McGill. Break it."

"Any idea on how I'm supposed to do that, Primus?" I asked, thinking that perhaps Graves didn't grasp the incredible girth of this monstrosity, this edifice of technology. Without a doubt, it was the largest single weapon I'd ever witnessed up close and personal.

It was on the scale of something a Skay would use—except instead of being an artificially intelligent being, a living reef of electromechanical and organic components, it was a single gun aimed at the heart of humanity.

"That part's up to you," Graves said. "Improvise, and do not fail. Graves out."

I lowered my arm. My tapper was now blank. That arm slowly sagged down to my side.

Natasha, who'd of course been listening in on this conversation, wormed her way close to me.

"What are we going to do, James?" she hissed.

"Have you got any bombs with you? Any real ones, I mean?"

She shrugged. "Some plasma grenades, crap like that. I don't think that's going to stop this thing from firing."

"No..." I said, "probably not. What if we took the battery packs out of all our weapons? What if we chained them together into a ball? Do you think that could work?"

She shook her head again. "That would take hours."

"Yeah, you're right," I said.

"I've got an idea," Harris said, crawling toward us. "Here, how about this: Everybody, give me their tapper feed. Just touch it right here."

As he went past, troop after troop, all of them dusty-faced, worried, tired—they looked like burning eyes in the dark and little else—they touched his device.

"I'll record it. Now, we'll just take our morph-rifles, hook them up to this here battery pack of mine." He was pulling out the thin, high-capacity battery from his teleport harness. "If I can just get half a charge," he said, "that's all I need. I can teleport myself back to base camp, and nobody needs to get permed. Nobody!"

"That's not going to destroy this cannon, Harris," I told him.

He looked at me like I was crazy. Then he laughed. "We aren't destroying this cannon, McGill. We could barely climb the outside of it. We haven't killed a single Silicoid since we got here. Wreck the cannon? No, I'm just trying to make sure nobody gets permed. It's very high-minded of me, just you ask anyone."

"Then how about I teleport back to base instead?" Cooper shouted. That earned him a venomous stare from Harris.

"It was my idea, and you shut up, Cooper," he said. "I've got half a mind to pull that stealth suit off your ass and shove you down the cannon barrel—just to see what happens."

Natasha snapped her fingers at that moment. "That's it," she said.

"That's what?" Harris asked doubtfully.

"It's not that hard to damage a big gun like this one," she said. "They have to be very carefully designed not to blow up in the first place. If we blocked off this barrel, for example, even if we just changed the physics a little bit unexpectedly, then the Silicoid engineers who designed it may not have compensated for that much error. It may actually cause the whole thing to misfire—or at least miss the target."

Harris was growling and glaring at everyone again. "Is anybody going to fill up my battery pack or not?"

"Yes," Natasha said to herself. "It's a good first step. Assuming a consistent design, these exhaust ports must occur at regular intervals. I've already plotted likely spots all over the structure."

"Huh?" Harris grunted.

"We've got to obstruct the barrel somehow. Our bodies are blocking this one, but we've got to plug up more of the exhaust chutes. Anything we can do to disrupt the way the cannon works is a good idea."

"Oh, for Christ's sake," Harris complained. "That's crazy talk. Just charge my harness up."

"Shut up, Harris," I said. "Or you're going first."

"Go first where?" he asked doubtfully.

I didn't answer him right away. "What we're going to do," I said, "is block up this exhaust port. Anybody got a puff-crete squirter on them?"

No one did, but we did have one dead body, a man who'd fallen and gotten hung by the monofilament wire that I'd helpfully given to the group that was following me up the ladder.

"How'd he hang himself?" I asked Clane.

Clane shrugged. "He's a recruit. Splats will splat."

That was pretty much a proverb in the legions, so I didn't press the issue.

Using the body, and as much spare equipment as we could, we stuffed a big wad of material in the middle of the exhaust tube. Sure, it might all get blown out behind us and do nothing, but we had to do what we could.

"All right," I said. "Next thing we're going to do—"

"James," Natasha said. "James, it's venting."

"What? What are you talking about?"

"Look, something's rising up the barrel."

It was true. A big puff of steam, smoke, gases, and grit was coming up from the bottom of the barrel that we were all sitting in the middle of.

"They're loading a projectile," she said. "Can you feel it?"

And we could. The whole cannon was shaking, rumbling. It was like a minor, distant earthquake, not as sharp as when the cannon had actually rotated around and aimed. But still, the motion was long and continuous.

Something was moving. Something *big* was shifting under our feet. It was a very disconcerting feeling.

"All right, we haven't got any more time. Here's what you're going to do," I said, crawling to the end of the line where the shaft was filling with vapors. At this point, you couldn't even see anymore.

Gases and drifting dust gushed up into our faces. We were all coughing and wheezing. It was like being in the cone of a volcano right before it went off.

"Clane, teleport your lights to these coordinates—the ones Natasha is feeding you right now. Have them plug their snap-rifle batteries into their harnesses. That should be enough juice to jump a few hundred meters."

"Oh, for shit's sake!" Harris complained.

"Before they go," I said, ignoring Harris, "hand me your plasma grenades, one at a time."

The grenades began to flow to my position. As they were handed to me, I activated it with a ten-second fuse, and tossed it out into the midst of the rising column of gases and fumes.

Dutifully, choking and wheezing, they all handed me their plasma grenades. Everybody had at least one on them. I tossed them over and over, one at a time, down into the abyss.

Men began to port out next, each with a weak blue gleam, rather than a powerful flashing glow.

"How is this even going to do any good?" Harris complained. "The cannon might not even go off for another hour!"

"In that case," I told him, "it's somebody else's problem. If this thing fires right now, we're all toast. Therefore, we're going to take action right now and do whatever we can."

That was the last thing I could remember from the hour we spent inside the space-cannon. I can vaguely recall I planned to throw men out into the barrel of the cannon, one at a time, hoping their tiny mass might somehow disrupt the massive projectile that the Silicoids were attempting to fire toward my beloved green Earth. But I don't know if I ever did that or not, because our communications were cut off at that point.

What I am sure of is that everybody in my unit died in those pitiful, wretched, curving tubes of crystal.

-46-

When I was eventually revived, I was surprised by the circumstances. I mean, I'd expected to catch a revive. When I was dying in that space-cannon, I didn't figure that I was permed.

After all, we'd transmitted our data up to the fleet using Natasha's high-powered tech-specialist machine. All that information had been relayed to a safe datacore. Unless everybody was knocked out, and nobody made it back to Earth, I was pretty certain to catch a revive eventually.

That said, I'd naturally expected to catch a revive aboard *Scorpio* and enjoy the flight home. Those long trips back to Earth were normally fun times for old McGill. The ladies aboard the ship were always in a relatively relieved and relaxed mood. They also tended to be somewhat bored...

A great recipe for success for a man like me was to take a happy woman and give her a heavy dose of boredom...

"I don't get this," said one of the bios, a male who seemed to be in charge.

"Orders are orders," said the second voice. She was female and much softer—more to my liking.

I didn't know either one of them, but that wasn't that unusual. There were tons of bios running around aboard *Scorpio*, after all.

"He's being revived way out of sequence," the male voice said.

"We got a priority queue change," the girl answered.

"Let me see it again."

There was some rustling of computer paper. Now, up to this point, I hadn't opened my eyes, but my ears were working pretty well. I knew I had two bios standing over me while I lay bare-ass naked on a cold table.

They were using one of those little turkey-baster things to suck nasty plugs and fluid out of my nostrils. They were probably severing the umbilical, running instruments all over my person to take my vitals, that kind of stuff.

I thought about sitting up and squinting at them. I kind of wanted to tell them to stop pawing at me.

But instead, I went along with the ride. I barely moved when they pricked me with needles and poked shiny lights into my eyeballs—all that irritating stuff. Oftentimes, a man learned more when everybody else around him thought he was out of it.

"This right here," said the prissy male bio. "It says he's going straight down to Legal."

"Ah," the girl said, "that must be it. Maybe our good centurion here was misbehaving on the campaign."

Was that a note of regret in her voice? Maybe she liked the look of old McGill, all stretched out on the gurney in my birthday suit. I began to entertain certain ideas.

But right then, a hard rapping began at the door. The girl left and answered it.

I dared to squinch one eye open and take a little look-see. A skinny, impatient, frowning man marched into the revival chamber. It was none other than Tribune Winslade.

"What's the holdup in here?" he demanded.

"Some people just take a while to get off the table, sir," said the male bio in a rather stern voice. I could tell he didn't fancy this interruption. Winslade was a big cheese, but this was bio-country. Every revival chamber was the holiest of holies to all the ghouls who ran them.

"Nonsense," Winslade said.

He marched up to my gurney where I lolled and gargled a little spit. I could hear his boots tapping rapidly on the tiles.

"McGill, you get your ass up off that gurney right now. I don't have time for any of this."

I took in a big snort of air and stretched, looking around. I pantomimed surprise when I saw Winslade glaring down at me.

"Whoa! Primus Winslade, sir, is that you? My eyes are still blurry. You know how it is after a long sleep and a—"

"Shut up, McGill. Get dressed. We're heading down to Legal."

"Whereabouts, exactly?"

"Floor negative forty-one."

For the very first time, a chill ran through me. Minus forty-one? If my numbers and memory served, that was in the middle of the detention area. One of the least pleasant regions underneath Central.

That was another thing. I could tell already I was inside Central, not *Scorpio*. Looking around at the walls and that ugly tile floor, I realized this wasn't the Blue Deck of any ship in the fleet.

No sir, the walls were solid puff-crete, and there were no bulkheads or anything. Somehow, I'd been revived on Earth, and Winslade was already standing around waiting for me. What's more—and what's worse—I was headed down to the brig.

To make a long story short, I was staggering along behind Winslade ten minutes later. He was my necromancer, and I was his shambling undead creation. Or at least, that's how I felt.

"Winslade, sir?" I said. "I'm not sure we should be leaving Blue Deck so quick. I mean… I feel kind of funny."

I was overdoing my physical state. In reality, I felt pretty darn good. Not as good as I'd feel with a six-pack and a hamburger in my gut, but good enough for being recently dead.

Winslade didn't buy any of it. He knew me too well. He simply crooked a finger over his shoulder, and I had no choice but to follow. I was, in fact, stalling for time, trying to think of any reason why we shouldn't go down to the depths of Central. The last few times I'd been there, I hadn't enjoyed the experience.

"Uh…" I said in the elevator.

To be flat-out truthful, I was contemplating murder. That had been my move the last time that Intel weasel had led me down here to my doom. Maybe it would work again.

Winslade seemed to be completely unaware of my thought processes. He was simply holding up his tapper and thumbing it impatiently. This man never seemed to have enough time to do anything.

"Sir?" I said.

"What is it now, McGill?"

"Sir, uh, what's this all about, anyways?"

He glanced up at me. Perhaps something in my eyes tipped him off. Perhaps for the first time, he realized that I was contemplating drastic action. He put his skinny hands on his hips and glared up at me.

"Don't worry. It's got nothing to do with *you*. As unlikely as it may seem, you're the hero of this sordid tale. You're the only one in this entire chain of command that isn't under scrutiny and investigation."

"Oh…?" I said. "Is that right?"

A big grin split across my face. Listening to him talk, I believed him. He seemed quite irritable, annoyed and upset.

"You're the final witness to be summoned," he said. "And it took a damnably long time to get you breathing again, too. Now, what's your story going to be when we get into the courtroom?"

"The courtroom, sir?"

"Well, yes, that's effectively what it is. A court-martial."

"Oh…" I said. "If it's not me, who's the guest of honor?"

"Graves."

While I blinked at him in surprise, the door swished open. We glanced outside the elevator. We were on deck negative forty-one, all right.

He stepped away, and I followed him. I asked a few more questions, but he simply shushed me and waved skinny fingers over his shoulder in my direction. He didn't even bother to look at me.

I gave up on the whole shambling zombie routine and began to walk straight and proud. The hogs that eyed us did so with dislike, but perhaps a hint of respect. That was just the way it should be. No hog deserved the time of day from a starman, in my point of view.

I fully expected to be dragged into an auto-court. Such chambers were an abomination of justice. In such places robotic judges squatted. They had tin cans for heads, a single arm to wield a gavel, and a shabby black robe that no one ever seemed to launder.

In such a place, I'd often been tried for various crimes. Most of the details I could no longer remember. I knew the routine, however.

The robot would demand my testimony and then pronounce his judgment. Invariably, the story ended with me incarcerated or dead.

But today, this wasn't the case. Instead of a robed robot, I was led into a large conference room. It was nice. It was *frigging* nice!

I'd never seen the like down here on my previous visits. There were no bloodstains on the floor, no whips hanging on the walls—none of that stuff. There were, however, gravity cuffs attached to each of the steel chairs that circled a holotable.

Winslade perched on one of these stool-like seats, and I squatted on another. The next man to walk into the room was Graves himself.

"Uh…" I said, looking around. "Where are the judges? The lawyers? All those guys?"

Graves didn't even bother to meet my eyes. He seemed to be looking down at the table, contemplating things that I had no inkling of.

Winslade glanced at me sourly. "All that will be made clear soon enough, McGill. Now do shut up."

Graves, without being asked, reached down and hooked up his gravity cuff. I watched as he attached it to his own wrist.

Winslade did the same. Then I looked down at the chains and manacles doubtfully.

I pointed at the jangling restraints. "Am I supposed to be doing this?"

"No, McGill," Graves said, still not lifting his eyes from the table. "You're in the clear. Don't worry about it."

I grinned. I grinned big. Sure, that was an out-of-place emotion to be having, but I couldn't help but feel happiness.

Usually, when everything went to shit, and there was an investigation to be had. That invariably involved a bunch of angry brass doing the investigating.

In most cases, I was the man left holding the bag by the end of any such inquiry, whether I was guilty or not. The man who everybody else blamed for all their troubles.

But not today, Satan, not today!

The next person to enter the chamber was a shocker. In fact, I wasn't even sure you could call him a person.

It was a Nairb. The hogs let him in, wrinkling their noses as the slappy, moist, green blob humped his way into the room. The Nairb took a seat and put his front flippers up on the table.

"I see," the alien said, "that we have all the culprits in attendance."

"Uh…" I said. "I was told I wasn't a culprit. I think I'm a witness."

The Nairb looked at me. "That's right, McGill," he said. "I spoke prematurely. Your status is that of a witness."

Right then, I realized who I was talking to.

You have to understand that to me, one Nairb looked the same as the next. But this boy, he knew my name. That was unusual.

There were very few Nairbs in the universe who knew my name. One was the Chief Inspector from the Core Systems. That snot-bag hated me, and he wanted me dead beyond anything.

Under different circumstances, I would have thought this was the Nairb who was officiating. But not today. Today, I was in the clear, so this guy must be the other solitary Nairb in the cosmos who knew me.

"Seven?" I said, smiling at him.

"The same," the Nairb replied.

"It's good to see you again, buddy! How've you been doing? How'd you catch a revive?"

"Human technology is faulty in the extreme," he said. "But in this rare case, it was able to replicate my form."

I frowned a bit. "Oh… but why didn't you go off with the Mogwa on their ship and get a revive on Segin?"

He did one of his shrugs—it was one of the best imitations of a human gesture I'd ever seen from a Nairb. "There were extenuating circumstances, let us say."

"Okay..." I said, deciding not to delve deeper into the subject.

Seven was definitely the only Nairb in heaven or earth that I considered to be an okay guy. If he didn't want to tell me something, I wasn't going to pry—at least not now.

Just then, at the head of the table, two more figures joined us. They flickered and glowed into simulated life, rather than walking into the room.

They were holograms. Both were standing, and both were known to me. One figure was the portly man known as Consul Wurtenberger. I knew he was a consul now, judging by the five starbursts riding on his shoulders.

"Hey," I said before the man could even speak, "hey Wurtenberger, did you make consul? Seriously?"

"I certainly did, McGill."

"Congratulations!"

He nodded coldly, as if he couldn't give less of a shit, but that was okay. Congratulating the brass on a promotion was never a bad idea in my book. Even if they pretended not to care—they always did.

"Let us bring this function to order," Wurtenberger said.

His hologram sat in the chair at the front of the table. It was weird to watch him do that, because his belly was so big, it went right through the table itself. Normally, it would have slapped that table and flopped over it. But as his hologram was incorporeal in form, it passed through solid surfaces without touching anything.

Wurtenberger pointed a thick finger at me. "I will hear your testimony first, McGill," he said. "What happened on the surface of Crystal World at approximately 10:23 AM on October 3rd?"

"Uh," I said, blinking a couple of times, "was that like... last week, or something?"

Wurtenberger's flat lips created an ugly scowl. "No," he said, "that was over a month ago when you and your legion were entirely wiped out on the surface of that miserable planet."

I stood up suddenly. "Wiped out? What happened?"

"That's what we're trying to determine," Wurtenberger said. "Sit down, Centurion!"

I looked around at Winslade and Graves, gaping.

Winslade looked annoyed. His little arms were crossed over his skinny stack of ribs, while Graves kept studying the table. He wasn't even looking at anybody. That was kind of odd for Graves…

I glanced over at Seven next. He wasn't freaked out, or upset, or worried. I could tell that much. He just seemed curious.

"Perhaps I can help prod the witness," Seven said, looking at me. "We're simply asking for you to recite the last things you remember. The final hour of your previous existence."

"Oh… oh yeah, sure. I can do that."

I quickly went over the whole thing about climbing the cannon and finding the exhaust port. I explained how we re-established communications with the fleet and the legions, and then watching the Silicoids ambush our troops out there in the open plains of Crystal World.

After a while, Winslade got bored and made a spinning motion in the air with one of his hands. "Can't we cut to the important part now?"

"Do not attempt to badger or corrupt the witness," Seven said sternly.

Wurtenberger glared at Winslade for a moment, and he fell quiet.

That made me blink and think a little harder. Apparently, I was getting to the important part. It had to be the entire reason I was sitting in this room right now. I was still drawing a blank on what exactly that was, however.

"Well…" I said, thinking back, "oh, yeah, that was when Primus Graves called me. He gave me orders."

"Regarding what?" Seven demanded.

"He told me to do my best to blow up the cannon. He said it was aiming at Earth, and we needed to stop it from firing at all costs."

Wurtenberger suddenly jumped to his feet. Again, his belly passed through the massive table, unharmed.

He threw a big, fat, accusatory finger in Graves' direction. "That's it! That is the testimony we've been seeking."

"Do you stand by your words, human?" The Nairb asked me. He was giving me a very straight stare, an inscrutable one if you asked me.

"Yeah...?" I said slowly, trying hard to figure out what lie I should be presenting instead of the truth.

That was the problem I was having right now. I considered myself to be a consummate liar—a true master of the art, one might say. But it's damned hard to lie, especially to lie appropriately, when you're not even sure what lie you should be telling.

That was where my brain failed me. Sure, if I'd figured out by now that I was supposed to say something important. If I'd needed to make it up, I could have done it, and I could have done it convincingly.

But I was baffled. So, I looked blank.

I let my jaw sag low, and I just stared at Wurtenberger's ghostly form with big, empty eyes.

"That's pretty much it," I said. "I ported my men around to the different exhaust ports. I threw every plasma grenade I had down into the barrel of that devilish gun before it could fire. Then... well... I don't know what happened after that."

Lifting my big hands high, I shrugged.

"It blew up," Seven said. "The entire cannon exploded. It was a total loss."

"Not only that," Wurtenberger said angrily. "Every single Silicoid, every single legionnaire, including the Saurians, the Claver troops, the Rigellians—all of them were annihilated."

"Oh... whoa, whoa, whoa!" I said. "Everybody?"

"Yes, McGill," Winslade told me. "Everybody was vaporized—including myself—for approximately ten square kilometers around the site. The blast was in the gigaton range. In fact, the mushroom cloud reached up high enough to stain the atmosphere and plateau in orbit over that dismal planet."

"Wow!" I said, thinking about that.

A big grin began to form on my face. It was the biggest grin I'd displayed so far today. I stuck my thumbs into my belt loops and leaned back proudly.

"That is some prideful news!" I declared, looking around at everybody. "That sounds like I completed my assigned mission with bells on!"

"I'm glad you're happy, McGill," Winslade snapped. "Do you realize what kind of a hole that explosion put in Earth's military budget?"

My face fell a bit. He had a point there.

All of Legion Varus, all of our gear, every gun, every piece of armor... Not to mention the revival costs... Yep, it was going to be expensive.

On top of that, it'd probably wrecked our coalition. Rigellians didn't believe in revivals in the first place. All those men on the ground—well, they weren't men, just little bears, but still—they'd all been permed in that one big final blaze of glory.

"So that's why you're upset?" I said. "Because of all the loss of men, all the loss of gear?" I looked around at the various people at the conference table.

Wurtenberger glared at everyone. "Not just that. We wanted to capture that cannon. Those were my explicit orders on that fateful day. The cannon was to be captured—disabled at the worst—not blown into space!"

"Well, sir..." I said, "if you don't want something blowed-up, you really shouldn't send in Centurion James McGill. Hell, everybody in Legion Varus knows that."

Wurtenberger nodded. He then turned to Graves. All this time, Graves had never really lifted his head, never really looked at anyone. He was just studying that table.

"Primus Graves," Wurtenberger said, "I am now going to pronounce my judgment."

At last, Graves looked up. His eyes weren't just steel-colored, they seemed to be *made* of steel.

He didn't say anything. He just stared at the hologram of the fat man at the far end of the table, daring him to do his worst.

"You have been tried and convicted upon the basis of eyewitness testimony of conduct bordering on treason. You must atone for great loss of life, diplomatic breaches, and an extremely expensive reconstruction bill. An expense, by the way, which I have half a mind to assign to the budgets of your dreadful organization."

Winslade looked nervous. His fingers fluttered over the table. I could tell he wanted to shout and squawk, but he didn't dare. "Consul, masterful sir," he said. "Might I beseech you not to do that? We're accountable for our own losses, of course. But to foist more financial burdens on our backs—well, you might as well disband the outfit entirely."

Wurtenberger eyed him angrily. "I've considered it. Legion Varus might do better if it was disbanded and rebuilt under new leadership.

"That is my recommendation," the Nairb said.

Damn it, old Seven, I thought to myself, *shut the hell up!*

That was the problem with having a Nairb as one of your buddies. He was always an accountant at heart—which was to say he didn't have one. You could trust him to count every bean on the table if there was a single bean to be counted.

Wurtenberger folded his hands on the table, or at least seemed to, and he studied us for a moment.

Finally, he shook his head. "No… technically, it was a successful mission. The extended costs, the breaches of diplomacy—yes, those are unforgivable. But I have to admit, against all odds, your legion achieved its stated goals."

Graves seemed relieved. So did Winslade. Only the Nairb, Seven, seemed agitated.

"I daresay," Wurtenberger said, "the reconstruction of this legion will be slow. It will be done with the lowest budget contractors I can find. It may well be years before your organization of ruffians is deployed in Earth's service again."

I gave a little whoop at this. I was looking forward to a long vacation.

Graves was still staring at Wurtenberger, perhaps waiting to hear the details of his own fate. I opened my mouth then, ready to protest, ready to just say that it wasn't Graves' fault, that it was all my idea—but I stopped myself.

It was too late for that. My big mouth had already sunk Graves. Telling a fresh whopper now wasn't going to help anything.

Then I looked at Winslade for the first time. I mean, I *really* looked at him. It seemed to me like he had just a little bit of a smirk playing underneath that scornful frown he was aiming at Graves.

Graves, of course, wasn't even looking at him. He didn't care what Winslade thought on the best of days. But Winslade, yeah, he was looking at Graves. I think he liked this situation. He liked the fact that Graves was taking the fall wholly and entirely on his own.

That led me to a fresh suspicion. Was Winslade really the one who'd given the original order to Graves? Or had Graves really gone rogue and ordered me to do something that went against a command from the brass?

I did some cogitating. I rethought, double-thought, then triple-thought the idea. When I was done, I realized that no, it wasn't Graves' style.

Primus Graves was the kind of guy who would stand on a ship and sink to the bottom of the ocean if he was told to. Hell, he would've welded his boots onto the hull on the way down.

There was pretty much no way he'd go against anyone's direct orders. So and therefore, the orders to blow up the cannon must have originally come from Winslade.

For the first time, I felt there was an injustice underfoot. I was a bit annoyed, and I frowned a little.

I wondered if there was a way I could reverse the tables on old Winslade…

I glanced back at Graves again. For the very first time, he wasn't looking at Wurtenberger, his judge and jury, but toward me.

He caught my eye, and he gave me a tiny shake of the head.

Graves wanted me to keep my mouth shut. If that's what he wanted, that's what I'd do. It was his funeral. I blinked a couple of times, and then I sat back, scowling.

Meanwhile, while all this eyeballing was going on, Wurtenberger—or at least his hologram at the head of the table—was listening to someone off-camera. He leaned to one side, and he seemed to be muttering to someone.

That seemed odd. Who could he be talking to? Who could be there, telling a consul what to do or what to think?

Maybe he had advisers. I shrugged because I didn't know, and I didn't much care.

Finally, Wurtenberger turned back to the camera pickup and spoke to us. "Gentlemen," he said, "my judgment has been carefully considered and is now final. Graves will be reduced in rank to that of centurion."

I stood up suddenly, my knees thumping into the table and rocking it a bit despite the fact it was *damned* heavy. I didn't even care about the burst of pain in my kneecaps.

"Hold on, sir!" I said. "That's plain crazy!"

Consul Wurtenberger glanced at me sourly. "Sit down, McGill."

Reluctantly, I sank back down and squatted on that little stool again. It just wasn't fair.

When something big and bad happened in the legions—meaning something expensive—somebody had to go down for it. That's just how things worked.

That someone was always an officer—usually a lower-ranked officer who couldn't defend themselves.

Today, it was Graves.

"The guilty party will be executed and incarcerated for a period of no longer than two years," Wurtenberger said. "After that, you may return to active service at your new lowered rank. Case dismissed."

Just like that, Wurtenberger blinked out. I was left in a quiet room again with just the three others who all looked serious but somewhat unsurprised.

"It is a suitable verdict," said the Nairb. "As a contracted representative of the Galactics, I approve."

He humped on out of the place after that, just the way he'd come, leaving a slimy trail on the deck. I stared after him, wondering what his new role here at Central must be. I was too befuddled by the entire miscarriage of justice I'd just witnessed to ask about it, however.

"Tribune Winslade?" I said. "That proceeding was horseshit, sir."

Winslade looked at me with scrunched-up lips. "No, it wasn't, McGill. It was necessary and appropriate—just as the consul informed us. Please don't get involved in things you don't understand."

I gaped, and I gawked, but I did shut up.

Ignoring me, Winslade called in some hog guards. They marched in and hustled Centurion Graves out of the room.

He was trussed up like a chicken, with all kinds of jingling chains and cuffs that no human ever born could break.

Watching this spectacle made me scowl, and I thought about killing a few hogs just on principle. I controlled myself with difficulty.

In the end, Graves was led down an echoing metal passageway to the brig, while Winslade and I went the other direction and boarded an elevator together. We began to ride up to higher floors, leaving that dismal dungeon behind.

"What the hell was that?" I demanded. "That disaster wasn't Graves' idea!"

"Have a care, McGill," Winslade said. "Please note that you were not the one left with the blame. Not this time. I do believe you owe me not only a thank you, but an apology for that."

"An apology?" I said. "What the hell for?"

"For letting you get away with the destruction of captured equipment. For disobeying standing orders, and for following Primus Graves' instructions over mine."

"What?" I said. "How the hell was I supposed to know that Graves wasn't following your orders?"

Winslade gave me a tight smile and waved a skinny finger up at me.

"That," he said, "that reasonable claim of ignorance, that's why you're not the one being executed in this hellhole. You should count your lucky stars and keep your mouth shut."

The elevator stopped, Winslade got off, but I rode on further. I was fuming and griping all the way up to the lobby.

-47-

Standing in the lobby for a full minute, I didn't even know where I was going next. But then, I had it.

It was high time I left Earth. It was time to go back to Dust World to find out what had been happening all these months while I'd been flying out to Crystal World, dying, and languishing in limbo.

I turned and set course for Gray Deck. Essentially, that was Central's version of the transmission station in the middle of the Great Sphere of Geneva.

I figured that by now, Galina had to be up and kicking again—literally. That made me smile for a moment. After all, she had to be happy with me.

I'd not only followed her instructions and gotten her to die in public, all that stuff, I'd also gotten her out of being promoted to consul. Old Wurtenberger had taken over the job in her absence. The job of running Earth was his problem now.

Galina was going to like that, I was certain.

On the way to the public Gray Deck, which was actually right near the ground floor and the lobby, I paused.

By chance, I'd glanced out the big front glass doors of Central. Now, those doors were, by anyone's standards, impressive. They were overly large, and overly expensive.

But that wasn't what had caught my eye. Instead, it was the city outside. It was just getting dark, about dinner time. Or, to be more precise, it was happy hour.

I stopped, and I stared. I gaped, in fact. People streamed around me. I was like a stone in a river.

At last, I slowly turned and headed towards those doors. I was like a moth drawn to flame. It had been so long since I'd had any fun. Ages since I'd sat on a bar stool, flirted with a girl who wasn't wearing a uniform, and had myself some good, old-fashioned, char-boiled bar food.

I knew a place called the *ElectroBite Bistro*. Right now, I couldn't think of anything else. It was close. Really close. Right outside Central, in fact. I didn't go there often, because there were too damn many people from Central in there, and it was too friggin' expensive by half.

But tonight, I made a beeline for the place. Gray Deck, Galina, Dust World—all that stuff could wait. It was high time for a little celebration.

As I counted it, this McGill had been gone for four frigging months. Sure, I'd spent a couple of those months dead, but that time still counted in my book.

I wanted a burger and a drink. So, sue me. Just you languish around dead for a few months, then see what you want to do when you wake up.

I made my way to the big, overpriced bistro, found a stool up at the counter and plopped my butt down on it.

Along about the time I was getting into my second beer, I began to wonder where the hell my burger was. That's when I heard a familiar voice behind me.

"Yes, thank you. I will no longer be needing your services."

"Are you sure about that… um… sir?"

I turned around on my stool, and I stared. Yes, it was Seven's voice I'd heard at the doorway. It had to be Seven, because I don't think there'd ever been another Nairb who spent time humping his way around the streets of Earth before.

A couple of hog guards were with him. They looked kind of befuddled. Maybe they had orders to follow Seven's ass around Central City, to make sure nothing happened to the guy.

Nairbs were so weak. If a seven-year-old kid in cowboy boots stepped on one of those flippers, well, there were going to be some broken bones, let me tell you.

"Sir, uh...?" said one of the hog guards, giving himself a scratch on the neck. His collar seemed to have become too tight all of a sudden. "We have orders to escort you wherever you go, once you leave Central."

"How irritating," Seven said. "Do you have to accompany me into this establishment?"

The guards kind of looked around at one another, and they shrugged. "I guess we could stay out here until you come out. You should be safe enough inside, I suppose."

"Very well," Seven said, and he humped away from them, leaving the two guys loitering at the door.

The hogs looked chagrined, but I smiled. Seven was humping directly toward the bar. He spotted an empty stool not far from where I was. I wasn't quite sure how he was going to get up there, but then I saw a waitress rush forward. She was all smiles and fluttery fingers. She grabbed up a chair and set it next to the stool with a practiced motion.

The Nairb, with equal alacrity and familiarity, climbed first the chair and then humped his way up onto the stool. There he perched with his flippers on the bar itself. His head swiveled eagerly, trying to catch the attention of one of the bartenders.

I took occasion to walk over to the waitress and put a big hand on her elbow. She frowned at that for a moment, but then smiled up at me.

"What is it, sir?" she asked.

"Hey there," I said. "Do you know that critter over there? The green guy who looks like a seal full of snot?"

She looked this way and that, and then leaned a little close. I liked that. She smelled nice, too.

"Yes," she said, "we all know him. He comes in here every day after work."

"After work, huh? Every day?"

I let go of her and nodded, thinking that over. She rushed away to get another order. After staring at her rear for just a few moments, I had a thought.

This Nairb must be a big tipper. No one got that kind of service—especially not from a real, human waitress, if you didn't roll out the credits. It was either that, or everybody here was scared of Nairbs. I wasn't sure which it was, but I was certain old Seven was getting some special treatment.

There was a seat open next to Seven. Without asking, I moved my beers and my sandwich—which had finally shown up—and took a seat next to the little green blob. I swigged down a big gulp of my beer. Then I glanced over at Seven. He was already staring at me.

I did a double-take. "Whoa!" I said. "I didn't even see you sitting there!"

"I believe that qualifies as a falsehood," he said.

"I swear it on my mother's grave," I said, solemnly lifting one hand and crossing my heart with the other.

The Nairb looked at me, unconvinced.

"Well..." he said, "whatever the case, I suppose you may attend me. As long as you're not yet another agent from Central shadowing my every step and my every activity. Do you plan to report back to Winslade or Wurtenberger concerning my personal habits?"

"Huh?" I said. "No, no, no! You know me. I like to drink and carouse more than most humans."

The Nairb seemed to consider. "Yes," he said, "my recent memories corroborate your claim very well. You shall be my companion for this evening."

"Uh..." I said, not totally certain that was going to be the funnest way to spend my time. It wasn't going to be the best way to get one of these waitresses or lady patrons to come home with me tonight, either.

But... what the hell? I was the one who'd come over and horned in on this Nairb's private party. The least I could do was have a conversation with him.

We talked for a while about Central and other bullshit. Drinks came, and they were consumed. What was weird about the Nairb was he never seemed to go to the bathroom. He did, however, swell up a bit.

This concerned me somewhat. I'd never really thought about the Nairb waste-processing system. You really didn't want to think about that when you were sitting next to one of them. You could kind of see all of his organs functioning and processing through that thin, semi-translucent flesh. Nairb skins didn't entirely hide their internal organs, and believe me, that wasn't a good thing. A normal human might lose his lunch just watching this guy eat something.

But as the night wore on, and he drank more, I came to wonder about how his body worked... Alien physiology was always quite different from human physiology. This Nairb was nowhere near as weirdly built as one of those Silicoids, mind you—but its body didn't function the way mine did.

We talked about a lot of things, and I learned that Seven had taken an official job here at Central. He was contracting for his home world, of course, like all of them did. That kind of befuddled me.

"But I thought you guys only worked for big people, you know, like the Galactics."

"Earth is now a small principality on the fringe of the galaxy," he said. "You're part of the Empire, but you're not entirely subsumed by it. That independent nature, and the fact that your budgets have achieved a level almost unheard of this far from the Core Systems, has resulted in a need for professional advisement."

"Huh..."

That kind of surprised me. Especially that part about a Nairb thinking Earth was rich. I hadn't known Mid-Zoners like Seven felt that way.

I guess we *were* rich—for our neighborhood. It was kind of like being the king of the hobos, you know? Not rich the way you would think of some dude in a mansion on the Riviera, but we were rich when compared to all the other hobos that lived in squalor around us.

"So, Earth has an official Nairb contractor?" I asked. "That's pretty cool."

"Again, you make odd references to ambient temperatures," the Nairb said. "I would prefer that you cease doing that. It's irritating."

He never seemed to get some of my idioms. I guess his translator box simply couldn't translate them correctly.

"Never mind then, never mind," I told him. "Are you working under Consul Wurtenberger or the Ruling Council?"

"Both," he said. "Technically, the consul is your sovereign. But as I have determined through investigation and observance, your government functions as an oligarchy in reality."

"An ola-what?"

"An oligarchy is a small group of elite individuals that rule a nation, or a planet."

"Oh…" I said. "You mean like kings and queens, lords and ladies, stuff like that?"

"Something like that, yes."

"Okay…" I said, "so you work for Earth Gov—for Hegemony at large. What do you do for us, exactly?"

"I serve as a liaison to the Empire. I advise your leadership on probable reactions."

"Uh… probable reactions? From who?"

"From the Galactics, of course, human. How is it I'm the one who is inebriated, and yet this conversation is so one-sided?"

I took a big gulp of beer before answering. "That's 'cause I'm a little on the dumb-side."

"Unfortunate…"

"Anyways, I think I get it. You're sort of a PR man. An advisor that tells us what we're doing right or wrong in terms of Galactic opinion."

"That is a crude but sufficiently accurate description of my function. It will suffice."

No matter how drunk he got, he still talked in a super-prissy fashion. I figured that was probably because his translator had been designed by another Nairb. Maybe he was actually using a ton of swear-words in his own language, but it was all being cleaned up and churned out as nice, concise language by his AI translator.

"Uh…" I said to him after I watched him consume perhaps his fourth or fifth strong beverage. He seemed to be getting kind of drunk. He sure as hell hadn't been eating anything, either. "You want some of my sandwich, or my fries, or something?"

He took one of the fries and nibbled on it. "Disgusting," he pronounced. "There's a distinct lack of appropriate seafood in this city, despite its proximity to large bodies of water."

"You're talking about the Atlantic Ocean, right? Don't worry. I'll fix you up."

I took it upon myself to order a shrimp cocktail appetizer. When it arrived, he ate it. He didn't really like the sauce much. I guess Nairbs weren't into spices. But he liked the shrimp just fine.

After he'd consumed every shrimp, including crunching down the tails, he thanked me for the tip on shrimp cocktails.

"You know," I said, "you gotta be careful with drinking too much booze every night. It starts to affect a person. It becomes harder and harder not to drink more."

He looked at me seriously. "You seem to perform this function without difficulty."

"Yeah, but, that's partly because I get killed a lot," I said. "You know, when a man gets a brand-new liver every year or so, the problem just takes care of itself. But I don't think you want to die regularly, do you?"

"The concept is unappealing," Seven admitted. "Frequent death? Just in order to have my body rebuilt? Isn't there a more civilized option, such as organ replacement?"

"Uh... probably, yeah... but I'm pretty sure we can't do that for a Nairb."

"Depressing. I don't wish to submit to the barbaric witch doctors you have out here on the rim. I just recently suffered death and revival."

"Oh yeah, on that invasion ship."

"I'm not anxious to repeat the experience."

Later on, when the Nairb had been sufficiently inebriated, he was definitely in a friendlier mood. "Tell me something about what's happened in the center of the galaxy," I asked him.

His head was down on the bar. He lifted it just long enough to talk, but he didn't open his eyes. "Like what?"

"Like... do the Galactics have an Emperor yet?"

He squinted at me, shaking his head. "They will never have an Emperor again. Not until one of the factions dominates—or quite possibly destroys the others."

"Ooh," I said, "that sounds bad. So… we don't really have an Empire anymore. We have a group of split-apart independent states."

"That is an accurate description," he said. "We're an Empire in name only. In truth, there are more like five empires. Each of the major Galactic species has an ally or two, except for the Skay. They are completely alone and find every other group intolerable."

"Or maybe," I said, "nobody else can tolerate them."

Seven actually laughed then. He slapped his flipper on the table, ordered another drink, and seemed to be honestly enjoying my company.

Eventually, I got bored with him, and I left him there at the counter.

As I walked out, I noticed the hogs were still standing around waiting for Seven. "Hey boys, how about I order you a couple of beers? I'll have the girls bring them out to the street."

"That would be nice of you, Centurion," one of them said. "I don't know how you can stand talking to that fish-breath freak for so long."

"Hey," I said, "just how often does this Nairb go out drinking at night?"

They looked at one another a little furtively. "Just between you and me," said the one on my right, "he does this every damn night. He gets drunk, annoys the staff, and eventually we have to carry him back to Central, to his quarters. It's disgusting."

The guy was working his hands in the air and rubbing at them like he was already thinking about how sticky they were going to get. I imagined that carrying the drunk, possibly barfing Nairb, back to his quarters could get messy.

I felt a bit sorry for these two boys, so I didn't harass them any further. I ordered them some beers, and I left, paying my tab with a healthy tip.

After that, I proceeded to check in on every girl I knew in the city. I found all of them were otherwise engaged, and the girls from Legion Varus hadn't been revived yet. I was among the first to be brought back to breathing.

Apparently, *Scorpio* had only returned and docked in orbit two days ago. The long process of reviving the rank and file was underway, but was by no means complete.

Disappointed, I found a hotel room and called my folks. I let them know I was fine, and I'd be coming home soon.

But I spent the night in Central City, alone.

-48-

The next morning, I had a small headache. I had to wonder how bad Seven was feeling. Damn, that little Nairb could put it away! He could pack booze like I'd never seen in an alien.

Giving my head a shake and taking a shower, I noticed that my tapper was going off hard right after eight a.m.

The first call was from my folks and Etta, who were all down there in Georgia Sector. They did one of those group-shot things where my dad held up his arm, showing his face and slowly panning around.

I saw my mom, then Etta, and... What the hell?

There was that guy, Derek. That friggin' hog! I'd totally forgotten about him...

Hadn't it been months since he'd left Dust World? Was he still hanging around my parents' house?

My eyes and my attitude began to darken automatically, but I did my best to hide that. I conjured up a big, fake grin. I waved at all of them. I even said hi to Derek. Right there, I considered myself to have done my good deed for the day.

Etta looked nervous. "Um... when are you coming home, Dad?" she asked.

"Pretty soon," I said, "I've got just a couple more things to clean up."

All four of them glanced at one another. What the hell was that all about? If my little girl was already pregnant, I swore to myself my first grandchild would be born an orphan by sundown.

I was thinking all these negative thoughts, but I still kept that pasted-on fake smile going.

"Don't worry none," I told them. "I'll be coming home soon. Real soon."

They all nodded, and then I spent some time listening to my mom prattle on for a while about her garden, the weather, and the neighbor ladies she liked to talk to. Eventually, they let me end the call.

Then I was able to get to the serious business of breakfast. About halfway through it, just past the hash browns and well into the eggs, my tapper started buzzing again.

"Goddamn it," I said, mumbling around a mouthful of food.

I looked at my tapper, and my first inclination was to swipe across it, declining the call. But I paused. Then I froze.

The call wasn't from my family members—or some loser like Carlos. It wasn't even one of the old flame girlfriends I'd tried to entice last night.

No, it was Public Servant Alexander Turov.

"Whoa..." I said. I swallowed big, threw down some juice, wiped my mouth with the back of my hand, and answered the call.

"Good morning, Mr. Servant, sir," I said. "To what do I owe this honor?"

Alexander squinted at me and didn't speak for a moment. "McGill," he said at last, "you are a very troubling individual."

"Uh..." I said, "troubling how, exactly? I mean like... today?"

"I realize that I sent you out to Crystal World with certain special instructions. In fact, I emphatically insisted upon their execution."

I blinked a couple of times. I had no idea what he was talking about. But then it struck me like a bolt out of the blue.

He *had* talked to me back at Central on that one day in the Intel zone, where Dixon and that guy Brinkley were working me over. He'd come in and saved me, but then he'd told me to do something... What was it again?

"...therefore," Turov was saying, and I tried hard to tune back into his words, "I have to consider myself partly responsible for your insane behavior."

I blinked and began to sweat, just a little.

"You mean, like…" I said, "when we blew up the space-cannon?"

"Yes, of course! That's exactly what I'm talking about. That was a critical piece of infrastructure that we wanted to capture and study. You had to know that. Everyone in Legion Varus knew that!"

Naturally, I'd known no such thing. People had mentioned it, of course. But it wasn't really my job as a mere centurion on the battlefield to make strategic decisions about what was blown up and what wasn't. My job was to do a mission, whatever I was told to do. To my mind, I'd executed that function flawlessly.

"Does this have to do with Graves, and Winslade, and all this business about capturing the cannon versus blowing it up?"

"Yes, of course it does, you idiot! Aren't you listening?"

"I'm *always* listening, sir. I've got ears so big, I can't help it. Just look at them." I reached up and cupped my right ear with my right hand, making sure the camera pickup on my tapper caught the action. "I can't hardly miss hearing a fart in a—"

"That's quite enough, McGill. I am sick of your earthy prattling and nonsense."

I lowered my hand away from my ear slowly and gawked at him, wondering where this conversation was going next. He stared at me for a bit, as if making a critical decision.

At last, he heaved a sigh.

"All right," he said. "In this instance, I'm going to forgive your incredible fit of destructiveness. But don't for a moment attempt to blame Graves or Winslade or any of these other fools, no matter what the investigations show. I know it was you, McGill. I know it was you because I told you to do it. That is the thing that galls me the most."

I was back to blinking and gaping again. I was only half-following this conversation. I looked down at my fine breakfast, which was growing colder by the minute. What I really wanted to do was eat the rest of it.

But I knew now wasn't the time for chewing. I took a swig of coffee and felt the caffeine hit my veins, waking me up just a little.

Then suddenly, I had it. This old bastard *had* given me an order, an imperative. He'd said, in fact, that he wanted me to break the coalition, to cause so much damage to the Rigellians and the Clavers that our military alliance would lay broken.

"Oh..." I said, smacking myself in the head with an open palm.

I'm not quite sure if it was the coffee, the adrenaline, old-fart Turov's hints, or maybe even that big smack in the head—but it was all clear now. It was all crystal-clear in my foggy brain.

"I have to confess, sir," I said, "you figured it out."

"I've figured out what? That I sent an ape to do a delicate job?"

"No, sir. I meant the part about how hard I had to work to engineer all those explosions and whatnot. It wasn't easy, but I followed your orders to a T. I honestly figured you'd be pleased."

Old Turov glared at me for a moment. "Pleased? You believed I would be pleased? There were imperatives handed down to capture that facility!"

"Yes, yes," I said, "but I figured that was all part of the cover-up. It gave me the perfect opportunity. Did I do something wrong, sir? Are the bears still happy? Is Rigel still wanting to go with us up against the Silicoids? Maybe I needed to kill a couple thousand more of their best troops—or blow up one of their ships."

Old Alexander heaved a sigh and closed his eyes. "I now understand Drusus and some of the warnings he gave me about you. Ridiculous references to bulls in china shops and something about doing surgery with a wrecking ball..."

I was enthusiastically nodding my head. I pointed one big finger and waggled it at the camera pickup.

"Yes! Yes!" I said. "That's me. If you want something done, and you want it done big, you just call old McGill. But I kind of thought you knew that, Servant, sir?"

At last, pinching up his lips tightly, he nodded his head. He seemed to force himself to relax.

"I accept your accusations because they are factual. Painful, but factual. You are like an evil genie in a bottle, McGill. Do you know that?"

"Uh... how's that exactly, sir?"

"An unwary man can make a wish, and you will grant it—but never in the manner that the wishing man envisioned."

I was back to blinking, but at least I was fake-smiling again. I just nodded and smiled until finally, he told me my well-overdue perming had been suspended, and that I was free to go about my business once again.

He did say one thing that I found memorable before he signed off. "Just think, McGill, if Earth had captured such a weapon. What if the Skay came to Earth again? What if the Mogwa send Battle Fleet 921? What if they resurrect that venerable formation of highly advanced ships? The Silicoid technology could have changed the course of history. It could give us an edge against the Core Worlds themselves."

"Against the Core Worlds? We're not going to war with them... um, are we?"

"Not yet," Old Alexander said. "Not yet, but there may come a day."

"But Servant," I said, "what about the other cannons? Weren't there other smaller ones dotted all over that planet? They had a defensive network."

"Yes," he said, "they did. And we have examined them. Some survived after you annihilated our ground forces. The Fleet technicians did their best to examine and duplicate the technology of the Silicoids. But they failed."

"But how did it...?"

"Underground, beneath that megalithic device, was the primary Silicoid city on the planet. The operators were destroyed. Their software, their computers—whatever they used to operate the defensive network—it was all lost."

I nodded, finally seeing why Old Alexander was a bit upset. But I didn't much care, and I didn't see how I was to blame. Not really. Graves had given me the order, and I had the feeling Winslade had passed it down to him. If old Turov wanted to fry somebody for it, he should look at those two.

After that, the old man complained a bit about Galina and how stubborn, intractable, and willful his daughter was. I could commiserate.

Then he finally signed off, and I went back to eating my eggs, which were now as cold and unappetizing as the proverbial witch's tits in the brass bra.

-49-

Some hours later, I made my way to Dust World. When I got there, I was frowning and mystified right from the get-go. There was quite a bit of activity going on in the tiny volcanic valley.

"Hey," I said, asking the new hog who'd come to replace Derek. "Hey, hog!"

He glared at me, but he nodded his head. People still had some respect for my officer's rank, and even more for the wolf's head patch of Legion Varus.

If you acknowledged an insult from a Varus man, if you made a big deal out of it, well, you might just end up as mulch for a revival machine. Just about every hog in Hegemony knew that by now.

So, the hog glared at me, but he nodded. He waited for me to say my piece.

"What the hell is going on over there?" I asked, pointing to a distant field across the lake.

The hog shrugged. "I don't know, Centurion," he said. "These Dust-Worlders are strange people."

"Don't I know it? What is that, some kind of hydroponic farm, or something?"

"Yeah, I guess so. There's been a lot of different folk going through this gateway lately. Contraband, too."

"Like what?"

"Like organic stuff, plants that I've never seen before…"

I looked at him sharply. "Stuff that's against regulations?"

The guy's eyes got a little squirrely then. They didn't meet mine. They squirmed off to the left, then the right, then the ground. Anything but my face.

"No," he said. "Nothing too far off regs. Just... you know... some odd specialty flora, I guess."

I knew what was going on right then. The kind of hog who got himself assigned out here at Dust World, why, that was a man who was being punished.

No one wanted to be here. Frigging *no one*—with the possible exception of Derek, who'd been chasing after Etta. I couldn't imagine another hog in the cosmos who wanted to get posted out here. Every hog who came out here to do guard duty had done something wrong back home.

What was this guy's crime? Could it have been bribery? Could it have been smuggling? The way he wouldn't meet my eyes, that triggered a response of suspicion in my heart. He'd done something bad. He'd done something wrong. And now he'd come to Dust World, and he was still doing it. I decided not to make a big deal out of it.

"Thanks a lot, hog," I said. "You've been very helpful."

Then, after touching my cap with my fingers briefly, I sauntered on down toward the village. My immediate mission was to find the best local beer I could and take a hit of it. They didn't have anything like that in the warrens and caves where the Investigator and his strange little family liked to work in their hidden laboratories. If I was going to get a few final moments of joy before visiting the Investigator and his stinking turd-tanks, I was going to have to do it right here, right now.

I was on my second clay mug of beer—which was just as bad-tasting as you might imagine—when someone appeared on my six.

I turned and glanced over my shoulder. It was Boudica. I'd felt her presence rather than heard or saw her.

She was staring at me. She had a half-dozen of her strange, knife-wielding followers crowding in behind her.

I was unhappy to see that her breasts were covered today. How unfortunate.

The entire bar had gone quiet, but I was in a pretty good mood, so I kicked off the conversation.

"Hey there, Boudica," I said, "long time no see."

"Indeed, McGill," she said, studying me carefully.

"Uh, is something wrong?"

"I hope not. Tell me exactly why you're here."

"Oh…"

I was beginning to wonder about a few things right then. I was curious about the behavior of everybody else in the bar, for example.

The barkeep was clattering around with earthen jugs and mugs. The serving girls had all vanished. Most of the patrons seemed to have all needed to take a leak at once, too.

Those who were left sat quietly at their tables, trying not to stare.

All of this indicated a couple of things to me. First off, Boudica had somehow intimidated these rough frontiersmen. That was a statement in and of itself.

Secondly, no one was freaking out or laughing and pointing at the bare-chested dudes in their leather pants. That could only mean that they'd met Boudica's thugs before, and more than that, that they feared them.

Boudica was quite a bully. She reminded me of a gang leader, or something like that.

I stood up and walked toward her, putting on a bit of a swagger. My latest mug of ale was half gone, but I offered it to her anyway. "A lot of dust flowing around out there," I said. "This'll cut it out of your throat."

She eyed the beverage dubiously for a moment, but then she took it and tossed it down. It was, after all, something that the locals relished. She grimaced a bit, then gave me a thin-lipped smile.

"Why are you here, James?" she asked.

"Hell, don't you know?" I said. "I'm here to see you!"

She blinked once, then twice, then she dared to smile.

I began to lie then, and I went big with it. "I couldn't think of anything else the whole time I was out there on Crystal World," I said. "All those boring women in uniforms…"

I reached out some fingers, running them over her red tresses. She watched those fingers with mild surprise.

We had, in fact, had a few good times together about four months ago, and I was ready to relive them.

But she batted my hand away. It dropped to my side, disappointed.

"No," she said, "you did not come for me. I traveled to Death World the last time we parted ways. Did you forget?"

"Uh…"

"You came for that vile woman—Imperator Galina Turov."

"Oh," I said, because of course she was right. I had come back for Galina. I'd pretty much left Boudica at the Great Sphere, knowing she was bound for Death World. I'd half-figured she'd never come back.

But here she was. What's more, she was playing the part of a suspicious girlfriend.

"Is, uh, Galina revived yet?" I asked.

Her eyes stared at me like two coals smoldering in a fire. "She was revived."

"Okay then! Maybe I should just escort her back to Central, and—"

"But then I put her down again," Boudica continued. "I found her intolerable."

"Huh…" I said, "so… you two ladies didn't get along? That's too bad."

Boudica shook her head. She was looking down again. I didn't quite know what to make of the situation.

Sure, Boudica was violent. And sure, Galina was a wild-eyed, fiery woman when she wanted to be.

I could well-imagine these two domineering, arrogant, and just plain evil females not getting along. That part didn't surprise me, not one bit.

"You guys are reviving her back again though… right?" I asked.

Boudica heaved a sigh. "Yes, yes. I can see already you prefer her over me."

"How's that?" I asked, immediately drafting a long list of surefire excuses.

But she dashed them all. "Because," she said, stepping closer, "you never came to look for me again. You never came to find out how I was faring. Instead, you immediately came here to learn if your true girlfriend was back out of purgatory yet."

"Now, hold on," I said. "I left Galina dead. In fact, I got her killed right in front of you. Don't you think that kind of situation was more pressing? You wanted to go to Death World."

I pointed in the direction of the grove I'd seen. "And what's with all the big plants over there? Those aren't any native species I've seen before."

Boudica reached up and slapped my hand down. "Never mind about that," she said. "If you want to see your woman returned to life, if you want her to keep breathing after she rises from the disgusting muddy waters the Investigator stirs and fawns over, then you will come with me now."

She turned away and began to march out. Her six stooges followed. I threw some credits on the bar and walked out after her. Boudica ignored my attempts at conversation and lighthearted jokes the whole way out to the Investigator's lair.

As we got close, I began to gape at the difference in the flora that I was seeing as we approached the entrance to the underground warren.

"Lookie at that!" I said. "That's not like one of the big, weird, waxy flowers. That's not even a reed."

I kept pointing out obviously non-native plant species that were surrounding us. In fact, we were soon cast into a green gloom. Some of the plants reached twenty or thirty meters tall. Nothing so big had ever been seen living on Dust World before. Nothing. I was certain of that.

"Where are you getting the water from?" I asked.

Boudica, although she had been giving me the silent treatment for most of the walk out here, finally paused and pointed toward the lake. She did so in the manner of a person pointing out the obvious to an idiot.

"We pump it from the great lake," she said. "How can you be so ignorant? You are living proof that brain-size does not indicate mental capacity in any way, shape, or form."

"Oh…" I said, glancing back at the very deep, cold lake. "Of course."

Shaking her head, she turned and led the way into the echoing passages. When I finally arrived at the Investigator's dimly lit, illicit revival operation, I wrinkled my nose at the stinks.

The various tanks gurgled and released fetid, nauseous gases. There were more of them now, and they all seemed to be active. The stench was worse than ever before.

Floramel was there. Not the Investigator, just Floramel. Etta, of course, the other competent aide that usually worked in these strange underground chambers, was safely back on Earth—and I was glad for that.

Floramel was bent over a subject, rubbing at it, cleaning it off, it seemed. Then I recognized the shape. She was small, and she was dirty—but she was familiar to me.

"Galina?" I asked.

"McGill," a voice said from behind me.

I turned. It was Boudica. Her eyes were dark with anger, and I got the feeling it was directed at me.

She pointed a long finger toward Galina, who was getting her hair unmussed and hosed off by relatively fresh pond water—pumped up from the lake, I assumed. Mud streamed all over the floor.

"Take that harpy from this place and never return! I don't want to see either of you on my planet again!"

I gaped at her, but I didn't respond. I sensed that perhaps I shouldn't.

Boudica left then, and after I gave her rump one final, lingering stare, I turned back and approached the less than attractive-looking Galina.

She was naked, and she was covered in mud—but mostly, she was pissed off.

"Get away from me, you skinny witch," she said, fighting with Floramel.

Floramel seemed unperturbed. She continued to wash the mud off Galina in the manner in which a groomer might handle an ornery dog—a feisty, small dog that didn't like getting its nails clipped or its fur cleaned. At last, she let Galina go.

Seeing me, Galina snatched up a dirty towel and wrapped it around herself. She glared at me as if I'd killed her, as if I'd stuck her in a stinking mud-tank. Some people really need to learn the fine art of gratitude.

"James," she said, shaking a bit. I wasn't sure if the shaking part was due to the cold pond water or sheer rage. "Get me out of this place. Right now!"

Floramel, looking at me over the smaller woman's shoulder, spread her eyes wide and nodded rapidly. She seemed to think that was an excellent idea.

I could tell there was trouble in the henhouse. During my absence, Etta had taken off, Boudica had apparently killed Galina at some point, and Floramel seemed to want everybody out of her laboratory as fast as possible.

Looping a big guiding hand around her small shoulders, I gently steered Galina out of the laboratory. I found some minimalist clothes for her. As Dust-Worlders lived on a very hot planet, they rarely wore more than a short skirt and a tunic. It was better than nothing.

I took her out of there. She stumbled, cursed, and mumbled death threats to everyone who dared come near. I decided not to even go by town, even though I was craving a fresh jar of ale in a clay pot.

There was no time for that, and I sensed that Galina wasn't in the mood.

I led her to the gateway posts where the hog guardian stopped us. He scanned Galina's tapper and gaped in astonishment.

"An imperator?" he said.

"That's right, you idiot," Galina hissed at him. "Step aside, or I'll have you flogged just for fun—just out of spite."

The poor bastard hurried away. In fact, he kept going, glancing over his shoulder until he was at least fifty meters away. He wanted nothing to do with either one of us, I could tell.

Then we stepped through the gateway posts and vanished.

-50-

I managed to get Galina to the streets in Central City, and I summoned an aircar to take her back to her place.

The ride was an angry one, but every minute I sensed that her mind was knitting back together. As certain facts were being remembered, she was indeed beginning to function again.

"And the nice thing about it," I was saying, keeping up a steady prattle despite the fact she was giving me the silent treatment, "is the sheer and obvious one that you have returned to your finest and prettiest self."

She glanced at me sidelong. She was leaning forward, hunched, her hair a bedraggled mess with some mud still in it—but I didn't have the heart to tell her that part.

"You look absolutely great, Galina," I told her.

"You vicious liar!"

"Come on, beauty's way beyond skin deep. You've got your youth back. All you need is a good shower, maybe a makeover… or a haircut… something like that."

"Shut up," she said.

Galina never liked looking ugly, not for one minute, not even in the repose of death.

"Uh…" I said, as the aircar began to lower itself, setting us down in the street outside her front door.

She had a really nice place, a small estate you might even call it. The house was about three stories high and had a big basement underneath as well. That was full of wine bottles, but she hated it when I drank one of them.

I eyeballed the house, remembering many happy—and unhappy—events that had occurred inside.

"What happened at Crystal World?" she finally asked. "What happened to the universe while I lay dead in that tank for months?"

"Uh..." I said, "are you talking about the first time you were dead, or like... the second time?"

She snarled and hissed. She outright *hissed* at me.

She opened the car door and moved to get out. I opened the opposite side, paid the AI that was driving the aircar, and the two of us were left in the street amid a whirlwind of grit and autumn leaves.

Galina brushed past me, heading for her smart-gates. I knew those iron spiky gates didn't want to let me inside any more than she did.

"Galina?" I said. "I got you out of being the consul."

She slowly turned to face me. "What do you mean?" she said.

"Your daddy chose Wurtenberger over you. That's okay... I hope...?"

She paused. She studied the ground, and then she looked back up at my eyes. "So... the plan worked?"

"Yeah, it worked perfectly!"

She showed me her teeth. "No, it didn't work *perfectly*. That crazy bitch girlfriend of yours, Boudica, started a fight with me—and she had me killed. Again!"

"Oh..." I said, "you mean like... with knives and all that?"

"Yes, exactly like that. Twice on Dust World, I was stabbed to death by a dozen insane aborigines with knives!"

I nodded and rubbed at my chin thoughtfully. "That sounds bad enough to put almost anyone in a mood. But you got your way," I said, spreading my hands wide. "You're off the hook. Your plan worked. You'll never be consul now."

"You didn't follow my plan, you bastard," she said. "You tricked me. You led me out there, and—"

"Listen, listen," I said, taking a step forward. I didn't touch her, though. I didn't yet dare. "Galina, your original plan was unworkable. How the hell was I supposed to take you somewhere in public, and like, shoot you in the head or something? While everybody watched? That was never going to work."

"You tricked me," she said. "You tricked me. You got me killed, and then you got me killed again."

She put a hand up to her bedraggled hair and pulled it away in horror. "I must look like some kind of a leper."

"How about we go inside?" I said. "You feed me a drink, you get yourself cleaned up, and I'll bring you up to speed on everything that's been going on over the last four months."

She breathed through her teeth for about ten seconds. Finally, she turned away, opened her smart-gates, and walked through.

To my surprise, she held the gate open for me to follow.

Smiling, I let her lead me into her home. My swagger was back in every step.

Galina let me stay that night. After she cleaned up, she was looking and smelling great again. She must've put something like two hundred goopy products into her hair alone.

She was almost greasy with all that lotion and soap on her skin, but I pretended not to notice. We made love that night, although she was somewhat reluctant, and still a little bit angry.

I'd done what she'd asked, and I'd come back for her after the campaign was over. Despite all this, she still seemed to be holding a grudge. Go figure.

In the morning, she kicked me out after breakfast, saying she had a lot of work to do at Central. She was squawking about her position as an imperator being in jeopardy for having been AWOL for so long.

I believed that, but I also believed she was butthurt by the way she'd been treated on Dust World, and by her own daddy. Kissing the top of her head, I left her, and I finally made my way back down to Georgia Sector on the sky train.

There, I was greeted by four people. My mom and pop, of course, squealed with joy and gave me big hugs with their ancient, leathery hands.

Damn, I thought, these old fossils might need to get killed and revived again one of these days. Sure, they were taking a lot of longevity drugs... but there were limits.

Then Etta stepped closer. She looked a little worried.

Derek, who stood behind her, looked like he was going to shit himself.

"Daddy?" Etta said. "We've got something to tell you. Something important."

My jaws clamped down, squeezing up tight. That made the muscles in my cheeks bulge. I could feel it.

Here it comes, I thought.

I couldn't help but study her belly. It didn't look swollen to me, no more so than the last time I'd seen it, but I knew a woman could oftentimes hide a pregnancy, maybe for four months or so. After that, it became really obvious.

"Daddy?" Etta was saying. "Are you listening, Daddy?"

I looked up again and met her eyes. "What's that again, girl?"

"I know this has got to be a shock, but... but we're married now, Daddy. Me and Derek."

My jaw sagged low—lower than low.

A pregnancy, a grandbaby, those kinds of things I could understand. But a marriage? That was a permanent connection to this snot-nosed little hog.

Derek fluttered a few fingers at me. He raised his eyebrows hopefully and took two steps forward. He raised a hand.

What was that for? Did he want some money or something?

A couple of cold seconds went by.

My parents both looked nervous, staring at me and glancing at each other. Etta was talking again, but I didn't even hear her.

I was just staring at that hand Derek was holding out to me. Was it trembling, just a bit? I was disgusted.

Sure, this hog was about Etta's age. He was of a reasonable height and athletic build—but he was just a normal man. I bet he could barely fight. I bet, in fact, that if my daughter really wanted to take him, she probably could, especially if she got the drop on him. I'd taught her well, and she was a ruthless scrapper.

At last, I heaved a sigh. Then I forced my knotted-up cheek muscles into a tight smile. Next, I took that hand. I shook it firmly.

"Welcome to the family, Derek," I heard someone say.

I realized later… that someone was me.

THE END

Books by B. V. Larson:

UNDYING MERCENARIES
Steel World
Dust World
Tech World
Machine World
Death World
Home World
Rogue World
Blood World
Dark World
Storm World
Armor World
Clone World
Glass World
Edge World
Green World
Ice World
City World
Sky World
Jungle World
Crystal World

Visit BVLarson.com for more information.

Printed in Great Britain
by Amazon